BEYOND

THE

GATES

BEYOND
THE
GATES

An HOA Mystery

Linda Lovely

LEVEL
BEST BOOKS

First published by Level Best Books 2025

This novel is entirely a work of fiction. The names, characters and incidents portrayed in it are the work of the author's imagination. Any resemblance to actual persons, living or dead, events or localities is entirely coincidental.

Linda Lovely asserts the moral right to be identified as the author of this work.

Author Photo Credit: Danielle Dahl

First edition

ISBN: 978-1-68512-904-0

Cover art by Level Best Designs and Linda Lovely

This book was professionally typeset on Reedsy.
Find out more at reedsy.com

Dedicated to the kind readers who rate and review books you enjoy.

Every author loves you. Please keep reading, rating, and reviewing.

Praise for Beyond the Gates

"What could be a better backdrop for murder than a Homeowner's Association? In *Beyond the Gates*, Linda Lovely spins a twisted murder set in South Carolina's lush low country. Kylee Kane, a bride-to-be, juggles wedding preparations with sleuthing as she dives headfirst into the investigation of Maury Campbell's death—his golf cart crash is just the beginning of a deadly cover-up. With a cast of unforgettable characters and a plot that keeps you guessing (not to mention the most EVIL HOA ever imagined!), *Beyond the Gates* is the perfect cozy mystery for readers who crave Southern charm, suspense, and more than a little danger."—Carla Damron, award-winning author of *The Orchid Tattoo*, *The Stone Necklace*, and *Justice be Done*

"*Beyond the Gates* is the fourth novel in Linda Lovely's HOA mystery series but the first I've read. It won't be the last. The main protagonist is Kylee Kane, a retired Coast Guard officer and investigator. She's smart, funny, loyal and compassionate, but she doesn't take crap from anyone. When a family friend is found dead after apparently running his golf cart into a tree, authorities and the HOA board are ready to dismiss it as an unfortunate accident. But Kylee doesn't buy it and as she starts following where the clues lead certain people get nervous about what she might find...certain people who would kill again to keep their secrets to themselves. Producing a great novel is all about developing strong characters and a compelling storyline and author Linda Lovely has done that deftly with *Beyond the Gates*."—Kevin Kluesner, author of the Cole Huebsch Mysteries

"What do stolen jewels, a murder, and a wedding have in common? Retired Coast Guard Captain Kylee Kane, of course! In the fourth installment of

An HOA Mystery Series: *Beyond the Gates*, author Linda Lovely treats the reader to a trifecta of intertwining plots that will keep readers hooked until that last satisfying page."—Lynn Chandler Willis, award-winning author of bestselling crime, mystery and suspense

"Set in beautiful coastal South Carolina, *Beyond the Gates* combines intrigue and excitement with characters I fell in love with. Every writer's goal is to keep you turning pages until dawn. Author Linda Lovely has done a masterful job, creating a mystery to keep you up till dawn and then make you late for work."—HG Lewis author of *An Unlikely Warrior*

"Even if you've never dealt with a homeowners' association, Linda Lovely's HOA Mystery series is a must read. Kylee Kane, a former Coast Guard investigator, serves as a security consultant for an HOA management company owned by her fiancé, Ted Welch. In *Beyond the Gates*, the fourth novel in the series, a family friend reports her husband Maury fatally wrapped his golf cart around a tree in Stillwater Cove, Kylee and Ted suspect murder. As Kylee tries to unearth the killer before her upcoming wedding, she's kidnapped. Now she must draw on her lifetime of water skills to stay alive in the unforgettable bang-up ending."—Nancy G. West, author of the Aggie Mundeen Rom-Com Mysteries and the forthcoming YA thriller, Risky Pursuit.

CHARACTERS & HOMEOWNER ASSOCIATIONS

(No worries. You'll meet them gradually.)

Welch HOA Management Company

- Ted Welch, owner *(retired U.S. State Dept.)*
- Kylee Kane, security consultant *(retired U.S. Coast Guard)*
- Grant Welch, Ted's son, Citadel Cadet
- Myrtle Kane, Kylee's mom, receptionist
- Frank Donahue, construction & maintenance
- Robin Gates, IT & website

Stillwater Cove HOA

- Archer Highsmith, president
- Quentin Teacher, board member
- Lisa Queensbury, board member
- Jack Durham, Security Chief
- Maury Campbell, golfcart crash victim
- Velma Campbell, Maury's widow
- Richard Ryebread, Campbell neighbor
- Dr. Perry McMahan, HOA's veterinarian

Hullis Island HOA

- Chief O'Rourke, head of security
- Theft victims: Evie Miles, Tony Baldwin, Doug Fisher
- Martha Evatt, Myrtle Kane's friend
- Babsie Talbott, Care Committee Chair

Hullis Island HOA (Cont'd)

- Babsie Talbott, Care Committee Chair
- Beth Talbott Reiner, Babsie's stepdaughter
- Suzie Becknell, Care Committee
- Anna Whitner, Care Committee
- Ella Dent, Babsie's former maid

Lighthouse Cove HOA

- Howie Wynne, financial consultant
- Mike, Howie's husband, a lawyer

Law Enforcement

- Sheriff Eileen Baker
- Deputy Josie Muschel, Sheriff's Office
- Deputy Nick Ibsen, Sheriff's Office
- Lt. Alysha Carter, U.S. Coast Guard
- Captain Harvey Reed, U.S. Coast Guard
- Glen Jenkins, District Attorney

Other

- Betsy DeJong, funeral director
- Mimi Jones, Grant's girlfriend, a birder
- Carl Jones, Mimi's father, a birder
- Olivia Tucker, Kane family attorney
- Dr. Hardesty, Kane family veterinarian
- Jim Whitner, banker

iii

Chapter One

Kylee Kane

Sunday Afternoon, December 15

"Kylee, is the chocolate ready yet?" Mom asks.

I snap to. I may be a fifty-one-year-old, retired Coast Guard captain, but Mom will always outrank me. I peer into the top of the double-boiler.

"Nope, the semi-sweets haven't melted, let alone the paraffin."

"Well, keep stirring." Mom moves a tray of white-jacketed maraschino cherries from the refrigerator to the kitchen table. She chuckles as she slaps Ted's pilfering fingers away. "These aren't ready. Not until your bride-to-be dunks them in chocolate."

I glance out the window. This cold, blustery afternoon is perfect for candy-making. Since I was a kid, I've always helped Mom make gifts and, okay, snarf down vast quantities of homemade chocolates every Christmas. At least every Christmas I could make it home.

Ted Welch—I still have trouble realizing he's my fiancé—was more than happy to tag along, saying, "I assume you need a taste-tester."

Mom glances at Ted as she coats more cherries with fondant. "I hear you have a new crisis," she teases. "Saw a post on that Earful app about a holiday display in Lighthouse Cove. Fifty-five riled-up neighbors have commented. I bet the community's directors tossed the kerfuffle to you like a hot potato."

1

Ted hangs his head and temporarily quits petting Mississippi, the black cat curled in his lap. Keokuk, the second black cat Mom adopted, is rubbing against Ted's leg, angling for a way to jump up.

"You had to bring that up, Myrt." Ted groans. "Happy holidays, indeed. Wish I could block everyone in a homeowner association from connecting to that stupid social app."

"I'll second that," I agree.

Earful is our nickname for The All-Seeing Ear, a social media site that's supposed to link neighbors for the betterment of communities. While it lets neighbors post pet photos, recipes, and restaurant reviews, it's too often an echo chamber for misinformation, hurtful gossip, and conspiracy theories.

We call it Earful because we get an earful of drivel when we tune in, and too often, the malicious drivel is directed at one of the dozen homeowner associations Welch HOA Management counts as clients. Since Ted sweet-talked me into a gig as his firm's security consultant, I get to share those Earful headaches.

"I'd hoped to escape all feuds for an afternoon, Myrt," Ted says. "Remember Howie Wynne, the Lighthouse Cove financial consultant? He's the guy neighbors wrongly suspected of instigating a bogus swat raid. Anyway, Howie and his husband, Mike, arranged their outdoor Christmas lights to spell 'Tis the season to be GAY'. Some neighbors consider that blasphemous. They'd like to run the gay couple out of the Lowcountry—or at least Lighthouse Cove—but for starters, they want the HOA to force them to take down the lights."

"Can they do that?" Mom asks.

"The short answer is no. Nothing in the covenants or bylaws prohibit owners from using Christmas lights to spell words." Ted laughs. "And, believe me, the complainers have tried. Lighthouse Cove has more rules than Russian names have consonants. Howie and Mike made dang sure their display complied with every single caveat.

"Only white lights are permitted outside homes. Check. No household display can cast light beyond the edge of the property. Check. No lawn display can be wider than six feet or taller than four feet. Check."

Both Mom and I are giggling. "I suppose someone crept inside their yard to measure," I say.

"Yep," Ted answers. "The dimensions were one-half-inch smaller than the maximums. I think Howie and Mike watched out the window and laughed their heads off. Mike's a lawyer. HOA rulebooks like Lighthouse Cove's are thicker than the Oxford English Dictionary, but a sharp attorney can always outwit them."

Mom glances over at me. "Kylee Kane, are you stirring that chocolate or daydreaming? Surely, it's ready for dipping."

"I could answer with your 'watched pot never boils' gem, but the chocolate is indeed ready. Can't see a trace of white paraffin."

Mom sets a candy tray beside the stove for me to coat the cherries, then returns to the kitchen table to roll more fruit in the sticky white fondant.

A ringing phone makes me jump as I scissor the first cherry between two forks for a quick dunk in the chocolate bath. "Ted, can you get that? Mom and I are at a critical stage here."

"Sure. Can't have any candy-making interruptions delay my taste-testing job."

Ted rocks back in his kitchen chair to snag the wall-mounted phone behind him, unceremoniously dumping Mississippi in the process. In this household, a landline still trumps cell phones.

"Hi, Velma." Ted's cheerful greeting is quickly followed by a sharp "Oh, no!"

"Is that Velma Campbell?" Mom asks. "What's happened? Put her on speaker. My hands are covered with goo."

As Velma's anguished sobs fill the kitchen, I fumble the cherry precariously teetering between fork tines and watch it sink beneath the bubbling chocolate.

"Maury's dead, murdered. The bastards say it's an accident." Velma's words escape in an anguished rush. "They made me leave him."

My throat tightens. Maury dead? It can't be.

"Slow down, Velma," Ted pleads. "Help us understand what's happened. You're in Stillwater Cove?"

"Yes." Velma takes a ragged breath and starts over. "Maury left for the maintenance barn about ten and said he'd be home by eleven. When noon came and went, I got worried. He didn't pick up calls to his cell, so I went to look for him."

Velma's sobs force her to pause. "Oh, God, I spotted his golf cart wrapped around a live oak and Maury on the ground. His neck. It was all wrong. No pulse."

"Are you there now?" Ted asks. "Is anyone with you?"

"No, I'm in our house. Jack, the security chief, strong-armed me into his ATV. I fought him." Her voice lowers to almost a whisper. "They made me leave Maury. And those detestable security thugs acted like they'd just stumbled across a deer carcass. Smoking and flicking cigarette butts toward his body."

"Did EMS come?" Mom asks.

"Yes, I called 911, though I knew my Maury was dead. A security guard arrived almost instantly, then EMS, a sheriff's deputy, and finally the coroner."

I stand open-mouthed at the stove. Tears sliding down my cheeks.

Two nights ago, Ted and I joined Mom and her significant other, Frank, for dinner at Maury and Velma's home. We all oohed and aahed at the Campbells' festive outdoor lights and Santa's hand-crafted reindeer on the front lawn.

"Did they say why you couldn't stay?" Ted asks. "Was there some danger?"

"Ha, just danger I'd speak the truth." Velma's tone sharpens. "I told security to question our neighbor, Richard Ryebread. That's when they carted me off to shut me up."

Mom uses her calm nurse voice. "I'm so sorry, Velma. We'll come right over. Together, we'll figure out what to do."

"I want answers," Velma says. "Maury didn't ram his golf cart into that tree on purpose. That security jerk claims Maury had a heart attack and lost control. Bullshit. He's seventy-eight, but his resting heart rate is around sixty. You know what an exercise fiend Maury is.

"This is a cover-up," Velma's voice vibrates with anger. "It was no accident.

Someone chased Maury into that tree. And, in my bones, I know it was Richard Ryebread."

A cover-up? If so, something always trips them up. We'll get Velma her answers.

Ted interrupts. "We'll head your way now, Velma. You can tell us the whole story then. It'll take us forty minutes to get there. You need to call and warn the gate. Since Stillwater fired our company, we need an owner invitation to enter.

"Make sure they know we'll arrive in two cars. Maury mentioned your security's been hassling invited guests if they come in multiple vehicles or show up before they're expected."

"Bless you." Velma's voice, hoarse from crying, ends as a whisper.

Mom uses the back of her sticky hands to wipe away tears, then heads to the sink to wash up. "Kylee, put the candy trays back in the fridge while I break the news to Frank. Ted, is Frank still in his workshop?"

"Yeah, he said he'd join us as soon as he finished cleaning his paintbrushes."

I close the refrigerator door, and Ted's arms wrap me in a tight hug. "We'll drive separately from Myrt and Frank," he says. "That way, they can stay longer, and we'll have our car to drive to the accident scene."

I nod. "Good idea. Could you make sense of what she was saying?"

"No. She's in shock," Ted says. "Talking face-to-face, we'll have a better idea if Velma's trying to find someone or something to blame for her loss or if she has valid reasons for thinking it's murder."

Chapter Two

Kylee

Sunday Afternoon. December 15

Ted backs his Lexus down the driveway and out to the street so Frank can exit his garage. I watch as Frank helps my petite mom climb into his beat-up truck. Once she's installed, he trudges back inside the house. When Frank reappears, he's traded his plaid lumberjack-style jacket for a rain slicker.

Bet Mom "suggested" the wardrobe change. Just like she once suggested what clothes Dad should wear.

Amazing how Mom and Frank act like an old, married couple. They're not married, but have cohabitated a year. Carryover habits? Both my widowed mother, Myrtle Kane, and widower, Frank Donahue, were happily wed for decades before losing their mates.

Mom moved in with Frank last Thanksgiving after an arsonist torched her house. Frank invited her to bunk with him to save money while her house was being rebuilt. Mom's always pinched pennies and enjoys giving gossips the proverbial finger. So her decision didn't surprise me.

By the time the new digs won an occupancy permit, Mom and her kitties had comfortably settled in with Frank. She sold her rebuilt house without spending a night inside.

My thoughts turn back to Velma and Maury. "Have you come up with any alternative theories to explain Maury's strange accident?" I ask Ted.

He shrugs. "Velma's convinced a heart attack wasn't to blame, but they can happen to anyone, even top athletes. Perhaps it really was a freak accident. The autopsy should provide some answers."

"Velma said Maury was headed to Stillwater's maintenance barn," I comment. "I thought the HOA directors fired Maury."

Ted nods. "They did. Maybe Maury's dismissal was handled more diplomatically than ours. He owns a house in Stillwater Cove. They couldn't confiscate his gate pass. Plus, they wouldn't want Maury telling neighbors the board screwed him. Could be the directors let him finish projects underway. They just said there'd be no future HOA repair jobs."

"How well do you know the directors? Stillwater Cove was a client for four years, right?"

Ted chews on his lip as he thinks. "The board changed about a year ago. I can't tell you much about the two new directors who are calling all the shots. Lisa Queensbury is the only holdover from the old board. From what I can tell, her only role is voting yes to whatever the other two want.

"Initially, the new directors were very complimentary. Said our company was doing a fine job. Then, boom, we were no longer needed. Half the time, I can't guess what's going through the heads of our HOA clients. I thought managing homeowner associations would be a piece of cake after twenty-plus years in the State Department managing embassy facilities in third-world countries. Boy, was I naive."

I laugh. "You should have warned me. I was just as naïve when I came on board as your security consultant. Didn't think there would be much for a retired Coast Guard investigator to do. Ha! Haven't had a chance to sail the River Rat past Savannah to the south or Charleston to the north."

We bounce along a series of winding country roads as we tail Frank's truck. Since water covers more than half of Beaufort County's half a million acres, the roads zig and zag through a jigsaw puzzle of marshes, estuaries, and sounds.

"Can you turn up the heater?" I pull my lightweight raincoat tighter. "I would have worn something warmer if I knew we'd be spending time outdoors.'Tis the season when the Lowcountry can't make up its mind. Yesterday, it was in the mid-seventies. Today, the wind chill must be in the low forties."

Outside the car, strong gusts churn the marshy waters that border this stretch of road. The wind is bullying black clouds all across the horizon. More trouble for our fragile dunes. That brings our destination to mind. Stillwater Cove is one of the few private enclaves lucky enough to have both a beach and a marina with easy ocean access. The marina, nestled within a protected sound, is chock-a-bloc with yachts that would make the River Rat, my thirty-eight-foot live-in sailboat, look downright puny.

"How many people live in Stillwater?" I ask.

"Not an easy question," Ted replies. "At least half the properties are second or third homes, and some owners only visit two or three weeks a year. It's hard to call them residents."

"Only seventy properties, right?" I ask. "How can such a small gated community afford a private golf course, clubhouse, marina, and all the other extras? Since Stillwater prohibits short-term rentals, there are no tourist dollars to subsidize amenities. The HOA fees must be outrageous."

"They are. Last I heard, every lot owner pays an initiation fee of $250,000 to join the club. They fork over another fifty to one hundred thou a year in annual dues, depending on whether they keep a yacht at the marina. Not a budget buster for most of the owners. They expect a five-star restaurant at the clubhouse. If they have a sudden hankering to play golf, they can tee off whenever they like. For yacht owners, there's also a marina with handy deep-water access. Stillwater owners frown on letting outsider riff-raff through the gates."

"Geesh, like us, you mean? How can Maury and Velma afford to live there? I realize Maury sold a profitable construction company when he retired, but a quarter of a million dollars just to join? That's a big chunk of money unless you have a million dollars or two in spare change."

Ted chuckles. "The Campbells have never given Stillwater Cove a red cent. Maury bought their isolated oceanfront parcel a decade before Stillwater Cove Club LLC snatched up the surrounding property and built an access road to the mainland. Their property is grandfathered, and they're exempt from HOA covenants and bylaws. In exchange for amending their deed to make the next owners of their property part of the HOA and subject to its rules, they have free access to all amenities. They also got a slip at the marina."

"Sweet."

"Maybe." Ted takes his eyes off the road to glance my way. "Maury told Frank they've never felt comfortable hobnobbing with Stillwater neighbors. They don't fit in. The guy next door—Richard Ryebread, the jerk Velma mentioned—hates the Campbells. He's angry they don't have to abide by the HOA rules. Still, Velma and Maury have felt the positives outweighed the negatives. A priceless ocean view, clubhouse, golf privileges, and a free boat slip. When they want to spend time with friends, they just leave Stillwater."

Lightning flashes on the horizon, and rolling thunder makes me feel like I'm in a surround-sound theater. In seconds, Frank's taillights disappear as a curtain of rain marches toward us. Ted turns his windshield wipers on high. Still the edge of the road vanishes.

"Crap," Ted swears as he slows his Lexus to a crawl. "Good thing we're in a no-passing zone. The double-solid lines are all I can see."

"If it's raining this heavily at Stillwater, the accident scene is going to be a muddy mess," I comment. "From Velma's description, it sounds like the security guards and first responders arrived in a flotilla of all-terrain vehicles and tramped the ground all around Maury's body. Wonder if anyone took photographs before the human traffic jam."

I assume the wooded crash site is covered with pine straw and rotting palmetto fronds. Even without this gully washer, I doubt we'd have seen any shoeprints or skid marks.

I quit talking so Ted could concentrate on keeping the car on asphalt and out of the bordering marsh.

* * *

The expression "it's raining cats and dogs" seems somehow inadequate to describe this torrent. Maybe "it's raining cows and horses." Yet, in any weather—rain, fog, hurricane—it would be hard to miss the massive stone and glass guardhouse looming in front of us. It makes the Hullis Island gatehouse look like Clark Kent's phone booth.

The Stillwater guardhouse is bigger than most normal-sized homes. Its mass, plus the sprawling mansions inside the gates, suggest this HOA is convinced size matters. Stillwater also appears unconcerned about electric bills. Prison watch towers would envy the powerful reach of this guardhouse's floodlights. The lights knife deep into the gloomy rain shroud.

Rain streams off the security guard's bright yellow slicker as he stands at attention outside the gatehouse. He had to venture out to check Frank's bona fides. When he saw our headlights, he probably felt it wasn't worthwhile to pop back inside.

"Good day. May I ask your business?" The burly guard's eyes narrow to slits. Does he think we look like burglars? But, hey, maybe it's the weather. The wind's spitting rain in his face, and a plump raindrop teeters on the end of his pug nose.

"We're guests of Velma Campbell," Ted answers. "She called to say we're expected."

"Your names?"

"Ted Welch and Kylee Kane. We know how to get to the Campbell home."

"Good," the guard replies. "Our owners don't like strangers roaming around the neighborhoods."

He hands Ted a square hunk of plastic. "Keep this on your dashboard at all times."

The gizmo resembles the devices popular restaurants give diners who are waiting for tables. Those gadgets beep and flashlights when a table comes free. Wonder what tricks this one might perform if we veer from our pre-approved destination?

Ted looks from the gizmo to the guard. "Huh, I'm used to getting visitor placards to put in the front window. What's this thing do?"

"It identifies who you are and who you're visiting. Have a good afternoon. You must return your auto ID box when you leave."

The guard hurries inside before Ted can ask anything more. A motor groans as the massive wrought-iron gates slowly retract to let us inside.

I grab the auto ID box off the dash and study it. "Imagine it has a tracking feature that tells security our car's location at all times. Seems like overkill given Stillwater's rather small size. Maybe it's to impress wealthy owners they're entitled to cutting-edge security."

"Maybe." Ted frowns. "But this technology doesn't really do much to prevent crime. Doesn't tell security where people go once they exit their cars. Then again, maybe they've covered that by installing night-vision cameras to track every movement inside the gates. I'm not sorry we lost Stillwater as a client."

Chapter Three

Kylee

Sunday Afternoon, December 15

The Campbell house sits on three-quarters of an acre. While that sounds large, the lot is quite narrow. Even developers who cater to buyers of super-sized mansions try to maximize the number of oceanfront properties they can sell.

I strain to pick out the Campbell mailbox on the beach frontage road. Once we reach it, we crunch down a private drive of crushed oyster shells for a good hundred feet before the elevated house appears.

Like all its neighbors in this coastal high-hazard flood zone, the Campbell home rests on stilts, ensuring its first habitable floor sits above sea level. However, the latticed space below the first floor isn't wasted. It provides parking for up to four vehicles. Of course, the vehicles that pull into the rear parking rows can't exit until later arrivals back out.

As soon as Ted's car slides under the protection of the house, Frank calls to us.

"Myrt's upstairs with Velma. I waited to make sure you made it through the Nazi checkpoint. Let's go up."

I know by "going up," Frank plans to ride in the Campbells' closet-sized elevator. I get why home elevators are becoming expected conveniences in beachfront properties. Who wants to schlep grocery bags up steep sets of stairs? But, being claustrophobic, I usually offer an excuse to avoid the tight confines. "I like the exercise. Think I'll take the stairs."

Today, I suck it up. With a deep breath, I scoot inside the elevator with Frank and Ted. We're shoulder to shoulder. None of us is petite. I'm five-foot-seven. Ted and Frank both top six feet. While Ted's slender, Frank's been expanding horizontally thanks to his sweet tooth and Mom's cooking. Never mind what I weigh. I decide not to peek at the elevator's posted weight limit.

The moment the elevator doors grind open, I hear Mom's voice. "Surely, they'll investigate. Find out where your neighbor was this morning."

With this home's open design, it's hard to have a private conversation, unless you whisper or hold your conversation in a bathroom with the door closed and the exhaust fan on high.

We hang our raincoats in the entry closet and head to the large eat-in kitchen, where the inviting smell of freshly brewed coffee makes me eager to wrap my hands around a warm mug. Mom and Velma cease talking as soon as they hear the three of us arrive.

Velma looks up from her seat at the kitchen table. Her eyes are red; her eyelids puffy. Tears have forged visible trails through her powder-caked makeup. Frank bends to kiss her cheek. Ted follows suit. I give her shoulder what I hope is a comforting squeeze.

Mom pops up to pour coffee and hand steaming mugs to each of us.

"Have you heard anything more from the authorities?" Ted asks.

Velma shakes her head. "I asked the coroner when I can claim Maury's body. He said I'd be notified once the autopsy is complete. Told me he had no idea how soon that would be given the holiday backlog. I'm not sure what that means. Do medical examiners take Christmas vacations, or do more people die around the holidays?"

Mom glances my way. "Kylee, can your deputy friend offer a better answer?"

"Maybe." I turn to Velma. "Do you recall the name of the sheriff's deputy at the scene?"

I mentally crossed my fingers, hoping it wasn't Nick Ibsen. A couple years ago, I had a much-regretted brief fling with the handsome Ibsen. When I discovered he was a misogynist jerk, I ran. My rebuff turned Nick into a vengeful enemy.

"If the deputy said his name, I don't remember." Velma closes her eyes. "He was young. Of course, most everyone looks young to me. But this one still had acne. Imagine he thought his wispy blond goatee made him look older. It didn't."

Good. Definitely not Nick.

Velma stares out the window. While the rain has slowed to a drizzle, the oceanfront windowpanes vibrate with each seaborne wind gust.

"Did you see any neighbors near the crash?" Ted asks. "Anyone who might have witnessed the accident?"

"I'm certain Richard Ryebread *saw* the accident since I'm convinced he caused it. Richard—or Dickhead, as Maury calls him—has been getting increasingly aggressive."

"Why? What set him off?" I ask.

"From the day he started building that oversized monstrosity next door, he's never stopped bitching at us." Velma's grip on her coffee cup turns her knuckles white. "He's irate we aren't required to pave our driveway. He complains his visitors must wonder why the HOA puts up with his next-door trailer trash. Dicky sees no difference between a dirt road and our crushed oyster shell driveway.

"Lately, he's been after Maury to take down all the trees along our property line," she says. "He claims they block what should be panoramic views from the windows facing our house. We planted those trees years before he built. Two months ago, several of the trees began to fail. Maury thinks Dickhead poisoned them. We complained to the Stillwater board, but since we don't fork over a king's ransom every year, our protest went nowhere.

"Two days ago, when Maury left the house, Dickhead took after him, screaming obscenities and threatening to sue us because we haven't chopped down the ailing trees. Says they're a danger to his property."

Velma's shoulders shake as a sob wracks her body. "I'm not exaggerating Dickhead's bullying. He must have chased Maury in his souped-up ATV.

That would explain the crash. If Maury was looking over his shoulder, he didn't see the tree. Richard Ryebread murdered my husband. He didn't need a gun or a knife, just malice."

Ted's look suggests he wants me to try and coax Velma back to less hypothetical ground. "Is it possible anyone other than Ryebread saw what happened?"

Velma shakes her head. "No. You'll understand when you see the site. The woods are real thick, and they're a long way from any house."

"Who responded to your 911 call?" I probe.

"Stillwater security officers were there in force. They ushered in an EMS crew, the deputy, and later the coroner. All told, six security guards showed up. That's not counting Jack, the bruiser-in-chief who hustled me home. I don't know any of these guards. We knew all of our old security guards by name. This board didn't keep a single one of them."

Seven security guards responded? How many officers would sleepy Stillwater need on duty on a rainy Sunday afternoon?

Though I'm curious about the size of Stillwater's security force, now isn't the time to get sidetracked. Ted can fill me in later. Our number one priority is to help Velma deal with her heartbreaking loss.

Ted sets down his coffee mug and eases his chair back from the table. "Velma, can you tell us how to get to the crash scene? We'll have a better understanding if we take a first-hand look. If we get lucky, we might pick up some clues to reconstruct how the accident happened."

"You can't drive all the way there," Velma answers. "Since you don't have a golf cart, you'll need to walk about a half mile from the road once you leave your car."

* * *

It's still drizzling when Ted pulls his Lexus to the side of the road. Before he can turn off the motor, a security car cozies up to our back fender.

"We've got company," Ted says. "That dashboard tracker must offer pinpoint accuracy."

The security guard jumps out of his car before we can unbuckle our seatbelts. Like the guard at the gate, he's wearing an oversized yellow slicker, and he's got the hood pulled up. Can't tell much more than his height—about average for a man, maybe five-foot-ten or eleven.

"Why are you stopping here?" he shouts.

He has to compete with the wind to be heard, but his gruff tone and volume make it sound like he's accusing us of invading a secret military facility.

Ted opens his car door. The guard barely gives him room to stand. Ted pretends the man's crowding posture is normal. Not meant to intimidate. "Velma Campbell asked us to look at the site where her husband had his golf cart accident."

Ted is taller than the guard, forcing him to look up. A prominent nose dominates the security officer's craggy face. Can't tell the color of his hair. The portion visible inside his hood is shaved military-recruit close.

"Any problem with us taking a look?" Ted asks.

The guard takes a small step backward. "No, sir. A tragic accident. Not much to see. I'll guide you in."

We trot after the security officer, who maintains a fast pace over the spongy ground. Wish he'd slow. I'm in tennis shoes, and the footing's dang slippery on the wet pine straw.

I involuntarily gasp when I spot the accordioned golf cart. The front end's twisted metal wraps halfway around the trunk of a large live oak. The tree and vehicle resemble a single, welded sculpture.

Can a golf cart go fast enough to collide with such force? When I visit Mom and Frank on Hullis Island, I often swear at the glacial pace of golf carts toddling along in front of my car.

Would a heart attack cause someone to floor the accelerator? Even so, is there enough horsepower to do this much damage?

Ted and I walk the accident perimeter under our babysitter's flinty gaze. So much for any hope of visual clues to help reconstruct the scene. It looks like someone used a giant Cuisinart to blend a mud pudding with pine straw lumps. Ted makes a few notes. I assume he's jotting down the golf cart's make and model.

Neither of us voice any thoughts. Any words we utter would be carefully relayed up the chain of command.

Are these people afraid of some liability claim? Are they hiding something? Protecting a wealthy someone, like Dickhead Ryebread? The security reaction oozes paranoia.

I chance a few innocuous questions. "Mrs. Campbell's husband told her he was headed to the HOA maintenance barn. I don't see any barn. Is it nearby? In what direction?"

The guard points to the west.

I risk a glance at Ted. He looks as perplexed as I am. When the golf cart crashed, it wasn't headed west nor was it headed east, back to the road. It was traveling due south.

The security officer steps away to talk on his radio. I use my cell phone to snap a few pictures while his back's turned. When he ends his conversation, the guard, who has never introduced himself, asks if we're finished.

Ted looks at me, and I nod.

"Yes. Thank you."

The guard clears his throat. "Um, I told our chief I accompanied you to the crash site and that Mrs. Campbell believes her husband was en route to the maintenance barn. The chief said she's mistaken. The gentleman had no reason to go there. Mr. Campbell turned in his keys to the barn last week. He had no way to enter."

Chapter Four

Kylee

Sunday Afternoon, December 15

As we leave the crash site, I'm surprised the brusque security guard doesn't sit on our bumper to make sure we head directly to the Campbell house. Then again, he doesn't need to—not with our dashboard tracker keeping tabs. Security will know if we make any unauthorized detours.

Can't wait to leave Stillwater, far too Big Brother for my taste.

Back at the Campbells, I reluctantly climb in the elevator with Ted. I quit holding my breath as soon as the door opens on the main floor.

Mom and Frank are sitting on the living room couch, heads together, for a whispered conversation.

"Where's Velma?" I ask.

"Packing a suitcase," Mom explains. "She's spending tonight with Frank and me. Did you learn anything?"

Before we can reply, Velma walks in, rolling a small suitcase behind her.

"Can't imagine why I feel spooked about staying here alone tonight. I've done it plenty of times before." Velma shrugs. "It's not that I imagine the Dickhead next door will attack me. He's undoubtedly confident security will dream up some reason Maury plowed into a tree for the heck of it. Stillwater wouldn't want any bad press for one of its precious big-money

18

owners."

"Why don't you stay all week with us?" Mom suggests. "We're happy to have you."

"No. I just need to escape for a night. Our son's trying to make it home as fast as he can. He's on assignment in Bhutan right now, and travel within the Himalayan range is complicated. He'll be here in two or three days. I need to get Vince's room ready. He's a vegetarian, you know. So I also need to shop for food he likes."

The new widow turns toward Ted and me. "What did you make of the accident scene? Were you able to see any skid marks?"

"We had a supervised visit," Ted says, reporting our fast interception by Stillwater security and the guard's insistence on hovering in the background throughout our visit. "But he didn't make any attempt to keep us away."

"When the golf cart crashed, it didn't appear headed toward the mainte-nance barn or back to the road," I add. "Can you think of a reason—other than being chased—for Maury to be headed south?"

Velma shakes her head. "No. There's nothing in that direction except marsh."

Her forehead creases. "Just wish I knew why all my calls to Maury went to voicemail. He always leaves his cell phone on when we're apart. It's probably still in the back pocket of his pants.

"I need Maury's cell to contact his work friends. His business contacts are all on his cell. He's worked with many of these folks for decades."

"If Maury's phone was in his pocket, maybe I can speed its return," I say. "An accident victim's clothes and personal belongings usually are sent to the funeral home."

I don't mention that authorities keep those items if foul play is suspected, and they're typically not released until after an autopsy.

Foul play? Would there be charges if a golf cart chase ended with a fatality? Highly doubtful if there are no witnesses.

Mom gets up from the couch and turns to Ted and me. "Why don't you two drive straight back to Beaufort? No point following us to Hullis Island just to turn around and drive home. Not in miserable weather like this."

Mom gets no argument from Ted or me.

After an extended round of hugs, Mom walks us to the elevator. "Ted, I'm scheduled to work tomorrow," she whispers. "Any problem if I take the day off?"

Like me, Mom and Frank work for Welch HOA management. For decades, Mom, an RN and former head nurse, was accustomed to being the boss. Even doctors quaked when she raised her voice. After winning a cancer battle, Mom wasn't ready to meekly watch the world go by. She's now Ted's three-days-a-week admin and receptionist.

Frank Donahue—Mom's housemate and significant other—sold his roofing company at his late wife's insistence. She worried Frank was too old to prance atop roofs like Santa. After his missus unexpectedly died, Frank jumped at the chance to be Ted's construction manager. He wasn't ready to retire.

"Of course, you can take the day off, Myrt," Ted says. "Things aren't exactly hopping at the office anyway. With the exception of the Lighthouse Cove uproar over Christmas lights, the holiday season seems to have imposed a temporary truce among warring HOA factions. People seem willing to postpone quarrels over lawncare or pickleball noise until the new year so they can spend time with friends and family."

* * *

Ted and I both breathe a sigh of relief when we drop off our dashboard tracker, exit Stillwater's gates, and head home. For the time being, I concede home means Ted's fixer-upper abode in Beaufort's Historic District and not the River Rat, my comfy, live-on-board sailboat. She's named after the dinghy Dad and I once sailed on the Mississippi River.

While the River Rat offers perfect lodging for a single woman, elbow room's scarce for a twosome, especially when one member of that twosome stands six feet plus. There's also a personal space issue. We're both accustomed to having some.

Still, I hope Ted's six-bedroom renovation project won't be our permanent residence. He bought the run-down edifice because he sees beyond its decay to the structure's pleasing architectural bones. He couldn't bear to see it demolished.

While I get his passion, I'm not enamored of the renovation side effects. Plaster dust coats every surface, including the omnipresent tarps. There's a constant (expensive) parade of contractors in and out, and I could happily live the rest of my life without waking to a jackhammer serenade.

The marauding tourists are another annoyance. Admittedly, my sailboat has nautical neighbors moored a few feet away, but, unlike Historic District gawkers, my fellow sailors don't wear binocular necklaces and think it's a-okay to peek in windows.

The unkindest cut of all? None of Ted's windows offers a view of the water. A sight that feeds my sense of place and well-being.

Nonetheless, I won't fuss about where we hang our hats for the foreseeable future. Ted has too much money invested in his architectural donnybrook to stop mid-renovation. Plus, his son, Grant, a sophomore at the Citadel in Charleston, needs a room of his own when he visits.

I've been quiet, letting Ted concentrate on driving. Now that the rain's let up, I want my curiosity satisfied. Was Stillwater Cove intent on Big Brother security when he managed the HOA?

"When Stillwater canned Welch HOA Management, you had me chat up the security chief who got sacked at the same time," I begin. "As I recall, you wondered if there'd been some security lapse and you were sharing the blame. But the ex-chief said his firing came out of the blue. No reason. The directors just said they'd 'decided to go with a different contractor.' Did you ever learn anything more?"

"No. Since we vetted Stillwater's security force, I figured a high-value theft or some other blunder might have prompted the board to axe us along with the security firm. I even asked Maury to do a little sleuthing. He quizzed a half-dozen owners. No one had heard a whisper about any security or management screw-up."

My eyebrows head skyward. "Makes you wonder if the directors got a kickback to award new contracts for security and management services."

Ted chuckles. "They obviously found a different security contractor, but the board didn't exactly replace us. They did hire a secretary to answer phones, so owners could talk to a human if they called, but the two new directors took on the bulk of the management chores."

Really?

"You're telling me Stillwater's directors are personally handling all the administrative crap you used to shovel?"

"That's the story. We were let go about two months after Quentin Teacher joined Archer Highsmith and Lisa Queensbury on the board. Like Archer, Quentin is a relative newcomer to Stillwater Cove.

"When Archer phoned to say Stillwater was bringing all management tasks in house, I figured somebody's favorite relative would be named a fulltime, inhouse manager, with at least one support person. But as far as I know, they've only added the secretary."

I'm stumped. Like many HOAs, Stillwater's biggest problem has always been finding owners willing to serve on its board. Second-home owners who only visit a few weeks a year have zero interest, while fulltime residents, mostly retirees, feel they've done their duty after a single term.

"How on earth does this board expect to recruit volunteers to serve as unpaid directors if the job includes actual work and not just monthly meetings?" I ask. "Managing a seventy-home HOA might be relatively simple if it didn't have Stillwater Cove's amenities—a clubhouse with a restaurant, swimming pool, and tennis and pickleball courts, not to mention a marina and a golf course. Owners phone with questions and complaints. Even if Stillwater contracted out management of each facility, oversight's essential."

"I'm stumped, too," Ted admits. "Before today, I didn't care. Not my problem. But security's insistence that Velma leave the accident scene and their shadowing us raises plenty of questions."

"My first question is about their security force," I add. "Velma said seven security officers showed up at the accident scene. Why would Stillwater Cove have even half that number on duty on a Sunday morning? And why do they need those high-tech trackers for every visiting vehicle?"

Ted adjusts the windshield wiper speed as a new round of showers replaces the drizzle. "Maury told me Stillwater recently doubled its security force. He couldn't fathom why they needed more officers. But he had no reason to complain since the Campbells pay no dues."

Ted pauses. "Speaking of unanswered questions, do you think Josie can help you get Maury's cell phone before the autopsy?"

"I'm not sure. Josie's on good terms with the medical examiner. If the coroner doesn't suspect foul play, the ME might release Maury's cell phone quickly, even if he hangs on to the rest of his belongings until after the autopsy.

"Too bad Josie wasn't the sheriff's deputy called to the scene," I add. "If she had any reason to suspect it wasn't a single-vehicle fatality, she'd have asked plenty of questions."

Josie Muschel and Lt. Alysha Carter are terrific friends. This past summer the three of us conned an assassin into helping us unmask an even bigger villain. Josie dubbed our informal investigative trio the Smart Gals Network. A group not even remotely akin to Beaufort County's Old Boys Network.

Ted's smartphone buzzes. He connects hands-free with Bluetooth.

"Hi, Dad," Grant says. "Thought I'd check in. You're still coming to pick me up Tuesday, right?"

Since the conversation's on speaker, I chime in with a 'hello' to let Ted's son know I'm on the line and listening in. Only polite.

"Hi, Aunt Kylee. Or should I start calling you Stepmom? You won't turn into one of those wicked stepmothers, will you?"

I laugh. "You have no idea what all I've planned."

I've loved Grant since he was a baby, and I'm pretty sure he feels the same. I go right along with Grant's good-natured kidding.

When I was a kid, Ted was my across-the-street Keokuk neighbor and my little brother's best friend. When Ted was nine, his mother died, and Mom took him under her wing. Ted practically lived at our house. Ever since, Mom's considered Ted a second son. And when Grant came along, Mom "adopted" him as a grandchild. That's why Grant calls her Grandma Myrt and me Aunt Kylee.

When I first stumbled into a romantic relationship with Ted, it felt weird. Grant adjusted to the change a lot faster than I did. He seems genuinely happy his dad and I will tie the knot in (*oh my Lord*) nine days. Our family members unanimously voted that we should marry on Christmas Eve. I wasn't actually asked to vote. The big day is Tuesday, December 24.

"Is it okay to invite Mimi to dinner on Tuesday?" Grant asks. "She's flying home from Cornell University that morning."

Aha, here comes the real reason for Grant's call. His girlfriend, Mimi Jones, interned with Welch HOA Management this past summer. She's a delight.

"Fine with me," Ted replies. "But be polite and call Grandma Myrt. She's the one planning your special homecoming dinner. Of course, if Myrt's cooking, there's never a scarcity of good eats."

Grant promises to call his grandma then rings off.

"It'll be fun to see Mimi," I say. "Can't wait to tell her about all the bird varieties I've identified since she put that birdsong app on my phone. Every time I hear a bird chirp, I check to see whether it's a Lowcountry native or a wintering visitor."

Ted chuckles. "Yeah, bird chirps get you to turn on your cell phone when fellow humans can't."

I fake a put-upon sigh. "I know the identity of all the humans who want to bug me," I quip. "I check for messages when it's convenient. I just refuse to be tethered to a cell phone. An old joke claims that aliens decide dogs rule Earth since humans pick up their shit and snap to attention when they bark. I swear aliens visiting today would decide cell phones rule people. Any time the hunks of plastic squeal, humans obey."

Ted rolls his eyes. "Okay, how about activating your cell now to order a pizza for us to pick up on the way home."

I chuckle. "Cell phones do have their uses. If we don't cook tonight, I can think of other enjoyable activities to occupy the time."

Chapter Five

Archer Highsmith

Sunday Afternoon, December 15

My security system squawks. I take a final sip of scotch before I buzz Quentin Teacher inside. "Come on up." I push a button to unlock the ground-floor elevator. I don't believe in welcoming uninvited guests.

As soon as Lisa Queensbury gets her nicely-toned ass in gear, our Stillwater Cove HOA board can meet. As usual, there will be no need to take minutes. No point bothering our owners with board decisions. Most don't affect them anyway. They can stay fat and happy in their monied cocoon.

Quentin makes a beeline for one of my couches and casually sprawls his long limbs across all the cushions. His polished wingtips rest on the arm of the couch.

I arranged Quentin's move to Stillwater a month after I settled in. Needed my protégé's computer skills and figured his ability to make friends easily would come in handy. Wealthy matrons practically drool whenever they see his handsome face or sneak a peek at his abs. His looks fit a wholesome boy-next-door stereotype. Stillwater's male owners are equally enamored. They enjoy his ribald jokes and his keen interest in anything they say.

"So, how was church?" I ask. "Snag any dates with horny pew warmers?"

"Sadly, not today." He shrugs and mock frowns. "Just got a few more do-gooders signed up to help with the drive to provide needy Lowcountry tykes with Christmas toys. My godliness—or is it goodliness—surprises even me."

"Not me," I say.

I'm suddenly irritated by Quentin's nonchalance. We have serious problems. Yes, I'm partly to blame for opening our conversation with a crack about horny churchgoers, but he needs to pay attention.

"You're paid quite well to pretend you're a cross between a humanitarian Nelson Mandela and a young Michael Douglas playboy. But don't bring your act in here today. The day's been more than a little trying."

Quentin gets the message. He sits a little straighter and removes his size-twelve shoes from my couch.

I do appreciate Q's ability to perform as our board's most affable, caring member. It lets me limit my owner interactions to an occasional club dinner, a now-and-then golf outing, and princely waves as I parade around the community in my golf cart. These goodwill tours tell owners I'm keeping a close eye on what happens in the community to protect their interests. Actually, I'm looking out for anything that would upset my boss, Mick Haney, his bottom line, and my share of the take. Unfortunate happenings like Maury Campbell's passing.

Once a month, I send email greetings and a neighborhood update. A fitting gesture given my image as an eccentric high finance entrepreneur. Owners believe my clairvoyant timing in buying and dumping Bitcoin let me amass an unseemly fortune before I turned thirty-eight. That explains how a bachelor like me can afford an oceanfront mansion and a sixty-foot yacht. No one raises an eyebrow at my frequent travel.

A new security alert tells me our third HOA director has arrived. I buzz Lisa up.

She frowns as she steps out of the elevator. At least, I think it's a frown. Botox injections and an over-enthusiastic plastic surgeon have severely restricted the woman's expressions. Lisa's stretched skin gives the sixty-nine-year-old a perpetual look of surprise.

While she claims to be sixty-two, Lisa's true age isn't all she hides from her

26

ultra-rich, conservative hubby and suspicious stepkids. Like me, Lisa has a carefully constructed legend that guards her secrets and hides her former identity.

Funny how things work out. Lisa never wanted to be a Stillwater director. Her husband insisted. Since business travel kept him from serving, he wanted Lisa on the board to protect his investment. He had no idea that his demand sent a fox into the henhouse. Fortunately, I know the foxy vixen's secrets and have ample leverage to force her to do as I ask.

"What's so important we have to meet on a Sunday?" the platinum blonde complains. Her butt's perched on the edge of a leather director's chair. Lisa looks prepared to bolt if the news is bad, though we both know Stillwater's only carry-over director won't budge an inch unless I say so.

Quentin grins. "Don't worry, Lisa. Whenever Archer commands our appearance, he's got headline news. Come on. Don't keep us in suspense, Archer. What's up?"

I award my protégé a glare as I get down to business. This isn't some social, let's sip our Bloody Mary's gathering.

"Jack killed Maury Campbell this morning."

I ignore Lisa's audible gasp as she crumples in her chair. Her ramrod posture forgotten.

"Don't worry," I continue. "We staged it to look like an accident. The coroner had no problems buying into our fiction that Maury's golf cart crashed into a tree and his neck broke when he was thrown free. A freak accident but an accident nonetheless."

"So, what's the emergency?" Lisa asks. "Sounds like you've handled the Maury problem. Nothing for Quentin or me to do beyond publicly moan about the man's bad luck."

Lisa has certainly perfected her snooty diction. It shouldn't bother me, but her haughty mannerisms annoy me even more than Quentin's cheek. The woman's gone so deep into her phony identity that her play-acting has become second nature.

"Our problem," I explain, "is the widow, Velma Campbell. Unfortunately, she discovered her husband's body before we were ready to call in the authorities. We hadn't quite put all the pieces in place. EMS, a deputy sheriff, and a coroner were all within earshot when Velma started mouthing off. She said the crash was no accident and started tossing around accusations."

Quentin sits up. "Did she accuse us—the board—because we fired him?"

"No," I say, "but the point is she injected a grain of doubt into our accident explanation. And her theory of the crash isn't totally bonkers. She suggested the Campbells' neighbor, Richard Ryebread, killed her husband. She thinks Richard was chasing Maury and, when her husband looked back at Dicky, wham! he smacked into a tree. While the idea of a high-speed golf cart chase is a bit of a stretch, it's easy to imagine Dicky Ryebread harassing Maury."

"So what?" Quentin asks. "Given that's not what happened, the widow won't find dipshit to back her conspiracy theory. Can't we just let her rave? Without any evidence, the authorities will assume it's her grief talking. That she can't accept the fickle finger of fate."

My cell phone rings. Since I'm expecting a call from Jack Durham, our security chief, I didn't have it muted. I hold up a hand to silence Quentin and Lisa while I take the call.

"Good," I say. "They've all left, and the widow is definitely not returning to Stillwater tonight?"

Good news. "Okay, Jack, tonight you'll join Quentin and me on a visit to the Campbell house. Make sure the gate knows to alert us instantly if Mrs. Campbell comes back unexpectedly."

I end the call, and return my attention to Lisa and Quentin.

"The problem, my fellow directors, is that Velma Campbell not only doubts Maury's death was an accident; she has friends. The new widow immediately invited Ted Welch, who owns the HOA management company we fired last year, to come poke around the accident scene with his nosy security consultant, Kylee Kane, in tow. We couldn't prohibit their visit without notching up their suspicions."

"Let's back up," Q says. "I know Maury was a problem. Heck, I'm the one he first confided in. But I thought we agreed firing him would be the end of it. If we took away his keys to the maintenance barn, we'd end his ability to snoop."

I grimace. "As it turns out, Maury made himself a spare set of keys. A guard spotted him going inside the barn this morning. Jack and I waited till he exited. Then we questioned him. Jack emptied his pockets, and I took his cell phone.

"He took pictures with his phone—photos that sentenced him to death. The only question was how to make it look like an accident. Jack broke his neck, and I hopped in his golf cart to move Maury's body a good quarter-mile from the maintenance barn. I spotted a big oak in the woods, and Jack crashed the golf cart into the tree. We positioned the corpse a few feet away."

"What about the pictures on his phone?" Lisa asks.

"Jack took the batteries out of the cell phone and smashed it. It's buried in three feet of pluff mud. No one's ever going to find it. We block all cell phone signals inside the maintenance barn. Before destroying the phone, I accessed the pictures and deleted the new ones from all devices. That way, even if the stupid phone uploaded to the cloud, the pictures are gone."

"Okay, I'm missing something," Q says. "What's got your asshole puckered? The afternoon downpour must have turned the crash site into mud soup. So what if Ted and Kylee guess something's fishy? They have no leads, nowhere to go. If they hassle Richard Ryebread, it only works in our favor. That hothead will respond like the homicidal maniac Velma says he is. A nice distraction."

"It's not quite that simple. We don't know if Maury shared his suspicions with anyone else before he took those pictures. If he did, we need to tie off any loose ends."

Chapter Six

Kylee

Monday Morning, December 16

Ted and I arrive at the Welch HOA Management office at eight a.m. En route, I picked up a dozen donuts, even though I'm unsure how many will come to our Monday morning meet-up. Since Velma's staying with Mom and Frank, Mom's taking the day off. Frank might be a no-show, too. But my motto is: when in doubt, don't skimp on donuts. So what if there are only three of us—Ted, me, and Robin Gates, our computer guru—hungry clients might drop by, right?

At our Monday roundtable we discuss any "emergencies" that popped up over the weekend, and we share our priorities and plans for the coming week. Our office is staffed a half-day on Saturdays. A number of HOA directors and owners have jobs that make it hard for them to connect with us on weekdays. On Sundays, the office is closed. An answering service alerts Ted to any true emergencies and records all other requests for us to handle come Monday.

I start a pot of coffee in a kitchenette at the back of our offices.

"Hey, Robin." I hear Frank's booming baritone greet the company's only youthful employee. "Have any hot dates this weekend? Us old fogies need to be reminded that some people have better ways to spend weekends than discussing arthritis and cataract surgeries."

"Listen, old man," Robin replies. "I recently read how old folks, meaning you and retirees your age, are the demographic hardest hit with STDs. You know, syphilis, gonorrhea, herpes. Maybe you should share what you and Myrt did this weekend."

The exchange ends with shared laughter.

Okay, when clients aren't around, our crew makes no attempt to be politically correct (PC). We're like an extended family, kidding and matching wits. Doesn't mean we're not absolutely professional when we interface with customers.

Our light-hearted banter lets off steam. Stress levels can soar when you're dealing with an owner incensed that a neighbor's truck is blocking his driveway or with a retiree disgusted that Welch HOA Management allowed a trash bin to overflow.

I greet Robin with a high-five as I pass her cubbyhole. "Don't take any guff off the old fart."

Frank peels off his plaid wool jacket, glances my way, and hangs his head. "Et tu, Brute?"

Ted grins and rolls his eyes. He's already seated at our break table and inhaling his first donut. I wait for the coffee to finish percolating, fill my mug, and join him.

Once we're all seated, Ted updates Robin on Maury's death and yesterday's visit to Stillwater. Since Maury handled occasional maintenance jobs for Welch HOA Management, Robin knew and liked him.

Ted tips his chin toward me. "Kylee will be spending part of her time this week interfacing with authorities on Velma's behalf."

He tactfully doesn't mention that I will try to find out more about Richard Ryebread and if there's any way to prove he was or wasn't involved in Maury's accident. I'm dead certain Stillwater security will not investigate.

Robin frowns. "Kylee, I hope you're still planning to make your two o'clock with Evie Miles. Evie went on Earful again this morning and repeated that no one at Hullis Island or Welch HOA Management takes people seriously if they're old and sick."

I sigh. One of Robin's most distasteful tasks is to monitor what folks are saying on Earful about us and our client HOAs, but we never, ever post. That's just what trolls hope we'll do to keep their attacks fresh.

"I'll keep the date with Evie if I have to swim to Hullis," I say. "Meanwhile, I'll check out every theft report filed with Hullis Island in the last two years. It won't make Chief O'Rourke happy, but maybe due diligence will convince Evie we're not dismissing her. It sure would be nice to have her say so on Earful. Evie has quite a following."

Before Ted took over the management of Hullis Island's HOA, Chief O'Rourke reported directly to the HOA board, which gave him free rein on everything from budgets to how he handled security complaints. Now that the chief reports to Ted, he strongly resents any questions about his operation.

Our meeting wraps at 8:45, and I head to my cubicle. I want a little privacy for my call to Sheriff Deputy Josie Muschel. Our office is housed in a failed convenience store that Ted bought solely for its central Beaufort County location. It offers easy access to Hilton Head, Port Royal, Beaufort, and smaller islands like Hullis. Ted gutted the interior and used carpeted wall panels to divvy up the space. Not fancy, but the fabric-covered walls offer a smidgen of auditory privacy.

I reach Josie on the first try. I'm glad she's at her desk and not responding to some law enforcement crisis. I explain why Maury's widow wants his cell phone ASAP, and Josie promises to check on the autopsy schedule and the phone. I refrain from sharing Velma's belief that Maury's accident wasn't due to solo driver error.

Next, I contact Hullis Island security and request a list of all theft reports received in the past twenty-four months. I expect there to be a half-dozen at most. Sleepy Hullis Island isn't exactly a high-crime community. The download surprises me—two dozen theft reports with eighteen cases remaining open. The six closed cases were solved after a "nanny cam" caught a plumber pilfering items during a renovation project. The discovery quickly linked him to thefts at five other Hullis repair projects.

Wonder if the open cases have any common threads?

These owners did not report service people visiting their properties around the time of the thefts, and there were zero signs of break-ins. Of course, that doesn't mean strangers didn't enter their homes and exit with valuables. Too many people in gated communities brag about leaving their doors unlocked. That nonchalance is an open invitation to theft.

A phone call interrupts my look-see at the theft reports.

"Hi, Josie. That was quick. What's the answer on the cell phone—can I pick it up?"

"Sorry, Kylee, can't help. I checked the log of the vic's personal effects. Other than clothing, it only lists a wallet, a watch, a pocket knife, and a wedding ring. No cell phone. I called the ME's office to double-check. They were rather huffy. Assured me no cell phone arrived with the body."

Josie pauses. "The widow's undoubtedly in shock. Maybe Mrs. Campbell isn't remembering clearly. Perhaps her husband left his cell phone at home. Maybe he started charging it and forgot to put it back in his pocket. See if Mrs. Campbell has one of those find-my-phone apps. That might locate it."

"Josie, have you heard any scuttlebutt about the possibility someone might have been chasing Maury before his golf cart ran into that tree?"

"No," she answers. "Why? Is that what the widow claims?"

"Let's say Velma's suspicious, and frankly, so am I. Ted and I visited the accident scene, and it didn't feel right. Maury's golf cart ran into a huge tree with considerable force. Why would Maury be driving like a bat out of hell in dense woods? And, if he was, wouldn't he be paying attention? Looking for big bad oaks?"

"The coroner believes he might have had a stroke, or a heart attack, maybe a seizure," Josie says.

"Okay, that's possible, but it doesn't explain why he'd be going so fast. Pretty reckless, and that wasn't Maury. Guess we'll know more after the autopsy."

I recall Velma mentioned there was a sheriff's deputy at the scene.

"Mrs. Campbell described the deputy at the scene as a young kid with pimples and a scraggly goatee," I add. "Anyone come to mind?"

Josie laughs. "Yep, he's older than he looks, but still wet behind the ears and semi-clueless. I'll pump him for his impressions anyway."

I thank Josie for her efforts. I'm not eager to relay the news to Velma. I sip my coffee as I try to marshal my thoughts. While Josie offered logical explanations for the cell phone to be missing, I doubt Velma will buy any of them.

Could it have fallen out of the golf cart when Maury was thrown from the wreckage? If so, wouldn't the first responders have noticed it? Or maybe Maury set it down in the maintenance barn and forgot to pick it back up? Of course, Stillwater security claims Maury never entered the maintenance barn.

I hope Ted can remind me how those find-your-phone apps work. If nothing else, maybe an app can pinpoint when and where Maury last used his cell.

I steel myself to call Velma. Until we get the autopsy report, I'm loathe to fuel her suspicions that Maury's golf cart collision was anything other than a tragic accident. A vanished cell phone will rev up her doubts. Would Richard Ryebread have a reason to steal the phone? Maybe if he thought Maury had videoed him poisoning the Campbell trees.

I postpone calling Velma. She's likely to ask if I've looked into Richard Ryebread's background. I haven't. Primarily because documenting that he's an asshole doesn't prove he chased Maury. Impossible without a witness or a shred of evidence that the fatality involved two vehicles. Still, it would help to know if he has a record of past domestic abuse or physical altercations.

A couple of quick queries net me zero items of interest. Richard Ryebread is the CEO of a company that manufactures and custom-modifies vehicles to withstand terrorist attacks. Customers include the U.S. Secret Service, the military, and law enforcement. Also, the people who like to think they're important enough to attract an assassin. That runs the gamut from sheikhs to movie stars. Of course, Dickhead's customers need a few million to purchase luxury, bullet-proof rides.

Good luck getting any dirt on Ryebread from law enforcement sources. I'll scan social media posts later.

Time to quit procrastinating and call Velma. Since I don't know her cell number, I phone Mom's landline. My call goes to voicemail. Must mean

Mom and Velma aren't at home. Mom always answers when caller ID reports her daughter's on the line.

A call to Mom's cell phone also goes unanswered. I leave another voicemail asking her to call back, noting I'll switch off my phone when I meet with Evie. Interrupting an interview to take a call would certainly juice up Evie's feelings that no one considers her important. And I'd agree. Unless someone's waiting to hear about a family member on life support, I can't think of a reason to halt an in-person conversation to answer a call.

"If we don't connect before two, I'll drop by after I see Evie."

Chapter Seven

Kylee

Monday Afternoon, December 16

I finish my background notes on Hullis Island thefts, then sort through the two-hundred-plus emails that accumulated in my inbox over the weekend. I even scan my Spam folder. Occasionally, something I'm expecting gets dumped there.

Next on the agenda? Researching golf cart accidents.

How rare are fatalities?

Not as rare as I expected. My first query pulls up an insurance company post about a handful of golf cart fatalities in South Carolina. The article suggests the absence of seatbelts and airbags contributes to the mayhem. If people hit their heads when they fall from carts, brain injuries can be traumatic.

Another article summarizes a decade-long study that tallied more than 150,000 hospital visits to emergency rooms caused by golf cart-related injuries.

I'm mildly surprised. It sometimes seems that golf carts outnumber cars in Beaufort-area HOAs. When my Mustang is dawdling behind these vehicular turtles, I'm convinced radar would clock their speeds under five miles per hour.

Actually, my research tells me most of these buggies can zoom all the way up to 12 to 15 miles per hour. The pace still seems glacial when your car can't pass. Golf course liability is partly to blame for the speed caps. Since golf cart accidents make up nearly fifteen percent of on-the-links personal injury claims, golf clubs have a vested interest in restricting their speed.

Maybe the accident rates aren't all that surprising. Golf carts do have a tall-skinny profile that makes them susceptible to tipping on uneven terrain.

Of course, folks who own their own buggies aren't restricted by golf course caution. Some electric models have enough pep to zip around at twenty-five miles per hour, while custom gas models can top fifty miles per hour.

Need to ask Ted about the make and model of Maury's machine.

Finally, I look into potential injuries in "low-speed" crashes. One article compared an unbuckled seatbelt passenger involved in a thirty-mile-an-hour crash to a person falling from a three-story building.

Yikes. Maybe Maury could have been thrown from his cart, even if he was going slow. But what made him run into that tree?

I'm startled when Robin taps me on the shoulder.

"It's one o'clock, Kylee. If you want to knock on Evie's door at two, you'd better get your rear in gear. If you're late, we're bound to see more posts saying we disrespect old folks."

"Thanks for the reminder."

Can't believe how I let online research suck me down rabbit holes. I totally lost track of time. My growling stomach reminds me I was glued to my screen through lunch. Good thing I bought a dozen donuts. I fill my travel mug with caffeine, swipe the last chocolate-iced donut, and snag extra napkins for my crumbly road meal.

* * *

En route to Hullis Island, I try to recall everything I know about Evie Miles. I first met the retired librarian about five years ago while spending a few vacation days at Hullis Island. Back then, I never dreamed I'd someday work for an HOA management firm. Mom introduced me to Evie at a reception that followed a sea turtle talk.

Despite the intervening years, I have a clear picture of Evie in my mind's eye. That's largely due to her hair—a thick, shoulder-length mane dyed the improbable color of a Macaroni and Cheese Crayon in an extended coloring set. I'm always surprised when I meet intelligent women who insist on dye jobs that make them look like dummies or at least color-blind. Do they avoid mirrors like vampires?

Nonetheless, Evie impressed me as quite intelligent. A natural conversationalist, her grin and laughter both came easily. I liked her. She definitely didn't seem the type of librarian who considers stern shushing her primary duty.

Despite the unfortunate hair shade, Evie clearly knew how to dress and accessorize. Though stout, she looked quite stylish. I remember complimenting her on a striking malachite necklace and earrings.

The copy of Evie's theft report indicates her current age is eighty-two. When we met, Evie and her older sister had just purchased an island home. The sister died three years ago, and Evie has lived alone ever since. Neither sister ever married.

Mom mentioned visiting Evie about nine months ago, shortly after the former librarian's cancer surgery. Being both a former nurse and cancer patient, Mom tries to support neighbors enduring treatment ordeals.

I find Evie's house easily. The attractive clapboard is painted a pale yellow with a front door and shutters in a contrasting hunter green. Her house is only three blocks from Frank's home. Both border the sixth hole of the golf course, though they're on opposite sides of the fairway. My finger is still hovering above the doorbell when the door swings open.

For a second, I'm convinced I'm at the wrong address. The frail woman who greets me is a mere shadow of the stout but robust lady I recall. Her thick mane is gone, and the remaining sparse hair is pure white. Evie's scrawny frame swims inside a heather cashmere sweater set, and without a belt, her green linen trousers would pool at her feet.

Evie smiles. "Thank you for coming, Kylee."

I'm glad to see her smile—even though fleeting—hasn't totally disappeared.

Evie ushers me into her living room. Oversized sliding glass doors take up most of the wall facing the fairway. In fact, I can see Frank's house across the links. Floor-to-ceiling bookshelves line the other three walls. I almost feel like I should present my library card.

I do a quick scan of the titles. They seem to be organized by genre first, author name second. "Looks like you're still passionate about books," I comment.

"Yes. No matter how my body betrays me, reading never lets me down. These days, I focus on lighter fare—mysteries, thrillers, historical romances. I can lose myself in books that entertain. I won't even start one of the popular dystopian tales."

"You've described my reading preferences to a tee." I chuckle. "My book club does force me outside my comfort zone. Fortunately, it's a no-shame club. If I start a book I don't enjoy, I stop. Too many good books waiting. No recriminations."

Evie carefully lowers her body into a club chair and motions me toward the loveseat opposite her. "Please, sit down."

There's a moment of awkward silence. Should I mention her illness, or would she rather I didn't? She must realize I've noticed how much her appearance has changed since we last met.

"I was very sorry to learn of your cancer diagnosis. Mom reports you've finished chemo and are well along the road to recovery."

Evie lifts an eyebrow. "That recovery road has huge potholes, as Myrt knows. It's good to talk with someone who's traveled the same path. Your mother never tried to discount the horrors I'd encounter, but she gave me confidence the journey would be worthwhile.

"Of course, you're not here to discuss my health. I'm hoping you share your mother's gift—the ability to listen. Our young Hullis Island Security officers dismiss anything us old, sick people tell them. They assume our minds are as feeble as our bodies. If we can't offer concrete proof of some thief breaking in, they blame the loss on dementia."

I hold up my hand. "Evie, let's start with a clean slate. As a Coast Guard investigator, I worked a variety of crimes. Let's pretend I'm the first person you've contacted about the theft. Start at the beginning."

Evie nods and begins her story. She was diagnosed with cancer ten months ago. Following major surgery, she underwent radiation and then chemo treatments. The last treatment was six weeks ago. After Evie "rang the bell"—a tradition the day a patient has the last chemo infusion—her bridge club friends planned a major celebration.

"They reserved a table at the Breakwater," she says. "I felt better than I had in months. I couldn't remember the last time I'd worn anything besides pajamas and sweats. Getting dressed up seemed another way to convince myself the worst was over.

"I put on a dress that had hung—untouched—in my closet for over a decade. I'd gained too many pounds to wear it, but hadn't given it away. Hoping someday I'd lose enough to wear it again.

"Of course, cancer wasn't the diet regimen I had in mind. Once I put on the dress, I decided to wear my best jewelry. I have a large, organized jewelry case. When I opened it, I was horrified. My diamond and emerald necklace and matching earrings were gone."

I stop taking notes for a second to ask, "Were any other pieces missing?"

"No. That puzzled me. I have other expensive pieces, though none as valuable as the diamond and emerald pieces. I have a gorgeous malachite stone an artist set in an intricate gold design, and I inherited a long, double-strand pearl necklace from my mother. Both were in the case."

Evie slides a sheet of paper across the coffee table that separates us. "An insurance policy rider covers my jewelry. To obtain the rider, I had to provide both valuations and photos of all my expensive pieces. The emerald and diamond flower necklace was valued at seventy thousand dollars. When the Hullis Island Security officer came to investigate, I gave him a copy."

The color photos are stunning. Evie included a pencil in the pictures to give some perspective on the size of the gems. I don't know carats from carrots, but the stones looked like very impressive rocks.

"The pieces are beautiful," I say.

Evie leans back and briefly closes her eyes. Picturing her lost treasures?

"Did you call Hullis Island Security as soon as you missed the jewelry?"

Evie shakes her head. "No. My friends were due to pick me up in five minutes. I didn't want to make us late for our reservation. I figured the jewelry would still be gone in the morning, and I'd deal with it then. Also, I planned to wrack my brain before I made the call. Was it possible I'd taken the missing pieces out of my jewelry box for some reason?"

I have a good idea why the security officer was skeptical about Evie's report. My own mother frequently complained about "chemo brain" and how the treatments made her forgetful.

"So what happened the next morning?" I ask.

"I spent hours searching the house," Evie confides. "I wanted to make absolutely sure I hadn't misplaced the pieces. I turned the place upside down. But even while I was searching, I felt certain the necklace and earrings had been stolen."

She looks at me and slowly shakes her head. "You're lucky you haven't gone through chemo, but your mother will understand. Though the treatments make you forgetful, you don't abandon lifelong routines. They're what keep you sane. My mom gave me my first jewelry box when I was sixteen, and I've had one ever since. Never in my life—not once—have I taken off a necklace and failed to put it in my jewelry case. I'm obsessive about everything being in its place, tidy.

"Also, between my cancer diagnosis and that celebration my friends planned, I didn't wear any jewelry. Not a ring. Not a necklace. Not even earrings. I felt why bother?"

Okay. Evie needs to be treated the same as any person who reports expensive jewelry missing. Her illness should carry no weight.

"When was the last time you wore the missing necklace and earrings?"

Evie chews on her lip as she thinks. "Last January. That's when I attended the wedding of my youngest niece—quite the formal affair. My brother has two daughters. The weddings for those girls cost a fortune. But that's not the last time I saw that necklace and earrings.

"I know it sounds morbid, but my cancer diagnosis prompted me to make decisions about how my valuables would be divvied up while I was still alive. I'd heard too many stories about heirs squabbling. So, I estimated the value of each piece of jewelry and created two lists that were roughly equal in value. Then, I invited my nieces to spend a weekend with me. Anyway, I gave them copies of the list, and we looked at the jewelry. Fortunately, the girls chose different lists to claim their favorite pieces. No arguments."

I make a note of the date before quizzing Evie about other folks who might have seen her diamond and emerald jewelry.

She laughs. "How about half of Hullis Island and dozens of people in Beaufort and Hilton Head? Before the cancer, I enjoyed dressing up for special occasions."

Her answer doesn't surprise me. I knew Evie was a big supporter of the arts and nonprofits that promote literacy and environmental protection. During the five years she's lived in the Lowcountry, she'd have attended plenty of dress-up charity events, where her jewels might have caught the eye of other guests or wait staff.

I follow up with questions about Evie's security system. While I didn't see a video doorbell, I noted a security control panel near her front door.

"I turn my alarm on every night before I go to bed," she says. "I turn it off when I wake."

"Do you keep your doors locked during the day?"

She sighs. "I did before I got sick. Then, I didn't have the energy to get up and answer the door. If I was expecting people, I left the door unlocked."

She snorts when I ask if she can list all the people who've been inside her house since her cancer diagnosis.

"Might be easier to give you a list of who didn't drop by. Of course, all my friends visited, and the folks on the Hullis Island Care Committee delivered meals.

"Come to think of it, I did have a couple of repair people in. I bought a new microwave when my old one quit working and had it installed. Also, the HVAC folks came for my annual fall inspection. Think that's it. I wasn't exactly in the mood for a 'This Old House' update."

I ask for the names of the microwave and HVAC vendors and, if she can remember, approximately when they visited.

Finally, I ask if she can show me her jewelry box. I want to see where she keeps it.

Evie leads me to her bedroom. The impressive cedar box takes up half of a long dresser. Hard to miss.

"Wow, it's beautiful."

"It is, isn't it?" Evie's tone communicates her pride. "Bought it in Peru. It's hand-carved cedar with native designs carved into both the leather and wood."

I glance around the room. With the drapes open—as they are now—someone skulking around the house could see this box.

But wouldn't a thief simply empty the entire box? Why take only two expensive pieces?

Evie opens the hinged top. The inside of the lid is a mirror. Below the lid, individual velvet cubbies hold Evie's most prized items.

She points at two empty spots. "That's where the missing pieces should be."

Evie closes the lid and opens the drawers that sit below the top. There are eight rows of side-by-side drawers, sixteen total. I'm duly impressed.

"You have some beautiful pieces." I find I'm unconsciously fingering the only jewelry I wear—my engagement necklace. Knowing I don't like to wear rings, Ted's proposal came with a custom necklace showing a man and woman in a row boat. Both have oars in hand.

When Evie and I return to the living room, I review the information I saw in the Hullis Island Security file.

"The officer said he checked your doors and windows," I begin. "He saw no sign of a break-in."

"Correct," she says. "Of course, I was gone a lot with hospital stays and doctor visits. Who knows? Maybe the thief crawled in a window. Fall weather's so pleasant; I often leave windows open. Not that hard to remove a screen."

I close my notebook. "Evie, give me a few days to do more research. I promise I'll be back in touch soon."

Chapter Eight

Archer

Monday Afternoon, December 16

Quentin seems a might put out he had to cancel his date for tonight. He planned to hook up with some hot Hilton Head tourist he met while picking up donated toys at one of the collection spots. Too bad. Q can wait another twenty-four hours to bed some bimbo.

Q has the brains but not the discipline. That's how he came to my attention. He was sure his tech start-up would make him a billionaire overnight. He failed to pay attention to market indicators and lost his shirt and the money he'd recklessly borrowed. I saw Quentin's potential and asked my associates to bail him out. Sometimes, Q likes to forget he's owned. Tonight's a reminder. I need his computer skills.

I'm so glad Velma was thoughtful enough to stop at the gate and add her house to our watch list. Nice to know she has no plans to return to Stillwater until late Tuesday.

Gotta love how helpful such ingrained habits can be. Even before Stillwater finished installing its gates, the HOA asked owners to let security know any time their houses would be vacant. Knowing no one was home, security would increase drive-by frequency and an officer would regularly walk the perimeter of the empty house to discourage trespass.

Naturally, we strongly endorsed the practice and continued it. Though we're not worried about thieves inside our HOA, we do like to know exactly who's in residence. It's also helpful to keep tabs on any residents known to take nocturnal strolls. Typically by two a.m., our owners—even the insomniacs—are all tucked in.

The widow's departure offers us an excellent window to tie up any remaining loose ends. While the grieving spouse is away, we can search the Campbell house and check Maury's computer files.

The man's unauthorized Sunday visit to the maintenance barn netted him limited clues about our endeavors. He snagged a few currency straps and used his phone to snap pictures of our shrink-wrap machine and some cages hidden under tarps.

Could I dream up explanations for those pictures if pressed? Sure.

"Why do you have straps to bundle cash?"

"Stillwater's golf club and restaurant take in a fair amount of cash. We stock the straps at the maintenance barn to bundle bills before making our bank deposits."

"What about the shrink-wrap machine and the cages?"

"The shrink-wrap machine is being repaired for our clubhouse kitchen. They use it to vacuum-pack items for the freezer. And, our security guards use the cages to humanely trap wild animals that become nuisances and to round up lost pets for owners. We also keep them for the convenience of our on-call veterinarian. His in-home visits are one more example of the extraordinary services we provide our owners."

My search of Maury's entire photo gallery did provide a few more worrisome snaps. On Saturday, he took pictures at the marina. Too many were focused on my yacht. I need to make sure he didn't jot down notes about any speculation. His wife or son might come across them while going through his desk or looking at his computer. If they don't look, I'll bet Kylee will.

Glad I had the presence of mind to use Maury's cell phone to delete their video doorbell account before Jack destroyed the phone. Quentin, Jack, and I can safely visit the Campbell home any time after dark.

Chapter Nine

Kylee

Monday Afternoon, December 16

I swing by the Hullis Island Security Office to copy all missing property reports filed in the last two years. As I'm stuffing the papers in my briefcase, a scowling Chief O'Rourke grabs my arm.

"What are you doing? You'd better not be removing any files."

"No, sir," I reply. "Just made copies."

He frowns. "Kylee Kane, our officers are professionals. We know what we're doing. I don't appreciate you poking around and second-guessing us. It sends the wrong message to owners. I heard you called on Evie Miles. Why are you listening to confused residents' conspiracy theories? It just stirs up more outlandish notions about non-existent crime."

I shake my head. "I beg to differ. When Welch HOA Management looks into complaints, owners realize their HOA takes their concerns seriously. If the Hullis Island Security investigation was indeed thorough and you did everything possible, we'll say so. That doesn't hurt your credibility; it improves it."

The chief releases my arm. "You always have a pat answer, don't you? Your boyfriend's company may have the right to nitpick how we operate and spend our budget, but you'd better not waste any of my officers' time on your wild-goose chase."

O'Rourke turns his back on me and stomps off. He doesn't expect an answer.

I'm quite aware of the Chief's opinions. Before Hullis Island hired Welch HOA Management, the volunteer directors on the Hullis board gave O'Rourke carte blanche. Never questioned his budget or policies. He hates that he now reports to someone who actually reviews budgets, makes suggestions to improve security, and follows up on complaints.

It's four p.m. Not enough time to return to the office so I head to Frank's house. I hope Mom and Velma have returned from wherever they ventured earlier. While I'm not eager to tell Velma her husband's phone is missing, she needs to know. It's possible the phone fell out of Maury's pocket before the crash.

* * *

I don't see any vehicles in Frank's driveway. That doesn't mean Mom and Velma aren't inside. The two-car garage has ample room for Frank's truck and Mom's Chevy Bolt. I don't expect to see Velma's car since Mom and Frank brought her here.

I climb the front porch stairs. I'm sure Velma is exhausted, emotionally and physically, and I wonder if she might be napping. Should I ring the bell?

Frank gave me a key to his house when Mom moved in. I've only used it once. It was summertime, and the deviled eggs I'd brought needed refrigeration. Leaving them on the porch till someone came home risked food poisoning.

I don't believe in invading anyone's privacy, lacking explicit permission. Mom's the same way. Of course, I have no worries about Mom climbing aboard the River Rat when I'm gone. Heck, it practically takes dynamite to get her to step foot on the boat when I'm holding her hand. Given her fear of drowning, getting in a tub represents an act of courage for Mom.

I give the bell a quick tap, and Mom answers the door.

"Come in, but be quiet. Velma's napping. She didn't sleep much last night. We spent the afternoon at the funeral parlor and with the Methodist pastor, making arrangements. Exhaustion finally forced Velma to close her eyes an hour ago."

"They're open again," Velma says as she enters from the guestroom to give me a hug.

Based on the shadowed skin below the widow's eyes, the nap wasn't long enough. She looks eggshell fragile and somehow smaller, as if the weight of her grief has settled on her shoulders.

"Let's sit," I suggest. I want Mom and Velma seated before I deliver my unwelcome news.

"Did you get Maury's phone, or do I need to pick it up?" Velma asks.

"Unfortunately, neither. My friend Josie, a deputy in the Sheriff's Office, checked the inventory of Maury's belongings. It didn't include a cell phone."

"What! That's ridiculous. Maury always put his cell phone in his back pocket when he left the house. Of course, he had it with him."

"Perhaps he lost it or set it down somewhere after he left the house," I suggest.

"No way. You don't know Maury. He is—was—obsessed with his phone. He bought a new iPhone two weeks ago. With Vince galivanting all over the world, Maury set up alerts on his phone. He wanted to make sure he had up-to-the-minute news about any country where our son was working."

Velma wraps her cardigan tighter. "Someone stole Maury's phone. It was expensive. Someone at that crash scene saw it and snatched it."

Velma is becoming increasingly agitated. Not good.

"If you're right, maybe we can find it. You say it's an iPhone, do you know the model?"

I pull my laptop from my briefcase and Google the latest iPhone model. Ted had already given me a refresher course on find-my-phone apps.

"Did you or Maury turn on the Find My Network option?" I ask.

She nods. "I think so. I'm terrible at figuring out all these apps. I just want to use my phone to talk, take pictures, and text. Maury always set my phone up for me. I remember he said he used the same Apple ID for both our phones to keep it simple. That way, he could always see my location."

"That's good. If your phone and Maury's have the same Apple ID, we should be able to use your phone to find Maury's—even if it's turned off. The Find My Network also can show the phone's location the last time it was powered on."

Though I'm no techie, I help Velma navigate the app.

Crap! Maury's phone can't be located? What does that mean?

I thought the app could find a phone even if it was switched off.

"The app does show Maury's phone was last active in that wooded area near the crash site," I note. "Perhaps it was damaged in the crash. That's probably why the app is no longer working."

Velma stares at the screen, then glances at me. "I want to go look for it. If it got jostled out of Maury's pocket by first responders, it could still be there under pine needles or palm fronds."

I glance at my watch. "Velma, it won't do any good to search tonight. The sun sets around five-twenty. By the time we arrived at Stillwater, it would be too dark to see anything in those woods. I'll search for it in the morning."

Velma sighs and glances out the window. Christmas lights are already coming on in the houses across the fairway.

"Okay. I already told Myrt I'm going home in the morning. Vince is arriving late tomorrow afternoon, and I have things to do before he arrives."

"I can pick you up here tomorrow and take you to Stillwater," I offer.

Mom shakes her head. "Nonsense. I'll drive Velma home. No need for you to make a Hullis detour. Besides, you can use an extra pair of eyes to search for the phone. When should we meet?"

"How about ten o'clock?" I suggest. "Tomorrow's supposed to be sunny. It should warm up by ten."

"I've got a roast in the crockpot," Mom adds. "There's plenty of food if you and Ted want to join us for supper tonight."

"Thanks, Mom, but we're already coming for supper tomorrow to welcome Grant home. Did he call you?"

Any mention of Grant and Mom's face lights up.

"Yes, I told him it was perfectly all right to bring the bird lady along. I enjoy chatting with Mimi. I know she loves to photograph birds; just hope she doesn't mind me cooking one. I'm making chicken parmesan, one of

Grant's favorites."

Mother frowns. "Velma, I apologize. Here I am prattling on about Grant coming home for Christmas when your Vince is coming home for his father's funeral. You know you and your son are welcome to join us tomorrow night."

"No, Myrt," Velma replies. "Vince and I need some time alone. On the phone, he'd already started yapping about me living alone so far from town. He's trying to push me into selling this house and moving to Beaufort. He needs to understand I have zero plans to make a snap decision."

"That's wise," Mom says. "When my Hayse died, it took me a good year to feel I was on an even keel, ready to weigh pros and cons, think rationally."

As I pack up my computer, I have serious doubts about tomorrow's treasure hunt. While I offered practical, innocent reasons for Maury's cell phone to be missing, my gut tells me the real reason is far from innocent.

Velma was too shocked by my cell phone news to ask about Richard Ryebread. I wish I could see a path forward there.

Should I call the man and ask to speak with him?

I need to make the effort, though I can't think of a single reason he'd agree to talk, let alone meet me. I'm smart enough not to step foot on his property uninvited. That would likely get me shot—or run over by a Humvee look-alike. Knowing what his company does, I wonder if his golf cart or ATV is a custom job. If so, could it have shoved Maury's golf cart into that tree without doing substantial damage to his own off-road vehicle?

Chapter Ten

Archer

Monday 6 p.m., December 16

"Hey, the house is all lit up. The widow must have come home."

I sigh. "Jack, think about it. Wouldn't we know if Velma Campbell is here? The gate has standing orders to warn us if and when she arrives."

Our security chief is aptly named. Jack is indeed a jack-of-all-trades. Killer being one of them. Obedient, yes. Brainiac, uh, no.

His bowling ball-shaped head bobs up and down as he considers my reply. I often wonder what's rattling around inside his thick skull.

Jack shrugs. "Okay, then, who do you suppose turned on all these Christmas lights?"

"Maury was a handy guy," Quentin answers. "Probably set a timer to automatically switch on the outdoor lights come dusk. Imagine they're programmed to shut off around the Campbells' normal bedtime."

"Oh." Jack's elegant reply.

I check out the Christmas display. Maury spared no expense in showing his holiday spirit. Old-fashioned, multi-colored light strands trim all the windows and edge the roof overhang. A floodlight shines on prancing, life-size reindeer—carved wood figures, not plastic blow-ups. No doubt, showcasing Maury's woodworking skills. A damn shame I won't be able to

51

use him for projects around my house. He should have kept his nose out of our business.

We park our three ATVs in shadows on the right side of the Campbell house. The part-time owners of the house next door are out of town. Unfortunately, I know the Ryebreads, who live in a Disneyesque mansion to the left of the Campbells, are in residence.

Dicky screamed at me for at least ten minutes this afternoon. He heard Velma had accused him of chasing Maury into that tree. Wanted to know what I was going to do to shut the bitch up. No point asking him to sympathize with a woman who'd unexpectedly found her husband's dead body. I assured Dicky the board would do everything in its power to make sure Stillwater neighbors and the Lowcountry at large, repeatedly hear the "true" story. That the fatality was a tragic, freak accident with no one to blame but fate.

I've warned Quentin and Jack that we need to take every precaution to keep from advertising tonight's visit. Some neighbors may not have heard about Maury's death and could drive over to view the Campbells' Christmas decorations, an annual tradition.

Gaining entry to the house isn't a problem. We changed our covenants to require owners to provide HOA security with keys and/or security codes to access their homes if we suspect some sort of problem when they're absent. If need be, we can easily fabricate justifiable emergencies—smoke drifting in the vicinity, water pooling near the foundation.

What we can't control are those damn video doorbells sending owners pictures of us entering their mansions. That's why I took the precaution of using Maury's phone to kill his home's video doorbell account. Glad I thought of it before Jack bludgeoned the phone and sunk it below layers of marsh pluff mud.

Quentin leads Jack and me into the house and straight to Maury's home office. Fortunately, the office sits at the back of the house, in the right-hand corner. Any light spill won't be seen by the Ryebreads or anyone coming up the driveway.

I switch on the overhead light.

The office isn't what you'd call tidy. His desk is cluttered with multiple stacks of paper and towering columns of wood-working magazines. A plastic in-basket overflows with junk mail. Imagine there's some rhyme or reason to the paper stacks—financial documents to be filed, bills to be paid? The magazines he's saved are dog-eared. Articles he wanted to re-read or reference?

A tall paper shredder sits beside his desk. I assume he used it to shred junk mail whenever his in-basket pile gets too high.

Handy. If we find anything we don't want the wife or son to read, we'll shred it. No need to haul it away.

"I'll go through the folders in that filing cabinet. Quentin, you fire up Maury's computer and search his hard drive and any thumb drives you find. He might have downloaded information to one of them.

"Jack, you search through these piles of paper and magazines. Look for any handwritten notes. Maury might have done some back-of-envelope ruminating about our enterprise."

"Rumin-what?"

I sigh. "Just see if Maury kept any notes about the maintenance barn, the marina, or Stillwater security. If so, put them aside for me to look at after I finish with the file cabinet."

"Bet you're happy Maury invited me into his office for our confidential meeting," Quentin says. "I couldn't believe he had such an ancient computer. I told him his antique operating system made him a prime candidate to be hacked.

"Maury just laughed. Explained he always left this computer up and running. He feared it might not start again if he shut it down. Said he had zero worries about online hackers since the computer isn't connected to the internet."

Jack looks up from a well-thumbed magazine. "That's pretty dumb. Why have a computer if you can't go online?"

"He did all his online work on his smartphone," Quentin replies. "Didn't update his desktop because he had some expensive computer-assisted drawing and financial management software that worked perfectly. He didn't want to fork over big bucks to buy the updated versions he'd need with an operating system upgrade. Thanks for your frugality, Maury, it makes my search a lot easier."

It takes the three of us a good hour to complete our assigned searches. I have to assume Maury was paranoid. He told Quentin he suspected Stillwater's security force was dirty. Maury thought the security guards were using the maintenance barn for unnamed nefarious purposes, and the board was oblivious.

With that mindset, he would make it hard for Stillwater security to find any evidence he gathered. After all, he knew security had the keys to his house and could enter whenever he and Velma were gone.

"I found zip," Quentin says.

"How about you, Jack?" I ask as I close the last file cabinet drawer.

Jack shrugs and hands me seven Post-it notes.

The writing couldn't be any harder to decipher if Maury'd penned them in hieroglyphics. He had his own unique shorthand. I spot a word that could be "marina" at the top of two pieces of paper.

"Quentin, take a look at these," I say. "Can you tell what this hen-scratching says? Is he talking about supplies for his own cabin cruiser or could the notes have something to do with Wavedancer?"

"Haven't a clue," Quentin says. "Why worry? None of the notes mention your yacht by name. I can't see anything that could be an abbreviation for Wavedancer."

"Yeah, but the Campbells were married a long time. After fifty years, maybe Velma can decipher these notes better than we can. We have a shredder sitting right here. Let's make good use of it. Feed it all the damn Post-It notes. I doubt the grieving widow will notice a few slips of missing paper in this messy man cave."

"What a waste of time," Jack carps.

"No, it isn't. We can't afford mistakes. The next shipment arrives tomorrow night."

Chapter Eleven

Kylee

Monday 6 p.m., December 16

I hear Ted whistling the instant I walk in the door.

"Sounds like you're in a good mood," I call out.

I find Ted in the kitchen pulling leftover pizza out of the refrigerator.

"Why shouldn't I be?" Ted responds. "'That infuriating woman of mine' is finally home."

"Say what?" I arch an eyebrow.

Ted grins. "That's what Chief O'Rourke called you when he phoned to harangue me. Let's see if I can remember his exact words: 'That infuriating woman of yours is stirring up trouble on Hullis Island. Can't you control her? Kylee needs to butt out of our investigations and stop encouraging doddering old biddies to spread rumors about a non-existent theft ring.'"

I start sputtering. "That pompous horse's patoot."

Ted laughs. "Don't worry. I told O'Rourke I have absolutely no control over you that you are your own woman. I added that I believed whatever you did was entirely professional.

"So what did you do?" he asks. "Why don't you start filling me in on your infuriating offenses while the pizza's heating? If your crimes take longer to catalogue, I'll listen while we eat."

"Sounds like a plan. I'm starved. However, I need a beer to wet my whistle for story time, and I'll need a couple more with the pizza."

While Ted slides the pizza in the oven, I fetch beers from the fridge. So nice to have a functioning kitchen. About went crazy during the lengthy kitchen renovation. Had to make do with a toaster, coffee pot, mini-fridge, and hot plate for weeks on end.

I sit at the kitchen table and twist off the bottle cap. Ted sits across from me and takes a long swig of his beer. Wish I could capture his expression. He always closes his eyes when he takes that first drink. One of his many quirks I've discovered since we started living together. Most of them—well, except for his fetish about which way the toilet paper unwinds—I find charming.

"Come on, spill," Ted urges after he swallows. His hazel eyes are wide open again and twinkling.

As we wait for the oven timer to ding, I share my search of reported Hullis Island thefts and my interview with Evie Miles.

"I believe Evie. The woman didn't misplace or lose her diamond and emerald jewelry," I conclude. "Someone stole them, and I think the thief has been quite active. I was shocked to learn Hullis Island residents have reported more than two dozen suspected thefts in the last two years. All but six are unsolved.

"Imagine O'Rourke's twitchy because his men dismissed those reports, one at a time. Chalked them up to old folks' carelessness or forgetfulness. He missed the big picture, the trend. When he learned I'd pulled twenty-four files, he freaked."

"As he should," Ted agrees. "That number's too big to be a coincidence. So what's your theory?"

"Don't have one yet. I want to look for any obvious links among the victims—same pest control, insurance companies, cleaning services, that sort of thing. Most victims are women. Only three men. The guys reported stolen watches and rare coins. I'd like to do a quick run-through of the cases with you at the office tomorrow. I need to leave by nine o'clock to meet Mom and Velma at Stillwater."

"Okay, I don't have any eight o'clock appointments. At least we can get a start. Why are you going back to Stillwater with Myrt and Velma?"

I quickly recap the saga of Maury's missing cell phone and Velma's determination to hunt for it.

When the oven bell dings, we cease talking business. Ted and I work together and live together. If we spend our out-of-the-office time discussing work, it's like we're on the job twenty-four hours a day. Plus we become very boring people. So, we try to talk about other things at dinner. And, after dinner, neither of us is allowed to mention work the rest of the evening.

I take a big bite of pizza. Just as good left-over as it was last night. In fact, I could have gobbled it up ice-cold. The beer tastes mighty good, too.

"Are you marking a calendar to cross off your remaining days as a swinging single?" Ted's grin is impish. "I know how excited you are about our *big* wedding."

I resist the urge to stab him with my fork. I suggested getting married at the courthouse with Ted's son, Mom, and Frank as witnesses and the sole attendees. If we wanted to do it up right, I figured we could treat our witnesses to dinner at a nice restaurant.

Ted calls our current wedding plan a compromise. I call it unconditional surrender. My mother said she'd waited her entire life to see one of her children marry, and, by gum, the ceremony was going to be beautiful and traditional. Family pressure is tough.

"Have you picked a dress yet?" Ted asks.

"Thinking about a clingy black silk with a plunging neckline," I reply. "Or maybe my dress uniform. Didn't get nearly enough wear out of it in the Coast Guard, and my medals will remind the pastor he'd better not try to sneak any obeying nonsense into the vows."

Ted laughs. "Don't think you have to worry about Reverend Pfaff. You made your feelings about the vows quite clear. Regarding the dress choice, I vote for black and clingy, though I'm surprised your mother hasn't bought you a dress."

"Mom knows there's a red line," I answer.

I nixed the idea of a bridal gown, multiple bridesmaids, flower girls, and ring bearer. However, I caved on a lot of other hoopla. At this point, Mom understands I've reached my limit.

Mom's compromise on the rehearsal dinner was to cap the guest count at thirty people. My number. Otherwise, I felt we'd be feeding half of Beaufort County. Mom and Frank have tons of friends, and Ted has lots of HOA clients with multiple directors. A thirty-person cap limits attendance to close friends and family.

There'll be no rehearsing either, and the meal will be a casual Frogmore Stew—boiled shrimp, potatoes, corn, and sausage—served on newspapers at the Hullis Island picnic shelter.

Hope it's not super cold December 23. The shelter, like a number of restaurants with outdoor seating, can fire up portable heaters. While they project heat, the radius is small. Guests will have to elbow their way to prime positions if it's in the thirties.

Since Ted wanted his son, Grant, to be his best man. I agreed to a maid of honor. Had my two pals in our Smart Gals Network flip for the slot. Lt. Alysha Carter, a young Coastie, won. I might have asked Kay Barrett, an older friend, but she's living in Europe with her new husband. Guess it's not that uncommon for ladies in their fifties to marry for the first, second, or third time.

The Christmas Eve wedding will take place late afternoon. Mom plotted all this, suffering little input from me. She determined four o'clock would give *her* guests time to spend the evening at home with loved ones or attend a candlelight Christmas Eve service.

In fact, the folks who scheduled the Hullis Island nondenominational chapel told Mom our wedding and the reception in the adjacent community center had to wrap by six p.m. A Christmas Eve service starts at eight o'clock.

"I know all the ceremonial pomp isn't your thing," Ted says as he polishes off his last slice of pizza. "But you've made Myrt very happy. Me, too. I'm excited Ed Hiller is preparing a Christmas Eve feast for our family. A unique present from a celebrity chef."

Ted grins. "I'm even more excited that we leave Christmas Day for a week, devoted solely to consummating our marriage in the sunny Cayman Islands."

"Yeah, like we haven't *consummated* plenty already." I laugh. "Won't your choice of honeymoon destination worry your clients? Maybe they'll think you picked the Caymans to launder money skimmed from their treasuries."

"First, the Caymans aren't the only island where dirty dollars can get an overnight make-over to clean green," Ted answers. "Learned that in the State Department. And second, the two of us haven't consummated nearly enough. To address that deficiency, I propose we head upstairs before Grant comes home, and you get all skittish about my son hearing squeaking mattress springs."

"So, it's okay if I scream tonight?"

"Be my guest. If you want, I'll scream, too."

Chapter Twelve

Kylee

Tuesday 8 a.m., December 17

T ed pulls into his parking spot just ahead of me. We don't drive to work together, since we usually need our cars during the day. Today, I head to Stillwater Cove in an hour to meet Mom and Velma while Ted has meetings at Lighthouse Cove and Rand Creek.

I don't dawdle going from my car to the office. I'm delighted it's sunny. But the wind is brisk and cold. True, it's not Iowa cold by any stretch of the imagination. I'd have thought this temperature on the seventeenth of December downright balmy when I was growing up.

My teeth chatter. I haven't picked up a Southern accent, but my body seems to have reset its tolerance for cold. Right now, it's in the forties. My body says that's a lie.

Since Ted and I are the first ones in the office, I make a beeline to the back to start coffee. Can't wait for a warm mug. Once it's percolating, I turn on the copier to create a second set of the Hullis Island theft reports for Ted. Then, with coffee and copies in hand, I head to his cubicle.

"I've arranged the reports sequentially, starting two years ago. As we go through them, I'll make notes on what we know about the victims. First up is Grace Shutt, who reported the theft of a black pearl necklace with double strands. Her husband bought it for her in Fiji while they were celebrating their fiftieth wedding anniversary. The insured value of the necklace is three thousand dollars, but the sentimental value is much higher. Mr. Shutt didn't make it to their fifty-first anniversary."

"I met Grace about three years ago," Ted says. "She was on a Hullis Island landscape committee looking into liberalizing rules that determine when residents can cut down palmetto trees on their lots. Nice lady. I believe she's a retired high school principal."

I nod. "I haven't met her, but Mom mentioned visiting Grace after she had a stroke. Understand she's fully recovered."

"Who's next?" Ted asks

"Second up is one of the few men who filed theft reports. Doug Fisher reported the theft of a rare coin. Let's see, he identifies it as an 'Early Eagle, Capped Bust Right, Heraldic Eagle' appraised at five thousand dollars. No other coins were missing from his collection.

"I've not heard Doug Fisher's name before. The report says he's forty-five and lives alone. Do you know him?"

"Yes," Ted says. "When Doug and his wife divorced, she got their primary residence, and he got their Hullis vacation house. He's a corporate consultant, who travels a lot. You'll want to do his interview by phone. He sold the Hullis house and bought a condo near the Savannah airport. I can give you his work number."

By the time Frank and Robin arrive, we've taken a cursory look at all the victims. The newcomers stop by to say "hi" before going to their workstations. Ted looks at his watch.

"It's eight-thirty. We'd better wrap up. I need a few minutes to prepare for my meeting."

I pack up my papers. The victims are predominately retired women, and I know several have had serious health issues—diabetes, strokes, heart attacks, or cancer. We've identified only one other common bond: the victims live alone.

I stop by to tell Ted goodbye. "My Stillwater visit should be brief. It won't take long to search the crash site for Maury's phone. There's really nothing else I can do to help Velma, except check on the autopsy schedule and how soon his personal items might be returned. After Stillwater, I'll try to interview Hullis theft victims who don't fit the typical profile. If I find a common thread among them, I may be on to something.

"How about you? When will you leave to pick up Grant?"

"Around lunchtime. Grant's last class ends at two. I never know how bad the Charleston traffic will be, so I'm leaving a little early to reach the Citadel by two. Once we return to Beaufort, we'll drop Grant's suitcase at the house, then head to Hullis. If you're home by five, we can all go together and make it to Hullis by six."

"What about Mimi? Are you picking her up?"

"No. Mimi said there were no guarantees the plane from New York would arrive on time. She'll drive herself."

We engage in a PG-rated office kiss. "Be careful," I say. "Charleston traffic can be brutal."

"You be careful, too," Ted replies. "Don't let those Stillwater goons strip search you before they let you through the gates."

Chapter Thirteen

Kylee

Tuesday 10 a.m., December 17

Before the Stillwater officer agrees to open the gates, he grills me. Then, he makes a show of going inside the gatehouse to double-check Velma's assertion that I'm a legit visitor and not on some terrorist list. He also hands me another tracker gizmo with a stern warning to keep it on my dashboard.

When I ask if Velma has returned to Stillwater, he grudgingly confirms that she came through the gate in another visitor's car about five minutes ago.

Good. They should be at Velma's house by now.

When I reach the Campbells' home, Mom and Velma are standing outside. Velma's oversized gestures suggest she's more than a little upset.

"What's happened?" I ask as I approach.

"Someone deleted our video doorbell account," Velma says. "That's what. It was working just fine before Maury's accident. I didn't know it was on the fritz until now. My cell phone didn't ding to alert me that Myrt and I were outside.

"Then I realized I didn't get a single alert last night. I should have. Stillwater guards are supposed to walk the house perimeter a couple of times each night when they know a home is vacant."

I frown. Living on a boat, I don't have a video doorbell. I know their purpose, but I'm clueless about how they work. "Could damage to Maury's cell phone have turned off the doorbell?"

"No," Mom and Velma reply in unison.

"Even if Maury's phone was destroyed, it wouldn't stop the app from sending alerts to my phone," Velma explains. "Maury programmed it to send to both phones."

"Could it be a dead battery?" I ask.

"Ha! That would be quite the coincidence," Velma scoffs. "No. Somehow, someone disabled it. I'm afraid to go inside, and I'm certainly not going to call Stillwater security to investigate. Could you call your deputy sheriff friend?"

"Let's hold off on sounding any alarms," I suggest. "At least until I take a look around. While I won't be able to tell if anything's missing, I can see if the house has been vandalized."

Velma and Mom are both shivering, and a stiff wind off the ocean has blown Mom's sparse white hair into what looks like a Mohawk.

"Go on, you two. Wait in Mom's car. No point volunteering to get frostbite. The gusts can practically blow you over. I'll be out in a jiffy."

I take my purse with me, and once I'm out of Mom and Velma's sight, I take out my gun. I got a permit to carry after encountering several people intent on ending my time on planet Earth.

I need less than fifteen minutes to peek in all the rooms and closets on the two upper floors. Neat as a pin. Except for Maury's office. But everything looks just like it did when I visited Sunday. Velma's a much better housekeeper than me.

Reluctantly, I came up in the elevator to speed my search; now I clomp down the stairwell to check it out. Before I walk outside to give an all-clear report, I put my Glock back in my purse.

Then I hear the yelling.

Velma and Mom are back outside the car. At the moment, Mom's voice is the loudest. She's giving what-for to a man I, unfortunately, recognize from yesterday's internet searches—Richard Ryebread, the pear-shaped, beetle-browed CEO.

My guess is the ATV he climbed out of is a custom job. If its wheels jacked the body up any higher, old Dicky would need a ladder to climb in. The monster machine looks like it was built for soldiers to ford the Amazon River and keep crocodiles out of snapping range. Serious overkill for Stillwater Cove and a round of golf.

"Who the hell are you!" Dicky demands of Mom. "Butt out. I'm trying to explain to my dimwitted neighbor that I had nothing to do with Maury running into a tree. Why did it happen? Probably because he's a dumbass and wasn't watching where he was going."

The man's face is much redder than his wispy, faded red hair. The wind has foiled his attempt to comb over his bald spot. A gust has plowed a wide part, exposing his pink scalp.

"How dare you!" Velma yells.

I run to separate the combatants.

"Mr. Ryebread," I shout. "You're not invited. That means you're trespassing. Please leave immediately."

"Who have we got here? Imagine you're a younger member of this defective gene pool." He smirks. "You're clearly not a Stillwater neighbor, and I don't have to listen to you."

"I think you do, buster. South Carolina is one of those states that doesn't shed a lot of tears if something bad happens to a dickhead who fails to leave a person's home once he's told to vacate the premises."

I hear Velma sobbing.

Crap, I meant to de-escalate the situation, not make it worse. I somehow need to channel Ted's trademark diplomacy.

My comment was stupid. What if this bully is packing a gun? Mine's back in my purse, within reach, but not for a quick draw.

Be the bigger person, the adult. Take a deep breath and step back.

"Mr. Ryebread," I lower my voice to a near-normal level. "Please leave. This isn't the time or place for a rational discussion. Mrs. Campbell just lost her husband. Have some compassion."

Dicky is vibrating with anger. His chest expands and contracts like a bellows.

"Don't think this is the end," he growls, staring at Velma. "I'll get you booted out of this house if it's the last thing I do. How dare you insult my reputation. You'll be hearing from my lawyers."

With that final verbal salvo, he stomps around to the driver's side of his ATV, climbs in, and backs down the driveway at kamikaze speed.

Yes, that ATV could push a golf cart into a tree and probably wouldn't suffer a dent in its reinforced front bumpers.

Mom puts her arms around Velma and leads her toward the house. While her sobs are subsiding, I know her heartbreak has just begun, and her rage is growing.

* * *

I carry Velma's overnight bag inside, and we all climb into the elevator. Mom gives the bag a sidewise look. "Are you absolutely sure you want to stay here tonight?"

Velma nods. "The dickhead next door may sic his attorneys on me, but he's not going to attack. He's mean but not stupid. You two would be witnesses if anything happened to me. Besides, Vince will be here late afternoon. I'll only be alone for a couple hours. I'll spend the time researching how to reactivate our camera and motion detector. If I can't figure it out, Vince can, or we'll buy a new one."

"Why don't you walk through the house while we're here?" I suggest. "See if anything looks out of place or strange before we search for Maury's phone."

Velma waves us toward the kitchen. "Okay. Myrt, make us a pot of coffee while I take a quick tour. We could all use a hot pick-me-up before we venture back outside."

I follow Mom into Velma's kitchen and pull a stool up to the breakfast counter. Mom's visited often enough that she knows where to find coffee, filters and mugs.

"Mom, I know zilch about video doorbells. Is Velma right to think someone may have tinkered with it?"

Mom nods as she fills the coffee carafe with water. "I think so. Especially since we all have a hard time buying the Stillwater version of the golf cart accident."

Mom pours coffee into three mugs when she sees Velma returning. A frown creates a deep furrow between the new widow's eyebrows.

"You look troubled. What did you find?" Mom asks.

"It's what I didn't find. Maury always keeps a Post-It note right next to his office phone. The note lists Vince's itinerary for the week. Maury keeps daily tabs on our son's scheduled visits. He keeps all that info on his phone, too, but he doesn't enter it into that old computer. No point. It's not connected to the internet. Anyway, that Post-It is nowhere in sight. In fact, I didn't see a single Post-it, and Maury always has five or more stickies scattered about with reminders of things to do."

While the absence of Post-It notes may have a logical explanation, I'm beginning to share Velma's alarm. Too many very odd coincidences and an unhinged next-door bully.

"Given all that's happened, do you still want to search for Maury's phone? I can do it for you," I volunteer. "Mom, can you stay with Velma until Vince arrives?"

Mom gives me an annoyed look.

Uh, oh. I momentarily forgot about tonight's welcome-home dinner for Grant.

"Don't be silly," Velma says, and saves my butt. "We'll go together to look for the phone. Then you two can skedaddle. I know Myrt's got chicken thawing to make chicken parmesan for the whole crew, and we went through recipes yesterday for a Death by Chocolate trifle."

Chapter Fourteen

Archer

Tuesday 10 a.m., December 17

I review the schedule one more time to make sure Quentin and I are in sync.

"At one a.m., an unmarked panel truck will arrive at the gate and be escorted to the maintenance barn," I begin. "Three Stillwater guards will be waiting to unload and help you bundle and shrink-wrap the bills."

"They're sending fifty million tonight, right?" Quentin asks. "What if we can't stuff that much inside the Wavedancer's hidden compartments?"

"I did the math. The cash will fit easy. Shrink-wrapped, fifty-million dollars in hundred-dollar bills take up about twenty-three cubic feet. That's a fraction of the sixty-foot yacht's hidden compartments. We'll get some twenties and fifties, but most bills will be hundreds. It's not going to be a problem."

"What if you're wrong, and we get a lot more twenties?" Quentin presses. "Will you leave what won't fit in the maintenance barn?"

"You better not be thinking about pocketing any excess. Don't invent problems before they exist. I'm more concerned about speed. I want to get the cash to the marina and onboard my yacht before any early birds show up to fish or cruise. I've tasked two guards to help with the transfer. When I arrive at Andros, our Bahamian crew will be ready to offload the cash.

"I'll stay in Andros long enough to make the trip look like a legit personal get-away," I add. "I'll let you know when to prepare for my return and this month's imports."

"When are you leaving?" Quentin asks. "Maybe this isn't a good time for you to be away. Maybe you should delay until Maury Campbell's six feet under, and any questions about his accident are buried with him."

"I don't like having that cash stored on Wavedancer any longer than necessary. But the currency is en route. We can't postpone delivery. While it doesn't make me happy, it is what it is.

"I had planned to leave tomorrow. The weather forecast has changed that. Too dicey. I'm hoping we can leave in a couple of days. Fortunately, cash doesn't need to be fed or babysat. It'll sit securely aboard the Wavedancer as long as the Coast Guard isn't tipped to make a surprise inspection."

Quentin looks me in the eye. "I could make that trip to Andros for you. Since you've got a captain, it doesn't matter that my oceangoing experiences have all been with Carnival Lines. Stillwater folks know we're buddies. You could say you're rewarding me with a break at your island estate for my contributions to the Stillwater board. A right friendly gesture."

Before I can tell Q to get real, my private cell rings. It's my throw-away used solely for company business. No mystery who's calling. I set up a Flintstone ringtone to tell me Jack's on the line.

I pick up. "What?"

"Maury's widow came back early, and she brought company again—Myrt and Kylee Kane. You know the buttinski mother and daughter who work for our old HOA management company. I was driving along the beachfront road and heard the roar of an engine. Sounded like a jet taking off. A second later, Richard Ryebread almost hit me, backing out of the Campbell driveway at warp speed.

"He screeched to a halt when he saw me," Jack continues. "Got out of his ATV and started yelling about the Campbell woman and her friends being a menace. He claimed one practically promised to shoot him. What should I do?"

"Nothing," I answer and glance over at Q. "Tell you what, I'll put Stillwater's super spy in play. It's high time Quentin called on the widow to offer the board's condolences. He can charm Velma and her buddies to tell him if they're planning to shoot off their mouths or their guns."

Quentin cocks an eyebrow and smirks. "Just call me 007. And if I'm successful, you can reward me with that trip to the Bahamas."

"You'd better be suave and charming. Not a good time for anyone to be poking around Stillwater asking questions. Not when we'll be up to our gunnels in greenbacks by morning. Give the widow our sincere condolences. Offer a memorial gift from Stillwater to one of the Campbells' pet charities. Tell Velma we'll have a talk with Mr. Ryebread. You need to buy us a little grace and elbow room to arrange our export."

Chapter Fifteen

Kylee

Tuesday Morning, December 17

Velma's doorbell chimes.

"See," Velma says. "My phone should have dinged to alert me that someone was outside. No alert. No image. No video app."

She hurries over to her security panel and presses a button. "It better not be Richard Ryebread," she mutters, before asking: "Who's there?"

"Hi, it's Quentin Teacher. If I'm not interrupting, I'd like to come up for a minute and offer the Stillwater board's condolences. I'd also like to see if there's anything we can do to make this difficult time easier for you."

The muscles working in Velma's jaw say she wants to tell Quentin to go fly a kite—or perform more difficult personal feats. I shake my head and whisper, "Invite him up. We could learn something."

Velma takes a deep breath. "I've unlocked the entry to our elevator," she tells the uninvited visitor. "It's on your right. Push M for the main floor."

Velma turns back toward us. "I hope I can hold my temper. Can't tell you how much I'd love to lay into anyone associated with the Stillwater board. But Maury did say if he needed to talk to a director, Quentin at least pretended to listen."

The three of us stand almost shoulder-to-shoulder near the elevator, waiting for the door to open. I attempt to park my face in neutral, but doubt

I can succeed. He'll be greeted with universal glares. Imagine we look more like a firing squad than a welcoming committee.

As Quentin steps from the elevator, he initiates eye contact with each of us. I've never met the man before. Ted's management contract with Stillwater ended shortly after I agreed to serve as Ted's security consultant. I never dealt with any Stillwater board members, just the former Stillwater security chief. He was a highly competent, retired MP, fired at the same time as Ted. The chief's dismissal wound up a blessing. He now heads security for a much larger Charleston-area HOA.

Quentin looks like a male model an ad agency might pick to sell beer, sporting goods, or, yeah, condoms. Athletic, with blond, surfer hair and contrasting chocolate brown, bedroom eyes. No man should be entitled to sport eyelashes that long. I peg him mid-to-late thirties.

Over six feet tall, Quentin obviously takes care of his body, and his wardrobe is sports chic. A casual navy puffer vest over a bright red polo shirt. Tan chinos with a crisp pleat.

I figure whatever Quentin does for a living, he works out of his house. Don't imagine he drove to Stillwater from a Beaufort office to make a ten-a.m. weekday sympathy call.

The man doesn't try to make physical contact with Velma. No hand extended for a shake. No arms outstretched for a hug. He's obviously read our mood. Hostile.

Instead, Quentin acknowledges Velma with the hint of a bow. "Our security force just informed us that Mr. Ryebread had a rather heated exchange with you a few minutes ago," he says. "I'll talk with him and make sure Mr. Ryebread understands he's not to come on your property uninvited.

"That wasn't my main reason for visiting," he quickly adds. "I learned about the situation with Mr. Ryebread while I was en route to offer condolences. I am very sorry for your loss, Mrs. Campbell. We've had few opportunities to talk, but I was privileged to spend considerable time with your husband. Maury was a valuable member of the Stillwater community. He will be sorely missed."

Velma doesn't say thank you or invite the man to sit and enjoy a cup of coffee.

"I didn't realize you had company." Quentin hurries his pitch along. "I wanted to tell you the board will be making a sizable donation in Maury's honor to any charity you believe appropriate."

Velma gives a non-verbal nod, indicating she's heard him.

"Is there anything we can do to be of assistance during this difficult time? I imagine family and friends will soon come to pay their respects. I'd be happy to ask the chef at the Club to prepare any meals or refreshments needed for visitations."

"Not necessary." Velma's tone is frosty enough to make alcohol freeze. "Friends have already volunteered to provide all we need."

Okay, if we want to learn anything, we need to engage beyond curt replies.

"Mr. Teacher, have you visited the crash site?" I butt in. "When Maury left the house the morning of the accident, he had his cell phone with him. It isn't listed among his personal effects. Could you inquire if anyone at the scene saw the phone? Maybe a security officer picked it up, put it in a golf cart cubby, and simply forgot about it."

"Oh, my," Quentin responds. "I'm sorry Maury's phone is missing, but I'm sure none of our security people have it. They would have returned it to Mrs. Campbell. But I'll make inquiries."

"*That* I'd appreciate," Velma adds. "We were just leaving to search the area for it. I need it to notify Maury's many professional friends. He kept all his business contacts on his phone."

"Then, please let me help," Quentin says. "I dropped by in my golf cart. It seats four comfortably. I'll be happy to take you to the crash site and help you search."

Velma glances my way, and I give a slight positive nod.

"All right," Velma says. "We'll just get our coats."

As I slip on my jacket, I decide introductions are in order—though I'm quite certain the director already received a complete report from the Stillwater gate on who arrived with Velma this morning.

"Mr. Teacher, I'm Kylee Kane, and this is my mother, Myrtle Kane. The

Campbells have been good friends for years."

"Please, call me Quentin. Do you mind if I call you Kylee?"

"Not at all, Quentin. What brought you to Stillwater?"

"Short story," he answers. "I'm a tech guy, and the type of work I do lets me work remotely. My friend, Archer Highsmith, invited me to visit him, and I fell in love with the Lowcountry and Stillwater. Who wouldn't?"

As the four of us crowd into the closet-size elevator, all conversation ceases. Fine by me, less oxygen wasted if we get stuck in this metal coffin.

* * *

Quentin's golf cart is a luxury model. The plush four-seater has a zippered weather enclosure to shield passengers from rain and wind chill. Now I understand why Quentin is wearing a puffer vest and not a beefier coat with sleeves. It will be interesting to see how enthusiastic he is about our cell phone treasure hunt once he's out in the elements.

I want to quiz him on the drive over. Can I come up with an excuse to ride shotgun? The seat of honor would naturally go to Velma. I elect to fib. Okay, lie.

"Velma and Mom, would either of you mind if I ride up front? I had a recent vertigo bout, and I don't want to chance sitting in a back seat."

"Of course," Velma says.

"Sure." Mom's agreement comes with a companion what-are-you-up-to look.

We're still in the driveway when I pose my first question. "I don't think I heard you answer when I asked if you'd visited the crash site. Have you?"

I figure he's got to say yes since he seems to know exactly where to take us. Once I get his yes, I can question when and who accompanied him.

"No," Quentin says. "This will be my first visit."

"Then how do you know where to take us?"

"Easy," he replies. "Our board carefully reviewed a security report on the accident. It included GPS coordinates and photos. I put the coordinates in my phone."

He takes a hand off the wheel, raises it to his head, and taps an earpiece. "I'm getting guidance."

Of course, my suspicious mind wonders whether the guidance is coming from a virtual GPS voice or an actual person telling him what to say and where to drive.

"I'd like to see that security report," I reply.

"I'm sure that can be arranged. I'm glad I have GPS. I doubt I'd be able to find it otherwise. Security towed the wrecked golf cart away after they searched it for anything salvageable for the family. They didn't find so much as a stick of gum in the glove box. So, as a courtesy to Velma, Stillwater paid to haul it to a scrap dealer. One less thing for Mrs. Campbell to worry about."

Yeah, real thoughtful. And you did it without asking Velma how she wanted to dispose of her property.

I pull my jacket tighter as we bump along. Somehow, the biting wind has found a crack in the cart's zippered plastic shell. We're off paved surfaces now, and despite my cushioned seat, my bottom bounces up and down with every washboard bump.

"Did Maury ever talk to you about the board's decision to terminate his employment?" I ask.

"Yes, yes, he did. I assured him it wasn't personal. This board just feels it's better to have in-house people. More reliable if folks are employees rather than contractors. Take Maury. Being retired, he and Mrs. Campbell did a fair amount of traveling. Even going overseas to visit their son."

I'm forming a follow-up question about how a single secretary can juggle the workload Ted and his staff once managed, when Quentin applies the brakes.

"This is it," he announces.

The site looks different than it did when Maury's mangled golf cart hugged the giant live oak in a deadly embrace.

We all shiver as we get out of the golf cart.

"Let's do a grid search," I suggest. "We can form a line to the right of the tree and move forward in tandem as we search the ground. Velma, you can tell us when we're, say, fifty feet past where Maury was thrown."

"Tell us what the phone looks like, Velma," Mom says. "Silver? Black? How big?"

"It's black, rectangular, maybe four by six inches," she replies.

I glance at Quentin. Why do I think he doesn't need a description?

In less than half an hour, we've walked the grid three times. Since I don't trust Quentin, I changed our line-up order each time. That meant every strip was inspected by someone other than Quentin. I feared if he actually spotted the phone, he'd step on it and grind it into the squishy ground.

"It's not here," Velma says. "I just don't understand. It didn't walk off by itself."

"Maybe an animal carried it off," Quentin suggests.

I stifle the urge to laugh. Right, an alligator or raccoon with a taste for plastic. Even if the man bats his super-long eyelashes at warp speed, I'm not buying.

On the ride back to the Campbell house, I decide the time is ripe to ask the question I'd been saving.

"Quentin, I understand your board no longer uses a management company. So, who handles all your administrative tasks?" I ask. "You know, owner complaints, clubhouse, golf club and marina inventory, damage from wind storms?"

A glib reply doesn't come quickly.

"Um, we do have a secretary," he answers after a few seconds. "She can answer most questions. Then, our president, Archer, is a young, energetic guy—really too young to be retired even though he can afford it. He enjoys maintaining contact with fellow owners, ensuring things run smoothly. And since he doesn't need the money, he does it gratis."

Quentin chuckles. "Of course, Archer also twists my arm to be generous with my talents. I maintain the website and have set up lots of automated systems."

What do you know? Two philanthropic men in the prime of their careers, electing to work for free. It's not like they're volunteering to help indigents. Stillwater owners could easily pay the tab.

"Does Archer twist Lisa Queensbury's arm, too?" I ask. "She's Stillwater's third director, right?"

Quentin coughs, an attack that lasts a good thirty seconds. A stalling tactic?

"Sorry," he says when his coughing jag ends. "As a matter of fact, Lisa's just as susceptible as I am to arm-twisting. She keeps watch over Stillwater's social agenda and makes certain our club services remain first-class."

When we reach the Campbell house, Quentin shakes hands with Mom and me and claims it was a delight to meet us. He's still reluctant to press the flesh with Velma. He acknowledges her with a nod.

"Again, please let us know if there's anything we can do. You have our deepest sympathies."

Chapter Sixteen

Archer

Tuesday Noon, December 17

"Come on up," I say when Q announces his arrival. "Let's hear how the widow received your condolences."

Quentin shivers as he walks in. "I didn't know I was going on a scavenger hunt in the great outdoors. Thought it was just going to be a social call. About froze my nuts off. Kylee Kane made us walk a gridline three times. And she shifted our positions each time. That woman definitely isn't a trusting soul. My charm assault didn't move her trust meter one iota.

"Richard Ryebread's antics didn't help any," he adds. "That guy's a real asshole. He all but advertised he was the type of person who'd chase someone to their death. Bottom line? We need to be very, very careful and watch Kylee Kane like a hawk. She asks way too many questions, and I don't see her stopping."

Hearing Quentin's verdict, I decide to call an impromptu board meeting. I offer Q lunch while we wait for Lisa Queensbury to get her fashionable ass over here.

"Are you going to talk to Ryebread, or should I?" Q asks as he slathers mustard on his ham and cheese sandwich. Then he laughs. "Geesh, I'm eating rye bread. There's one Ryebread I wish was toast."

I chuckle, too. The coincidence is amusing even if Dicky isn't. "I'll handle him," I say. "I'll suggest he take a holiday for the good of the community. Perhaps I'll offer some incentive, like a month of free dining at the clubhouse after he returns. No matter how much money these people have, they always like free."

"What about Lisa?" Q asks. "Maury's death upset her more than I expected it to."

"I'm not worried. Lisa's upset because the murder ups her risk if we get caught," I answer. "She'd be an accessory, and unlike us, she'd be loath to run and disappear. As far as Maury Campbell goes, Lisa could care less that he's no longer among the living. She saw the man as a member of the help caste, not a neighbor. The Campbells weren't eligible to be part of her social clique."

Q chuckles. "Lisa wouldn't be eligible to be Mrs. Queensbury either if her husband knew as much about her past as we do. That blueblood and his cronies would dump Lisa as scum if they ever learned about her former life. How do you suppose the woman managed to forge a new identity and get away with it for literally decades?"

I shrug. "It used to be easier before the internet and social media. But don't underestimate Lisa. She's smart, cunning, and ruthless. She wouldn't hesitate to murder anyone if she deemed it necessary and thought she could pin the rap on someone else."

A buzzer signals Lisa's arrival. I unlock the elevator and return to my seat.

When the elevator opens, a glaring Lisa stomps toward us. No hello. She reminds me of a novice bowler who pitches a ball down the alley, believing pure resolve will knock over the pins. She should know better. Her haughty act is wasted on Q and me. A gutter ball.

"Your blackmail may force me to stay on this god-awful board," she says. "But don't expect me to snap to attention and drop whatever I'm doing to help cover up your latest screw-up. I had to cancel lunch plans with the publisher of House Beautiful. It's hard to invent last-minute excuses that don't make you look like a jackass."

"Well, we both know you're mighty good at invention," I reply.

"Take a load off." Q pats the couch cushion next to him.

Lisa sniffs and toys with her black pearl necklace as she sinks into a chair across from us. Her silk suit and careful makeup say she was all primped for another performance as a high-society matron. Her platinum hair is definitely dyed, but Lisa's blue eyes and porcelain skin suggest she's always been blonde. The work she's had done is better than the average facelift. Very few wrinkles and no crepe or sagging skin beneath her chin. Too bad she can't manage a believable smile. However, her scowl remains quite credible.

"Lisa, I don't ask you to join us very often," I say. "Only when we need your social connections. So lose the attitude and listen up. We're keenly aware of your *friendship* with Babsie Talbott. I need you to pump Babsie for any personal information she can scare up on Myrtle Kane, her daughter Kylee, and Ted Welch.

"I want to know what they do when they're not at Ted's office and what they have on their calendars for the coming week. Use your leverage to prompt Babsie to do some serious digging. Lord knows everybody in gated communities like Hullis Island are bound and determined to find out any juicy details about their neighbors' lives."

Our meeting lasts less than half an hour. Lisa's not thrilled but understands her marching orders.

Chapter Seventeen

Kylee

Tuesday Afternoon, December 17

K nowing Mom is pulling out all the stops to cook tonight's dinner for her grandson and, oh, yeah, the rest of us, I shouldn't stop for a shrimp burger. But surely, I deserve a reward for not pulling out my Glock and putting a hole in Dickhead Ryebread or screaming "baloney" and rolling my eyes while listening to Stillwater's smarmy director, Quentin Teacher.

I also deserve a pat on the back (or, in this case, the stomach) for stoically entering a toy elevator for multiple stomach levitations and drops.

I get takeout to wolf down in my car. When my French fry count is down to ten, I pull out my cell phone to call Josie. I hope she has an update on Maury's autopsy and the release of his personal effects.

Unlike Ted, I have no hands-free Bluetooth option to chat and drive. Even if I had the technology, I'd abstain. I prefer to focus on one task at a time, and driving Lowcountry backroads can be challenging. Forests and marsh crowd the narrow roads. That means they're often flooded, and deer, raccoons, and other wildlife assert their rights to dart in front of cars whenever and wherever they want.

I recall the old joke about a newcomer who complains a deer-crossing warning sign is too close to her home. She demands the sign be moved and the deer told to cross in a more convenient spot.

Josie picks up on the second ring.

"Hi, Kylee. Perfect timing. Just got off the phone with the ME. He agreed to move Mr. Campbell's autopsy to the front of the line. It's slated for tomorrow morning. He's released the victim's personal effects to DeJong's funeral home. The ME said he couldn't see any reason to keep Mr. Campbell's clothing, and the only other items were a wallet, watch, pocket knife, and wedding band. The wallet held a fat wad of cash inside—three hundred bucks—so even if the autopsy reveals something suspicious, it's not some robbery gone wrong."

"Does his use of the word 'suspicious' imply he's thinking foul play's involved?"

Josie laughs. "Sounds like you think that, but I didn't get that vibe from the ME. So far, everyone seems to agree it's a freak accident."

"You're right. I'm skeptical. I'll let Velma know she can pick up Maury's belongings at DeJong's. Thanks a million, Josie."

"You're welcome." She sniffs like her feelings are hurt. "Even though I don't get to be your matron of honor."

I laugh. "Hey, I can't be blamed for a coin toss outcome. Besides, I'm confident you'll find a way for me to make it up to you."

Before I leave the restaurant parking lot and head to Hullis, I phone Velma with the news.

"Oh, Kylee, could you possibly swing by DeJong's and pick up the items for me?" Velma asks. "Since I'm unsure when Vince will arrive, I don't want to drive to Beaufort. He's renting a car when he lands at the airport."

"Of course," I answer. "But I can't stop by DeJong's until late afternoon, so I won't be able to bring the items to Stillwater tonight. I'm meeting Ted and Grant at about five for our command appearance at Mom's family feast."

"Tomorrow's fine," Velma answers. "With Vince coming, we have lots to talk over. Going through Maury's wallet can wait a few more hours. After I learned his cell phone wasn't recovered, I only cared about getting his wedding band and wallet. I need to make certain no credit cards are missing. If someone pocketed his cell phone, the scumbag could have helped himself to credit cards, too."

"I doubt you need to worry, Velma. The inventory said the wallet contains three hundred dollars. Most thieves would pocket cash long before they'd steal credit cards."

My phone duties complete, I head to Hullis with my stack of theft reports piled on the passenger seat. The reports include victim phone numbers and addresses. Though I realize some individuals may have moved in the intervening months or dropped landlines in favor of smartphones, it's a place to start.

As I told Ted, I want to contact the outliers, first. I'm hoping something will jump out in the interviews and help me figure out how the thief picks his targets. I'll leave female retirees for my next round of interviews. Since they're more likely to have overlapping contacts, it would be harder to spot which investigative threads to follow.

As I approach the Hullis gate, I realize it looks downright dinky compared to Stillwater's massive edifice. But size and showy stonework have squat to do with security. Both gates have a human officer posted, and visitors need a resident's authorization to enter.

The main difference is Hullis asks visitors to put a cardboard placard on the dash, while Stillwater insists on a high-tech tracker. I can't make an economic case for the extra cost. I also wonder—does Stillwater assign an officer fulltime to monitor gadget feedback and track where every car goes? If so, it must get danged confusing on a busy day with lots of guests and service vehicles.

Since I have both approved "family" and "vendor" decals on my windshield, I bypass the Hullis gate check-in lane and breeze through the residents' entrance.

When I reach the mid-island Chapel and Community Center, I grab a spot in the parking lot and scan the theft report at the top of my presorted pile. Tony Baldwin, age forty-nine, reported the theft of an Omega watch six months ago. He valued the Omega at close to six thousand dollars. The report lists the model as a Seamaster Diver 300M 42mm with a blue dial.

I phone Tony, fully expecting to get no answer or a recording.

"Baldwin, here," a male voice answers.

I quickly deliver my spiel about gathering more information on island thefts and ask if I can make an appointment to visit.

"You on the island?" he asks.

"Yes."

"Might as well meet now. Though telling authorities about my stolen watch has never done an iota of good. You got the address?"

"I do. Should be there in under five minutes."

I'm glad I have Baldwin's address. His home is in a neighborhood of some thirty look-alike cottages. Flowers, yard art, and the color owners choose to paint shutters seem the only way to tell the units apart. Hope Baldwin never tips too many scotch-and-sodas at the Club after nightfall. It would be very easy to pull into the wrong driveway after dark and fumble around trying to open someone else's door.

A silhouetted head hovers inside the front door's frosted glass sidelight. The gentleman is waiting for me. The wavy glass offers no clue about Baldwin's actual appearance.

He opens the door. "Come on in," he says. Then I hear the clip of nails on hardwood as a big, shaggy dog bounds down the hallway. I barely have time to brace myself before it jumps on me. Luckily, the mutt's teeth aren't bared, though drool cascades off its tongue and onto my top as it greets me.

"Down, Dixie, the lady doesn't want you slobbering all over her."

Dixie, a large golden retriever, doesn't listen. I pet her head with my left hand, as my right hand attempts to pry her paws off my chest. Glad my shoulder-strap purse lets me keep both hands free.

Sparring with the dog, it takes me a couple of seconds to notice Baldwin's attire. Unusual, to say the least. Up top, he's wearing a suitcoat, crisp white shirt, and red tie. Below the waist, he's rocking torn, gray sweatpants and fluffy bedroom slippers.

Baldwin leads me and Dixie down a hall and into a den.

"We need to talk in here," he explains. "I'm expecting a call from a client. If he phones, you'll need to usher yourself out. Clients don't like the notion someone might be listening in on our video calls."

Okay, that explains his attire. Apparently, he only needs to look the part of a professional while seated at his computer with the video range preset. Still, he's got my curiosity.

"What do you do?"

"I'm what the industry terms a marketing agent. I work with college athletes to negotiate NIL deals. You know—Name, Image, and Likeness contracts. I make sure the kids get the max they're entitled to and don't get screwed.

"But let's get down to business. I'm busy. And call me Tony, will you? Mr. Baldwin makes me feel ancient. Tell me what you want to know. Don't know what I can add to the report I filed with security. They were clueless. Didn't help at all.

"I loved that watch. I'm passionate about scuba diving. Head to dive spots like the Maldives or the Caymans at least twice a year, so I treated myself to the Omega. It helps with the image, too. Gotta look prosperous to gain the confidence of kids, but I'm not a gold chains or diamond earrings kind of guy."

I explain I'm trying to understand how and why the thief found individuals who happened to have high-value items in their homes. Items small enough to put in a pocket and stroll away.

"Can you walk me through what was happening in your life when your watch was stolen?"

He laughs. "Walk you through, that's funny. I wasn't walking anywhere. I played football in college and ruined my knees. They'd gotten so bad I needed two new ones. Over the doc's objections, I insisted on having both knees replaced at once. Didn't want to take any more time off than I had to. It's a competitive business, and when my butt's not in front of a computer, I'm traveling."

Okay, when the theft happened, Tony Baldwin was laid up just like Evie Miles after her cancer surgery.

I ask a series of questions about Tony's healthcare team. He visited a different hospital than Evie. No physician overlap. His surgeon belongs to a specialized orthopedic group. Evie's oncologist has a practice miles away.

No commonality with family physician. Tony had in-home visits from a physical therapist. Evie did not.

However, like Evie, Tony had a regular parade of Hullis Island neighbors coming and going. The Care Committee orchestrated most of the visits.

Could a member of Hullis Island's casserole brigade be a sneak thief? The idea seems preposterous.

I'm wrapping up our interview when Tony's phone rings. His shooing motion tells me to scram. Dixie dog follows me, and I carefully ease my body out the door to keep the mutt from climbing in my car.

Wonder if Dixie made friends with the thief?

Dang. Didn't get a chance to ask Tony for the names of his sympathy callers.

I make three more phone calls. After two local strike-outs, I try Doug Fisher's business number. He's the gentleman with the stolen gold coin. Doug answers and has time to talk. He tells a story similar to Tony's. The main difference is Doug had back surgery.

It's past time to call it a day. I need to visit DeJong's funeral home, before I run by the house to change clothes and meet up with Ted and Grant.

Unlike Tony Baldwin, I can't have a split-personality work wardrobe. Sweatpants are a no-go, even if paired with a spiffy silk blouse. Instead of bedroom slippers, I need to wear leather shoes. While mine are no-nonsense flats, I can't wait to exchange them for running shoes. Though tonight's family gathering is special, the dress is casual. Even Mom will be wearing a sweatshirt and jeans. Me, too.

Chapter Eighteen

Kylee

Late Tuesday Afternoon, December 17

DeJong's Funeral Home looks like a nineteenth-century Lowcountry plantation house—stately pillars, expansive front porch, tall windows. Yet, it's less than twenty years old. Guess the traditional copycat design is meant to convey stability and dignity.

I check the lot behind the building to make certain a funeral isn't in progress before I park out front on the street. The door opens before I can knock.

Betsy DeJong beams. "Hi, Kylee. Happened to glance out the window and saw you coming up the walk. Velma told me to expect you. Nice of you to save her the trip. I know she's anxious to welcome Vince home.

"Come on back. The package is in our office. All ready for you. "

I'm surprised to see Betsy in slacks. It's not like she's wearing jeans. She has on dress slacks and a tailored blouse. But, before today, I'd never seen her decked out in anything except dresses in gray or muted tones. And she's always wearing hose, and dress shoes with squat heels. Betsy must add cushions to those heels since she always glides past mourners without making a sound.

The DeJongs have no guests "slumbering" in any of the four salons accessed from the center hall. The right-side salons are connected by sliding panels and can be opened if a big crowd is expected for the deceased's viewing.

Betsy keeps up the chatter as I follow her down the hall. "By the way, congratulations. I hear you're getting married soon. Oh, sorry, I'm only supposed to congratulate the groom. Congratulating a soon-to-be bride makes it sound like she's darn lucky to snag a husband."

I laugh. "Congratulations are just fine by me. I do feel very lucky to be marrying Ted. I didn't think I'd ever want to marry, especially having been single for fifty years. Ted changed my mind."

We've reached the large office Betsy shares with her husband. While the office has a desk, most of the space is devoted to an informal seating arrangement that lets the DeJongs sit with the folks who've come to plan funerals for loved ones—or themselves. I've occupied one of those chairs on two occasions. I accompanied Mom when she made Dad's funeral arrangements and later when she insisted on pre-arranging her own funeral.

Betsy lifts a sturdy, reinforced bag off the desk. "The shoes are at the bottom," she explains as she hands it to me. "That's what makes it a bit heavy."

She looks a bit sad as I accept the package. "When we receive personal-effect packages, they always look too small," she says. "Like this is all that a person left behind."

Betsy coughs. "Though, of course, that's not true. Maury Campbell will be remembered by so many friends."

I nod. "Thanks, Betsy. I understand Maury's body will be released to you tomorrow after the autopsy. Has Velma determined a date for the funeral service?"

"Yes, the viewing is set for Thursday, and the Methodist Church will hold the funeral service at eleven a.m. on Friday. Imagine you and your family will attend."

"Yes, we'll all be there. Thanks for your help."

Before I start my car, I open the bag. A see-through, sealed plastic bag sits on top. Except for the clothes folded underneath, the bag lets me see all the items Josie mentioned—wedding ring, pocket knife, watch, keys, and wallet.

Hmm, there is one extra item—a brilliant deep blue feather, almost purple.

Why? Did the feather get snagged on Maury's clothes when the crash tossed his body to the ground? If so, I'm surprised it was included among his personal effects.

I don't believe I've ever seen a feather this color. I'll show it to Mimi tonight. If anyone can tell what kind of bird lost this feather, Mimi will know.

I glance at my watch. Uh, oh. I'm running late. Ted and Grant will be pacing the floor. They'll want to be on time for Mom's dinner. I hope my tardiness doesn't make it a close call.

Chapter Nineteen

Kylee

Tuesday Late Afternoon, December 17

"Hello, anybody home? Sorry I'm late, I'll be ready in a jiff. Fiancé? Soon-to-be stepson? Burglars? Anybody here?"

Hmm, no answer. It's five-fifteen. Ted expected that he and Grant would be home from Charleston long before now. I'm surprised they aren't impatiently tapping their toes at my tardiness. Maybe Ted and Grant decided to go ahead. I check my phone for messages.

Yep, Ted left a voicemail an hour ago. A horrendous accident in Charleston snarled traffic in the city. "Why don't you go on to your Mom's house? We'll get there as soon as we can. We won't bother stopping in Beaufort."

Dang. Should have checked my phone earlier. Maybe we'll arrive about the same time.

* * *

It's six o'clock, cold and dark, when I pull into Frank and Mom's driveway. Two cars are parked in the drive but not Ted's Lexus. I figure Mimi's dad loaned her his shiny BMW, and the Beetle definitely belongs to Mom's friend, Martha Evatt, a long-ago hippie, who hasn't lost any of her youthful passion. She's one of Mom's best friends and, thanks to Mom's sweet-talking, a fellow member of Hullis Island's HOA board.

I park behind the Beemer. Since I can't remember if Mom said Martha was staying for dinner, I don't want to block her exit. I figure Mimi's here for the duration. Good thing the driveway is both wide and long. There's still room for Ted to pull in behind me.

Seeing Mimi's ride reminds me to take the unusual feather inside. I open the door to the back seat and pluck it from the bag that holds Maury's personal belongings.

Hearing laughter and voices, I don't bother to knock before I walk into Frank's house. He never locks the front door when there's a gathering.

I'm not sure anyone notices my arrival. "Hi. Guess the party's already started," I say

Mom looks behind me and, seeing I'm solo, shakes her head before awarding me a hug. "Yes, the party's underway, but where's the guest of honor?"

Martha chuckles. "Were the 'boys' bad? Did you ground them at home?"

I explain Charleston traffic is to blame, rather than Grant's wicked, would-be stepmother.

Mom sighs. "Glad chicken parmesan is a dish that can stay warm in the oven without any harm. Take off your coat and help yourself to a drink, Kylee."

I do as I'm told and hang my coat on a peg in the entry. When I head to the front-room bar, I decide it's okay to enjoy one rum and Coke, since it will be hours before I get behind the wheel to drive back to Beaufort.

Martha pats the middle seat cushion on the couch. Mimi and Martha have claimed the end seats, and, as usual, Frank's ensconced in his worn Lazy-Boy. Once Mom returns from her kitchen vigil, she'll sink into the "petite-person" recliner Frank bought her so they could watch TV side-by-side.

"Great to see you, Mimi and Martha," I say. "How was the flight from New York, Mimi? Looks like it was on time."

"Yes. Amazing. We even had a tailwind and got into Savannah early." She grins. "Good thing I booked that flight and not one arriving in Charleston."

"Oh, I have something to show you." I pull the mystery feather from my sweater pocket.

Mimi's eyes go wide. "Where did you get this?"

"It's gorgeous," Martha says. "Very unusual."

"And quite illegal," Mimi adds.

"What?" I'm dumbfounded. "How can a feather be illegal? Birds lose them all the time. I often see them in leaf litter when I'm out for a run."

"Not from this bird, you don't," Mimi answers as she holds the distinctive feather by its tip and twirls it, showing off its rich color. "I'm almost certain it's from a Hyacinth Macaw, the largest of any parrots that can fly. Its cobalt-blue feathers are often trafficked."

"Do the parrots live in Florida?" Martha asks. "I'm pretty certain we don't have any native South Carolina parrots."

"You're right there," Mimi agrees. "This endangered parrot lives in central and eastern South America. Unfortunately, feather trafficking, habitat loss, and illegal wildlife trade are real threats to its survival."

Mimi turns to me. "Where did you find this?"

"Velma asked me to pick up Maury's personal effects from the funeral home. I peeked in the bag when I put it in my car. The feather was sitting on top of his clothes."

"What did you just say?" Mom asks as she returns from the kitchen. "How did a feather like that get mixed in with Maury's things?"

I shrug. "Maybe it was in one of his pockets, or it was lying on the ground and got stuck to his clothes when the EMTs moved his body."

Mimi shakes her head. "There's no way that feather got blown to South Carolina, even courtesy of a hurricane. Somebody brought it here. Was Maury a collector?"

Frank laughs. "The only things Maury collected were tools. Think his workshop has every woodworking gadget ever made. He certainly didn't collect feathers."

"Is it really illegal to collect feathers?" Martha asks. "I have a duvet and multiple pillows filled with them."

Mimi shakes her head. "The feathers of many birds aren't off limits," she explains. "That includes game birds and domesticated fowl like chickens and turkeys. But it's been illegal to collect the feathers of eagles and many other birds for more than a century. Back in the early 1900s, birds were often slaughtered for their feathers, since feathered ladies' hats were all the rage. In Boston, two women started preaching how wrong it was. They wore featherless 'Audobonnets' in protest and helped form the Audubon Society."

"Huh, never knew that," Frank comments.

"Glad we have our own ornithology expert," I add. "Sounds like you're getting a good education at Cornell University. How do you plan to use that knowledge when you graduate? Conservation? Research?"

Mimi glances my way. "Maybe I'll be like you, Kylee, and become an investigator. I could specialize in catching wildlife traffickers."

"What's that?" Ted asks as he and Grant walk inside. "Kylee, are you recruiting young women to join your Smart Gals Network? You, Josie, and Alysha are formidable enough."

"It appears our team might just need to add an ornithology expert."

Mom poses at the dining room entrance with her hands on her hips. "For the next hour, the only talk of birds should be praise for my chicken parmesan. Grant, come give your grandma a hug. Then, let's sit and eat before my reputation as a cook becomes endangered."

Chapter Twenty

Kylee

Tuesday Evening, December 17

Mom's cooking reputation is in no danger. Everything is delicious—chicken parmesan, Caesar salad, green beans almondine, garlic bread. While we eat, the conversation centers around our two college sophomores, who good-naturedly answer questions about their on-campus studies and lives. Somehow, the teens manage to clean their plates while undergoing their inquisition.

Then, the talk turns to wedding plans. Answering Mom's pointed question, I'm forced to confess I still don't have a dress. To pause the inquisition, I quickly stand and start clearing the table. A good excuse to escape to the kitchen.

I bring in the dessert plates, and let Mom have the honor of carrying in her fancy trifle. It's really pretty, with its eight layers showcased in a glass bowl. The presentation is greeted with a round of applause. Years ago, we clapped in appreciation of one of Mom's creations. Now, applauding outstanding desserts is tradition.

And this dessert deserves it. Here are the repeated layers—crumbled brownies soaked in Kahlua, chocolate-caramel mousse, whipped cream, and, finally, chunks of homemade toffee.

I'm almost too stuffed for a serving of Death by Chocolate. *Almost.*

It's after eight when we leave the table and settle in the living room with cups of coffee. Mom tells Grant to bring in dining room chairs so everyone has a seat, but Mimi offers an alternate suggestion. "The floor's fine."

That's the clue for Mimi and Grant to demonstrate how limber they are as they turn into decorative rug pretzels.

Mom glances at Martha. "At dinner, we heard how our youngest members have fun. How about sharing your afternoon entertainment?"

Martha laughs. The happy sound always prompts me to picture the devil-may-care hippie in her heyday. Martha's brown eyes sparkle as she toys with the ends of her long gray braid.

"We played hide-and-no-seek." She giggles. "I was visiting with Bonnie Vidler, when we heard someone climb the stairs to her porch. Bonnie shushed me and whispered, 'Don't utter a peep. I bet it's that busybody Babsie Talbott, and I have a surprise for her.' Bonnie checked her phone, and indeed, the video doorbell showed Babsie's bony body on the porch.

"Popeye's Olive Oil look-alike rang the bell. When Bonnie didn't answer, she pounded on the door. 'I know you're in there,' Babsie said. 'I just want to help. As the head of the Care Committee, I can arrange meals, transportation, whatever you need to see you through this ordeal.'"

Martha laughs again.

"I'd try to imitate Babsie's high, squeaky voice, but I'd damage my vocal cords and your ears. Anyway, this is when Bonnie unleashes her snarling pit bull, Diesel. Once he starts growling and barking, I think Babsie wet her fancy pants. Didn't realize her toothpick legs could pump so fast. She dashed down the stairs in a New York minute."

Mimi looks alarmed. "Did Diesel catch her? Did it attack? I can't believe your friend really sicced a pit bull on someone. That's not funny."

Martha chuckles. "Diesel is an audio program. Bonnie's grandson, who doesn't like the fact his grandmother lives alone, created it to scare off ne'er-do-wells. He even rigged up stereo speakers. The soundtrack not only features barks and growls but what sounds like paws pounding in for the kill. It won't work on Babsie twice, but it was sure fun the first time."

Mom nods. "Babsie is a pest. Some people like their privacy. They don't want people—even alleged do-gooders—invading their homes when they look and feel like hell. I told Babsie and the Care Committee to pound sand when I was being treated. The only people I wanted to see were Kylee, Martha, and a few more close friends. I wasn't keen on feigning polite responses to strangers. If I felt bad, I could snarl at Kylee. I didn't have to pretend."

"Yeah, I remember those snarls," I say.

"Payback for your teenage years," Mom quips.

"How come you think Babsie won't fall for the audio again?" Frank asks. "Maybe she assumed Diesel rushed to the door and couldn't get out."

"Unfortunately, once Bonnie shut down Diesel, Babsie heard Bonnie and me laughing our heads off. I was peering through the transom when she turned and screeched, 'Why are you so mean to me? I'm just trying to help.'"

"Babsie's reaction doesn't surprise me," Mom says. "That woman loves to play the victim. When her husband died, she loudly bemoaned how widowhood would mean fewer social invitations since she was no longer part of a couple. Hardly mentioned her husband's passing in terms of missing the man. It never dawns on Babsie that her behavior is what prompts people to cross the street to avoid her."

The conversation turns to more pleasant topics, and soon, it's time to leave.

* * *

I follow Ted's taillights as his car winds around the dark road's many curves. While there's a sliver of moon above, clouds keep any moonlight from lighting the way. It's hard to distinguish black asphalt from bordering marsh.

My thoughts keep returning to Babsie Talbott and the Hullis Island Care Committee. Was there one Care Committee member who visited every victim's house? The Committee boasts quite a large roster of volunteers, and they rotate duty. Would the victims even remember which Care Committee members delivered their tuna casseroles and seven-layer salads. I seriously doubt Babsie has kept detailed records.

Should I ask for Babsie's help? The woman and I don't enjoy what you would call a cordial relationship. While I didn't run her off with a virtual pit bull, my bark might have been just as scary when she refused to leave my ailing mother alone. We repeatedly told her, "No, thank you," before I got mad.

What possesses Babsie to be so pushy and oblivious to how she makes other people feel?

Babsie's husband died three years ago. She's stayed alone in their oceanfront mansion. Her late husband was quite wealthy, so his passing hasn't forced her to get a job to pay the bills. Maybe loneliness is what makes Babsie such an annoying nuisance.

Chapter Twenty-One

Archer

Wednesday 2 a.m., December 18

T he truck is right on time. No surprise. Mick, my boss, makes sure everyone who works for him knows there's no excuse for being tardy. "You better have contingencies," Mick preaches. "Unless someone's picking your charred bones from the wreckage, a traffic accident is no excuse."

I parked inside the Stillwater gate to lead the truck to our maintenance barn. This is a new crew's first delivery. Hope they've been told they're expected to stay and help unload.

I phone Quentin, who's waiting at the barn, to tell him we're en route. "Should be there in under ten minutes."

The hidden, graveled service road isn't used by residents. The meandering route is far from straightforward. There's no way a truck or car could navigate the more direct path Maury favored to reach the barn in his golf cart. Damn trees are too close together.

Quentin's waiting outside when we arrive. He uses a flashlight to help direct the truck driver as he backs up to the sliding barn door. Though it's the middle of the night, we don't risk any exterior lights. The barn's few windows are covered with black-out shades.

Once the truck parks and its rear door opens, I order the driver and his partner to help unload. I assume the answering grunt is a "yes." Given the size of the brutes maybe they could lift the truck's front end and let the boxes slide out the back.

Did they know they were transporting fifty million dollars? Though Mick puts the fear of God in everyone, I doubt he'd want the truckers to ponder the temptation of grabbing a few million and trying to vanish.

The thought of Mick's likely revenge makes me shiver. Failures aren't tolerated. What would he do to me if authorities shut down this expensive operation? I sold him on the idea of trafficking endangered species to improve his return on investment and my piece of the pie. "Why waste a return voyage with zero cargo?" I argued.

This Maury Campbell mess has frayed my nerves. Now I keep worrying that I'm doubling the chance some newly-appointed Coast Guard captain will want to show off his authority, stop the Wavedancer for a search. Recent luxury yacht accidents would give a cowboy captain a ready excuse for a yacht safety check.

Would they find anything? Maybe, maybe not. Should I tell Mick we need to find different cargo to import? My Swiss bank account has grown quite chubby, but not as fat as I would like. Reducing my share of profits doesn't eliminate the risk I face running Mick's money-laundering show.

Stop worrying. Exporting or importing, the risk is small. Maury's departure makes it smaller.

In fifteen minutes, the transport is emptied, and the truckers and their vocal grunts depart. I never heard either utter an actual word. Entirely possible they don't understand or speak English.

Knowing Mick, maybe he prefers deaf-mutes, knowing how tough it would be for them to rat him out.

I help Quentin, Jack, and two more security guards open the boxes. The bills are loose, but tightly packed. One denomination per box. We use a machine to count out one hundred bills, then wrap a bank strap around them. Next, we build a brick of ten straps and shrink-wrap it.

I look at my watch. Crap, this is taking too long. The sun won't rise till a little after seven o'clock, but the sky begins to lighten before six. That's when eager-beaver fishermen first arrive. I can't have some busybody owner start asking why Stillwater security officers are carting containers onto the Wavedancer. Curiosity is an unwanted enemy.

I turn to Jack. "Tell the guards waiting at the marina to go home. We need to reschedule moving the merchandise."

I head home, disappointed and bone-tired. Hope tomorrow holds less drama. Maybe when Maury's son arrives, he'll succeed in getting his mother to leave Stillwater and put her house on the market.

That would be a relief. If Velma's not an owner, there's no reason to let Kylee or Ted through our gates.

Chapter Twenty-Two

Kylee

Wednesday 8 a.m., December 18

I pack my essentials in a small travel bag and head downstairs to have breakfast with Ted.

Wow. Grant's not only up, he's manning the stove, flipping sizzling bacon strips in a frying pan.

"I'm impressed. Even though you're on break and can sleep in, you're up early and cooking. It smells great. Is any of that bacon for me?"

"Yep, I'm making enough for all three of us. Dad's getting the newspaper. He says the paperboy misses this yard nine times out of ten. Want your eggs over easy or hard?"

"Over-easy," I reply. "I'll get the toast started as soon as I dump this bag and grab a cup of coffee."

"What's with the bag?" Grant's forehead wrinkles. "You going on a trip? Fleeing before you're expected to say 'I do'?"

I laugh. "Nothing so dramatic. I'm going to stay on the River Rat until the wedding."

Grant frowns. "Because I'm here?"

"No," I reply, though his presence *is* part of the reason. It won't be long before Grant graduates and begins his adult life. That's bound to lessen how often Ted gets to see his son. I want them to enjoy some quality time together now, without a third wheel.

"I've neglected the River Rat the last few months," I explain. "I need to take care of maintenance issues and get her all buttoned up before we leave on our honeymoon. Somehow, I was unable to convince Ted to spend our honeymoon on the River Rat, cruising the Intracoastal. We could have saved a pile of money."

Ted walks into the kitchen. "While I believe in togetherness," he interrupts, "living aboard the River Rat for more than one night is outside my comfort zone."

I chuckle when I spot the bedraggled newspaper in his hand. "Guess Butch got the paper again."

Ted sighs. "Our neighbor's dog thinks he's doing me a favor by fetching the paper and delivering it along with a pile of drool. But, back to the River Rat. Why can't you stay here and do whatever needs doing to get your boat shipshape?"

"Between helping Velma, attempting to ID a jewel thief, researching wildlife trafficking, and, oh, yes, buying a wedding dress, I have zero free time during the workweek. I'll tackle boat projects early mornings and evenings.

"There's another advantage to staying on the River Rat. If Mom happens to come up with any new ideas for the wedding, she won't come pester me. The River Rat is a perfect safe house."

"You make fun of your Mom's fear of the water, but how's it different from your phobias about heights and confined spaces?" Ted asks.

I roll my eyes. "Maybe you should develop some fears. Like the fear of pissing off your bride-to-be a week before the wedding."

Both men laugh.

Grant slides eggs onto the waiting breakfast plates. "Sit down and eat while your eggs are still over easy."

* * *

After breakfast, I phone Velma. I'm certain she'll be up by now, though I hope a phone call won't wake Vince. Beaufort's a long way from Bhutan, and he's probably suffering from jet lag.

"Hello." Velma sounds out of breath.

"Hi, it's Kylee. Just checking in. Will you be home this morning? If so, I can bring Maury's belongings over first thing. That assumes I'm allowed through the Stillwater gates."

"Oh, Kylee. I meant to call you last night. Vince isn't here. He's temporarily stuck in Taiwan. His plane was late, and he missed a connection. With the holidays, everything is booked. The next possible flight with an open seat doesn't leave until tomorrow, and there are weather problems. I need to change all the funeral arrangements. With Vince's travel delays, I don't want to take chances. I'm moving the service to Saturday."

"Are you staying alone on Stillwater until he arrives?" I ask, then rush ahead to assure her I'm not advocating any permanent move.

"While I agree you shouldn't make any big decisions now, I'd feel better if you weren't alone at Stillwater. Not until we figure out how your video doorbell account got deleted or why someone snooped in Maury's office when you were gone. I'm also concerned about that bully next door."

"Those things worry me, too," she admits. "But I don't want to leave my home and live in some hotel or at a friend's house. I can't explain it, but being here, where every room has so many happy memories, is a comfort. I'm staying put."

A tap on my shoulder prompts me to turn. Grant motions for me to cover the receiver.

"Dad told me about Velma's problems," he says. "Ask Velma if she's had a chance to install and set up a new video doorbell. If not, I can do it this morning."

I ask and Velma admits she hasn't done a thing.

Grant grins. "Tell her I'll buy one and set it up. Don't have any other plans this morning. Dad's tied up in meetings, you're deserting me, and Mimi's not free until two o'clock."

I share the idea with Velma. She seems relieved to accept Grant's offer.

"I have to come to town this morning to visit DeJong's and talk with the pastor about rescheduling the funeral service," she says. "I'll leave an envelope at the Stillwater gate with a spare house key inside. I'd be hesitant to give those security thugs a housekey if it weren't for the fact they already have one."

"What? Stillwater security has a key to your house?"

I'm shocked. None of our HOA clients would dare suggest security should have that kind of blanket access to private homes.

"Yes, the covenants were changed about nine months ago." Velma's reply has an angry edge. "They claim it's for everyone's protection, since many Stillwater owners are gone more than they're here. The HOA now requires security to have a way to enter every house in the event of an emergency like a gas leak or a fire."

Yeah, or a severe case of HOA nosiness.

"Will you come out with Grant?" Velma asks. "I need to tell the gate who's coming."

"Yes, it'll be easier for Grant to install and test the video doorbell if I'm with him. I'll bring Maury's belongings, too. Where should I leave them?"

"Just put them in the living room. I really appreciate this."

"Oh, I almost forgot to ask. Did Maury collect feathers?"

"Heavens, no. What a strange question."

"It's just that I noticed a gorgeous blue feather sitting on top of Maury's clothes when I picked up his belongings from DeJong's."

"Do you suppose he picked it off the ground?" Velma asks.

"Mimi believes the feather's from an endangered parrot that lives in South America."

"My word," Velma says. "How odd. There's no way he'd have a feather from South America. Must have gotten mixed in with Maury's things by accident."

Maybe. Maybe not.

* * *

Grant and I coordinate our schedules. I'll pick up a few groceries and drop them and my travel bag at the River Rat. I'll also chat with whoever's in the Beaufort marina office to let them know my honeymoon travel plans. While I'm tackling those errands, Grant will drop Ted at the office and drive to a big box store to purchase a video doorbell.

I give Grant a hug, and kiss Ted goodbye. I'm almost out the door when a thought occurs to me.

"Grant, while you're at the store, why don't you pick up two trail cameras? I'd love to see what kinds of creatures are active on Velma's property after the sun sets. Hidden cams would let us monitor any unauthorized comings and goings. If someone found a way to kill her video doorbell once, they might do it again. Or they might enter her property from the oceanside, out of the doorbell camera's view. If so, hidden trail cams could catch them."

"Sure, good idea," Grant answers. "I've got Dad's credit card."

Should I call Velma and ask her permission?

No. She's already stressed out and nervous. We'll put them in. Then, tell her about the added security. If she doesn't want them, we'll take them down.

Chapter Twenty-Three

Archer

Wednesday Morning, December 18

I listen to the recordings with growing alarm. Damn glad we put the bugs in the Campbell house when we searched Maury's office.

How the hell did we miss that feather?

Jack searched Maury's pockets long before the widow arrived and called 911. He removed everything the man pocketed while he was inside the maintenance barn.

Velma is suspicious about her video doorbell's failure. She doesn't buy that their video account was accidentally deleted. I regret shredding Maury's Post-It notes, too. The missing notes have only strengthened Velma's conviction intruders visited her house after Maury died.

Water under the bridge. What now?

Should I dream up an explanation for the feather and casually mention it to Velma? That feather is bound to increase Kylee Kane's determination to stick her nose in my business.

And I can't forget to warn Jack and Quentin that the Campbell house will soon have a working video doorbell. Fortunately, I see no need to revisit the widow's house. Our bugs are providing good intelligence. Still, we need to keep an eye on Kylee whenever she's inside Stillwater's gates.

Chapter Twenty-Four

Kylee

Wednesday Morning, December 18

I'm in the office reviewing Hullis Island theft reports when Grant returns with our spyware.

"Ready to storm the Stillwater gates?" he asks. "I've never been there. Should be interesting. Want me to drive?"

"No, we'll take my Mustang, so your dad has wheels. After we finish at Stillwater, I'm coming back to Beaufort. I can drop you at home or here."

"Here. I'm hoping Dad will spring for lunch, and Mimi says she can pick me up at two—wherever I happen to be."

I chuckle. "I'd invite you to lunch with me, but it might prove a harrowing experience. I'm meeting Josie and Alysha. My Smart Gal Network comrades have volunteered—make that insisted—on becoming wardrobe consultants. They've promised I won't get a bite to eat until I buy a dress for the wedding.

"The upside is they're treating me to a shrimp burger and fries at Port Royal's Fishcamp once I commit to a dress," I add. "Whatever I buy will definitely be roomy enough to fit no matter how many fast-food splurges I enjoy before Christmas Eve."

"Maybe I'll ask Dad to take me to the Fishcamp," Grant says. "I love shrimp burgers—okay, any burgers—and I'm not worried about how my suit fits. Grandma's made it clear that Dad and I will appear in suits and ties with polished shoes and boutonnieres of her choosing."

I shake a don't-you-dare finger at Grant. "Keep your father away from the Fishcamp while we're eating. Can't have him joining Alysha and Josie to gang up on me if I haven't bought a wedding dress."

**

When we're almost to Stillwater, Grant's cell phone sounds with the ominous warning notes from the movie *Jaws*.

"Hi, Dad." Grant grins, then switches his cell to speakerphone mode. "He wants to talk to you."

"Velma phoned me when her calls to you went to voicemail," Ted begins. "She figured you were en route to Stillwater and hoped I could reach you. Velma forgot to ask you for one additional favor—to check on their boat."

"Did Velma say why? What am I supposed to check?"

"The day Maury died, he was planning to finish repairs on the boat. Velma is worried he left tools topside or hatches unsecured. With new storms predicted by the weekend, she wants to make sure everything's shipshape."

"Did she give you a slip number? I've been on the boat, but it's been a while. I'm sure I'll recognize it, but I'd rather go directly to the slip with no detours. Stillwater security would probably waterboard me if they thought I was wandering about, casing boats in the marina."

"The boat's in slip number twelve. It's on the finger of docks directly across from the biggest yacht in the marina, Archer Highsmith's Wavedancer."

"Okay. Shouldn't be a problem if the Stillwater Gestapo doesn't bar us from the marina. They certainly felt we needed a babysitter when we left the Campbell house to look at Maury's accident scene."

"Good luck," Ted says. "If security won't let you drive to the marina, you can always ask Alysha for a Coast Guard escort. Doubt security would dare stop them."

About five minutes after Ted's call, the Stillwater gates loom ahead. It's chilly, and the wind is gusting, but I'm thankful it's sunny. Rainy weather would make hiding trail cameras and checking the Campbell boat a lot less pleasant.

"Good grief, you'd think they're guarding the entrance to a forbidden kingdom," Grant raves. "Are they expecting an invasion? Someone should photograph these gates for video game graphics."

I chuckle at his reaction.

A guard stands outside the building, awaiting our arrival. He's probably been at attention since he heard our car approaching. Where does Stillwater find these guys? Ex-military?

Maybe, but being ex-military myself, I hate to think so. There's something off about the Stillwater security officers. Their polite formality feels like a thin veneer. They seem cut from a different cloth than the security folks I interact with day in and day out at our client HOAs. Even Chief O'Rourke, who gets his back up about my 'help' with investigations, doesn't give off this kind of barely-contained hostility.

"Are you expected?" the guard demands when I power down my window.

"Yes." I give my name and explain Mrs. Campbell has asked me to take care of some items at her house. "I believe she left an envelope for me."

He goes inside to retrieve the envelope along with the gizmo we'll be ordered to keep on our dash. I accept the envelope and tracker and thank him.

"We're good. I know the routine," I add.

I expect to hear the deep growl of the heavy gates grinding open. Nothing happens.

"Ma'am," he says. "I need to know how long you'll be here and the name of your passenger. Am I to understand you two will stay together while you're here?"

I'm tempted to answer that we need two trackers since we plan to split up immediately to case as many mansions as possible, but I bite my tongue.

Grant gives his name, then adds, "Don't worry. My mean stepmom won't let me out of her sight."

Oh, Grant. It's not wise to give smartass replies to these guys.

While the guard glares at both of us, he does open the gates.

We park outside the Campbell house, and I give Grant the house key.

"Could you take Maury's personal effects inside and leave them upstairs in the living room? Then, while you work on installing the new video doorbell, I'll scout locations to hide the trail cams. I have a distinct feeling security may visit soon, and I don't want them to catch me mounting cameras."

It takes a few minutes to find good camera sites. Several palmetto trees are ideally positioned to provide back-of-the-house panoramas, but the trees are too tall. Trail cameras attached to their trunks would be too easy to spot, and there's no ladder handy to climb high enough to use palm fronds as camouflage. Not that I'd voluntarily climb a ladder with these unpredictable wind gusts.

An overgrown wild tea olive offers a solution. I secure the camera to an interior branch. True, it's not invisible. If someone's searching for it, they'd probably find it. But I'm hoping the smug security guards would never imagine an owner would install any exterior surveillance beyond a doorbell camera. Not given their outstanding protection from marauders.

I decide to check on Grant's progress before I install the second camera. He's taller. Maybe he'll spot a good, higher location for trail cam number two.

"How's it going?" I ask.

"Almost finished," he answers. "I programmed it to send alerts to Velma's cell phone number and to your cell, too. Figured you'd want to keep tabs."

"Great idea."

We turn at the sound of a car crunching up the crushed-shell driveway. "Gestapo alert," Grant says.

"Yes, let's see what they want."

I walk toward the cruiser to talk to the heavyweight exiting the car. "Is there a problem, officer?"

"I'm checking on your progress," he says. "We keep a close eye on houses when we know the owners are away. Are you about done?"

I figure there's no point stalling. "Yes. We're getting ready to head to the marina to check on the Campbells' boat."

The man's bushy eyebrows knit into one long, black, furry caterpillar. "Mrs. Campbell didn't tell security you had permission to go to her boat."

"Well, she specifically asked me to check it." My teeth are clenched, but I try to avoid raising my voice. "If you don't believe me, I'll phone her, and you can ask."

I whip out my cell. Velma's number is now on my frequently called list. "I'm sure she won't mind being interrupted. She's just arranging her husband's funeral."

The guard stammers. "That won't be necessary. Uh, I can escort you to the marina."

"No, thank you. We know the way."

He gives me a sideways look before he gets back in his car, turns the vehicle around, and leaves.

"Wow," Grant says. "Sort of makes you think these guys have something to hide."

"You think? There's no 'sort of' about it for me."

Chapter Twenty-Five

Archer

Wednesday Morning, December 18

"She's going where?"

Why is Kylee heading to the marina?

The multiple bugs we planted inside the Campbell house have let me listen in to every phone call Velma's made or received, no matter where she is in the house. That's why I knew Kylee was coming to Stillwater and had arranged for a video doorbell replacement. But Velma never mentioned their boat or the Stillwater marina on any call.

Before he was killed, Maury snapped lots of photos of the marina and Wavedancer with his cell phone. Some of those pictures were taken weeks ago. Did he share some of the older ones online?

I know for certain he was unable to share the photos he took inside the maintenance barn. I didn't worry much about the marina pictures stored in his photo gallery. They weren't exactly incriminating. But if Kylee saw them, she might be asking why Maury took them.

On the other hand, Kylee's visit to the Stillwater marina may be totally innocent.

After I thank Jack for passing along the heads-up from one of his security people, I ask: "There's at least one guard aboard Wavedancer right now, correct?"

"Yeah, one on the yacht, one patrolling the marina."

"Tell whoever is onboard to stay out of sight until he gets an all-clear that Kylee's gone. I don't want the presence of extra security boosting Kylee's curiosity about my yacht."

I start pacing as soon as I hang up. I don't like Kylee wandering around the marina. I tell myself she has no reason to imagine the Wavedancer is being used to launder money. Still, I feel uneasy. I don't like it.

Damn the weather. If it weren't for the fierce Atlantic storms, we could load the money before dawn, and I could set sail tomorrow. Not a chance with the predicted high seas and gale-force winds. A launch tomorrow would be riskier than keeping the Wavedancer moored at the Stillwater marina.

I decide to leave the money in the maintenance barn for the time being. Now that Maury's gone, only my people can go inside the barn. And, unlike the marina, the area around the barn isn't frequented by any owners.

We'll wait and transfer the money to Wavedancer right before I set sail.

I wish I'd never heard of Kylee Kane. We always planned to fire Ted Welch's HOA management company, but, as soon as he brought an ex-Coast Guard investigator on staff, the management change became a priority. Any person with a Coast Guard tie gives me heartburn.

Kylee might be able to sic one of her old Coast Guard buddies on me. While the Wavedancer could easily pass a cursory safety inspection. A more dedicated search could betray some of the Wavedancer's best-kept secrets.

Mick warned me. "Don't dick around with the U.S. Coast Guard. They can board any vessel subject to U.S. jurisdiction whenever they want. They don't need warrants or probable cause. If you know what's good for you, don't do a damn thing to arouse suspicion."

Should I sideline Kylee?

It would have to look like an accident. It wouldn't need to be fatal. Just something to incapacitate her. Keep her in bed and out of my hair until I can sail off with Mick's fifty million. I'll have to give it more thought.

If Kylee visits Stillwater again, we should have advance warning from the bugs inside the Campbell house. Maybe we can arrange a unique welcome.

No, forget that.

If there's an accident, it can't be anywhere near here. Time to brainstorm with Quentin.

Chapter Twenty-Six

Kylee

Wednesday Morning, December 18

Since the Stillwater marina is on the backside of the peninsula, it's somewhat protected from angry ocean swells. But offshore gusts? Not so much. A strong one rocks me as I step out of my Mustang. Salt spray stings my face. Dang, it's cold. Can't help but shiver.

While there are no whitecaps in the cove, the boiling water looks like someone lit a fire underneath. The weatherman says the windchill is in the low forties. My body's chill tolerance is stuck in the mid-fifties. An unusually long stretch of warm weather in November and December didn't help reset my internal thermostat.

"I hope the Campbells' boat has a cabin," Grant says, "and isn't some open-deck fishing tub."

"Fear not. Two decades ago, when the Campbells built their Stillwater house, the only way to and from the peninsula was by sea. No land route. So they bought a reliable, wide-beamed motor yacht. Her cabin sleeps four, and she's got a compact galley and bathroom. Her twin inboards can power through rough seas."

I glance around the marina and spot the Soup Can with ease. What else would folks with Campbell as a last name christen their boat? The Soup Can's thirty-five-foot length barely classifies her as a yacht, and she looks puny next to her honking big neighbors.

"Guess I didn't need a slip number," I add as we approach the marina's multiple piers. "I should have realized the Soup Can would stick out. She's too old and small for the Stillwater elite. Plus, they need all the fancy navigation systems. Without them, they couldn't find their way to the nearest buoy."

"Do the owners actually captain them, or do they hire someone?" Grant asks.

I answer as we hurry down the pier. "Most of these owners don't captain their yachts."

"Gee, if you get tired of investigating HOA shenanigans, you can sign on as a yacht captain," Grant teases. "Bet they'd provide you with a nifty uniform. You'd never have to go dress shopping again."

I roll my eyes. "Come on. Let's check the Soup Can—Maury always called it a boat, never a yacht. I want to return to my Mustang's excellent heater as soon as possible."

The Soup Can's top deck looks shipshape. Ropes neatly coiled. Bumpers securely fastened. I climb down into the cabin. Everything looks tidy in the cabin where Velma and Maury used to sleep when they were building their house. Looks like Maury and Velma still keep a few clothes here.

When I reach the galley, I find Maury's unfinished project. He was in the midst of installing a new breaker panel. The old one's disconnected; the new one is lying on the counter, waiting to be wired up.

I don't mess with electrical wiring. I'll call the electrician I use to finish the job. Velma will just need to make sure he's allowed through the gates. As long as the Soup Can remains in port, the absence of electrical power for another day shouldn't be a worry.

I return to the main salon and find Grant peering through a porthole. He doesn't budge as I approach, and I'm sure he hears me.

"What's got you so focused?"

Grant holds up a photo packet bearing a drugstore label. "Maury—at least I assume it was Maury—paid to have these prints made. They're all of that monster yacht across the way. The name on her stern is Wavedancer."

"Let me see those photos." I leaf through the snapshots. Not exactly artistic endeavors or very shocking. Several show a couple of security guards leaving the yacht with what look like pet carriers. The rest show security patrolling the yacht's deck or the adjacent pier.

"The pictures all include the Wavedancer, the HOA president's yacht," I comment. "Not sure why Maury took these pictures. Best I can figure, he didn't like HOA security focusing on a single private yacht."

Grant looks puzzled. "Okay, but why so many snaps of guards with pet carriers?"

I shrug. "I don't know. Why would Maury care if Archer Highsmith takes his pets with him on cruises. Maybe it just irked him that HOA guards were running personal errands for the board president. Let's show the photos to Velma. Maybe she'll know the answer."

"I found something else," Grant says and opens a cigar box. "Look. Another feather, some weird scales, and a ball of fur. Do you suppose Maury was gathering stuff to make some sort of shaman charm? Then there's this Post-It note with two words—'dollars' and 'animals.' Dollars has an arrow pointing toward animals, and animals has an arrow pointing back to dollars."

Unlike the feather packaged with Maury's personal effects, the one in the cigar box is a brilliant scarlet and looks too long to come from a cardinal. I'm clueless about what creatures might have donated the strange scales or white fur. I can't think of any native Lowcountry candidates.

My rationale for Maury to take the photos of Archer's yacht doesn't feel right. Maury wasn't paying the guards' salaries. Why should he care how HOA dollars were spent? My gut tells me the pictures were meant to document something more sinister. Something related to the keepsakes in that cigar box? Smuggling?

I turn to Grant. "Let's take that cigar box with us, and I have one more idea. When that security guard showed up at the Campbell house this morning, I didn't have time to place our second trail cam. Bet there's a handy spot above deck where we can aim it at Wavedancer. Maybe nighttime video will offer more clues."

Chapter Twenty-Seven

Kylee

Wednesday Noon, December 18

I t's noon by the time I drop Grant at Ted's office and find a parking spot near Gigi's Boutique in Bluffton. That's where Alysha and Josie told me to meet them when they phoned. A glance at the boutique's window display makes me want to turn tail and run. Sure, my friends will be unhappy, but I can't imagine this boutique has anything remotely appealing to this fifty-one-year-old. The boutique clearly caters to the young and the hip. I'm neither—unless the fact my body is getting a bit more hippy counts.

Josie barrels through the shop's front door and grabs my arm. "Get in here," she orders. "We've found the perfect outfit for you."

I groan. "Sure you have."

While Josie's in her mid-forties, she dresses very stylishly when she's not in uniform. Her clothes always complement her curvy, fit figure. Josie says her teens scold her if she thinks about buying an "old-lady" get-up."

It doesn't really matter what Alysha, a svelte twenty-something, wears. She always looks like she's posing for a Vogue cover.

I can't begin to imagine what these two friends think I should wear. Something white and frilly? Or a dress that features racy leg slits and neckline plunges that would reveal my pasty winter skin. Heck, even with a summer tan, I'm not inclined to flash thighs or cleavage.

Josie tugs my arm again. "I know what you're thinking. You're wrong. Come back to the dressing room. We weren't sure about your size, or if the outfit we picked runs small, so Alysha has two sizes you can try."

Surprisingly, the one saleswoman in the shop practically hides behind a rack of clothes. She remains mute, too. She does seem to smirk as I'm dragged to the fitting room at the rear of the store. Obviously, my buddies prepped the woman to keep a safe distance from a reluctant and possibly foul-mouthed clothes shopper.

Alysha's in the dressing room. She's removed one of the dresses from its hangar and is getting it ready for me to try on.

"Come on, you need to get down to your knickers," Alysha says. "Don't even think about leaving your knee socks on; you'll ruin the effect."

The dress that's still waiting on the hangar calms my worst fears. The material looks soft and comfortable. The skirt is flowing, not tight. The top has a modest scoop neckline and three-quarter-length sleeves. And thankfully, it's not white. With my white hair, I avoid white clothes. If I stand next to a stucco wall, I'll practically vanish. This outfit is primarily burgundy, though a white, upside-down V starts just above the waist, providing a bold contrast.

"It's calf-length," Alysha begins, "and best of all, you'll be able to reaffirm that Ted isn't the only one to wear the pants in your family." She laughs. "It's a color-blocked, cropped jumpsuit. If you're standing still, your mom will never know the skirt is really like formal culottes."

I laugh. "Okay, you got me with the pants line. Let's see how it looks when I put it on."

Not bad.

The fit is perfect. The inverted V that starts below my boobs flares below the waist. Each step I take creates a swirl of burgundy and white. Reminds me of the season's scarlet and white poinsettias. I think (hope) Ted will like it. Of course, he won't have a chance to object before he sees me walking down the aisle on December 24. I have no plans to give Ted or Mom a preview.

"Thanks!" I turn and hug both women. "It's perfect." I drop my voice to a whisper. "I never would have dreamed of looking here. Of course, I may not think it's perfect after I see the price tag. Am I going to faint?"

"Nah," Josie replies. "But if you do, we'll revive you once we get to Fishcamp."

I whip out a credit card to pay the one-hundred-fifty-dollar charge for the outfit. It's more than I typically spend, but Josie assures me it's hundreds, maybe thousands, less than what today's brides shell out for their one-time wardrobes.

While I'm paying, Josie and Alysha abandon me to look at accessories in the front of the boutique.

"Hey, look at those two. They're practically strolling arm-in-arm." Josie's exasperated tone says whoever the pair might be, they're not on her friends list.

Where I'm standing, I can't see any passersby, though I know the street's bustling with panicked Christmas shoppers. Santa is set to arrive in seven days.

"Who are you talking about?" Alysha asks Josie.

"Those two rich witches with all the shopping bags—Lisa Queensbury and Babsie Talbott," Josie answers. "Lisa's the platinum blonde wearing the fur-trimmed coat. Babsie's the skinny-minnie in the high-heeled black leather boots.

"When my kids needed braces, I did some moonlighting, providing security for high-society galas. That's when I met those two pills. Both snooty pains in the ass. Thankfully, there was only one event when I had the displeasure of listening to haughty demands from both of them at the same time."

I hurriedly sign my credit card slip so I can join Alysha and Josie at the front window. Of course, I know what Babsie looks like—Martha's description of her as a possible stand-in for Popeye's Olive Oil is cruel but accurate. However, I've never laid eyes on Lisa Queensbury, Stillwater's third director and the only holdover from the board that was in power when Ted counted the HOA as one of his clients.

Both women are dressed to kill. High-heeled leather boots. Camel hair coats trimmed in fur. They're looking at a jewelry store's window display and carrying on an animated conversation. Probably discussing which sparkly gifts Santa should bring them.

From a distance, I can't really see much of Lisa's face. Still, I peg her as being in her sixties, but maybe that's because I know Babsie's age. Lisa's lustrous fur hat sits on carefully-styled platinum blonde hair.

I'm not at all surprised that the women know each other. I've heard both their names in connection with Beaufort County cultural events. They probably serve on many of the same committees—or museum boards, given their wealth.

"Okay, they've disappeared inside the jewelry store," Alysha says. "Unless one of us can come up with a reason to put the two in handcuffs, let's go eat. Josie, you can tell us all about said witches once I have a steaming bowl of she-crab soup in front of me."

"Amen," I say. "Shopping is fini! Let's eat lunch."

Chapter Twenty-Eight

Kylee

Wednesday 1 p.m., December 18

I use a napkin to wipe my greasy fingers and tell myself to make this my last dive into our shared basket of onion rings. When I look across the table at Josie and Alysha, I thank my lucky stars for my new friends.

After I retired, I sorely missed my Coast Guard buddies, especially fellow women officers. We applauded each other's accomplishments and laughed (better than crying) at misogynist backlash from a few service Neanderthals.

This spring, when I accidentally fell in with Alysha and Josie while working a case, I found my new tribe. To outsiders, it would seem we have little in common. Josie is a born-and-bred Southerner. Six years younger than me, she's the mother of two teenagers. She works as a Beaufort County Sheriff's Deputy.

I hail from Iowa, have never married, have no children, and I'm a fifty-one-year-old Coast Guard retiree.

While Alysha is a fellow Coastie, she graduated from the Coast Guard Academy two decades after me. Plus, the young, ebony-skinned lieutenant grew up in California. Unlike Josie and me, she has to deal with barely-disguised racism as well as anti-female taunts in her choice of career.

What do we have in common? We've survived and demonstrated our professionalism in male-dominated professions. We take no crap. We love chasing down villains, and we rely on humor to help us through rough patches.

"What's that shit-eating grin about?" Josie asks. "Are you thinking ahead to finally consummating your marriage? Since you're single, you must be a virgin, right?"

Both women chortle.

I lower my head like I've been whipped. "I had been thinking what good friends I have, but, now...."

I raise my head and grin. "Hey, speaking of friendship, Josie, why were you surprised to see Lisa Queensbury and Babsie Talbott chumming around together? Don't one-percenters tend to fraternize with peers in their exalted social strata?"

Josie holds up a hand while she finishes chewing an onion ring. "Both women want to be—no, that's not strong enough—*need* to be queen bees. My dad raised bees. If two would-be queens hatched at the same time, they'd fight to the death. Narcissists don't like to share the spotlight or accolades. In my dictionary, these two women are pictured adjacent to the word narcissist."

"Knowing Babsie, I agree with your assessment," I say. "Babsie likes to portray herself as a member of the noblesse oblige, selflessly ministering to Hullis Island's less-fortunates by running the Hullis Island Care Committee. In reality, she never actually lifts a finger to help—she doesn't bake cookies, clean houses, run errands, or take people to their doctor appointments. She just orders her committee minions to do as they're told.

"Nonetheless, she's shocked and hurt if anyone fails to accept her as the island's rich, nattily-dressed Mother Teresa."

"What's Lisa's story?" Alysha asks Josie.

"Beyond her witchy personality, I don't know a lot about her. She's married to Dwight Queensbury, a New England tycoon. He retired but still serves on a dozen boards and travels a lot. Lisa's his second wife and not fond of her stepchildren. They're adults, so she doesn't have to play mother. But I've overheard her talking about them. Not in a loving way.

"Afraid that's it. Mainly I've been the recipient of Lisa's attitude—'I'm the queen, you're a peon.'"

I chuckle. "Maybe the women get together to complain about their stepchildren. Mom told me there were rumors the Talbott offspring—products of the first Mrs. Talbott—seem none too fond of Babsie. When I marry Ted, I'll be a stepmom, too. Think that might get me invited to join Babsie and Lisa for lunch?"

"Not a chance," Alysha says. "Grant loves you, so you'd have nothing to bitch about. And the one outfit we picked out for your wedding would be only marginally acceptable for one of their society bashes. No designer label.

"Then there are your purses." Alysha waves a hand at my large over-the-shoulder carry-all. "We know you pick handbags based on how nicely your Glock fits inside. These women have different criteria."

I laugh. "I think I'll let that fashion comment wrap up our lunch. Besides all the onion rings are gone. I'm exiting before you start critiquing my shoes."

My good mood fades when the thought of shoes reminds me of the bag holding Maury's personal effects.

"Josie, don't forget to call me when you get Mr. Campbell's autopsy report."

"I won't. It'll be late afternoon."

Chapter Twenty-Nine

Archer

Wednesday Afternoon, December 18

My personal security system alerts. I glance at the video and spot Jack lumbering toward my door. Wonder what supposed emergency is prompting an in-person visit. It's been an hour since he confirmed Kylee and Ted's son, Grant, exited through the Stillwater gates.

I wish I'd thought to search the Campbell boat, but can't imagine Kylee's marina visit netted any intelligence. The pair were on the boat less than half an hour, and I suspect the guard aboard the Wavedancer followed orders and stayed out of sight until the snoops departed.

I buzz Jack in.

"What's the freakin' emergency?" I demand the second he exits the elevator. No sense wasting words with Jack.

"It's that woman," he says. "Kylee Kane. The Wavedancer guard kept an eye on her and that kid when they were messing around topside on Soup Can, the Campbell boat. He watched them install a camera and point it right at your Wavedancer."

"They what?"

Good God.

"So, once the guard knew about the camera, I suppose he popped up on

125

deck and waved."

"No, sir," Jack replies.

My sarcasm is wasted on him. Not necessarily a bad thing.

"Since the Wavedancer's backed into its slip, the guard was able to sneak off the back of the yacht, where the camera wouldn't see him."

Jack's rare smile says he's pleased with himself and his security.

"I was sure you'd want that damn camera removed. So I had the guard circle around from behind, grab the camera, carry it to the end of the pier, and let it sink. That woman will never know what happened or who did it."

I close my eyes. My temple throbs. I want to strangle the meathead.

"Oh, I'm sure it'll be a *big* mystery. Kylee won't need mug shots or badge numbers to know Stillwater guards did the deed. Why didn't you call me first?"

Jack shuffles his feet. He may not recognize sarcasm, but he can read my anger.

"Uh, well, lately, you seem pissed whenever I ask you what I should do. I, uh, thought you wanted me not to bug you so much, to act on my own."

"You're wrong," I say through gritted teeth. "Don't do shit unless I tell you to do it. I don't want to hear you say another word, just nod if you understand me. Then get the hell out of here."

I glare at Jack's retreating back. How am I going to clean up this mess? As soon as Kylee discovers the camera's gone, she'll know security was keeping an eye on the Campbell boat and cared enough about the camera to get rid of it. That's sure to get her antennae twitching. God, my head hurts. I need to think.

I'm glad Jack slunk out without uttering any more excuses. Not sure how much longer I could have controlled my temper.

My throat's sore. The cursed wet, cold weather and constant aggravations. I head to the kitchen and shake a Cold-EEZE out of the bag. Chase it down with a bottle of spring water. No improvement. Maybe I should try to sweat out an incipient cold. Besides, I do some of my best thinking on my rowing machine.

What made Kylee point a camera at the Wavedancer?

I concede my rage at Jack is partly anger at my own failure. Quentin and I searched the Campbell house for any shred of evidence he might have left behind, but I forgot all about his damned boat. We should have searched it, too.

What did Kylee find that prompted her to aim a camera at my yacht? Or did Maury blab to someone that he witnessed suspicious activity aboard Wavedancer?

Don't go there. Maury had a lot of friends. Can't ask Jack to break all of their necks.

If Kylee installed one camera, did she set up more? Maybe not on the boat, but on the Campbell property. Possible. But if I search for one, that new video doorbell will video me in the act.

Okay, why should I care about a trail cam on Campbell land? We're done with that house.

Kylee has met Quentin. Maybe it's time for her to meet me. Mick didn't pay for my advanced degrees so I could break people's necks. Organized crime needs organizers, managers to keep the business end running smoothly. That's me. Time to do my job. I'll visit Ted's office this afternoon, and hope Kylee's at her desk. If not, Ted can pass along my humble apologies combined with a veiled threat.

Chapter Thirty

Kylee

Wednesday 3 p.m., December 18

"Y ou look happy," Ted says. "Did the Smart Gal Network score a shopping success? Or are you still toying with the idea of marching down the aisle in military dress whites despite Myrt's don't-you-dares?"

I flash a thumbs-up. "Success. I bought what I plan to wear. It's very pretty, and no, you can't see it until December 24. Mom won't get a peek either until she walks me down the aisle."

Though it's unusual for a bride to be escorted to the altar by her mother, Mom's delighted to be doing the honors for Dad. She's certain my father and my younger brother, who died way too young, will both be watching from above, proud as punch.

I look past Ted's cubicle to see who else is working in the office this afternoon. I see Frank, Robin, and, to my surprise, Grant, who's sitting in my cubicle. He's intently staring at the computer screen. I sneak up behind him and shake the back of his swivel chair.

Grant jumps.

"What gives?" I ask. "Thought Mimi was going to pick you up for another birding stake-out—or is it a make-out date? And what are you doing on my computer?"

Grant laughs. "Mimi's en route, and I'll surrender your computer. Robin set me up on it, with an assignment to look for any interesting posts on Earful. When I finished, I downloaded a game I've been wanting to try. Figured you'd want to keep it. Lots of aliens to give you shooting practice."

I give Grant a friendly slug on the arm as he quits the video game and relinquishes my chair. We both look up when the bell attached to the office front door chimes.

"Hey, Mimi." Grant stands and waves her over. "Aunt Kylee just asked if we were still planning to scout rookeries this afternoon."

Mimi joins us. "While I've been wanting to visit a rookery on Pinckney, I'd really prefer to check out birds in Stillwater Cove. Ever since I saw that deep blue, almost purple feather, I've been wondering how a Hyacinth Macaw feather could wind up here. This parrot species is affectionate and beautiful. It's no surprise people want them as pets even though they're endangered in the wild.

"Unfortunately, people who buy macaws often aren't prepared to properly care for them. These parrots are really big, and normal cages are too small. When the parrots are outside their cages, their sharp bills can gouge deep holes in furniture—not to mention human flesh. They also escape.

"If a pet Hyacinth Macaw is trying to survive in Stillwater Cove, it's in trouble. Its natural habitat borders tropical rainforests. Yeah, we have rain, but the parrot can't be loving this cold. Temperatures may dip below freezing before Christmas."

Grant frowns. "Somehow, I don't think Stillwater would approve Operation Parrot Rescue. This morning, the guards practically ran Aunt Kylee and me off at gunpoint, and we had the equivalent of an owner-authorized hall pass. They seemed peeved an owner had the nerve to let us lowlifes visit her house and boat."

Mimi sighs. "A first step would be to see what species of birds are living in Stillwater. Think they'd let me record bird songs for a few hours. I wouldn't take pictures. The parrot's caw is quite distinctive."

Mimi's idea has some merit. "While I doubt Stillwater would approve a scientific expedition, you've given me an idea to rattle the HOA dictators.

They can't know when or how we came by that feather. I could say we found it in the Campbell yard and showed it to an ornithologist. The upshot is we believe it comes from an endangered parrot that may be in peril." I grin. "I can suggest we contact the newspapers and TV stations to help organize a community search."

Grant chuckles. "They'd croak at the thought of media swarming Stillwater. Hey, why don't you check your cell phone? Let's see if the marina trail cam has captured any interesting video."

"Good idea." I dig my cell phone out of my purse and toss it to Grant. "You set it up; you can check faster than I can."

A flurry of keystrokes and thumb swipes only serve to deepen Grant's frown and trigger a few mild curses. "The camera is gone. No signal, nothing."

"An internet outage?" I ask.

"No. The response would be different. Someone either removed the camera's batteries or destroyed it."

"You're sure?"

"Pretty sure."

The front door chime prompts us to look up. Ted's office doesn't get a lot of traffic. Most clients contact us by phone, email, or text. If they want a face-to-face meeting, they expect us to visit them, not vice versa. That's why I'm half expecting Mom and Velma will be the new arrivals.

The stranger looks too young to be one of Ted's clients. HOA directors tend to be age fifty and up. I peg this guy as early forties. Ted moves to greet the man, hand outstretched for a handshake, like he knows him. Maybe he is a client.

"Hello, Archer. I'm surprised to see you here. What can I do for you?"

Archer quickly ends the handshake. "If you have a couple of moments, I'd like to chat with you and Ms. Kane. I need to apologize for our security team's overzealousness and explain the reasons."

"Of course," Ted responds.

Ted quickly walks toward my cubicle with the man I now know is Archer Highsmith trailing him.

"Kylee Kane, let me introduce Archer Highsmith, the president of the Stillwater Cove HOA," Ted says.

Archer reaches out to shake my hand. "Pleased to finally meet you, Ms. Kane." His firm grasp, dark brown eyes, and neutral expression give no hints.

While Ted introduces the Stillwater president to Grant and Mimi, I study Archer. He's tall. Just a titch below Grant's six-foot-three, and he looks fit. His hair, a dirty blond, is stylishly cut, and his face is quite tan. Either he frequents a tanning booth to keep his summer bronze from fading to winter white, or regularly visits warmer, sunny climes.

Duh, he does own a yacht. That would make island visits a piece of cake.

With introductions complete, Ted suggests we sit down at our "conference" table. Unless there are visitors, Ted never gives our hand-me-down table such a lofty name. This is where we pig out on morning donuts and eat brown-bag lunches.

Once we're seated, Archer places his hands on the table, palms up. A gesture to show he has nothing to hide?

"Kylee and Ted, I need to apologize," he begins. "I just learned our security team destroyed a trail camera that was attached to a strut on the bow of the Campbells' boat."

I stifle the urge to open my mouth and start yelling about trespass and destruction of private property. Under the table, Ted tightly grips my leg just above my knee. A clear signal I should let Archer finish his mea culpa before I explode.

Okay, let's hear his excuse. He'll probably say the camera invaded his privacy.

"The security guards were doing a routine marina check when one noticed a trail camera pointed directly at my yacht." he continues. "They assumed a thief placed it to case the area and determine the best times to come on board and steal valuables.

"The guards were angry someone had breached security. They destroyed the camera before they learned that you, Ms. Kane, had just left the Campbell boat. Since the camera wasn't there before your visit, I assume the camera belongs to you."

Archer takes a deep breath. "While I apologize for the destruction of property, I must ask: Why were you attempting to video my yacht?"

My heart adopts a jackhammer beat. What's my excuse? Then it comes to me. Thank heavens Mimi dropped by.

"We certainly weren't trying to spy on your yacht, Mr. Highsmith." I attempt to make my tone convey indignation at the very idea. "That trail camera was placed to monitor birds. Mimi, the young lady you just met, is studying to be an ornithologist, and she's been bird-watching with her father for years. I showed her a distinctive feather I found on the Campbell property. It made her fear an endangered species of parrot escaped captivity and was not equipped to deal with the deep freeze we're expecting. We were trying to document its existence and were considering alerting the media."

"If you found the feather on Campbell property, why didn't you put the trail camera there? Why were you surveilling the marina?"

Archer's raised eyebrows and sarcastic tone showcase his skepticism. His lips twitch into a smug sneer. Archer thinks I've motor-mouthed my way into his trap.

"Oh, but we did put a trail camera in the Campbell yard," I answer. "We just thought it would be good to stake out a second site."

Archer's chair scrapes as he pushes it back to stand. "Given your explanation, I'll make sure you're reimbursed for the cost of the camera," he says. "But Stillwater Cove does not allow any private surveillance of our facilities. That includes the marina and all of our commonly owned land. Surveillance is forbidden for very good security reasons. With your background, Ms. Kane, that's something you should realize."

"Oh, I do." I go for my most sincere tone. "I understand your security concerns completely."

Let the jerk ponder my sarcasm. Let him wonder what Archer Highsmith security worries I've come to completely understand.

Ted's hand tightens on my leg beneath the table. Okay, I'll shut my trap. Scored a point or two.

Archer's attempt at a smile comes closer to a sneer. His straight white teeth provide a gleaming contrast to his tanned cheeks.

"I did have one other reason for dropping by," he adds. "Has a time been set for Maury Campbell's funeral service? The board would like to alert the community about the arrangements. I'm sure many neighbors will want to attend. I know Quentin, Lisa, and I plan to be there. We will also make a sizable donation to whatever charity is named as a tribute in lieu of flowers."

"A nice gesture," Ted replies. "Unfortunately, the arrangements aren't firm yet. Velma's son, Vince, is stuck in Taiwan due to travel snafus. Velma can't confirm a date for the service until she's sure Vince will be home."

As soon as Archer's out the door, Grant, Mimi, Robin, and Frank surround Ted and me. While they could hear snatches of our conversation, they demand a word-by-word replay.

The verdict is unanimous. Archer Highsmith is very antsy about people taking an interest in his yacht, and Stillwater's security team is guarding it like it's Fort Knox.

Mimi grins and holds up a fist. "You owe me. I gave you that bird rescue excuse for spying on Archer's yacht."

Mimi and I bump fists. "Yeah, Archer didn't buy it, but what could he do? Call me a liar without any security goons around to back up his scare tactics?"

Chapter Thirty-One

Archer

Wednesday 3:30 p.m., December 18

That lying bitch. *Monitoring birds, my ass. I listened to her phone conversation with Velma. She didn't find that damn feather on Campbell property. The feather was atop the personal effects Kylee collected for the widow. But I couldn't call her a liar. How would I know she was lying? Couldn't say the bugs I put in Velma's house let me hear everything the widow says while she's inside.*

I pound the steering wheel. Then, the idea that Kylee might be looking out the window and laughing turns my anger to icy control. I start the car. Don't let them witness my frustration.

I drive downtown and pull into one of the metered parking spaces at the Beaufort Marina. Didn't someone tell me Kylee keeps a sailboat here?

I think Kylee understood my implied threat. She'd better not pull any more stunts to spy on Wavedancer. Her message was loud and clear, too. If I give her shit, she'll go public about endangered birds and promote a media shitshow.

Worse, she could call in the cavalry. In her case, the Coast Guard calvary.

I'd feel better if the bitch were dead—or at least had pressing personal problems to keep her too occupied to hound me. I just need a few day's grace until I leave for the Caribbean.

Hmm. A nice, bed-confining illness could do the trick.

At the downtown parking pay station, I swipe my credit card for a half hour on the meter. Plenty of time to chat up whoever's working at the marina store. I didn't get this job solely for my brains. Mick knew I'd spent time around boats, though as crew, not owner.

Before going inside, I scan the piers. Quite a few empty slips. Not surprising. If I were cruising the Intracoastal over the holidays, I'd make plans to be farther south come Christmas. Of the sailboats moored here, I focus on one that seems to have been given a prime slip. Probably because the slip has been rented long-term. The River Rat is the name painted on her side and stern. She's big enough to be a live-in. Let's confirm Kylee's the owner.

A young lady behind the counter slowly leafs through a magazine. Doesn't stop to read anything. Maybe it's all pictures. When the twenty-something notices me, her face lights up. No other customers. *She's bored. Good.*

I walk to the counter. "Hi, my nephew asked me to check out area marinas willing to rent slips for six months to a year," I begin. "Are all your slips for transients, or do you reserve some for longer-term use?"

I don't even need to mention Kylee's name. In no time, the Chatty-Cathy tells me all about the River Rat and Kylee Kane. She volunteers that Kylee's getting married soon. Hopes she'll still keep the River Rat at the marina to go on day sails, even if she doesn't call the sailboat home.

"Once they're married, they'll likely live in that big house her fiancé owns in the Historic District. Guess you'd call it a mansion even though it was kind of a dump when he bought it."

I ask a few more questions unrelated to Kylee to keep her talking.

"Where could my nephew shop for groceries, if he didn't want to get in a car and drive?"

"Oh, that would be tough," she says. "A lot of our customers walk to downtown restaurants for coffee, snacks, and take-out dinners. But your nephew would need to drive or Uber to get actual groceries. It's not far to Publix on Ladys Island, or the Food Lion in Beaufort Town Center. In fact, I saw Kylee carrying Food Lion grocery bags to her sailboat early this morning. Guess she hasn't said a final goodbye to life aboard the River Rat yet."

I return to my car and call Lisa.

"What did you dig up?" I ask. "Let's hear about the Kane woman's daily routine, what she eats, every damn detail."

Lisa huffs. "What am I? A private detective? Babsie only knows island gossip. She's not a family friend, closer to an enemy. Zero love lost between Babsie and Kylee's mom. Here's the sum total of everything I found out. Kylee and her lover, Ted Welch, regularly visit Kylee's mother, Myrt Kane, on Hullis Island. Ted's ties to the Kane family date back to when he was a little kid. Since someone torched the widow Kane's Hullis house last Thanksgiving, she's been shacking up with Frank Donahue, also widowed.

"Babsie says Kylee retired young to help her mother when she was undergoing cancer treatments. Once Myrt got better, Kylee decamped to live on a sailboat at the Downtown Beaufort Marina. Rumor has it that the lovebirds—Kylee and Ted—spend most nights at his place. Babsie added that Ted's college-age son is home for the holidays.

"Oh, Myrt's reserved the Hullis Island Chapel and Community Center from four to six p.m. on Christmas Eve for Kylee's wedding. That's it. All I can tell you. Haven't a clue what the woman does when she's not visiting Myrt. If you want to know what she eats, whether she flosses, or how often she pees, you can damn well order one of your security thugs to tail her."

"Okay. You made your point. But tell Babsie to keep digging and provide updates."

Actually I think I learned everything I need to know from the marina store's Chatty-Cathy. But you can never have too much intelligence.

"By sheer coincidence, I saw Kylee in the flesh today," Lisa adds. "Babsie and I were shopping in Bluffton. I suggested the outing so we'd have time together, and I could grill her. Turns out, we weren't the only Christmas shoppers. Babsie spotted Kylee coming out of a dress shop with two friends. I'd met one of the women, a deputy sheriff, who has worked security at a few black-tie events I organized. Haven't a clue who the other friend might be. A willowy black woman. Looked elegant enough to be a fashion model.

CHAPTER THIRTY-ONE

Quite a bit younger than Kylee and the deputy."

"What's the deputy sheriff's name?"

"Like I'd remember?" Lisa huffs. "It's not as if I planned to add the deputy to my contacts. Her last name sounded like Muscatel, a wine I figured she might sneak out of a paper bag while she was working."

It shouldn't be hard to find out who the deputy is. Not many women in the Beaufort County Sheriff's Department.

Unfortunately, I'm fairly certain I know the black woman's identity. Sorry to learn the striking Coast Guard lieutenant pals around with Kylee.

Chapter Thirty-Two

Kylee

Wednesday 3:30 p.m., December 18

As soon as Mimi and Grant leave, I phone Alysha.

"Hi, Kylee," Alysha answers. "Don't tell me you're having second thoughts about your wedding dress. I devoted half of my day off to help Josie scout for an outfit that said 'you'—pretty, bold, practical."

"No second thoughts. I'm thrilled with the dress. My call has nothing to do with clothes. I've been retired a few years so I'm not up-to-date on the Coast Guard's smuggling challenges. I assume drugs remain a top priority, but not sure about other contraband priorities. Do any involve cages?"

"Cages?" Alysha's voice jumps an octave. "What mess are you sticking your nose in this time?"

"It's probably nothing, just humor me. Before Maury Campbell died, he took photos of Stillwater security guards removing cages from a yacht. Maury thought enough of the pictures to make prints."

"We're not talking human-sized cages, are we?" Alysha asks. "Sure as hell hope not."

"No. They looked more like pet carriers. Something people might use to take a medium-sized dog to the vet."

"If you think the cages are used for smuggling, my first guess goes to exotic pets. There's a brisk black-market trade in reptiles—snakes, lizards, even

138

crocodiles. Some idiots will pay tens of thousands to own illegal reptiles as well as endangered animals, from monkeys to tigers. Other animals are killed so black-marketers can sell their horns, fur, and meat. Some yahoos seem to think ground-up pangolin scales or tiger penises will make them more virile or ward off cancer. Of course, smugglers don't need cages to transport horns, meat, or powder."

"What about birds?" I ask.

"Rare birds are smuggled, too," Alysha answers. "I think you'd better tell me what you suspect."

When I fill Alysha in, I'm greeted with an unexpectedly long silence.

"You suspect Archer Highsmith of smuggling?" Her tone suggests I'm loco. "That's absurd. Archer is friends with Captain Harvey Reed, your pal who commands the Coast Guard cutter Oakum based out of Tybee Island. Shortly after Archer moved here, he visited all of our facilities in the Charleston District. Said he wanted to show how much he appreciated the Coast Guard's efforts to keep pirating threats away from our shores.

"I've been aboard his yacht," she adds. "He hosted a party for all the Coasties in the district who could come. Great food and drinks, a local band. And I didn't see a single rare bird or even a suspicious feather. Why would a smuggler give Coasties a chance to spend time on his yacht?"

Because he's smart. Keep your enemies close.

"He also donates funds to a boater safety program to teach newcomers the rules of the sea and navigation essentials," Alysha adds.

If we were talking in person, I'd hold up my hands. Enough already.

"Okay, okay," I say. "Archer should be nominated for sainthood. But just suppose my suspect isn't the 'honorable' Mr. Highsmith. I'm trying to understand why a smuggler would traffic exotic pets instead of drugs. Drugs have to be easier. They don't need food, water, or oxygen, and they can be shoved into all kinds of nooks and crannies."

Alysha sighs. "Okay, I'll humor you. It is lower risk. Penalties for trafficking endangered species—or illegal animal products like ivory tusks—are a lot less severe than they are for smuggling drugs.

"People convicted of trafficking endangered animals typically get less than two years in prison," she adds. "Though one big-time smuggler was sentenced to prison for five plus years. Prosecutors blamed that guy for having a hand in the massacre of more than one hundred elephants and rhinos."

I nod. What I expected.

"That's a big difference," I comment. "As I recall, a first-time offender smuggling fentanyl might get ten to forty years. He might even be ineligible for parole."

"True," Alysha says. "But smuggling animals is less lucrative, too. Archer's sixty-foot yacht must be worth four million dollars. Add another what—three million?—for his oceanfront mansion. Why would a financial wunderkind risk prison for a few million more? Wouldn't it make more sense for him to try for another killing, buying and selling something like Bitcoin? That may be risky, but the risk doesn't come with a prison term."

Alysha has a good point.

"I admit it," I say. "What you say makes sense. *If* Archer really is a financial wizard. That's the story. But, as we both know, some people invent their pasts. Take on new identities. Who knows, maybe Archer's really a front guy for organized crime."

Alysha laughs. "Yes, Beaufort County is a hotbed of organized crime."

"Laugh if you will," I say. "But I plan to check this guy out every which way. Tell you what. I'll bet you a dinner at Ombra that Archer Highsmith is not as squeaky clean as you think."

Once again, I've triggered Alysha's laugh. "Bet accepted, I haven't had one of Ombra's Italian specialties in ages. But we need to agree on terms. Archer's *dirty* rating should relate strictly to criminal proclivities. No fair counting things like ditching a former wife or back-stabbing a competitor."

"Done. The man's dirty."

"Fine. I'll start pondering what to order at Ombre's—champagne, an appetizer, soup, entrée, and, of course, dessert."

Chapter Thirty-Three

Archer

Wednesday Late Afternoon, December 18

I phone Perry McMahan's office. I hear a cacophony of yelps and barks in the background as soon as Sherry, his receptionist, answers. We're strictly phone buddies. Sherry's never laid eyes on me or my dog for good reason.

"Afraid I need Dr. McMahan to take a look at Whiskey," I say. "But I can't bring her in for an exam before six o'clock. I hate to ask, but could you see if the doc can stay after hours? I'd really appreciate it."

"I'm so sorry Whiskey's feeling poorly again," she purrs. "Let me ask if six o'clock will work for the doctor."

A couple of minutes later, Sherry returns to the phone. "Dr. McMahan will be happy to wait for you. I'm sorry I won't be here. One of these days, I'd love to meet you and your sweet Whiskey. I can't stay past five o'clock, though. That's when I pick my little one up from daycare."

"Oh, that's too bad," I fib. "You have such a lovely voice. I bet you're even more delightful in person."

I'm good at meaningless verbal diarrhea.

I had zero worries about the doc's availability. Neither did Whiskey. The mutt's worries are long behind her. She's been dead going on thirty years. Whiskey wasn't exactly my dog, just the closest thing to it. I was one of the

141

neighborhood kids who fed her scraps. We called the flea-bitten beggar Whiskey because she spent most nights huddled next to a homeless drunk.

The doc knows whenever I call for an after-hours consult, he'd better be there. And my visits are always timed to occur after Sherry leaves the office. Otherwise, I'd need a real pet to haul to the vet's office.

I hope Perry hasn't delivered the damn parrot to the buyer. Usually, I depend on Perry to keep the maximum number of imports alive and healthy. This time, I hope he can turn over a dead bird. If so, I can arrange for the ornithologist coed and Ted's son to visit Stillwater and find the poor escaped parrot's corpse.

Boy, would that frustrate Kylee.

She could speculate all she wanted about how an exotic bird wound up inside Stillwater Cove, but she couldn't attack the theory. After all, she was the one who suggested a pet owner might have allowed it to escape. Permitting the would-be ornithologist to visit would be another demonstration that Stillwater Cove operates with absolute transparency. Nothing to hide.

Chapter Thirty-Four

Kylee

Wednesday Late Afternoon, December 18

I log into the background service we use to check out new hires for clients. HOAs want anyone who works security or can access homeowner data and financial accounts to actually have studied and worked where they say they have. HOAs also want assurance their potential employees have no criminal records and don't make a habit of spewing hate rhetoric online.

Let's see if Archer Highsmith and his equally-oily director Quentin Teacher can pass the sniff test. On a whim, I add the third HOA director, Lisa Queensbury. Wish I knew the last name of the jerk who heads Stillwater security. I'd love to check that thug out. Unfortunately, the first name, Jack, isn't a big help. Maybe Velma knows the man's last name.

I enter what public information is available on Archer, Quentin and Lisa— full names, current addresses, and ages. I add the skimpy bio info Archer and Quentin provided to Linked-In. Lisa isn't on Linked-In. I find no social media accounts for any of them. Unusual, but not exactly a predictor of criminal activity.

The men are both single. Maybe they subscribe to dating apps. I'll have to ask our computer guru, Robin, what those apps might be and if she can scour them for any insights into my suspects' interests and behavior.

I order background reports and hope they will arrive tomorrow.

I shut down the computer. Time to try and set up more interviews with theft victims. I'm reaching for my cell when it rings. It's Josie.

"Hey, Kylee, I knew you wanted a summary of Maury Campbell's autopsy report as soon as it was issued. It lists the cause of death as a broken neck and the manner of death as 'undetermined.' Since there were no witnesses to the accident, it is impossible to know how the victim's neck was broken."

I sigh. "I understand the reasoning, though that 'undetermined' will leave Velma in emotional limbo. Did the autopsy indicate any possibility a heart attack or stroke caused Maury to lose control of the golf cart?"

"No. Heart was healthy. No signs of a stroke. Only anomalies were three broken ribs, and bruises on his chest, arms, and legs."

"Bruises? If his neck broke on impact, why would he have bruises from injuries sustained in the wreck? Maybe I'm off base, but if your heart isn't pumping, how can blood pool to create bruises?"

"You'll have to read the whole report to find the answer to that," Josie says. "I'll send it. By the way, Alysha called after you named Archer Highsmith as a prime smuggling suspect. While she thinks you're way off base with Highsmith, Alysha agrees Stillwater Cove would be an excellent base for smuggling. The marina has direct access to the Atlantic, and the sheriff's department doesn't typically venture inside the gates. In fact, with the exception of Mr. Campbell's death, I can't remember the last time a deputy set foot in Stillwater."

"But you do have the authority to go in gated communities whenever you want, right?" I ask.

"You bet. We don't need an engraved invitation from Stillwater Security or even a request from a property owner to check things out. Stillwater Cove may have gates, but it's part of Beaufort County."

"Good to know. I can't shake the feeling that something is very wrong inside those gates. I'm glad Alysha hasn't completely dismissed Stillwater Cove's bad vibes."

I figure there's still time to try and set up Hullis Island interviews for tomorrow morning. I leave voice messages with another of the male theft victims and one of the younger, working women. No actual humans answer their phones. I hope one of them calls back to confirm availability tomorrow.

Then, on a whim, I search my Hullis Island Community Directory. I look up Babsie Talbott, and what do you know, it lists both cell and landline numbers.

I pause before punching in the number. How am I going to sell Babsie on a face-to-face meeting?

"Hello!" Babsie's high-pitched squeak is unmistakable, and her hello isn't quickly followed by a "sorry I missed you" message. Wow. I've actually made contact with a human.

"Hi, Babsie. This is Kylee Kane calling. I'm researching a Hullis Island security matter, and I think you can provide some helpful background. Do you have time to see me tomorrow morning?"

Silence. I do hear her breathing. I hang on. Curious. Is she going to hang up? Tell me to go to Hades? Express outrage that I have some nerve asking for help after I was so rude when Mom was sick.

"What time would you like to come by?" she finally asks.

Her tone is as pleasant as it can be, given her unfortunate glass-shattering vocal range.

"Uh, is nine o'clock too early?" I fumble.

"Not at all. I try to do everything possible to support the Hullis Island community."

I hang up and giggle. People don't often surprise me. Babsie's cordial response is one-hundred and eighty degrees opposite of my expectation. Maybe she's not always the egotistical, self-centered witch prior experience suggests.

Chapter Thirty-Five

Archer

Wednesday 6:00 p.m., December 18

I check the parking lot to make sure there are no emergency veterinary patients. Perry's station wagon is the only car in the lot. While he only lives a block from his office, the doc drives to work. Perry could use the exercise. He has to be one hundred pounds overweight.

The doc opens the front door while I'm still ten feet away. He's been watching for me. As soon as I'm inside, he tries to lock the door. His chubby fingers fumble on the first attempt. His whole body is trembling. A wiggling bowl of Jell-O.

"What's the emergency?" Perry's double, make that triple, chins ripple with each word he speaks. "Please don't tell me the next shipment has arrived. I haven't begun to prepare for new arrivals or their delivery to buyers. You told me the shipment wouldn't arrive before late January."

"Calm down, Perry," I say. "If anything, this shipment will be even later. Maybe late February. Storms in the Atlantic have postponed my departure, and I always stay in Andros for a while. Want it to look as if I'm just there to unwind and tune up my suntan. However, I do need a couple of small favors. Let's go to your office. Sit and relax while I explain what I need."

Perry waddles through the large reception area to his office. I know another door leads to his examination rooms and surgery suite. I should know—we paid for the building and everything in it.

That's how we bought Perry. The newly minted and financially broke vet couldn't find a welcome in any existing veterinary practice, and he didn't have the money to set up shop. His slovenly appearance and nervous tics definitely factored into his rejection by overworked Lowcountry vets. They thought Perry might repulse clients. We didn't care if Perry ever scored any clients. We set him up in business to be our vet.

To my surprise, Perry now does a brisk business treating all manner of pets. High demand for vet services negated any hesitancy clients might have had about Perry's appearance or mannerisms. And, as it turns out, he's actually quite good with animals. Just not people.

While Perry may no longer need our financial backing, his debt will never be wiped off our books. Not as long as he's useful.

The oak chair behind his desk creaks as Perry slowly lowers his body into its oversized seat.

"What kind of favors?" he asks.

"I assure you they're small ones," I answer. "I need your help with a human animal, a woman with a snooping disorder. I need her to fall ill. It doesn't need to be fatal, mind you. I just want her out of commission for a few days. Too sick and weak to pry into our business."

Perry shakes his head. His eyes, shadowed by the overhang of his fat brow, dart nervously back and forth.

"I told you from the beginning I'd do what you asked with animals. I won't do anything to harm people."

"Relax your sphincter already," I say. "It's not as if I'm bringing the woman into one of your exam rooms to be put down. Whatever you concoct to make her ill, you won't be involved in the delivery. I'll take care of that. I simply need you to search your pharmacological treasure trove and come up with a recipe to cause bad, flu-like symptoms. Then give the concoction to me. I'll take care of the rest. You'll never know the woman's name. No danger of anyone tying her illness to you."

His head drops as he accepts defeat. "Let me think," he says. "I just don't know."

"Take your time," I reply. "We've got all night. But let me add a few more caveats. The toxic mix has to be something I can easily add to food or a beverage. It should be odorless, and, if it has a taste, it needs to be mild enough that whatever she's eating or drinking will mask it."

Perry doesn't protest further. He just starts typing on his computer keyboard. I don't begrudge him a little time to research. Perry doesn't get my kind of request every day.

Meanwhile, I pull out my phone to check in with Deputy Nick Ibsen, my friend in the Sheriff's Office. When we fired the old security crew, I invited Nick to be our new security chief. At the time, he wasn't interested. Nick was convinced he'd be the next Beaufort County Sheriff. But he did accept a handsome payment to help us ID recruits for our Stillwater security force.

I told Nick we needed ex-military types, like him, without criminal records. They had to pass the necessary background checks to carry guns and have arrest powers within Stillwater.

On the other hand, I told Nick to look for men, who'd only been able to land dead-end, low-paying jobs after leaving the military. I figured bitter men would follow orders—any orders—in exchange for outrageous pay.

"Hey, Nick," I begin. "How's Beaufort's finest doing in the fight against Lowcountry crime?"

"Good," Nick answers. "Hope you're calling to invite me to another party on your yacht."

"Soon," I promise. "Probably February. Meanwhile, I could use a little intel. One of our residents, Maury Campbell, broke his neck in a golf cart accident, and the crazed widow is insisting someone killed him. She won't accept it was an accident. Could you get me a copy of the autopsy report? I'm sure it'll prove the death was accidental."

"I heard about that accident," Nick says. "I'll email you a copy of the report. No problem."

"These ridiculous accusations are causing me headaches," I add. "Somehow, the widow's convinced Kylee Kane to start poking around, and Kylee may be leaning on some woman deputy to help her. I think the friend's name is Josie."

"They're both bitches," Nick interrupts. "Kylee is a menace, and Deputy Josie Muschel, is just like her. Another bitch who thinks her shit doesn't stink. Damn woman doesn't know her place. I was Josie's partner once. Never again. I'll be happy to help."

Good to know. I'd heard Nick and Kylee had a history. That she figured somehow in forcing him to withdraw his name as a candidate for sheriff. Apparently, she still sticks in his craw.

"Great. Just keep an eye on this Josie woman. See if she's doing favors for Kylee. Somehow, Kylee has gone from imagining that golf cart crash was no accident to hallucinating that I'm smuggling endangered parrots on my yacht. Ludicrous."

Nick laughs. "Sounds like another of her hare-brained conspiracy theories. I'll sniff around, see what Josie's up to."

"The only positive is Kylee's marrying Ted Welch next week," I add. "Hope she'll soon be too busy to be a pain in the ass. Maybe Josie will throw her a bachelorette party, and you can catch Kylee driving under the influence. Bet you'd like to throw her ass in the drunk tank."

"Now, that would be fun," Ibsen says. "I could only pray she'd resist arrest."

I laugh. "Thanks, man. And don't worry, my next party will include just the kind of ladies you prefer. Beautiful and willing. No uppity bitches allowed."

When I end the call, I notice Perry is staring at me and no longer focused on his computer screen. If he eavesdropped, he probably assumes my target is Kylee Kane. I don't care.

"What have you got for me?" I ask.

"I found two options," he says. "The first is propylene glycol. It's a colorless, odorless, and tasteless liquid I sometimes use as a solvent. It's added to lots of food products and considered quite safe in small doses. But a high dosage could make someone real sick. A plus is that it breaks down quickly in the body, a family physician would never suspect it.

"But I think Pyrantel is a better choice," he says. "It's used to deworm animals and people. Again, it's generally safe for humans, but overdoses can cause nausea, vomiting, and weakness. She'd start feeling symptoms in a couple of hours, and they'd abate within a day or two. But she'd still feel weak for several days.

"Best of all, anyone can purchase Pyrantel over the counter," he adds. "You could mix the powder into drinks or food. It supposedly has a slightly bitter taste, which you could mask in a spicy dish or a sweet drink."

"Do you have the powder on hand?" I ask. "If so, how much do I need to use?"

"Yeah, I have it," he says. "How much does your target weigh?"

I shrug. "I don't know. Best guess is 130 pounds."

"Okay, let me figure it."

I wait impatiently while he keys info into his computer.

"For an average adult, the dosage would be two and one-half to three teaspoons. Double that would be about two tablespoons. Don't go more than two tablespoons if you want it to look like ordinary food poisoning or flu. Maybe one and a half tablespoons?"

"Good. Give me four tablespoons. I might need extra if I need to doctor a dish served to two or more people."

Perry leaves to retrieve my overdose prescription. When he returns, he doesn't sit down. He's expecting me to leave.

"Sit, Perry. Remember, I told you I needed a couple of small favors. Have you already delivered that Hyacinth Macaw parrot to its buyer?"

"No. The bird didn't make it. You have to keep a closer watch on temperature and oxygen levels inside enclosures. That parrot was in bad shape when she arrived. I tried everything I could to keep her alive, but she died yesterday."

"So where is it?"

"What do you mean, where is it? The buyer isn't going to fork over fifteen thousand dollars for a dead bird."

"No, but a dead bird in the hand has real value to me."

"I buried it out back. I don't use my normal cremation disposal service for illegal animals. Too risky."

"Let's go out back. We're going to exhume the poor creature and give it a new purpose in death."

Chapter Thirty-Six

Kylee

Wednesday 6:00 p.m., December 18

Ted taps me on the shoulder, pulling me away from my computer screen. "Time to call it a day. Grant just called and wants to eat at one of his favorite restaurants tonight. I'm meeting him at Dockside on Ladys Island. I know you plan to spend the night on the River Rat—much to my sorrow—but, at least, join us for dinner.

"We haven't had a chance to talk since Archer Highsmith's unexpected visit. I want to hear if there are any new Stillwater developments or if you've made progress on the Hullis Island theft puzzle."

My stomach's rumbling. Why does it seem that pig-outs, like today's lunch, only give my tummy the idea it deserves equal treatment at the next meal.

I grin. "Sure, I never get tired of seafood."

* * *

Grant's waiting for us in Dockside's entryway. In season, there's often a wait for a table. On an off-season Wednesday, we're immediately ushered to a prime table beside a window. Across the water, I see sailboats and docks twinkling with Christmas lights.

A smiling waiter wearing a Santa hat arrives almost instantly to take drink orders. I opt for a beer. Feel like it's earned. Ted orders a scotch, and Grant goes with lemonade. When we're eating at Ted's house, Grant's allowed to drink beer. But he's not twenty-one, and he knows better than to order alcohol when we're out.

"You first," I motion at the Christmas lights across the bay. "Have tempers cooled down over the 'Tis the season to be Gay' display at Lighthouse Cove?"

"I wish." Ted groans. "More neighbors have gotten in on the act. Residents must have bought every string of white outdoor lights in stores from here to Savannah. They're using the lights to spell everything from END BIGOTRY to END TIMES. Some are serious, some poking fun at the uproar."

"So have the neighbors who are disturbed—and, yes, I did choose that word as a double entendre—uncovered some new covenant objection to use against Howie and Mike?" I ask.

Ted sighs. "Afraid so, they're now claiming 'Tis the season to be GAY' is, in fact, a political sign and political signs are only allowed in the six weeks prior to any election."

"Are any of the directors buying in?" Grant asks.

"A couple have, but they're in the minority. Since half of the HOA's directors are out of town visiting family, we met by Zoom. I told the board it would need a neighborhood vote to change the covenants and prohibit using lights—or anything else—to spell one or more words on owner lawns. Unless the word is the name of a candidate or political party, I told them I didn't see how it could be classified as a political sign."

"That's that, then?" I ask. "Game, set, and match to Howie and Mike."

"Not exactly. Two directors wanted to bring a covenant change up for a vote. The change would prohibit any neighbor from displaying a word or word art on their property. But I explained the covenant change process takes at least ninety days. We'd be halfway to Easter before the matter was resolved. My advice? Do nothing. It'll blow over. The two angry directors didn't like my advice. When things got heated, the board tabled the discussion. We meet again Friday."

Grant shakes his head. "If neighbors don't like the display, they don't have to look at it. It's not harming anyone. Seeing the word gay won't convince visiting grandkids to become homosexuals. What's the big deal?"

The waiter returns with our drinks, and I take a sip before voicing my thoughts.

"The people who freak out were quite happy when gays were firmly locked in closets. They knew homosexuals existed. They simply preferred to imagine all gay people were low-life perverts. Discovering that gays might actually be happy, productive professional couples like Howie and Mike violates their worldview. Especially since the evidence they're wrong lives next door."

I turn to Grant. "So, what about you, Stepson? Did you and Mimi have an exciting outing after you left the office?"

He laughs. "No, unless I'm spying for you, my life is pretty tame. We made a short visit to the Pinkney Wildlife Refuge. The best birding on the island is around the Ibis Pond, less than a mile from the parking lot. Mimi wanted to check what species of ducks might be wintering there."

Grant grins. "Okay, now I'll impress you with my newfound knowledge. We counted several green-and-yellow wood ducks, a few baffleheads, and blue-winged teals. Oh, and some dabbler ducks. They were fun to watch, wiggling their tails in the air when they dunk their heads for underwater snacks."

Ted raises an eyebrow. "I think you made up dabbler ducks. Is Donald Duck a dabbler?"

We all laugh. I'm glad I came. My mood is much improved.

When our food arrives, I'm amazed at the pile of food on Grant's plate. The boy has gone whole hog, or I should say whole ocean, with a Captain's Dish of oysters, stuffed clams, fried shrimp, scallops, and flounder.

"Think you can eat all that?" I ask.

"You bet—and I'll have room for dessert."

Though I considered a Bistro salad with seared salmon, I decided the chilly evening called for a hot dish. When the waitress places a heaping serving of my favorite seafood pasta in front of me, I'm not sorry. Ted's steak arrives, along with a baked potato and salad.

"Steak at Dockside?" I ask. "Isn't it against the rules to eat beef at a seafood restaurant?"

"Not if that's what you have a hankering for," he answers. "I've had steak here before. It's delicious."

We're all quiet for a few moments as we dig into our eats.

Between bites of blood-red sirloin, Ted asks, "And you, Ms. Sherlock, did you come up with any new theories about why Maury was taking pictures of Archer's yacht? Or were you working on cracking the Hullis Island theft ring this afternoon, while I was negotiating Lighthouse Cove peace terms?"

I hold my fork like it's a microphone. "I'll lead with my most shocking news. I scored a nine a.m. interview with Babsie Talbott tomorrow. I told her I thought she might have background that could help me look into a Hullis Island security concern. The woman didn't ask me to describe the security concern. She agreed to an interview without any clue what I wanted to discuss. Kinda bizarre?"

Ted sets down his fork. "Bizarre is right. Maybe Babsie's planning to turn the tables and grill you once you're in her web. Though I can't imagine you could share any gossip she hasn't already heard."

Grant chuckles. "Is this the woman who fled Diesel, the audio pit bull, thinking she was under attack?"

"One and the same," I answer.

"Uh, oh. If she knows you're friends with Martha, she might be seeking revenge. Watch out when you step on her porch."

"Any more ideas about why Maury was taking photos of Archer's yacht?" Ted asks, moving on to a new topic. "Archer tried hard to mask his anger when you invented that bird-watching excuse for aiming a trail cam at his yacht. He didn't succeed. His jaw and neck gave him away. All those muscles were straining to keep him from yelling."

I look at Ted. "I believe Archer's using his yacht to traffic endangered animals," I say.

"Yeah, Dad," Grant jumps in. "Did Kylee tell you we found a cigar box on the Campbell boat with another unusual feather, plus some weird scales and a patch of fur?"

"No." Ted's eyebrows ratchet up. "This is the first I've heard of that news flash."

"I called Alysha and told her about my smuggling theory," I report. "She didn't buy. At least where Archer was concerned. He's been really cozy with the Coast Guard. Hosting parties for Coasties on his yacht and donating to boat safety programs. To hear Alysha talk, Archer should be canonized.

"She did admit to Josie that Stillwater Cove would be an ideal base for smuggling. Direct access to the Atlantic, and no risk of pesky sheriff's patrol cars driving past when contraband is being loaded or unloaded."

Grant waves his hand. He wants to add something, but he can't talk until he finishes chewing.

"I just thought about that Post-It note we found in the cigar box," he says. "Maybe Maury's arrows between the word dollars and the word animals indicate both are cargo. The dollars move offshore; the animals move in."

Definitely possible.

"Great idea, Grant," I say. "I hadn't thought beyond the notion that selling animals was bringing in dollars."

"Not so fast," Ted says. "Last I knew, there were far cheaper and easier ways to smuggle cash out of the country. Using an expensive yacht seems overkill when you can pay mules to hide bills in luggage or stuff cash in car cavities. It's not like there are dogs at every customs checkpoint to sniff out cash."

Grant laughs. "You're out of the loop, Dad. The Citadel invited a dog trainer to give a talk during a class on border security. Customs now has dogs that alert on cash. They can smell the kind of ink used to print American and European currency. It has a distinct odor. At least to canines. That's forced organized crime to scramble and look for more creative ways to get cash out of the country."

"I'm out of the loop, too," I admit. "I've heard money is the root of all evil. But I didn't know it smelled, too."

Ted frowns. "This is all very interesting. It's also frightening. Kylee, I hope we can talk Velma into staying away from Stillwater until we learn more. And I don't want either of you going through those gates without me."

155

"I'm not planning any visits. Grant and I visited the Soup Can because Velma wanted us to check if anything needed to be secured since Maury never had a chance to finish repairs he'd started. I called Wally's Marine Repair, and Wally's going to install a new electrical panel on the Soup Can. He did a great job replacing mine several months ago."

Ted signals the waiter that he wants the check. My mention of the Soup Can reminds me to check in with Velma. Since dinner is over, I figure it isn't a violation of our cell phone rules to call Velma. I hope she has an update on when Vince will arrive. Nuts. My call goes to voicemail

Maybe Velma left me a message. I check my voicemails. Only one, and it's not from Velma. As I listen, an involuntary shiver races down my spine.

"Listen to this." I play the message on speaker so Ted and Grant can hear.

"Kylee, this is Archer Highsmith. I've given more thought to the notion an escaped pet parrot might be in danger inside our HOA. I'm going to launch a search for the bird tomorrow. And I'm inviting you, your ornithologist student, and any other folks you'd like to join in to meet Quentin and me at the Stillwater Clubhouse at noon. I'll treat for lunch, and we can plan the search, starting at the Campbell property where you found the blue feather.

"Please call before nine tomorrow to let me know how many people to expect so I can make the necessary arrangements."

Ted, Grant, and I are all open-mouthed.

"Are you both free for lunch tomorrow?" I ask. "I hear the Clubhouse restaurant is a five-star treat."

"You can bet I'll be there," Ted says. "And I hope Frank's free to be part of the team."

"I need to call Mimi," Grant says before he gives a worried glance at his dad. "With you guys along, you think it's safe for her to come, don't you?"

Ted nods. "I can't imagine they'll try to pull anything tomorrow. I just wish I knew why Archer decided to make this gesture. I'm sure he has something up his sleeve."

Chapter Thirty-Seven

Archer

Wednesday 9 p.m., December 18

I keep checking the time. I sent Kylee my gracious invitation as soon as I left Perry. I expected her to instantly accept. How could she turn down a free meal and the chance to snoop? Why hasn't she called?

My phone vibrates. Finally. Crap, it's Lisa, not Kylee.

I don't bother to say hello. "Did you get more background on Kylee?"

"Not exactly," Lisa replies. "Babsie has a face-to-face meeting with Kylee at nine o'clock tomorrow morning. She wants to know if there are any specific questions she should ask. That's why I'm calling. Babsie only agreed to meet the woman because I asked her to keep digging for information."

While I want to know more about Kylee and her close ties, she can't suspect she's being profiled.

"What excuse did Babsie use to set up a meeting?"

Lisa laughs. "Babsie didn't set it up. Kylee asked for the sit-down, and Babsie almost told her to take a hike. Kylee didn't give an exact reason for the meeting. She just said Babsie might have background to help her with a security investigation. Of course, Babsie knew Kylee has been interviewing theft victims. She gets that's why Kylee wants to talk with her. Every victim has dealt with her Care Committee. Babsie actively dislikes Kylee and her mother, and she had no desire to share details about the Care Committee.

Babsie only agreed because she knows you have us over a barrel."

"Babsie sounds smarter than I imagined," I reply. "Give me a few minutes, and I'll text a list of questions I want answered."

After I hang up, I hunt up a pencil and paper. I always find it easier to brainstorm if I'm not staring at a blank screen. I like to scribble down thoughts, stare at them, and scratch them out if I change my mind. With paper, the process feels like I'm making progress. On a computer, my thoughts seem to disappear into a black hole.

What do I want to know?

First up, it would be handy to know what Kylee likes to eat and drink.

Second, where is Kylee spending her nights? Is she alone on her sailboat?

Naturally, I'd love to know what she thinks that feather means and why she's so interested in my yacht. Too bad I can't see a way for Babsie to coax Kylee to spill on those topics. That's something I need to work on myself. If she accepts my invite to lunch and a bogus parrot search.

Chapter Thirty-Eight

Kylee

Thursday 7 a.m., December 19

I usually sleep like a rock on the River Rat. Not last night. I kept chewing on the two surprise developments—Babsie, who cheerfully agreed to a face-to-face, and Archer, who proposed I bring a bunch of outsiders through the Stillwater gates to conduct a fully sanctioned parrot search.

Mind you, I didn't come up with any answers, just found new bags under my eyes when I looked in the mirror. Time to get dressed. That presents a new puzzle. What to wear? I doubt I'll have time to change clothes between my Babsie meeting and my rendezvous with Ted, Grant, Frank, and Mom. We're all piling into Ted's Lexus for the ride to Stillwater. Mimi's dad is bringing her. He's a birder, who passed along his passion to his daughter.

While I tried to discourage Mom from joining the search party, my efforts were futile. Robin wanted to come, too. But she is the only one left to sit in Ted's office and answer phones.

I typically give little thought to my work wardrobe. In winter, I pick sweaters and trousers warm enough for the day and absent of any telltale grease spots. My trousers come in three colors: black, gray and tan. They all pair with any of my brightly-colored sweaters.

My work shoes are black leather with squat heels. If I'll be mucking about in marsh mud—a definite possibility today—I don boots.

Okay, wear the heels, bring boots to slip on before the search.

I slip on the gorgeous cashmere sweater set Mom gave me last Christmas. It's bright red and will look great with black slacks. I assume the outfit will pass any prissy dress standards the Stillwater Club enforces. These days, snooty clubs occasionally require men to wear jackets, but mostly, they've given up on dictating how women dress. Other than nixing bare midriffs or bare feet. Neither was a danger in December.

＊

I arrive on Babsie's doorstep at five minutes till nine. I hear someone's heels clicking. Practically sounds like a tap dance as the greeter scurries to answer the door.

Whoa. It's Babsie herself. No uniformed butler or maid. The only time Mom stopped by the Talbott house, she encountered both a maid and a butler. Mom couldn't believe both were dressed like they'd just been cast in a BBC mini-series on the Royals.

Babsie's lips twitch up at the corners, a not-quite smile as she welcomes me into the sprawling home's palatial front hall, lit by a crystal chandelier. An ocean of marble stretches in every direction. No wonder I could hear Babsie's high heels clicking. And, yes, at nine in the morning, she's wearing high heels and diamond earrings. The heels bring the scrawny, bird-like woman's head almost even with my shoulder.

The hostess takes my long, purple puffer coat and hangs it in a closet among several furry companions. Babsie's coats all feature fur. Some have fur collars; others have fur linings and cuffs. A mink coat, stored in a see-through protector, wins top-dollar honors, though it probably doesn't get much wear, given PETA outrage.

Wonder how many hairy rodents sacrificed their lives for Babsie's collection.

"Coffee is ready," she says. "I thought we'd talk in the solarium. On a beautiful day like today, the sunshine really makes the room feel warm and comfortable."

I try to ignore what her whiny, high-pitched voice is doing to my nerve endings. The woman is being quite friendly, overlooking our past frosty encounters. So buck it up. Think of Babsie's voice as a physical disability, one she can't help. Be compassionate.

"Coffee and sunshine sound great."

I follow Babsie to the back of her home. En route, I try to peek into adjacent rooms, but most have closed doors.

"It is nice to see sunshine today," I say to make conversation. "It's forecast to reach near sixty this afternoon, a nice change. We need to enjoy it while we can; a cold front is coming."

The solarium has a gorgeous ocean view, showcasing a section of the Hullis Island beach that contains impressive dunes. Dormant sea grass sways in the gentle breeze and sunlight makes the blue water look as if it's been dusted with sequins.

"I'd find it very hard to resist spending all day in this room," I tell my hostess. She waves me to a seat of honor—a cushioned loveseat with the best view.

While the outdoor scenery is impressive, the solarium's many plants scream neglect. Yellow leaves, drooping stems. Good grief, the ailing plant nearest me hosts a giant cobweb. I look up and catch sight of an ambitious spider that's crocheted its way clear to the ceiling.

Babsie must not spend much time in this room, or she needs glasses. Guess she hasn't checked up to see if her maid is dusting and watering plants.

When my hostess said coffee was ready, I didn't expect her to pour from an elaborate silver service. It looks strangely out of place. Like the solarium, the silver service appears neglected. Swatches of tarnish smudge the small cream pitcher. A hurried polish job.

Babsie hovers above the tray, waiting to pour coffee in my cup. "Should I leave room for cream or sugar?" she asks.

"No, thanks. I drink it black," I say.

"Me, too." She giggles and carries her delicate porcelain cup to the chair across from me.

"Have you eaten at the Club lately?" she asks before I have a chance to explain why I've come.

"No," I answer. "Mom and Frank dine there a couple of times a month, but when we come to Hullis Island for dinner, it's usually because Mom's invited us for a home-cooked meal."

"I asked about the Club because they've added some spicy new entrees, and I just love them. Do you like spicy food?"

"Mildly spicy," I answer. "I'm not into habaneros or food so hot tears roll down my cheeks. One of my favorite dishes is Kung Pao chicken."

Babsie frowns. "Is that Chinese? I never eat Chinese. But I do like spicy dishes, especially if I have a good chardonnay to come to the rescue. Are you a wine connoisseur?"

Okay, Babsie wants to pretend this is a social call. I'll play nice. Let her get comfortable.

I laugh. "No. I'm actually allergic to wines. But I'm no teetotaler, I enjoy bourbon, rum and beer."

"Oh, does that mean you won't be serving champagne at your wedding reception? The Hullis Island rumor mill is all abuzz about your wedding to the handsome Ted Welch. Are your girlfriends throwing you a bachelorette party? Will you have a rehearsal dinner before your Christmas Eve service? Do you have some exciting honeymoon plans?"

Geez, Babsie's packed so many questions in there, I'm not sure which one to answer first.

"Yes, despite my *advanced* age, my friends plan a ladies-only send-off Friday night, and we'll have an informal rehearsal dinner in the Hullis picnic shelter Monday. The wedding is set for four o'clock, Tuesday, Christmas Eve, and champagne will be served. I just don't plan to drink any. Ted and I are leaving the day after Christmas for the Caymans."

"Oh, how wonderful," Babsie gushes. "Can't imagine how you have time to help with any Hullis Island investigation with all your exciting wedding plans."

Thank God. We've gone hither and yon, but we're back to my reason for being here.

I put down the delicate cup. "Yes, the investigation. I think you may be able to help me."

"Really?" Babsie's eyes widen in surprise. It's as if I didn't tell her an investigation prompted this visit. "I can't imagine how I can help. What is it you're investigating?".

Babsie frowns as I tell her about the eighteen unsolved Hullis Island thefts and explain that all the victims I've spoken with have one thing in common— they were visited by members of her Care Committee.

"I hope you're not implying one of my committee members might be a thief?" Babsie's voice has risen to a pitch that could compete with an operatic soprano.

I prepared for Babsie's objection. While I do think the thief—or his or her accomplice—might be a committee member, I figured suggesting that possibility would prove counter-productive.

"No, please let me explain," I add quickly. "It's conceivable that the thief befriended one or more of your regular volunteers. Then, he used those friendships to coax the volunteers to reveal details he could use to select targets. For example, the people delivering meals or taking patients to doctor appointments could innocently pass along information that would tell a thief time periods when no one would be home."

"Oh, my heavens," Babsie exclaims. "Does this mean the thief could live on Hullis Island?"

"Perhaps," I say. "The thefts have taken place over a two-year period. I'd really like to talk with volunteers who've been with your committee that entire time. Maybe they can recall if someone ever seemed overly curious about the individuals they were helping."

Babsie nods her head. "All right," she says. "I can immediately think of one woman you should interview. Suzie Bucknell. She lives alone and never seems to travel. She's always ready and willing to bring meals or take neighbors to doctor's appointments. I'll write down her phone number and address. Just give me a minute. I'll be right back."

This almost seems too easy. I stand up and walk to the solarium's wall of windows. I notice a snow fence set to help prevent beach erosion. It brings to mind the old saying, "Fences make good neighbors."

Maybe the reverse is true, too. Do neighbors make good fences?

Babsie quickly returns with phone numbers.

"I've been concerned about Suzie for a long time." She drops her voice to a conspiratorial whisper. "The whole island knows Suzie's a hoarder, and I wonder if she can even help herself. Maybe. If she sees something that strikes her fancy, she just takes it."

Babsie reverts to hostess mode and fiddles with the silver service. "Would you like another cup of coffee before you leave?"

"No, thanks. I've taken enough of your time. Plus, I have a noon appointment at Stillwater Cove and need to return calls before then. But thank you for your hospitality."

Then, as planned, I casually ask a final question, hoping it will appear to be an afterthought.

"By the way, as committee chair, you've had contact with every theft victim. Has anyone chatted you up and seemed overly interested in your neighbors with medical issues?"

Babsie's pleasant veneer vanishes. I wouldn't be surprised to see lightning bolts spring from her narrowed eyes to shoot me down.

Up to now, she's done an admirable job hiding how she really feels about moi.

A vein in Babsie's skinny throat performs jumping jacks. "My friends would have no interest in hearing gory details about some neighbor's collapsed uterus or colon dissection. And I'm not stupid," she snarls. "When someone tries to get cagey, I see through it. Like now. I don't need an *investigator* to explain how scammers can trick gossips into saying too much."

The way Babsie spits out 'investigator' my profession is a step far below prostitute. Glad I got Suzie's contact info before my clumsy attempt to ask Babsie if she might be the committee's loose lips.

Time to extract my humble coat from Babsie's fur chest and leave before I get skinned.

Chapter Thirty-Nine

Archer

Thursday 9:30 a.m., December 19

I check my watch. Lisa's calling earlier than expected.

"So, what did Babsie find out from her chat with the ever-prying Ms. Kane?" I ask

Lisa laughs. "When she phoned, Babsie was steaming. Kylee had the nerve to imply that she, Babsie Talbott, would be stupid enough to be tricked into gossiping with a low-life thief."

I smile. "Family ties can be amusing, but let's save sharing Babsie's histrionics for another time. Did she learn anything useful?"

"Not sure. You wanted to know what Kylee likes to eat and drink. She is allergic to wine. Doesn't touch it. Not even champagne. She likes moderately spicy food but nothing too hot, like with habaneros. One of her favorites is that Chinese dish with chicken and peanuts. Think it's called Kung Pao chicken.

"Kylee's wedding is indeed scheduled for late afternoon Christmas Eve. A bachelorette party is set for Friday, and there's a rehearsal dinner Monday at the Hullis Island picnic shelter. Also, the bride and groom will fly to the Caymans, the day after Christmas for their honeymoon."

"That's it?"

"Yeah, that's all she wrote," Lisa replies. "And I seriously doubt Babsie will do any more digging unless I promise it will bury Kylee. Babsie's scared. She thinks she's a suspect."

"And I'm sure she is," I reply. "Tell Babsie it's over. You will not help her fence any more merchandise. How many decades have you known Babsie? Has she ever changed? She'd squeal and finger you if she thought it would win an advantage. We don't need any added reasons for Stillwater Cove directors to be investigated."

Lisa's intake of breath is audible. "Babsie wouldn't give me up."

"Right," I scoff. "If I were you, I'd help Babsie direct Kylee's suspicions in a different direction. You've got more brains than Babsie. Figure it out. Unlike Babsie, I know you're too smart to be a snitch. You'd never suggest Quentin and I are anything except stand-up citizens. We all know Mick doesn't handle it well if people disappoint him."

I hang up. Time to arrange a departure and a resurrection. I call the Club and ask to speak to the chef, Jean-Paul.

"As I explained earlier, Quentin and I are entertaining seven guests for lunch today. I'm sorry this request is coming so late, but I'm hoping you can prepare your popular seafood special that has a spicy kick. And I'd also like you to add Kung Pao chicken to the menu. I understand it's a favorite dish of our most important guest."

I listen to Jean-Paul whine. I cut him off when he says Kung Pao chicken is a no-go because he doesn't have any peanuts.

"For god's sake, send one of your helpers over to the golf club. They have bags of peanuts for sale. Buy as many as you need.

"Oh, and just for today, I've added a waitperson to your serving staff. He'll be the only person waiting on our table. His name is Lanny, and he should arrive soon. Don't worry. Lanny knows what he's doing. He'll meet the Club's high standards."

With luncheon matters straightened away, it's time for that resurrection. I go to my refrigerator and extract the large plastic container holding the parrot's corpse. The parrot's a monster—almost three feet from beak to tail-feathers. Glad that Perry keeps plastic containers for folks who want to take their treasured pets home for backyard burials.

The parrot doesn't look as colorful as it did alive. When we first dug it up, I wasn't sure we could use it. But Perry performed some magic and cleaned it up. He tweezed out visible bugs and used a hair dryer to blow dirt from the feathers. He even applied a little oil to return some gloss to the plumage.

Before I head downstairs, I grab a coat and a pair of gloves. I'm not about to handle the mangy thing with my bare hands. The doc may have missed a maggot.

As arranged, Quentin's waiting for me in his four-seater golf cart.

"Where to?" he asks.

"The Paynter house to the right of the Campbells," I answer. "I looked up information about this parrot. It tends to nest in the hollows of Mondavi or palm trees. We have neither, but there are lots of palmetto trees on the Paynter lot. And best of all, the palmettos are near the frontage road, far out of the reach of any doorbell cameras."

"How will you convince your searchers to focus on the Paynter lot?"

"Kylee claims she found the feather on the Campbell property. So, that's where the search should start, right? They're bringing a couple of birders along—the college kid and her dad. Imagine they know more about this parrot's habitat than I do. If they don't suggest heading to the palmettos, I will."

Chapter Forty

Kylee

Thursday 10 a.m., December 19

I grab a mug of coffee and join Mom and Frank. Since they didn't have to go into the office this morning, they haven't moved from the breakfast table. Frank's working a crossword puzzle, and Mom's making a grocery list.

Ted and Grant are due in an hour to pick all three of us up for our Stillwater Cove lunch and search outing.

Frank asks Mom for help with a crossword clue, which launches a back-and-forth that leaves them both laughing. It's obvious they're in love.

I'm delighted. I think Dad, who passed away ten years ago, would be, too. Like many seniors who fall in love, Frank and Mom see no reason to get hitched. Mom's almost eighty. She didn't worry much about gossip when she was younger and doesn't give a fig about it now. There are practical reasons to stay single, too. Changes in marital status often create pension and trust complications.

I kind of wish I could follow Mom's example. Seems silly to get married for the first time at fifty-one. It's not like we plan to start a family. However, making our relationship official should lessen my awkward feelings about sleeping with Ted with his twenty-year-old son down the hall. Also, Ted's HOA clients tend to be older conservatives.

I love Ted. Unconditionally. A marriage license won't change my feelings or commitment a bit, but it will make Mom and Ted's father happy. The one thing it won't change is my name. If someone yelled "Kylee Welch," I'd look to see who else shared my first name.

"What are you looking all googly-eyed about?" Mom asks. "Off on your honeymoon already? Come on back. Time to dish about your visit with the high-pitched, high-horse. Was Babsie a real witch?"

"All in all, my visit with Mrs. Talbott was very interesting," I answer. "She was quite the gracious hostess. Then, just before I left, I asked a question that implied Babsie—just like her lowly Care Committee members—might have blabbed and provided a thief with the info needed to target his victims.

"If Babsie's bony arms had enough muscle, she'd have tossed me out the door. She was seriously insulted."

Mom laughs. "Sounds like Babsie. Everything's always about her and her image."

"I agree. Babsie didn't seem to feel any outrage about folks being victimized when they were already suffering. But boy, did she get her back up when her behavior came into question.

"Before the blow-up, Babsie gave me the phone number for a Care Committee member, who volunteered throughout the two-year period. Babsie believes she called on all the theft victims. She also mentioned—sort of off-the-record—that this woman might be unable to control her impulses."

I pull out the sheet with the names. "Do you two know Suzie Bucknell?"

Mom and Frank break out laughing. It takes Mom a couple minutes to control her mirth long enough to speak.

"That's rich," Mom says. "Of course, Babsie threw Suzie under the bus. She's nominating her to either be an unwitting dupe or the actual Hullis thief. Bet she hopes it provides the perfect excuse to cut Suzie from the committee. She's tried everything else."

"What in heaven's name are you talking about?" I ask.

"Poor Frank had to listen to all my tales about Babsie's efforts to remove Suzie from her committee. Let's see, how do I put this kindly? Suzie isn't

169

the most attractive person. She's obese. Her housedresses look more like tents—used, bedraggled tents. Something happened after Suzie's husband died. She refused to toss any of his former possessions. Then she started picking up the discarded furniture and appliances neighbors put out at the curb for trash pick-up. Suzie's house has to be bulging at the seams. Not sure what all she's hoarding.

"Babsie asked the board for the authority to name committee members and reject other volunteers. We all knew Babsie wanted to dump Suzie because her appearance detracted from the committee's image. The Board said no, and it was unanimous. Anyone who wants to serve on a committee is welcome. We weren't going to change that policy. Whatever Suzie's flaws may be, she has a heart of gold and a real Midas touch as a baker."

I'm chewing on Suzie's penchant for taking home items she sees in the gutter. Maybe Babsie isn't totally off base. What if a gold coin or a necklace caught Suzie's eye?

"Bear with me a minute; Suzie may be a sweetheart, but given her behavioral change, could she be a kleptomaniac? Maybe we're not looking for a thief, who sells valuables to make money. Maybe the jewelry and coins are stashed in Suzie's house where she can admire them."

"No way," Frank says. "Doesn't compute. The thief only steals a single item—the most valuable option—from each household. A kleptomaniac would be driven to take whatever caught her eye. That wouldn't always be the most expensive option, and she wouldn't stop at one bauble."

I sigh. "Okay, okay. Just a passing thought. I agree with your logic. Mom, can you suggest any other Care Committee members I should interview?"

"Absolutely," Mom answers. "You'll get a completely different perspective from Anna Whitner. Anna had the nerve to suggest Babsie should step down as chair of the Care Committee and let someone else take a turn. Anna was fed up with Babsie's dictatorial style. While she didn't come right out and call Babsie an autocratic witch, her opinion was clear."

"Okay, got it. I'll plan to visit both women. Between the two of them, they probably know all their fellow committee members. They can also give me a better idea of how the committee works. In fact, if you'll excuse me, I'll try

170

to arrange interviews for late this afternoon. I also need to check in with Velma. I missed her last night. I should update her on Archer's lunch and parrot search invitations."

"Do you suppose Velma will join in?" Frank asks.

Mom shakes her head. "Not a chance. She can't bear to be around any of the directors—Archer, Quentin, or Lisa. She feels the Stillwater Cove board treated her husband badly in life as well as in death. Velma suspects they either conducted or authorized the search of Maury's office."

I excuse myself and move to the guest room and its cubbyhole desk. I succeed in making tentative appointments with both Care Committee members. I'm meeting Anna Whitner at her house at five o'clock and Suzie Becknell, the alleged hoarder, at the golf course cafe at six p.m. I was disappointed Suzie suggested meeting at a public spot, but there was no way to diplomatically say I wanted to visit her house to see if the hoarding rumors were true. Now, I won't know if Suzie's house is just cluttered or has become a health and safety hazard.

My final call is to Velma. I owe her a lot of explanations. I hope she won't be mad that I didn't ask permission to place those trail cams.

Velma doesn't interrupt as I race through my news headlines.

"I'm glad you added that trail cam in the backyard," Velma says. "You or Grant will have to show me how to use it. You mentioned two trail cams, where did you put the second one?"

Next, I detail our unexpected discoveries aboard the Soup Can. The packet of photos Maury took of Archer's yacht and the cigar box we found, holding a second feather, unusual scales, and fur.

"I thought keeping watch on Archer's yacht with a trail cam might provide some answers, but all it did was alert the HOA president that I'm poking about. He is furious."

Finally, I confess my lie about how I found the first feather. That's what led to Archer's surprising invitation to join him for lunch and a parrot search, with said search starting on Velma's property.

"Do you want to come to lunch with us? Or join the search?"

"No, thank you," Velma replies. "I don't trust myself to be within six feet of any of those vipers. I doubt I could restrain myself. For starters, I'd spit in their faces. Once you're finished, just come to the house and give me an update. Bring everyone—except Archer and Quentin."

* * *

I hear footsteps pounding up the porch steps to the front door. I figure it's Grant's energetic approach.

"Looks like our ride to Stillwater has arrived," I call to Mom and Frank as I open the door. Ted immediately sweeps an arm around me for a hug and a smooch.

"Missed you last night," he whispers.

"Absence makes the heart grow fonder," I reply.

"How could mine grow any fonder?" Ted answers. "Can't wait to whisk you away to the Caymans so I have you all to myself."

"I'm more than ready for that, too," I agree. "Meanwhile, we have a date to go parrot hunting."

"And don't forget eating," Grant adds. "I sure hope the Stillwater Club restaurant lives up to its five-star reputation."

Chapter Forty-One

Kylee

Thursday Noon, December 19

As we approach the Stillwater gates, Ted turns his head slightly to address his passengers. "Prepare to exit and submit to a pat-down," he teases. "Security knows I'm bringing in a carload of terrorists."

As usual, a security officer is outside waiting for us.

"Mr. Welch," the guard says. "You and your party can proceed directly to the Clubhouse. Do you need directions?"

"Uh, no," Ted answers.

Grant, who's sitting between Mom and me in the backseat of Ted's Lexus, covers his mouth to muffle his laughter.

"The other two members of your party arrived a few minutes ago," the guard adds. "They should be waiting for you at the Clubhouse."

"Thanks," Ted says.

When the gates finally grind open, and we're through the checkpoint, we all burst out laughing.

"What, not even a dashboard tracker to monitor us?" I comment. "Guess it's who you know. If you're Archer Highsmith's guest and will be dining at the Clubhouse, you're part of the in-crowd."

* * *

I'd seen the Stillwater Clubhouse from a distance but not up close. Impressive.

Beautiful stonework, gleaming natural wood trim, and the entire driveway is paved in bluestone. Ted pulls into the entry circle to drop Frank, Grant, Mom, and me at the front door before he parks. A uniformed doorman rushes to open the car door for Mom.

"If you'll give me your keys, I'll be happy to park your car for you," the doorman tells Ted.

I pop out the opposite side of the Lexus before the doorman can finish helping Mom. It gives me the heebie-jeebies when men scurry around "to help the little lady." Yes, I know. It's chivalrous. But I don't like playing the frail, helpless woman who can't open her own door.

"Thanks," Ted says and hands the doorman his keys.

Inside, I spot Mimi and her dad, Carl Jones, seated on one of the deep couches in a conversation pit. A massive river-rock fireplace anchors the room. Mimi and Carl stand as we enter through the glass doors.

While we're walking toward our two ornithology experts, Archer and Quentin round a corner carrying drinks.

"Oh, there you are," Archer says. "We were just fetching drinks for Carl and his charming daughter, Mimi, while we waited. Would you like to relax with some cocktails, or should we go directly to the dining room?"

Grant grins. "If I have a vote, the dining room. I'm starving."

"Hey, son, you're getting a little ahead of yourself," Ted says. "I believe we need to make introductions first."

Archer had met everyone except Mom and Mimi's father. However, Quentin had only met Ted, Mom, and me. Both Archer and Quentin seem determined to ooze charm. They greet each person as a best-friend candidate.

Archer leads us to the dining room, where a large round table's been reserved for the group. The table offers views of the golf course and the ocean in the distance. The clubhouse occupies the crest of a man-made hill. The Lowcountry is named that for a reason. Hills are scarcer than hen's teeth.

Maury said they hauled in truckload after truckload of fill to build a hill to an elevation that afforded spectacular views. He always worried that their aggressive construction schedule didn't allow for proper compacting of the fake hump's fill before work on the clubhouse began.

"I'm sorry Velma won't be joining us," Archer says. "How is she doing?"

"Velma is expecting her son, Vince, to arrive later today," I answer. "There have been a variety of travel delays, but he should arrive tonight. Good news on that front. We will stop by and visit Velma after we finish our search for the mystery parrot."

Quentin uses the parrot mention to segue into a series of questions for Carl and Mimi. He encourages them to share everything they know about Hyacinth Macaw parrots. He also fakes curiosity about Carl's involvement with organizations that track and count migratory birds.

As I listen, I think how one wrong conversational turn made Babsie's hospitality vanish. Would the Stillwater directors act the same way? If I ask a question that puts them on the spot, will it shatter their friendly veneer?

A waiter arrives to take our drink orders and tell us about the day's lunch specials. He describes a spicy seafood medley that's served over rice. Then he mentions Kung Pao chicken, and the hairs on the back of my neck prickle. Not a menu selection you'd expect at an upscale restaurant that specializes in seafood and steak. And a weird coincidence since I told Babsie Kung Pao was one of my favorites only three hours ago.

Babsie and Lisa are friends. Is she chummy with Archer and Quentin, too?

No one orders alcoholic beverages, not even our hosts. When the waiter returns with our drinks, he asks if we're ready to order. He wants me to start.

"There are so many excellent choices. I'm having a hard time deciding," I say. "How about if I go last?"

Archer frowns as he studies his menu.

Is there nothing he likes, or did my ordering delay annoy him?

I'm surprised when Archer orders the Kung Pao chicken. Maybe the chef put it on the menu because it's a favorite of his boss, the HOA president.

Frank opts for the Chinese dish, too. As usual, Mimi, our vegetarian, inquires about a meatless entrée and winds up with eggplant parmigiana. Everyone else at the table orders the spicy seafood special.

When it's my turn, I ask for a steak, grilled medium-rare, and a side salad with oil and vinegar dressing

"That's a surprise," Ted says. "I was sure you'd order Kung Pao chicken."

I glance toward Ted. "Your steak the other night looked so delicious I decided I'd treat myself to one. The Stillwater Club is known for its seafood and corn-fed beef. As an Iowa native, I'm fond of just about everything corn-fed."

As the luncheon conversation turns to Lowcountry topics, including the weather, Archer appears more and more glum.

"I had hoped to leave for Andros yesterday and spend the holidays at my place in the Bahamas," he says. "Winter storms have delayed my departure."

"Tell us about your place in Andros," Ted says. "I know Andros is the largest island in the Bahamas chain, but that's all I know. How did you pick it as your island retreat?"

"I love to dive, and Andros borders some of the best scuba diving in the world," he answers. "Andros isn't as developed as other islands in the Bahamas. That's partly because it's so hard to get from one part of the island to another. In some ways, it's like the Lowcountry, creeks and estuaries make straight-line travel nearly impossible. Unlike the Lowcountry, Andros has few connecting roads or bridges to span the creeks, so travel's mainly on the water."

"Andros," I say. "The name rings a bell. Oh, right, the U.S. Coast Guard base there has a reputation for running down drug smugglers."

"You're correct," Archer replies. "My place is on North Andros, and the Coast Guard is based out of AUTEC, the U.S Navy facility where they check out new submarine captains among other things. I'm a big fan of the Navy and Coast Guard. Try to show my appreciation any way I can. I don't want to worry about my yacht being boarded by pirates when I leave port here or in the Bahamas."

"Did you know Kylee was a Captain in the Coast Guard?" Grant asks.

CHAPTER FORTY-ONE

"No, I didn't know that," Archer says. "Thank you for your service, Kylee."

Archer is lying big time. When he was berating me for pointing a trail cam at his yacht, he said I should know better, given my background. Maybe he didn't know my rank back then, but I'll bet he now knows everything from my bra size to my exercise routines.

"I loved serving in the Coast Guard," I say. "And I try to keep up with all of the challenges. Trying to interdict smugglers is a big one these days. Ships are used to smuggle a lot more than drugs. Criminal networks increasingly rely on boats to launder money and traffic endangered species, which has become a multi-billion-dollar global enterprise."

As I hoped, my conversational gambit prompts Mimi and Carl to expound on the trafficking of birds and other endangered species.

Once our entrees are served, the talk mainly focuses on food, with several sincere compliments to the chef. All of us except Archer are members of the clean-plate club. Guess I should be glad I ordered beef. I eat steak rarely, but this one is definitely worthy of a red-meat splurge.

Our waiter returns to clear dishes and offer desserts or coffee. Most everyone promptly declines, saying they're too full. I wonder if Grant can resist the temptation of the chocolate caramel mousse. He looks wistful after he glances at his dad and says, "No, thanks."

Guess Grant doesn't want to be the one to delay Operation Parrot Rescue.

Chapter Forty-Two

Archer

Thursday 2 p.m., December 19

I can't believe the bitch ordered steak!

After all the trouble I went to. I ordered Jean-Paul to cobble up Chinese slop, even though it meant buying up peanut packs from the golf shop. I recruited Lanny, one of our security guards, who briefly worked as a waiter after his military hitch, to be our waitperson. His one job? Making certain the right spicy order was plated in front of Kylee Kane.

Did Kylee have a premonition, or was she just in the mood for steak?

Guess I'll never know. If she'd behaved as predicted, Ted would be holding her head in a few hours while she puked her guts out. It wouldn't look like food poisoning since Frank and I would have eaten the same meal. It would be blamed on some bug she picked up, maybe chatting up Babsie.

I hope no one noticed the brief non-verbal communication between Lanny and me. After Kylee ordered, he discreetly pantomimed adding a teaspoon of sugar to a cup and looked at me with eyebrows raised. I gave my head an almost imperceptible shake to say no. The confounded woman hadn't ordered a thing that could mask the bitterness of my special ingredient.

I signal Lanny to bring me the bill and sign for it, adding a nice tip for him. Though he didn't perform any extra service, he made a good show of being a first-class server.

"Ready to try to sight and possibly capture a rare bird?" I ask. "Since Kylee found the parrot feather on Campbell property, our search should start there. Let's meet at the access road next to the Campbell driveway and divide into teams."

I look directly at Kylee. "Can you give us a more precise idea of where you found the feather?"

"Of course," she fibs. "It was near the tea olives in the front yard."

I turn to Carl and Mimi. "Do you two have any suggestions about where a homeless parrot might look for shelter?"

"Most nest in tree hollows," Mimi says. "So, maybe we should look for trees?"

"Great suggestion," I say. "Thank you, Mimi."

Glad someone is singing the tunes I pre-selected.

"Why don't we split into three groups and move from the access road to the ocean on the Campbell and Paynter lots. The Paynters are visiting family in Boston, but they gave permission. I assume one of you asked Velma's permission."

"Yes," Mom answers. "Velma won't be alarmed when she gets an alert on her video doorbell. The camera mysteriously stopped working, but the new one is performing just fine."

Like daughter, like mother. Sarcastic. Trying to get a rise out of me? I'm not biting.

"Wait," Mimi says. "I know Dad, Grant, Kylee, and I have cell phone apps that recognize bird calls. Let's make sure one of us is in each group,"

"Good idea." Carl beams at his daughter. "And I brought along a few whistles so we can alert others if we find something."

What a great idea. The group starting on the Paynter property will blow a whistle in no time. Then, I'll offer to bury the damn bird, and we'll be done with this charade. Kylee will be all out of excuses to keep tabs on my yacht or snoop around the maintenance barn.

Chapter Forty-Three

Kylee

Thursday 2 p.m., December 19

We divide into three-person groups to search the two properties where owners have green-lighted our trespass. Archer explains that the owner of the Ryebread property, aka Dickhead, refused to grant permission for a search party on his land.

I regret claiming I found the mystery feather on Campbell property. My alleged find gives Archer a reason to confine our parrot search to the area near the Campbells.

Since the lots are narrow, the upcoming walk-about with our bird-chirp apps should finish in no time. I'm confident Maury pocketed that blue feather while he was in the maintenance barn, or it stuck to his clothes when he was thrown from the golf cart. Either way, the parrot that lost the feather is unlikely to be anywhere near the Campbells.

Maybe, when we strike out here, I'll suggest we target the heavily wooded Stillwater Cove common area. I've rehearsed two arguments. One, moving the search there won't require any homeowner permissions, and two, the acreage's natural vegetation should make the area appealing to a lost parrot.

Archer, who has anointed himself search commander, clears his throat. Guess he's ready to hand out our assignments.

"Grant, Quentin, and Frank. You search the left side of the Campbell property, the portion that borders the Ryebread's. Quentin knows where the property line is and will make sure no one strays onto Ryebread land.

"Myrt, Carl, and Kylee. You'll straddle the two properties, traveling up the right side of the Campbell property and the left-hand swath of Paynter land. That includes those wild olives where you say you found the feather, Kylee. And, finally, Ted, Mimi, and I will search the right-hand side of the Paynter lot."

Archer's face lights up. He's enjoying himself. Does calling the shots for the outdoor activity rekindle some Boy Scout memory, or is he smiling because he knows this is an exercise in futility and we won't find a dang thing?

"Is everyone ready? Make sure your whistles are handy, and your birdsong apps are turned on." He says before waving the troops on. "Okay, let's go."

As he studies his phone, Carl signals the need for silence with a finger to his lips. "Keep as quiet as possible," he whispers. "The app has already identified three winter visitors by their songs—Baltimore Orioles, Cedar Waxwings, and Yellow-Bellied Sapsuckers."

Despite Carl's admonishment to stay quiet, I chuckle. "I thought sure the bird's name was made-up, given all those childhood taunts—'What are you, a yellow-bellied sapsucker?'"

I quickly make a zipping motion over my lips, promising I'll maintain silence from this point forward.

A blast on a whistle pierces the quiet. It's followed by three more sharp whistle toots.

You're kidding me. Mimi's group actually found something?

We hustle toward the right side of the Paynter property, where Ted, Archer, and Mimi huddle within a small stand of palmetto trees.

When we reach the group, Carl kneels beside his daughter and slips an arm around her shaking shoulders. Her eyes brim with tears. "I wanted to find the macaw, but not like this," she says.

By now, the searchers who were furthest away have joined the mournful circle around the dead bird. The parrot is huge. From my Google queries, I knew these birds were sometimes called the "Great Danes" of the parrot world. They can measure more than three feet from the top of the head to the end of the tail. But, somehow, the measurement hadn't given me a clear visual reference. This creature must be really magnificent in flight.

Carl gently extends one of the parrot's wings; then he repositions the corpse to extend the opposite wing. The wing span looks like it's five feet. Wow.

"I wonder what killed it," Carl says. "Neither of its wings are broken."

"Guess we'll never know," Archer says. "I'm sorry your search ended this way. I'll make sure the parrot is properly disposed of so it won't be torn apart by vultures or other carrion eaters. Our veterinarian comes to Stillwater twice a month. He's due tomorrow. He'll handle the disposal."

Carl carefully scoops up the parrot and cradles it like a baby. "That's kind of you to offer," Carl says. "But we need to take this parrot to the Feathered Friends Clinic in Charleston. If it is a lost pet, it may be microchipped. This one doesn't have an ID band around one of its legs, but the owner might have opted to microchip it. These days, the microchips are really tiny, and only a local anesthetic is needed. It's over in seconds. No traumatizing the bird."

Ted frowns. "Isn't it illegal to import Hyacinth Macaws?" he asks. "Why would an owner want to microchip a pet and have an illegally trafficked bird traced back to him?"

Carl nods. "He wouldn't. But these parrots are also bred in captivity, and it's legal to buy and own these domestically-bred parrots as pets."

Mom shakes her head. "Then why on earth would anyone buy an illegal parrot?"

Mimi moves her thumb and index finger together in a "money-dummy" pantomime. "I read up on this. The hyacinth macaws are difficult to breed. Most chicks don't make it to adulthood. A domestic macaw from a legitimate breeder might cost between fifteen- and twenty-five thousand dollars. Some breeders have multiple-year waiting lists.

"If you don't want to wait and don't mind dealing with traffickers, the cost might drop to ten thousand dollars."

I overhear Frank's stage whisper to Mom, "Guess I shouldn't complain that chicken breasts now cost more than three dollars a pound."

Mom punches Frank's arm, but she can't hide her grin.

Though Mom loves to watch wild birds and listen to their songs, she quit putting out bird feeders years before she left Keokuk. Mom discovered her adopted black cats, forerunners of Mississippi and Keokuk, treated bird feeders like hunters treat salt licks. They hid nearby to wait for opportunities to pounce.

I turn to Archer and Quentin. "I am grateful to the board for allowing us to search for the parrot and for the excellent lunch. Thank you."

"You're welcome." Quentin flashes a big smile.

Archer mouths the same words but looks as if he has indigestion. Maybe it was providence that whispered I shouldn't order the Kung Pao chicken.

Archer and Quentin climb in Archer's gleaming red Corvette. As it leaves, I see its vanity license plate "AIMHIGH." The departure leaves the rest of the search party intact at the initial rendezvous site.

Carl carefully wraps the bird in a large sheet of plastic and places it in his trunk. When he closes the trunk, he turns and looks down the road, watching our hosts travel out of sight.

"I wanted to make sure they had no plans to return," Carl explains. "I've come across a lot of dead birds. None like this one. When I touched its feathers, they felt slick, kind of waxy. I've visited museums when taxidermists were preparing specimens for natural history exhibits. This bird's feathers had the same sort of unnatural sheen. I'll be very interested in what the Feathered Friends Clinic can tell us about this parrot's life and death."

"You're kidding," Grant exclaims. "You think maybe they stole a stuffed parrot from some display so we could find a bird?"

I smile. Never in a million years would Grant's idea have occurred to me.

Carl chuckles. "Good guess, but no. This bird's innards haven't been touched. It hasn't been stuffed for display. It is just weird. I can't tell you how, but I'm sure the vets at the center will know."

Once we wave goodbye to Carl and Mimi, I pile back inside Ted's Lexus along with Mom, Frank, and Grant for the short ride from the access road to the Campbell house.

Velma's outside waiting for us. Her very first act is to give Grant a hug.

"I can't thank you enough for installing the new video doorbell," she says. "It's returned a little bit of my peace of mind. Now, at least, I can see trouble coming before it arrives."

Chapter Forty-Four

Kylee

Thursday 3 p.m., December 19

Velma is prepared to play hostess. She's baked two varieties of cookies, still warm from the oven, and offers us a choice of hot chocolate or lemonade to accompany them.

I suppose baking gave Velma something to do besides rage at the Stillwater board or worry about Vince, who's now flying in from across the globe.

Once we're all seated in the living room, Ted recaps our sanctioned and supervised search for a mystery parrot minus a feather that somehow got returned with Maury's clothes.

"Carl, who's been a bird-watcher for decades, thinks there is something strange about the dead parrot we found," he adds. "He plans to take it to the Feathered Friends Clinic and see if their veterinarian experts can provide some answers. We'll let you know what he finds out."

"There are definitely some strange goings on within Stillwater Cove," I add. "I think Maury suspected what they might be."

While I'm afraid Maury's suspicions are what got him killed, I don't want to suggest he was murdered. Not without proof. At the moment, Velma still believes her husband's death was an accident—even if she thinks being chased by a neighbor led to the crash. How much worse to imagine a premeditated murder? Someone leaning over Maury to snap his neck.

"Kylee, this morning you mentioned finding a cigar box on the Soup Can," Velma says. "Did you bring it?"

I retrieve it. As Velma looks inside, a frown creases her forehead, making a deep furrow between her eyebrows.

"Maury never showed any of these things to me." She shakes her head.

Next, I hand Velma the packet of pictures. "Did Maury tell you why he was taking pictures of Archer's yacht?" I ask.

Velma thumbs through the snapshots. "How odd. You found these on the Soup Can?"

"Yes," I reply. "We had a hard time imagining why Maury took these photos unless it had to do with the security guards being paid to tote pet cages for the HOA president."

"Those pet cages sure don't belong to Archer," Velma comments. "The man doesn't own a single pet."

"Are you sure?"

"Absolutely, I've heard Archer comment more than once that he'd never own a dog, a cat, or any other creature. He thinks pets are too much of a bother for a single person who enjoys travel."

"Okay, let's go back to the items Maury stashed inside the cigar box," I suggest. "The scarlet feather obviously came from a bird. But do you have any idea what creature these scales might have come from? Or how about the animal that contributed the white fur?"

Velma fingers the white fur. "It's so soft. It definitely wasn't donated by our cat, Marshmallow. Her fur is a lot more wiry. The scales sort of resemble miniature angel wing shells, the way they're shaped, and their striations. However, the color looks more like sand. I admit, I'm stumped."

A single tear meanders down Velma's cheek. "Why didn't Maury tell me what he was up to?"

Ted, who is seated next to Velma, covers her hand with one of his own. "My guess is Maury was trying to protect you. He couldn't quite get his head around what was happening and thought he should get his ideas sorted out before saying anything."

From across the living room, Frank nods his agreement. "Ted's on the right track, Velma. Maury was meticulous. Always wanted to have all his ducks in a row before he started any project. And you meant the world to him. If Maury thought there was any danger, he'd have done his darndest to make sure you were out of harm's way."

Silence descends as our thoughts focus on Maury and the honorable way he approached every aspect of life.

Finally, Velma clears her throat. "Maybe we should take the scales and the fur to a veterinarian. Stillwater has a vet, who visits at least twice a month, and I think he's scheduled to be here tomorrow.

"Some Stillwater pet owners don't want to be bothered scheduling routine care off-island. The visiting vet program is supposedly another Stillwater perk. I've never met the man, but I could book a time to see him. Maury and I have always relied on Dr. Hardesty. Myrt, you use him, too, don't you?"

"Yes," Mom answers. "I would forget about asking the opinion of any vet who depends on the Stillwater board for revenue. That must be the vet Archer said he'd tap to dispose of the dead parrot. Why don't I take the cigar box to Dr. Hardesty? If he can't give us answers, he'll suggest who can."

"I second Mom's suggestion," I add. "I don't trust anyone or anything tied to the Stillwater HOA board."

I stop with the trust comment. I'm not ready to spout off that the Stillwater board is trafficking endangered species, and that's what prompted Maury to photograph Archer's yacht and stash strange keepsakes in a cigar box. My theory explains why Maury is dead, and it explains why Archer, or one of his flunkies, searched Maury's office and shredded all those Post-It notes. They were scared Maury was on to their game.

I assume they're using the maintenance barn to store merchandise until it can be stowed onboard the yacht or sent on to U.S. buyers.

Finding a way to prove my suspicions is a different kettle of fish. And I don't intend to flap my gums and accuse anyone of murder or trafficking endangered species without concrete backup.

Chapter Forty-Five

Archer

Thursday 3:30 p.m., December 19

Thank God for the let-it-all-hang-out gabfest in Velma's living room. Now, I know exactly what they're thinking. The situation is both better and worse than I feared.

So, think. Examine each of their assumptions and figure out how to de-escalate.

One: Maury's photos of Wavedancer. Even Kylee admitted Maury could have taken them to document that salaried HOA employees are running personal errands for me.

The counter? Dummy up payments from my personal bank accounts to show I was paying guards to moonlight. Not illegal, or even unethical.

Two, why were the guards taking cages off Wavedancer when I have no pets or need for pet carriers?

One possible rebuttal comes to mind. The cages are gifts for a friend, who visited me in the Bahamas, and admired the craftsmanship of pet carriers offered by a street vendor. I brought them back as presents. Lame, but no way to disprove it.

Three. What happens if this Feathered Friends Clinic can determine the dead parrot was previously buried, dug up, and cleaned for an above-ground curtain call?

Okay, I'm drawing a blank. I could hypothesize that a wild animal dug the bird up. But how did the parrot get spiffed up? Can't blame that on some wild creature's fetish about cleaning up prey before it feasts.

Four, and maybe the toughest, how to explain the animal detritus Maury collected? Thanks to their ornithology friends, Kylee is likely to learn that the scarlet feather, like the blue one, comes from an endangered parrot.

I doubt a local vet will be able to ID the scales or the white fur. He won't treat pangolins or Roloway monkeys in his practice. Who studies scales? And, surely, lots of mammals have white fur.

But what if these connections to endangered creatures can be confirmed? How can I explain their presence in Stillwater Cove?

I can't.

But Kylee and company can't prove Maury found these items on Stillwater property either.

It's a stalemate. There's no way Kylee could coax a judge to sign off on search warrants for the maintenance barn or Wavedancer. All she can do is speculate about where Maury picked up his unusual prizes. He could have found them anywhere. And I doubt there's some carbon-dating option to determine how old they are. Maybe Maury found his treasures thirty years ago.

Still, after we transfer the cash to Wavedancer, I'll order a deep clean of the maintenance barn. Make sure not a single hair, feather or scale remains.

When Perry comes tomorrow, I'll tell the vet to contact our exotic pet buyers and explain deliveries will be delayed. I won't risk bringing back endangered species on this Bahama run. Our Andros vet can keep the critters healthy for at least another month. No point pushing our luck.

I just wish Kylee didn't have Coast Guard creds. I have built plenty of goodwill with the Coast Guard command in this district. But Kylee has friends in high places, too. I need to sail as quickly as possible with the fifty million dollars stashed in the maintenance barn.

And I need to make certain Kylee is in no condition to call in Coast Guard favors. That's something she can't do if she's no longer breathing.

Chapter Forty-Six

Kylee

Thursday 5 p.m., December 19

I'm off to visit with Care Committee member Anna Whitner. Ted chauffeured Mom, Frank, and me back to Hullis Island with time to spare. I actually had a chance to wash up in Mom's bathroom before my appointment.

Anna and her husband, a vice president at a Beaufort bank, live on a peninsula finger of solid ground surrounded by marsh on three sides. All the peninsula houses resemble giant, glass geodesic mushrooms. They sit atop pedestals that form the interior core, including kitchen and baths. From the core, eight glass-fronted rooms open like petals to offer panoramic views.

Anna's house has no elevator. My climb up the metal stairs is noisy. These folks don't need a video doorbell; they can hear anyone coming. My suspicion is confirmed when I see Anna waiting for me at the entrance door.

My attractive greeter is young for Hullis Island. I'm guessing mid-forties. She's dressed in a sweatshirt and jeans, and she's wearing fluffy bunny slippers. A far cry from Babsie's high heels and diamond earrings.

"Kylee, I presume." Anna looks delighted to see me. "I don't get much company. Come on in and have a seat. I have a fresh pot of coffee brewing but it'll be a few minutes."

She ushers me into a living room with long-range vistas of marsh, water, and sky. I prefer to contemplate the ocean, but I understand the marsh attraction. Serene. Lots of interesting birds and wildlife.

"Thank you for agreeing to meet with me," I begin and dish out the same spiel I served up to Babsie this morning.

Anna grins. "I was curious how you'd appeal for my help. I knew why you were coming. I'm friends with Evie Miles. She thinks you're determined to actually investigate the theft of her jewelry. I'm glad. Despite what Hullis Island security may think, Evie doesn't hallucinate or misplace items. She's sharp as a tack. When she was going through her cancer treatments, we talked about books. And, when she got better, I asked Evie to be one of my beta readers. I'm an author, and Evie knows a good book when she reads one. She's ruthless about telling me where I need to cut and what plot points don't compute."

"What do you write? I love to read."

"Mysteries." Anna smiles. "Which makes my job a lot like yours—figuring out plausible motives and separating red herrings from actual clues as I construct a plot. You suspect someone on the Care Committee is either the thief or the thief's insider source of information."

I open my mouth to object. Anna holds up her hand. "Don't bother with a sidestep soft-shoe. I'm not angry. I wholeheartedly agree with your premise. I'm just going to point you in a new direction. I think Babsie is the thief."

"You do? Why?"

"Babsie doesn't actually lift a finger to help neighbors with cooking, cleaning, or transportation. And she never volunteers to sit with someone so they feel less alone. But she does visit everyone who is helped by the committee. On her first visit, she spends a lot of time walking through every room in the house. Allegedly to see if there are mobility issues that need to be addressed. She never finds any. And, she regularly checks in with committee members. But she only asks about doctor appointments for our well-heeled neighbors. Never exhibits the same curiosity about individuals unlikely to have expensive trinkets."

It's my turn to hold up a hand. "Whoa, Anna. I'm not a Babsie fan. But you mentioned the importance of motives earlier. Babsie is a rich widow who lives in what most people would consider an oceanfront palace. She's always attending some Lowcountry gala, and I doubt she wears the same outfit twice. Why would she risk all that to steal jewelry that's probably worth less than what she has in her own jewelry box?"

"Good questions," Anna says. "Let's have a cup of coffee, and I'll give you a few more clues."

Anna serves the coffee in large, sturdy mugs, and her cookies come in store-bought wrappers. Again, a huge contrast with Babsie. Already, I like Anna, and I can't wait to read one of her books.

Anna and I are both quiet as we take our first sips of coffee.

"Okay," Anna says. "Here's my first investigative suggestion. You need to chat up Babsie's former maid, Ella. She now works full-time for Jerry Schevers. I hear Ella had a front-row seat for Babsie's nuclear melt-down when she learned the details of her husband's trust. Apparently, hubby didn't trust Babsie to spend money wisely, and he wanted to ensure his two daughters were the primary beneficiaries. So, he named his daughters as the trustees. The girls have absolute say over whether an expenditure Babsie is contemplating will be authorized."

"Holy cow," I interrupt. "If you're right, restraints like that would chafe Babsie's britches big time."

Anna laughs. "Correct. And that gives you motive. Babsie needs an independent source of revenue to fund designer clothes and lavish trips. While my banker husband tells me it's next to impossible to ferret out trust details, I bet the stepkids would be delighted to fill you in. Ella says the girls hate Babsie's guts. I also imagine a felony conviction would give the Talbott daughters an excellent shot at cutting Babsie entirely out of any trust benefits."

"You've been more than helpful." I grin. "Of course, maybe you're handing me a bunch of red herrings to lead me away from the real thief. In your mystery, would it be you?"

Anna laughs. "Could be. You'll have to decide."

"Do you have any more helpful tips? Like how someone like Babsie could find a fence to handle stolen goods?"

"Hey, I can't do all your work for you," Anna says. "But please keep me posted. If you run into any more investigative roadblocks, maybe I can tell you what my heroine would try."

Though I'm half tempted to tell Anna that I've encountered what seem like insurmountable roadblocks in the Stillwater Cove mystery, I restrain myself. Maybe another time? Let's see how Anna's initial clues pan out.

* * *

The golf course café is practically empty. In winter, it only serves breakfast and lunch and closes at six-thirty—earlier if no golfers appear for nineteenth-hole beers and bragging rights. I assume Suzie chose the café for our meeting because the location would ensure our conversation would be relatively quiet and also brief.

A quick glance around the café tells me Suzie isn't here yet. I take a seat at a window table beyond the eavesdropping range of the few remaining golfers. Today's appearance of the sun probably tempted a number of golfers to the links course. However, the winds must have been brutal on the oceanside holes.

The café door opens, and Suzie walks in. She looks exactly like Mom described. A big woman. Her exact measurements are hidden by a tent-like dress with a hem that touches the edge of her boots. We're not talking fashionable knee-high leather boots, but what look like hiking boots. The boots and the feet encased inside seem far too tiny to support her body.

I smile and wave her over. She doesn't look pleased to be here. It's hard to tell Suzie's age. Her face is too plump to have wrinkles. But, from Mom's description of the widow, I put her in her mid-seventies. Unfortunately, I have the feeling this interview will be nothing like my visit with Anna.

I introduce myself as a waitress arrives to take our orders. I'm coffeed out so I ask for a lemonade. Suzie opts for hot chocolate.

Once again, I attempt to ease into the interview by saying I primarily want to know if Suzie recalls anyone who seemed overly curious about ailing neighbors who needed help from the Care Committee.

"No," Suzie answers. "Since my Donnie died, I'm afraid I've become sort of a hermit. I can't remember anyone asking me anything. Mostly, I just chat with the neighbors I call on for the Care Committee. I like helping out when people are ill or laid up. I love to bake, and it gives me an excuse to make homemade cookies or coffee cakes." She pauses and waves a hand at her middle. "As you can see, I certainly don't need baked goods sitting around the house to tempt me."

Her alto voice is melodious. It makes me wonder if she sings. I decide the woman could use a compliment.

"Suzie, you have a beautiful voice. Do you sing in a choir?"

She blushes. "Yes, besides baking, that's my other passion. I sing in the choir at the Methodist Church every Sunday."

"Oh, then you must know Velma Campbell," I say. "I think she also sings in the choir."

"Yes." Suzie frowns. "The minister told us about Maury's passing. I'm so sorry. I know how hard it is to suddenly be alone after you've been married for forty or fifty years."

"Do you have any thoughts about how the island thief picks his victims? It's hard to believe this has been going on for two years?"

The waitress delivers our drinks, and Suzie stirs her hot chocolate to melt the marshmallows on top.

"I've thought about it," she confesses. "I really despise whoever is doing this. These poor people are already feeling down and depressed, and the thief counts on the authorities dismissing their theft reports. Security officers assume they're too addled to know what happened to their jewels.

"These days, so many islanders have video doorbells you'd think the thief would be caught on camera," she continues. "The problem is folks have no idea when they were robbed. A week or a month may go by before they discover a single item is missing. Even if they save those door videos in the cloud, what would they prove? They'd show dozens of people coming and going. How could anyone know which visitor was the thief?"

I nod. "Exactly. That's the problem."

Reluctantly, I have to bring up the rumors about her being a hoarder. I mentally squirm at the need to turn the conversation in this direction.

"Suzie, I've heard you hate to see Hullis Island neighbors discarding items that may still be useful. That you sometimes salvage them. What do you do with them?"

The woman blushes again. This time, it's not because I've complimented her.

"I've heard all the whispers," she says. "Babsie is the main person encouraging them. Suggesting I'm a hoarder and maybe an out-of-control kleptomaniac. Well, it's partly true. I find waste appalling. People throw out a chair because the upholstery has a tiny tear. Or they ditch an end table with a wobbly leg instead of applying a little glue. Yes, I can't help myself. I take the discards home, but they don't stay there, stacked in some rickety floor-to-ceiling pile. If you doubt it, come on home with me.

"I fix what I can. It gives me something to do besides baking and eating. Then, I donate them to thrift shops. People give up on things too easily. Replace them with something new and shiny that they'll throw away, too, just as soon as it shows a little wear. It makes me mad."

And people do the same thing with neighbors. Suzie being one of the discards.

I vow to stay in touch with this woman after we find the thief. Suzie is someone worth knowing.

"I absolutely agree with you," I say. "And I don't need to see your house. I believe you. Thanks for your help."

Chapter Forty-Seven

Kylee

Thursday 7 p.m., December 19

T hough I miss Ted, I'm glad to have an evening to myself. I take a long pull on my beer while I wait for the microwave to ding. A Swanson chicken pot pie. One of my childhood favorites on days when Mom didn't have time to cook.

Ideas are scampering around in my head like hyper puppies, and I can't corral any of them long enough to decide which ones matter and which ones are crap.

Tomorrow is Friday, December 20. Maury's funeral service is now set for Saturday afternoon. As Mom gleefully pointed out this afternoon, that's when the wedding rigmarole will start to consume most of my waking hours.

Somehow, I need to find time to pick up table decorations, flower arrangements, party plates, and the wedding cake. It also might be nice to have time to shower, shampoo, and maybe even clip my nails. I'd hate to stab Ted with a long toenail on our wedding night. Oh, yeah, and I need to pack for our honeymoon.

I have to admit it. There's no chance I can wrap up my investigation into Hullis Island thefts or discover what criminal shenanigans are going on at Stillwater Cove before Ted and I leave for the Caymans.

But maybe I can pose questions and assemble enough quasi-evidence to persuade the Sheriff's Office to reopen the Hullis Island theft cases or even convince the Coast Guard to search Archer Highsmith's yacht when it leaves port.

The microwave dings. I pull out my pot pie and sit down at the River Rat's compact dining alcove. I pull the cover off my entrée. The escaping steam tells me it should cool a little longer before I chow down. I grab pencil and paper.

I head the sheet, "Chores for Tomorrow."

One. Talk to Ella, Babsie's former maid. See if she can confirm Anna's story about the Talbott trust, and find out if she knows how to reach Babsie's stepdaughters.

Two. Check in with Carl to find out if the Feathered Friends Clinic has offered any news about the dead parrot.

Three. See if Mom's vet can provide clues about the creatures who donated the scales and fur in Maury's cigar box.

The vet? I knew something had been niggling at the edges of my brain.

Velma mentioned that a vet spends two days a month at Stillwater Cove, and Archer volunteered to have said vet bury the dead parrot. If, indeed, Archer and his colleagues are trafficking endangered species, they'd need a vet to check out the new arrivals and provide care until the exotic pets can be delivered to buyers.

Maybe that's why Stillwater Cove offers on-island pet care. It wants residents to become accustomed to seeing the vet inside the gates. They won't be curious about him spending so much time there.

I absently fork a bite of the pie and, instantly, scald my lip. Way to go, Kylee. Want to show up for your wedding with blistered lips?

Still too hot. I reach for the phone and dial Velma.

"Hi, Kylee," she says. "I'm only answering calls if I can recognize who's calling. You can't imagine the number of calls I've gotten since Maury's obituary was published. Most from friends, but, unbelievably, also charlatans. They must think if I'm grief-stricken, I'll listen to their phony condolences and buy whatever they're selling."

197

"Oh, Velma, that's awful. Is Vince there? You ought to let him answer the phone."

"No, Vince is exhausted from all the travel, and I think it's just hit home that Maury is really gone. That he won't see his father again. The calls are just an annoyance. I can hang up on scammers as easily as Vince can.

"Everything is set for Saturday's funeral service. I'm so glad we could schedule the funeral before Christmas. I can't prevent Vince from associating the holidays with Maury's death, but I felt holding the service between Christmas and New Years would make it even worse. Then, there are Maury's friends wishing to pay their respects. I didn't want to take them away from their families during Christmas and New Year's celebrations. By the way, I totally understand if you can't make the service, what with your wedding only days away."

"Of course, I'll be there, Velma. I hope I have an opportunity to talk with Vince while he's home."

"Right now, he's very angry," she comments. "I hope the Stillwater Cove directors don't show their faces at the funeral service. I'm afraid Vince might just punch them out—Lisa Queensbury included."

"I know Ted and Grant will be serving as ushers," I say. "They can make sure the Stillwater directors are diplomatically turned away." I pause. "I hate to impose on you. But I do have a small favor to ask. Could you look up the name of the veterinarian who regularly visits Stillwater Cove? I'd very much like to ask him some questions."

"Sure, I'll text you the information in a little bit. Anything I can do to help nail those bastards is not an imposition."

I have one more call to make. I can't call it a night without talking to Ted.

Ted answers on the first ring. "Hi, honey," he says. "I planned to give you until eight o'clock before I bugged you. I really miss you. Sure you're not ready to abandon the River Rat and join Grant and me?"

"I miss you, too. But the answer is no. I'm still on overload, which tends to make me crabby. Don't want you to see my cranky side before Tuesday. You might change your mind about saying I do. Then there's your dad's Sunday arrival. You're going to be plenty busy. Think about the Caymans.

CHAPTER FORTY-SEVEN

We'll make up for lost time."

We talk a few more minutes. But, following our rule to not discuss business after dinner, I don't tell Ted about my visits with Anna and Suzie. Those details can wait for the morning.

"Goodnight," I say. "I'll see you at the office. I know Mom plans to stay home and bake for the church reception following Maury's funeral. Will you be in all day?"

"I have two meetings," Ted says. "I should be back in the office about eleven. How about you?"

"I'll arrive late morning, same as you. I'll call if that changes. Love you."

Chapter Forty-Eight

Archer

Thursday 8 p.m., December 19

Dammit. I listen to Velma's side of her phone conversation with Kylee a second time. What information did Kylee ask Velma to text her?

The bugs in the Campbell house have a serious drawback. They don't let me hear the caller's side of conversations, and I can't know what info is speeding back and forth via text. Too bad the Campbells aren't among the landline holdouts. It's hard to bug someone's cell phone when it's always in a pocket.

Kylee's latest call makes one decision easy. We'll skip Maury's funeral service. The board can send a big floral arrangement. Let it go at that. No point provoking a scene and get more Lowcountry tongues wagging.

The call didn't help me decide what to do about Kylee. Perhaps nothing.

She's almost out of time to interfere. She may suspect Babsie is the Hullis Island thief, but there's zip to prove it. And she has no inkling there's a Stillwater Cove connection. Sure, Maury's autopsy and the dead parrot have raised a few questions, but there's no hard evidence. Ditto for Maury's photos and his stupid cigar box treasures.

At most, Kylee has three days to unearth something startling enough to prompt the Coast Guard to search my yacht. And, if they search before

Monday, they'll find nothing. The weather in the Atlantic should improve enough to load the cash pre-dawn Monday and leave. Come the weekend, wedding-related commitments should take Kylee out of the picture.

Okay, that's settled. It's stupid to try and sideline or kill Kylee now. It would just up the risk of discovery. Maybe I will take Quentin with me to the Bahamas. Once we make it to Andros and unload the cash, we're in the clear. We can pause all operations for a while—money laundering and animal trafficking. Make sure it's safe before we resume.

Chapter Forty-Nine

Kylee

Friday Morning, December 19

I look at the clock. Holy moly. It's seven-thirty. I didn't set an alarm. Usually wake up at six-thirty. My body must have decided it needed some catch-up sleep after the prior insomnia-ville bout of tossing and turning.

I brew a pot of coffee and recheck my to-do list. First order of business is to phone Jerry Schevers and ask if Ella, Babsie's former maid, works for him. I'm hoping the answer is yes, and he'll tell me how to contact her. If not, it's another investigative dead-end. I have no idea what Ella's last name might be or where she lives.

I down a half-cup of coffee before I feel alert enough to make the phone call. I hope Mr. Schevers is not out golfing. He and my father were golfing buddies before Dad passed away. I look the number up in the handy-dandy Hullis Island community phone book. The guide provides phone numbers, addresses, and as much extra info as the residents want neighbors to know. That usually includes pet names, and, not quite as often, the names of children.

A woman answers the Schevers' phone on the first ring. Could it be Ella? Nope, don't ask. I'm not one hundred percent sure Ella currently works for Schevers. The woman who picked up the phone might be Mr. Schevers' significant other and could take offense at being asked if she's Ella.

"Hi, could I speak to Mr. Schevers?"

"Who's calling?"

"Kylee Kane."

In less than two seconds, Mr. Schevers' booming voice comes on the line.

"Hey, Kylee," he says. "What are you investigating now? Have I been implicated in another murder or some other criminal enterprise?"

More than a year ago, I spoke with Mr. Schevers when he was among several Hullis Island residents cheated by a scoundrel. Said scoundrel wound up with an arrow in his chest. Luckily, Mr. Schevers' tone is teasing, not irate.

"You raise an interesting possibility, sir," I tease back. "While I have no knowledge of any criminal activities, I'd be happy to listen if you want to confess."

He laughs. "No, don't think so. And call me Jerry."

It's funny. I have no problems calling Mom and Frank's friends by their first names. Not sure why it feels awkward to address members of the older generation informally if I don't know them well. Guess Mom's lessons in manners have stood the test of time.

"Actually, I do hope you can help with an investigation," I say. "But it has nothing to do with you. I'd like to get in touch with a woman named Ella. She used to work for the Talbotts. I was told she may work for you now."

"She does," he answers. "In fact, it was Ella who answered the phone. Do you want me to put her back on?"

"Uh, no. I think it would be better if I sit down with her in person and explain the situation. Will Ella be at your house all morning? If so, could I come by for a few minutes?"

"It's fine with me, but not if you're investigating Ella. Has someone claimed she did something wrong?"

"Absolutely not," I answer. "I'm hoping she might be able to tell me a bit about her time with the Talbotts. I'd really like to reach the Talbott daughters and I don't know how to contact them."

"Come on over, then," Mr. Schevers—Jerry—says. "If Ella can't help you, I probably can. I played golf with your dad and John Talbott. I know John's girls. Are you at Frank and Myrt's house?"

"No. I'm in Beaufort, so it will be about thirty minutes."

Excellent. Wish every request was granted so pleasantly.

* * *

The older woman who answers Jerry Schevers' door isn't dressed like Hollywood's idea of a maid. She's wearing a comfy flannel shirt, baggy cotton pants, and tennis shoes. Her dark, curly hair has very little gray. She has a lovely mahogany complexion and expressive brown eyes. I guess the woman to be my senior by perhaps ten years.

"Hi, I'm Kylee Kane," I say. "Are you Ella?"

"Yes, I'm Ella Dent, come on in. Mr. Schevers told me to expect you. He's not here. He thought we might need some privacy. I told him that wasn't necessary. I'd be happy for him to hear anything I have to say, but he's a very thoughtful man. Would you like some coffee?"

Ella has a faint but definite accent.

"That would be great," I answer. "Are you from Great Britain? I detect a bit of an accent, but you've obviously been in the States for years."

"You have a good ear," Ella replies. "I immigrated from Bermuda, schooled by British teachers. I've lived in the States for forty years."

"Take a seat in the living room, and I'll go get the coffee," she says.

"I remember there's a nice kitchen nook, and I bet it's close to the coffee pot," I say. "Why don't we sit there?"

I don't beat around the bush as I explain what I'd like to know. Either Eva will help me or she won't. She'll tattle to Babsie, or she won't. When I finish my explanation, Ella laughs.

"I worked for the Talbotts for twenty years," she says. "And, until Babsie came along, I always was treated like family."

She waves a hand at her clothes. "I dressed like this. Not in some absurd maid costume with a skirt and hose, like Babsie insisted. The first Mrs. Talbott died five years ago. By then, both girls had graduated from college, married, and had their own families. Mr. Talbott was lonely. Babsie saw it and pounced. He'd only known her a few months when they got married."

I interrupt. "Have you stayed in touch with the Talbott daughters?"

"Of course. Beth Talbott, now Beth Reiner, lives in Charlotte, and her sister, Marianne Talbott, now Marianne Skinner, lives in Columbia. Whenever Marianne visits Beth, they come to Beaufort, and we get together for lunch."

I decide it's time to dive into the trust rumors. "I've heard that Mr. Talbott created a trust and made his daughters the trustees. Do you know if that's true? I'm trying to determine if money problems might prompt Babsie to seek funds in some less than honorable ways."

Once again, Ella laughs. She's enjoying this.

"Boy, oh boy, is the rumor true. I was in the room when Beth and Marianne showed Babsie a copy of the trust and explained the terms. Told her she was entitled to live in the house until she died or remarried and that she'd receive a modest monthly allowance with the same conditions. The girls warned Babsie she was not allowed to spend or commit any money for household maintenance or changes without prior approval.

"I thought Babsie would have a heart attack right on the spot. She was beyond angry. Vowed she'd fight to make the trust null and void. She reckoned her three years as Mrs. Talbott entitled her to the house and at least half of the estate. The girls basically said bring it on. I don't think Mr. Talbott had been in his grave a week before Babsie called an architect to talk about major renovations. Having to cancel her grand plans was a major humiliation."

I ask Ella if Babsie's "modest" monthly allowance was enough for her to live comfortably.

Ella grins. "Guess that depends on who's defining comfortably. It isn't enough for Babsie to keep a maid and a butler, though Chester, the butler, and I had already given notice. It also probably isn't enough for Babsie to buy new designer outfits every week.

"To answer your question, most normal human beings could live quite comfortably on what Babsie's being handed for her three years as Mrs.

Talbott. Look, she has no housing expenses. The trust pays all the related bills—utilities, insurance, property taxes. But, no, I heard Babsie rave that she'd been given a pittance, and it was a huge injustice."

Ella provides contact information for Beth and Marianne and offers to give them a heads-up that I'll be phoning. "They'll be happy to help you, especially if there's a possibility you can tie Babsie to illegal activities. They'd love to kick her out of the Talbott house and permanently out of their lives."

Chapter Fifty

Kylee

Friday Morning, December 20

When I leave the Schevers house, I stop to say hello to Mom before heading to Beaufort. Inside, the smell of freshly baked cookies assaults my cut-back-on-sweets promise.

I hear the oven door close and a cookie tray slide onto a wire cooling rack. I don't want to startle Mom with hot cookie trays in process.

"Hi, Mom," I call out. "Just popping by for a minute."

"Kylee, what a surprise," Mom says as I enter the kitchen. "Want to help? I've made a batch of chocolate chip cookies and a batch of sugar cookies. You could ice the sugar cookies while I make brownies. There'll be a crowd at Maury's service. Vince is worn out from travel, and Velma didn't want to subject him to a family viewing before the funeral. That means some folks who might have only paid respects at a viewing will come to the funeral."

"Sorry, Mom, I can't help. Call Martha. She's always eager to lend a hand. I just came from the Schevers' house, where I had a very interesting conversation with his housekeeper, Ella, who is the Talbotts' former maid. Ella put me in touch with the Talbott daughters, and I have a lunch date with Beth in Beaufort."

Mom gives me a puzzled look. "Is this about the Hullis Island thefts?"

"Yes," I answer. "Why?"

"You need to check your voice messages," Mom says. "Chief O'Rourke called here about ten minutes ago. Said he'd left you a voicemail but wanted me to relay a message if I saw you first.

"What's the message?"

"The chief says you need to stop pestering people about the Hullis Island thefts. He arrested the thief this morning."

"What? Who?"

Mom shrugs. "He didn't say, and he didn't give me a chance to ask. Just left the message for you to butt out and hung up."

Did he arrest Babsie? How did O'Rourke gather enough evidence?

I call Hullis Island Security and ask to speak to the chief.

"Sorry, he's unavailable. Chief O'Rourke is in Beaufort and won't be returning to the office today."

"I understand he made an arrest," I say. "Can you tell me who he arrested and the charge?"

"No, ma'am. That's why the chief is in Beaufort. He took the suspect into the County Detention Center and is doing the paperwork. I don't feel I can release any information until it's official."

I hang up. I can't believe the chief took time out to gloat before all his I's were dotted and T's crossed.

No surprise, my next call is to Josie.

"Hi, Kylee, thought you might be calling. I saw the Hullis Island chief brought in a suspect for those thefts you've been investigating. Did you uncover the evidence and hand the chief a suspect on a gold platter?'

"No. I don't even know who the chief arrested or why. As far as I know, there is no evidence."

"Huh. I overheard O'Rourke talking with Nick Ibsen. I know, one of your favorite people. Anyway, the chief said he got an anonymous tip. He went to the suspect's house, and she agreed to a search without a warrant. They found one of the stolen items, a missing gold coin, in the drawer of some antique table. Do you want me to find out the woman's name and call you back?"

"Yes, please."

I have a sinking feeling I know who's been dragged off to jail, and I'm equally sure she's been set up.

No way would Babsie consent to a warrantless search of her house. But Suzie? Yeah, she'd figure she had nothing to hide. I feel sick. I am ninety-nine percent sure the anonymous tipster is Babsie. But how did she plant the coin? Did Suzie welcome her into her house?

My phone buzzes. "Yeah, Josie. Give me the bad news. It's Suzie Bucknell, right?"

"Yes, Suzanne Eloise Bucknell. Did you suspect her?"

"No, I think my prime suspect set her up, and I'm going to prove it. Is Suzie in custody?"

"Yes, she's only charged with possession of stolen property. Guess they need more time to put together a credible case to charge her with that whole string of thefts. After the officers found the coin, they tore her house apart. Didn't find any other valuables."

"Will Suzie need to post bail?"

"I'm not sure. She has no priors, and the theft of the gold coin didn't involve any violence. Sounds like she may not be the type of criminal suspect a judge would consider a public menace, but he might consider her a flight risk, if she's got money."

"Suzie's a widow, lives very modestly, sings in the Methodist Church choir, and bakes for neighbors when they're ill. And I don't think she has the kind of money she'd need to be a flight risk."

"Then maybe she won't be required to post bail."

"Thanks, Josie. Appreciate the info. Got to go. I want to be there for Suzie and make sure she knows there's at least one person who doesn't believe the charge. I'm on Hullis Island, so it'll take me a while to get to Beaufort. Maybe Ted can get there sooner."

I quickly make my next call.

"Welch HOA Management."

It's Grant's voice. Guess he's filling in for Mom. "Grant, is your dad there?"

"No, Dad had that follow-up meeting with the Lighthouse Cove directors who are all hot and bothered about the 'Tis the season to be GAY' sign. After that, he and Frank were going to Rand Creek to discuss financing for clubhouse renovations. Want him to call you when he's free."

"Don't bother. I'm leaving Grandma Myrt's in a couple of minutes and heading to the Beaufort County Detention Center. I think an innocent woman is being set up to take the rap for that string of Hullis Island thefts. I want to make sure she's treated well. I'll pay for her bond if need be."

"Whoa," Grant says. "Do I know her?"

"It's Suzie Bucknell. Doubt you know her. In fact, I just met her yesterday. But I'm confident she's innocent, and I have a good idea who the real thief is. Tell your dad I'll fill him in as soon as I can."

Mom stops shoveling cooled cookies from oven sheets to oversized Tupperware containers.

"I've been listening in, and I second your opinion," Mom says. "I'd go see Suzie myself and try to bring her home if I wasn't knee-deep in cookie dough. I also told the church ladies I'd bake a ham and scalloped potatoes. And I still have to take Maury's cigar box to my vet."

"Give me the cigar box," I say. "I'll stop by the vets after I do what I can to help Suzie."

After our long-time attorney moved to Europe, her old clients, including Mom, Frank, Ted, and me, were forced to find a new lawyer. We couldn't have settled on a better advocate than Olivia Tucker, Esquire. Though the paint on her shingle has barely had time to dry, Olivia's super smart, energetic, and determined—qualities that more than make up for inexperience. She's also youthful enough to love new challenges.

I phone Olivia's office, and she agrees to meet me at the Beaufort County Detention Center. Meanwhile, Olivia says she'll find out if Suzie's been processed and if the court schedule will allow her to go before a judge for arraignment this afternoon.

"Do you know who owned the stolen coin?" Olivia asks. "If he'll go on record that he agrees Ms. Bucknell should be released on her own recognizance, it could help."

"Think I can manage that," I say, "as long as Doug Fisher answers his phone."

Luckily, Doug answers his business line, and I explain my belief that Suzie's being railroaded.

"Hey, I still have withdrawal symptoms when I think about Suzie's brownies," he says. "I can't imagine Suzie being a flight risk. I'll be happy to sign a statement supporting her release without bond and send you a scan."

Chapter Fifty-One

Kylee

Friday Morning, December 20

When I arrive at the Beaufort County Detention Center, I find Olivia pacing up and down the sidewalk in front of the building. She's wearing her usual lawyerly uniform, a dark blue pants suit with sensible shoes. Everything about Olivia is, well, sensible. She keeps her brown hair cut short, wears minimal make-up, and doesn't carry a purse. She just tucks a wallet in a briefcase that she can sling over her shoulder to keep her hands free.

Olivia's plump and very average-looking until she engages with you. Then, her whole face lights up. She smiles when she sees me.

"Hi, Olivia," I say, "have you sprung my friend yet?"

"No, but I did get here in time to stop that putz Deputy Nick Ibsen from badgering the poor woman. If he could get away with it, he'd use a baton on suspects to make them confess. Suzie was surprised when I told her I'd been hired to represent her and that Ibsen's interrogation was over until we talked. I told Suzie you were totally in her corner."

"Should we go inside? Can I see her?" I ask.

"No, you won't be able to see her. I only need a few minutes to bring you up to speed. We're not freezing, so let's talk outside. There's no one to listen out here."

Olivia fills me in, and I give her a copy of the signed statement from the stolen coin's owner, requesting Ms. Bucknell be released on her own recognizance. Olivia says there's nothing more I can do and that she'll handle Suzie's first appearance this afternoon.

"If Suzie's released, which I'm almost certain she will be, I'll drive her back home," Olivia says. "I got this. Will keep you updated. Don't worry."

* * *

I drive to Ted's office to update him on the latest developments. I have plenty of time before my meeting with Beth Talbott Reiner.

Once I arrive, it's obvious Ted and I aren't going to have a private conversation as Grant and Robin hurry to greet me.

"What's happening?" Grant asks. "Did you spring the lady you think is being railroaded?"

I chuckle. "Yeah, I pulled my Glock and demanded they open her jail cell. No, I didn't need my Glock. I unleashed a more powerful weapon, Attorney Olivia Tucker. Come on. Let's go to our conference-slash-break table and I'll give a full report so everyone can hear."

Ted gives me a kiss. "That includes me, right?"

"You bet," I say.

I finish, and there's a moment of silence.

"It's kind of evil genius," Grant says. "Friday is the day everyone on Hullis Island carts trash to the curb for pick-up, and Babsie knew Suzie would do an early scouting trip to beat the disposal crew, looking for salvageable items. Babsie carts an antique table to the curb and slips a stolen coin inside. She watches Suzie make her pick-up, waits long enough for her to get it to her house, and makes an anonymous call."

"That's exactly how I see it," I say, "with one exception. The anonymous caller was a male from a burner phone. Maybe it was Babsie's fence. Among other things, I need to prove that the antique table came from Babsie's house. I hope to confirm that and a little more when I meet with Beth Reiner. She's one of Babsie's stepdaughters. We're meeting at Panini's at two o'clock for a late lunch."

Ted looks at his watch. "So you're skipping out on Grant and me again? Choosing someone else for a lunch date. I'm beginning to get a complex."

"Don't worry. You'll be with me for lunch. That is if you consider your name on the credit card buying lunch as being there. This is a Welch HOA Management expense, right? I am investigating HOA thefts.

"But, before I abandon you, have you come up with a peace proposal for Lighthouse Cove?"

"Yeah, Dad, did the board make a decision?" Grant asks. "Are they still afraid someone might get a mob together and storm the offending property? Tear the lights down?"

"That's been my worry—that things might escalate beyond competing displays. So, I talked to Howie and Mike, asked if they'd consider changing their wording to 'Tis the season of LOVE'. The answer was 'yes' if the board showed some concern about neighbors harassing them. I talked the board into holding a February town hall with Reverend Pfaff as moderator. Much to my relief, Howie and Mike agreed to rework their display. Will it calm things down? Have to wait and see."

I applaud. "Here's to the peacemaker. See, all those years in the State Department paid off. You're equipped to negotiate neighborhood spats."

Ted stands. "Sarcasm from my fiancée. Come on, Grant. Let's go get something to eat. Frank, Robin—do either of you want to join us?"

Ted gets a "yes" from Robin and a "bring me back something" request from Frank.

"What are you going to do until two o'clock?" Ted asks.

"I'll deliver Maury's cigar box to Dr. Hardesty. I hope he has a clue what creatures the scales and fur came from. I'll also ask about his competitor, Dr. Perry McMahan, the veterinarian who visits Stillwater Cove at least twice a month. Dr. Hardesty probably knows if McMahan treats exotic pets."

After the lunch bunch leaves, I look for the background reports on Archer, Quentin, and Lisa. They should have come in yesterday. Since I never made it to the office, I haven't seen them yet.

I log onto my computer, and sure enough, they're there. The information for all three is surprisingly sketchy. Because Archer and Quentin both own their own companies and have been self-employed since they got out of college, there is zero information on prior employment. There are birth certificates and driver's licenses. College transcripts do verify their academic claims. No complaints against their companies. No records of arrests or dismissed charges. Just suspicious blanks.

Lisa Queensbury's backgrounder is equally surprising. I'd just added her name to be thorough. Didn't really expect any criminal activity to show up unless you consider outrageous conspicuous consumption to be a crime.

But, as it turns out, Lisa doesn't even have a birth certificate. The report notes she was born in rural Saskatchewan, Canada, and all public records were destroyed by a 1985 forest fire that wiped out an entire town. None of the records—birth and marriage certificates, taxes, school enrollment—had been digitized, they are totally lost.

I promise myself to study Lisa's history in-depth when I have time. Right now, I want to make another call before I drive to Ladys Island. I pull out my cell phone, then put it away. I grin, wondering if Ted might consider buying me a burner phone on the company's nickel. I don't want my cell number captured when I make this call. I use the company's landline.

A cheerful woman answers, "Dr. McMahan's Office, how can I help you?"

"Hi, my name is Margie Bonnet," I answer. "I just moved to the Beaufort area, and I want to establish a relationship with a veterinarian to make sure my parrots will get proper care when they need it. Archer Highsmith recommended Dr. McMahan."

"Oh, yes, Mr. Highsmith is such a nice man. It's too bad that his golden retriever, Whiskey, has so many problems. I've spoken with Mr. Highsmith many times, but we've never met. He can't ever seem to bring Whiskey in before I have to leave the office."

What a shocker.

"Would you like to make an appointment so Dr. McMahan can meet your sweet birds?"

"Yes, I would. But I'm so busy getting settled. You know how it is when you move to a new town. Today, I just wanted to ask where your office is located and Dr. McMahan's normal business hours. Also, if there's an emergency, is he available on weekends?"

If Dr. McMahan is dirty, I seriously doubt his receptionist has a clue. Otherwise, she'd be a little more cautious about volunteering all sorts of information to any stranger who happens to call.

By the time I say goodbye to Sherry (we quickly got on a first-name basis), I have driving directions to the Port Royal office. I know Dr. McMahan lives in a "cute" tan house with black shutters "right around the corner." That's so he can scoot to the office in minutes, if there's an off-hours emergency. I've also learned which days of the month the doc visits Stillwater Cove and that his Port Royal office closes at noon on Saturdays.

Now, I need to decide how to use the info. My poor parrot might have an attack at any time. What are his symptoms? I need to come up with some, plus a good name for my pet. Something more original than Polly. I got it, Tattler. And I hope the doc will tattle, too.

Chapter Fifty-Two

Kylee

Friday Noon, December 20

"Hi, Kylee," Dr. Hardesty's receptionist, Geena, welcomes me by name. "Your Mom called, and the doctor's expecting you. He's with a patient right now, but I can squeeze you in for a few minutes after that."

"Great," I say, and take a seat.

There are two women in the waiting room. One has a small dog curled at her feet. The pooch is clearly out of sorts. He didn't bother to raise his head when I arrived. Neither did his owner, who's engrossed in swiping through something on her smartphone.

The other waiting room occupant has placed a pet carrier on an adjacent chair. Inside the carrier, a peeved cat stalks back and forth. Ms. Kitty's back is arched, and she's hissing. Her owner looks almost as irritated. Probably because she was here before me, and I'm getting "squeezed in" ahead of her.

I understand her ire. I also know my mother has earned her preferential treatment. Mom is a long-time volunteer at a no-kill animal shelter just down the road, and she's also one of its generous donors. Dr. Hardesty, a fellow champion of the shelter, often donates his time to spay and neuter feral cats. Two of which now reside on Hullis Island and are named Mississippi and Keokuk.

Mom has always adopted black cats, knowing their bad-luck reputation makes them unpopular adoption choices.

Dr. Hardesty walks his latest patient, a poodle, and the owner, who's carrying the pooch, to the waiting room. "Remember, one pill in the morning, one at night. Hide them inside something Ruby likes or a pill pocket so she'll swallow and won't spit them out. Call me if she doesn't perk up in a couple of days."

Dr. Hardesty spots me. "Oh, Kylee, come on back. I hear you want some help with a mystery."

I open the cigar box, show the doc the contents, and ask his thoughts about identifying the creatures who once sported the scales and fur. I explain we've already identified another feather as belonging to a Hyacinth Macaw parrot. "I assume this red feather is from another endangered bird, but I have no idea how to go about identifying the fur and scales."

Dr. Hardesty nods. "Can I keep these for a while? I can't give you answers, but I know who to ask. Some folks who graduated vet school with me now teach at our alma mater, Cornell University. I'll talk to them. As far as the fur goes, a DNA study might be possible, but it would take time. The scales are a different proposition. To my eye, they look distinctive. If you suspect they come from an endangered animal, my colleagues may be able to do a visual match with threatened species. I'll send them pictures."

I thank Dr. Hardesty, then ask offhand if he's heard of Dr. McMahan.

He chuckles. "Yes, I hear he has lots of business. He cares for some exotic pets in addition to the usual. Don't know how he financed a practice right out of vet school. Maybe he has a rich uncle. He asked me to consider hiring him as an associate. I wasn't in the market. I won't bring someone on board until I'm ready to retire."

Dr. Hardesty pauses. "I hope Dr. McMahan's people skills have improved," he adds. "He never could seem to look me in the eye, and when we shook hands, I almost felt I needed a towel to dry off. He was so nervous, he jiggled, and the sweat poured off him in buckets."

I thank Dr. Hardesty again and leave. As I pass through the waiting room, the cat owner gives me the stink eye. I nod a greeting. "Beautiful cat," I comment.

* * *

I reach Panini's fifteen minutes early. It's one of my favorite restaurants on the Beaufort waterfront and an easy walk from the River Rat for take-out or eat-in dinners. All the staffers know me. I won't get hassled for occupying a two-top with just a cup of tea while I wait. As it turns out, Beth Reiner is early, too. I've barely taken my seat when she arrives.

Since we'd never met, we'd traded descriptions, including what we'd be wearing. My short, curly white hair and purple puffer coat are hard to miss. While Beth spotted me first, she was easy to recognize. My guess is we're about the same age, height, and weight. However, Beth's long hair is a glossy chestnut, and her coat is bright red.

I stand as she approaches, and we shake hands.

"Tell me what you're investigating and how dear old Babsie fits in," Beth begins. "Believe me, nothing could surprise my sister or me. We've been in shock ever since Dad married that witch without making even a cursory inquiry into her past. Marianne and I weren't opposed to Dad finding a new love. We were all for it. But Babsie? From the outset, we pegged her as a self-centered gold-digger."

The waitress arrives and we both order shrimp BLT paninis and iced tea. Of course, since I'm not a born-and-bred Southerner, I order my tea "unsweet."

I quickly offer Beth a summary of my investigation into the Hullis Island thefts and what I learned from my interviews with victims along with Anna, Suzie, Babsie and Ella.

"That clears up one mystery." Beth delivers the line like it's a guilty verdict. "One day, I surprised Babsie when I dropped by to retrieve some of Mom's porcelain pieces. The dining room table was littered with pages torn from local magazines and printouts of Facebook photos. Babsie tried to gather them up. She obviously didn't want me to see what she was up to. I figured it was some ridiculous research effort to stay up on the latest fashions. But the photos were of older women—not the demographic Babsie likes to emulate. Now I understand. She was using a big magnifying glass to assess the value of her victims' jewelry. I could see circles drawn around necklaces and rings."

I shake my head at Babsie's callous research. Then, I tell Beth about today's arrest and why and how I think Suzie's been set up.

"Can you describe the antique table?" she asks. "If so, I can tell you if it's one of the antiques Mom collected and where I last saw it in our house. And, yes, it is still our house. Ella was right. At least Dad had the good sense to set up the trust the way he did. He'd been married to Babsie for a year by then. Guess he realized his wife's only financial concerns centered on how quickly she could spend money. So, what did the table look like?"

I share Olivia's summary. Suzie picked up a pretty, mahogany gate-leg table from the curb in front of the Talbott house. She didn't even notice the table had a small drawer until Chief O'Rourke opened it and pulled out a gold coin.

"Damn her," Beth says. "It's our table all right, and you can bet your bottom dollar Babsie picked that lovely table for her scheme because she knows Marianne, and I love all of Mom's antiques. She had no call to take it to the curb."

It occurs to me that Beth and Marianne may have run their own background check on Babsie after she became their stepmother.

"Did you and your sister ever do a background check on Babsie? If so, what do you know about her life before she married your father?"

Beth rolls her eyes. "Yes, though we never told our father, Marianne and I hired a private detective to check her out. We only found sleaze, nothing criminal. Before marrying Dad, Babsie got her hooks into two older men she thought would be meal-tickets. I'm sure she hoped they'd kick the bucket quickly and leave her sitting pretty. One guy was smart enough to insist on a year-long engagement. He died before the year was up, and Babsie didn't get a dime.

"Her second entry into the marriage lottery was a bust, too. That patsy croaked on schedule, and his will left Babsie everything. But, as it turned out, he was a bigger swindler than she was. He'd been under investigation for a Ponzi scheme, and his estate was frozen. In the end, his victims, thank the Lord, stripped the estate bare before greedy Babsie got her claws into it."

I frown. "Did the woman do anything besides marry old men?"

Beth nods. "Yep, there was a record of one earlier marriage when she was in her thirties. This one was brief, too, but not because the husband fell off the perch. The two got a no-fault divorce. No salient details in the divorce records. It didn't look like any money changed hands. They were both poor and no kids."

I pause in my panini eating. "So, when she wasn't married, how did she put food on the table? Did she hold a job?"

"Only found records for one job. Babsie worked as a hostess at a Las Vegas club for five years. That's all she wrote in terms of official employment. What's even stranger is there's no proof Babsie was ever born. Supposedly, all the public records that could have confirmed her birth, her parents, and her schooling were destroyed in a fire."

The hairs on the back of my neck prickle.

"Don't tell me," I say. "Babsie was born in a small rural town in Saskatchewan, Canada."

Beth gives me a strange look. "Did you get your own background report on Babsie? Were you just trying to see if our information matched?"

I shake my head. "No. I just reviewed a background check on a Lisa Queensbury, another Beaufort County resident. That backgrounder claimed Lisa's birth records and family history went up in flames in some Podunk town in Saskatchewan, too. Quite the coincidence."

"Do you suppose they're sisters?" Beth asks.

"Possible," I answer. "Or it could mean they used the same forger to cobble together past histories that would survive background checks. Either way, it's very interesting and quite suspicious."

After lunch, Beth and I promise to stay in touch. As soon as I can get a picture of the antique table that held the gold coin, I'll send it so Beth can confirm the table came from the Talbott house. In turn, Beth will send me the private detective's full report she and her sister commissioned on Babsie.

Can't wait to compare it with Lisa's. I wonder if the reports show the same maiden name. When I read Lisa's, her maiden name seemed irrelevant. I can't remember it.

I pull my coat a little tighter as I walk to the River Rat. Josie is picking me up at six o'clock to chauffeur me to my bachelorette party. In theory, she's driving, so I don't have to worry about how much liquor I consume. In reality, I think Josie and Alysha fear I might be a no-show. I love my friends, but this feels weird and over the top. Who holds a bachelorette party for a woman who's crossed the mid-century mark?

In my cozy galley, I make a cup of hot tea. It's been a pretty day, but the wind is picking up, and the River Rat is rocking. I actually don't mind. Reminds me I'm on the water.

I check my cell voicemail and cross my fingers that Olivia Tucker has called to say she's sprung Suzie from the detention center. The poor woman must be in shock. Suzie's never had so much as a traffic ticket. Then, wham, at age seventy-seven, she's arrested, handcuffed, fingerprinted, searched, and interrogated by Nick Ibsen, who doesn't need any method acting lessons to play the role of bad cop.

I listen to Olivia's message and grin. Suzie has been released on her own recognizance. Olivia drove her home and shot lots of photos inside Suzie's house. She attached some of her snaps. Chief O'Rourke's crew made zero attempt to be neat. The house is a mess, but the photos support Suzie's claim. She's a recycler, not a hoarder. Mom and Frank's house is packed with more furniture and bric-a-brac than Suzie's is. I get angry thinking about Babsie's callous slander.

One of Olivia's photos shows a small, antique gate-leg table. I call Olivia. "Thanks so much for your fast response today," I begin. "I owe you."

Olivia chuckles. "Money, maybe, though Suzie insists she wants to pay my bill. But gratitude, no, you don't owe me a thing. It's a real high to champion an innocent client, especially one who's being railroaded. And you are one hundred percent right. That's Suzie."

"I looked at the pictures you sent," I add. "Is that gate-leg table the one that held the stolen coin?"

"Yes," Olivia says. "Suzie picked it up from the curb in front of the Talbott house this morning, first light. She'd had it all of an hour before Chief O'Rourke arrived on her doorstep."

"Okay, I'm sending the table photo to Beth Reiner, she's one of Babsie's stepdaughters. Beth says she can verify that the antique table is part of the first Mrs. Talbott's collection."

"That's helpful," Olivia says, "though it's not proof. If Babsie claims she put that table out six months ago, it may be hard to dispute her. Your chief and that despicable Nick Ibsen will both say, 'So what? Who cares who owned the table before it wound up in Suzie's house? Suzie hid the gold coin in its drawer.'"

I sigh. "How are we going to prove Babsie framed Suzie?"

"We'll figure out something. Hey, shouldn't you be getting ready for tonight's party?" Olivia asks. "It'll be fun. Can't wait."

I groan. "If you say so."

There's a second voicemail. "Hi, Kylee. It's Josie, and I'm not calling to hassle you about tonight's shindig. Check your emails. I sent you the complete Campbell autopsy report. When you get down in the weeds, it answers your question about pre-mortem and post-mortem bruising."

I fire up my personal laptop and print the report. I do a little scanning to find the word "bruise," then read with care. Here's my plain English translation of medical speak. The ME couldn't tell if the bruises on Maury's arms, legs, and chest (where he had cracked ribs) were caused by trauma before or during the accident. That's because a broken neck may or may not cause instantaneous death. Death can occur seconds or minutes after the initial blow to the spinal cord. In addition, even if death is instantaneous, blood may circulate for several seconds after the heart stops beating. That may be long enough for bruising to occur.

Crap. No help.

I suspect Archer had one of his henchmen question Maury before he broke his neck and killed him. Maybe his interrogator kicked him in the ribs. Maybe the bruises on his arms occurred when Maury struggled. One goon must have held him down so another thug could snap his neck.

The way I picture it, Maury died before his killer or killers faked the golf cart crash. They pointed his golf cart at a tree, revved the engine to full speed, placed weights on the gas pedal, and let her fly. Afterward, they positioned Maury's body in a plausible spot and removed the golf cart rigging. The murder was staged as an accident.

Frustration doesn't begin to describe how I feel.

I'm dead certain Maury was murdered, and equally confident Suzie is innocent. Do I have any indisputable evidence of either? No.

Maybe a little partying isn't such a bad idea. A few drinks sound mighty good. So does forgetting this quagmire for a while.

Chapter Fifty-Three

Kylee

Friday Night, December 20

Josie's right on time. "Hey, girl, ready to party?"

"Why not?" I answer. "Sitting around contemplating my belly button isn't helping to solve any mysteries, and I suspect new clues aren't going to drop from the sky."

"That's the attitude," Josie says.

"I'd still like to know where you're taking me. And who's going to be there besides you, Alysha, and Olivia?"

Josie chuckles. "Yeah, you always want to know everything. All will be revealed shortly. Sit back and relax. In fact, I brought along this sleep mask so you could take a little snooze. I bet you haven't been sleeping much. Humor me and put it on. I'll wake you when we get there."

* * *

"Wake up, we're here!"

Geez, I can't believe I actually fell asleep. I was exhausted. I slip off the sleep mask and try to blink myself awake. I haven't the faintest where we are. We're parked in front of a large, very dark house. Not a single light shows through its windows. No sound either, except for the pounding surf.

The ocean can't be more than fifty feet away.

I laugh. "Okay, I guess you did have trouble scaring up friends. Looks like even Alysha didn't make it. Is this a ghost tour or a girls' night out?"

"Just keep walking." Josie urges. "Climb the stairs. The front door's unlocked."

Inside, it's pitch black. I fumble for a light switch.

"Surprise!" the loud yell practically bursts my eardrums, and I'm blinded by the sudden bright light.

When I can finally see and hear, I start to cry. There must be fifty women. Many are Coasties, retired and active, who have served with me over the years. Robin is there, along with at least a dozen Welch HOA clients who've become fast friends. Martha and Mom head a contingent of older ladies from Hullis Island. Plus, there are friends from the downtown marina and sailing club.

Then, I spot the biggest surprise and really start blubbering. Dana steps out of the crowd. Dana, who shared peanut butter sandwiches with me in kindergarten at Garfield Elementary, and snuck smokes with me when we cruised Main Street in a 1947 Plymouth her dad fixed up. It ran fine. You just didn't want to look through the holes in the floor. Since our graduation from Keokuk, Iowa Senior High, I've only seen Dana once. But I recognized her instantly.

When we finish hugging, I notice my newest friends are here, too. Anna Whitner's arm is draped around Suzie Bucknell's shoulders, and Olivia, right beside them, gives me a two-thumbs-up salute.

The evening goes by in a blur. There's a ton of finger food, and Julie, the bartender, will concoct any drink you choose. I request a frozen pina colada. It's my go-to celebration drink, even when it's cold outside. The first one tastes wonderful. I soon stop by for number two.

A DJ plays music curated from my youth. We sing at the top of our lungs, dance, and tell stories. I introduce Dana to my newer friends. I can't believe Dana's flying out at six a.m.

"Have to," she says. "My husband, two sons, and their families are waiting for me in Puerto Vallarta. A two-week holiday. I was lucky to find a way to make Charleston a stopover."

Mom joins Dana and me. "I'm so glad I stayed in touch with Dana's folks so I could track her down for this reunion."

Dana laughs. "I keep meaning to ask how all of you Keokuk, Iowa, folks wound up in Beaufort County, South Carolina."

"Hayse and I retired to Hullis Island," Mom explains. "In part, because Kylee was stationed nearby with the Coast Guard, and we figured we'd see her more often. Then, Ted visited Hayse and me, liked the area, and saw a business opportunity once he retired from the State Department. Plus, Ted's son, Grant, hoped to attend the Citadel in Charleston."

I smile. "Very fortunate decisions. Otherwise, we wouldn't be having this party, and I wouldn't be marrying Ted on Christmas Eve."

Before the evening ends, I find Josie and Alysha and give them huge hugs.

"Thank you so much. This is more than I ever expected. I love you guys."

I'm happy and exhausted when Josie drops me back at the River Rat. It's three o'clock in the morning. I'd better sleep fast. I promised Ted and Grant I'd meet them at nine o'clock for breakfast. Maury's funeral service starts at eleven a.m. We need to arrive at the church around ten. Ted and Grant will be ushering, and I'm helping Mom prepare the luncheon for mourners after the service.

I'm glad there will be no graveside service. Velma has arranged for Maury to be buried in their Minnesota hometown.

At funerals, I'm usually able to hold myself together while I'm in the church. But there's something about seeing a loved one lowered into a grave that makes me go from silent tears to sobbing. I'll never forget my little brother's graveside service. The bagpipes and the ceremonial salute by his fellow firefighters totally did me in.

Chapter Fifty-Four

Kylee

Saturday 9 a.m., December 21

"Somebody had a good time last night," Ted teases before giving me a kiss. "Have to admit you don't look exactly bright-eyed and bushy-tailed."

My response is a yawn. "More like bleak-eyed and tucked-tail, but I'm too tired to run. Didn't get home until three o'clock. I could say I'm sorry you weren't there, but I'd be lying. It was a fantastic girls' night out, with the 'girls' ranging in age from Mimi to Mom. And plenty of surprises.

"You remember Dana, my oldest friend. She dropped by between planes. Said she had to make sure you had improved over the pest she remembered from grade school. Suzie Bucknell was another surprise guest. Thanks to Olivia, Suzie arrived without handcuffs or an ankle monitor."

I see—and smell—that Grant's frying bacon again. "Hey, Grant, you're spoiling your dad and me. But I'm not complaining."

"I cooked, but it's serve-yourself," Grant says. "Scrambled eggs and bacon on the stove. Toast just popped up. Get your own coffee. We're fresh out of tomato juice, and I'm not offering any hangover remedies."

I laugh. "Not needed. I quit with the alcohol after two delicious pina coladas. I knew I had to get up early, and I didn't want to compound my lack of sleep with a headache."

We help ourselves and take our usual seats at the dining room table.

"You didn't call last night," Ted says. "Not complaining. I know Josie carted you away at six o'clock, but I'm curious about what you learned yesterday."

I fill Ted and Grant in on my Babsie discoveries, starting with her anger at being cut off from the Talbott money trough. I end with the Lisa Queensbury and Babsie Talbott background overlap.

"That's some coincidence, Lisa and Babsie being born in the same dinky town in wild west Canada," Ted says. "I've met both women. I wouldn't be surprised to learn they're sisters. Same coloring, snub noses, and similar, uh, top-heavy build on thin chassis."

Grant laughs. "Think Dad's saying they have big boobs despite being skinny."

I chuckle. "Your dad's right. I can't wait to compare their backgrounds in detail. Wonder if they claim the same parents. If they are sisters, they certainly haven't broadcast the fact. Wonder why?"

Grant waves a strip of bacon that's about to reach his mouth.

"I have news, too. The Feathered Friends Clinic got back to Mimi's dad. The parrot wasn't microchipped, and the vets estimate it had been dead at least seventy-two hours before Carl delivered it to them Friday afternoon. They agreed the bird's feathers had been cleaned and said the parrot didn't naturally expire in the condition it was found. A necropsy—an autopsy for animals—indicated the bird suffered the equivalent of a human heatstroke. That pointed to prolonged confinement in a hot space."

Ted shakes his head. "The Stillwater Cove situation is sounding worse by the minute. I always thought Archer and Quentin couldn't be trusted. Now I wonder if Lisa is neck-deep in some illegal activity, too."

We take our dirty dishes to the kitchen and put them in the dishwasher. I thank Grant once again for making breakfast. We all tarry in the kitchen. None of us appears eager to leave the house. Not to attend a funeral.

Ted puts an arm around Grant. "Let's go, son." And we leave. Grant and Ted in dark suits, white shirts and subdued ties, me in a black dress that has seen too much wear on somber occasions.

* * *

The Carteret Street Methodist Church may not be one of Beaufort's oldest churches, but it has been around for almost a century and a half. I find its stained-glass windows awe-inspiring. Sun streams through them as the beautiful tributes begin. At too many funerals, the officiating clergymen just dust off old sermonettes and make no attempt to talk about the deceased. That's not true of Reverend Pfaff. He speaks sorrowfully about Maury Campbell and his virtues, reminding the congregation of all the ways in which Maury will be missed—as a wonderful husband, father, and friend. The tears start in earnest when the choir sings and Suzie's rich alto soars.

Mom and I are seated with the ushers—Ted, Grant, and Frank. We chose to sit in the rear to quickly reach fellowship hall and do final buffet prep while the mourners filed out of the sanctuary. We know most will stop to speak to Velma and Vince. We expect half of the packed church to stay for the luncheon.

* * *

I'm replenishing the sliced ham on the buffet when Anna Whitner approaches. I didn't know Anna was a friend of the Campbells, but I'm not surprised. Anyone who lives in Beaufort County for more than ten minutes seems to have a tie to everyone I know.

"Kylee, I'd like you to meet my husband, Jim Whitner," Anna says. "The Campbells have been customers at Jim's bank for more than twenty years."

"Maury was a wonderful man," Jim comments. "Still can't believe he's gone. Just over a week ago, he was in my office at the bank, and we were chatting and laughing. Maury dropped in the Friday before he died."

The Whitners move on down the buffet line. As soon as everyone's fed, I want to talk more with Jim Whitner. I'd like to know if Maury's bank visit could have any relationship to his Stillwater Cove suspicions.

When everyone has gone through the line, I fill my own plate. Ted and Grant are seated at a table for eight, and an empty chair undoubtedly has my name on it. However, I've zeroed in on another empty seat. The one next to Jim Whitner. I stop by Ted's table long enough to whisper, "I need to talk with a banker. Explain later."

I reach the Whitner table and ask if the empty seat is taken. Jim and Anna immediately invite me to sit down.

Anna starts the conversation by telling Jim how I recruited Olivia Tucker to represent Suzie Bucknell and make sure she spent no time in jail.

"Seeing Suzie singing in the choir today was a bright spot in a sad day," I say. "I'm so glad you and Olivia brought her to the party last night, Anna. Today, however, I need to focus on another investigation, and you may be able to help me, Jim."

The banker looks startled as I explain my belief that Maury Campbell suspected a smuggling operation was underway at Stillwater Cove. I lower my voice. While the others seated at our table seem engrossed in their own conversations, I don't want to be the one starting wild rumors at a funeral.

"That explains it," Jim confides. "The Campbells have several personal accounts with our bank, and, for years, we handled Maury's business accounts, too. But that isn't why he came to see me. Maury asked me to explain how banks prepare money for shipment. He wanted to know how we band different denominations—twenties, fifties, and hundreds—and if we ever shrink-wrap them. He also asked if just anyone off the street could buy the color-coded bands, especially the mustard-colored ones, for hundred-dollar bills."

I interrupt. "I'm sorry, Jim, but I'm as clueless as Maury was. How do banks prepare bills for shipment?"

"The denomination doesn't matter," Jim explains. "Bankers call the bands we wrap around bills straps. There are always exactly one hundred banknotes in every strap. So, for example, a strap of twenty-dollar bills would be worth two thousand dollars, while a strap of hundred-dollar bills would be worth ten thousand dollars.

"Ten currency straps make up a bundle. So, a bundle of hundred-dollar bills would be worth one hundred thousand dollars."

I hold up my hand again to pose a question. "You say Maury specifically mentioned mustard-colored bands. Tell me about the color coding."

Jim nods. "The American Bankers Association specifies different color codes to help people quickly count stacks of currency in, say, a vault. The straps used on twenties are violet, and the ones used on hundred-dollar bills are a mustard color. Anyone can buy these straps off the internet. My guess is a multi-denomination currency pack of three hundred straps would cost just over ten dollars."

I nod my understanding. "And what about shrink-wrapping?"

Jim raises an eyebrow. "You seem to be asking the same things Maury asked. I told him ten-strap and larger bundles are often shrink-wrapped. That forces the air out so they can be packed in smaller spaces. It works like those bags advertised on TV to vacuum-pack clothes so you can cram more in a closet or suitcase."

I grin. "Maybe I've seen too many movies like The Sting where only the top bills in a strap are real, and dummies have been placed beneath. How would a bank on the receiving end of a money transfer know it was getting real bills with no phonies stuck in the middle?"

"Each denomination of real US currency has a unique weight due to the special paper and inks," he explains. "The straps are weighed against a counterweight equal to the weight of legit notes."

Jim's face clouds. "Do you think Maury stumbled on a smuggling operation, and that got him killed?" Jim's voice is a hoarse whisper. No doubt to keep his sudden insights private. Maury's funeral service, filled with mourners, is not the time or place to speculate out loud.

"It's possible," I keep my voice just above a whisper, even though all our tablemates have finished their meals and moved away. "But it could be coincidence. The smugglers, if they exist, may not have known Maury suspected them. The golf cart crash could have been an accident. We've yet to discover real proof, but believe me, I'll keep on trying."

Anna and Jim both nod. "Let us know if there's any way we can help."

I check with Mom to see if she needs another pair of hands to clean up and package the unused food.

"No," she says. "Reverend Pfaff has an arrangement with a soup kitchen and homeless shelter. They come and take everything that isn't eaten to supplement evening meals."

I catch up with Ted and Grant. "You deserted us again," Ted says. "Can I expect this to continue after we get married?"

"Absolutely," I reply. "When you can't provide the clues I need."

I tell them all about Maury's conversation with the banker. "I think you were absolutely right, Grant. Archer's yacht is being used to export cash and import endangered species. I need to convince Alysha and the Coast Guard to search Archer's yacht."

"No," Ted says. "You need to convince the Coast Guard to search his yacht when he sails for the Bahamas and not before. Odds are he waits until the last minute to load illegal cargo. At least that's what I'd do."

"Too bad I can't think of a single piece of evidence Josie can use to get a warrant to search the maintenance barn. I'll bet that's where they stash the money until it can be loaded."

When we leave the church, Ted drives straight home. I kiss him goodbye before I head to my car. No point going inside just to come back down the stairs and drive away.

"We'll see you tomorrow for Sunday brunch at Hullis Island, right?" Ted asks. "No skipping the meeting with my father."

"I'll be there," I promise. "I just have a lot of things to do today and tonight, including packing for our honeymoon."

Ted and I are both nervous about his dad's visit. After Ted went off to college, Otis Welch joined what Mom always called the "holy roller" congregation for their reputation of rocking and rolling if they believed they'd been touched by the Holy Ghost. Otis believes women were put on earth to have babies and shouldn't work outside the home. Afraid I don't fit that mold.

I'm counting on the fact that Otis accepted our wedding invitation to mean he's accepting me as his daughter-in-law.

* * *

233

As soon as I'm onboard the River Rat, I call Alysha, and, unfortunately, get her voicemail. I leave a message, sharing what I learned from the banker. "You don't want to believe Archer is dirty, but Maury uncovered signs that cash was being bundled and readied for transport," I conclude. "I hope this is enough to prompt a search of Wavedancer when she leaves port."

Since I can't think of anything else I can do on the investigations, I decide to pack. For most people, one of the drawbacks of living on a boat is the lack of closet space. Luckily, I'm no clothes horse. My wardrobe is simple and spare.

As I peer into my closet, I accept that it may be a little too spare for a honeymoon. True, we'll spend—I hope—most of our time in bed or in the water. My birthday suit and a couple of swimsuits meet dress requirements for those activities.

However, Ted also has arranged special dinners during our visit. He has seen me wear my one black dress to multiple funerals. Not a good memory jogger for a honeymoon. I should have at least a couple sexy, colorful summer dresses plus a pair of dress sandals to wear with them. Those items aren't hiding in my closet, and I can't imagine finding them in any Beaufort County store at Christmas time.

Sigh. No time to shop online. Hope I can find something I like in the Caymans. My lackluster closet does simplify packing. I have plenty of extra room in my suitcase to bring back any island finds.

Thinking about my suitcase makes me wonder how Archer Highsmith would hide huge amounts of cash on his yacht. Based on Maury's conversation with the banker, Archer's minions—probably security guards—use regular bank straps to bundle cash. They also employ some sort of shrink-wrap machine to vacuum-pack multiple straps in plastic.

But where would Archer hide see-through plastic bundles of cash on Wavedancer? He couldn't risk them sitting in plain sight. Transporting endangered species is even more problematic. Where does he hide his cargo?

While Archer appears to be on great terms with the Coast Guard, his yacht could suffer storm damage or mechanical problems and require assistance.

CHAPTER FIFTY-FOUR

There must be secret compartments.

I'm super frustrated.

I need to stop endlessly revisiting the same roadblocks. Do something useful.

I spend the next couple of hours handling boat maintenance chores I've neglected. I feel good about the River Rat. She's fine to sit here while I honeymoon. Come tomorrow, I'll have zero time to spend on her.

I'll also have zero time to try and uncover something—anything—Alysha can use to guarantee a Coast Guard search of Archer's yacht. And I strongly suspect the improving Atlantic weather means Archer's Wavedancer will leave Monday with a boatload of cash. The countdown is now a matter of hours.

I hate thinking a crime is in progress and there's no way to stop it. I can't storm the Stillwater Cove gates and break into the maintenance barn. I'd be arrested, and Ted would not be happy about his fiancée being in the pokey on our wedding day.

There is one loose end. That vet. Dr. Perry McMahan.

Based on Dr. Hardesty's description, the man is a jangling bundle of nerves when he's around humans. Maybe I can surprise him.

I need him alone, without Stillwater Cove directors or security goons around to tell him what to say and do. Then maybe he can be tricked into giving away some tidbit of information. Something, anything I can use to get the authorities to act.

Time's running out. What have I got to lose?

Chapter Fifty-Five

Kylee

Saturday 5:30 p.m., December 21

I drive to Dr. Perry McMahan's veterinary clinic. Yep, it's closed. No lights, and the doc isn't in. No car in the small graveled parking lot out front. Dr. McMahan's home address isn't listed in any online search engine. Maybe he just bought it, or perhaps he's renting or leasing.

Time to start my neighborhood crawl, looking for what the McMahan's receptionist considers a "cute" little tan house with black shutters. It's dusk, but I can still distinguish house colors. I cross my fingers, only one house fits her description.

The veterinarian's office is in a mixed residential-commercial neighborhood. As the traffic in this area increased, several homeowners sold out to lawyers, insurance agents, and other professionals looking for affordable office space. But there are also homeowner holdouts reluctant to move.

My first two-block saunter finds brick houses with black shutters and dirty-beige, aluminum-sided homes with green or burgundy shutters. No match.

I strike gold on my second two-block foray. A small one-story house with beige siding and black shutters. A station wagon is parked in the driveway. The house doesn't have a garage.

There's no name out front, just a house address. But the cute mailbox seems appropriate for a vet. It's painted to look like an orange tabby cat with black stripes and a Cheshire grin. I'm hoping anyone who owns an attack dog—the doc included—would not install a kitschy cat mailbox.

Then I recall that McMahan is the veterinarian of choice for owners of exotic pets and wonder if he has his own menagerie of poisonous frogs, pythons, and black widow spiders.

There are lights on in the front of the house. Someone's home. I pull in at the curb and turn off the car. I take a deep breath and switch on the small, handy-dandy digital recorder inside my purse. From past use, I know it can pick up and record conversations even when it's zipped inside a purse pocket and out of sight.

I walk to the front door. No sign of a video doorbell. The doc probably invests plenty in security for his veterinary office—where he stores all manner of drugs—and doesn't feel the need to worry about home safeguards.

He may feel differently after this evening's home invasion.

I don't actually see a doorbell, so I knock. I can make out voices, but they sound as if they're coming from a TV or radio and not a live, in-person conversation. Hope I'm right. I should have considered the possibility Archer or Quentin might be here. They would not react kindly to my visit.

Seeing the doc's driveway only held one vehicle—a station wagon—I took that to mean he had no visitors. But I didn't scan the entire block. I turn and do a one-eighty, considering the silhouettes of all the vehicles parked within sight. A few pickups and two homely compacts. Relief. Not a single vehicle I can imagine Archer or Quentin choosing to drive.

I knock again. Louder this time. I hear footsteps, not light. There's heavy breathing on the other side of the door, but it doesn't open.

"Doctor McMahan?" I call. "Could I speak to you for a few minutes? It's about a parrot. I called your office yesterday. They said you treat parrots."

The door opens halfway.

Based on Dr. Hardesty's description of the man who wanted to join his veterinarian practice, I'm somewhat prepared for Dr. McMahan's appearance. But not totally.

He's huge. My guess is over six feet tall and at least four feet wide. Three hundred pounds. Maybe more. He's wearing a flannel shirt with farmer-style bib overalls. I haven't seen many of those since I left Iowa. His thick, curly blonde hair is the most normal thing about his appearance. Boat-size moccasins cover his sockless feet. Doesn't look as if he has immediate plans to leave his house. Not in this weather.

With his brow overhang and chunky cheeks, the doc's eyes are deeply recessed. I can't tell their color. But I do see they're jerking hither and yon, moving from me, to the outdoors, and back to his living room. Trying to assess an escape route? Just my presence makes him nervous. I'm optimistic I can get him flustered enough to spill something meaningful.

"What about a parrot?" he asks. "I didn't get a call from our emergency paging service."

He pauses. "Wait. Why are you here, at my house?"

I smile. "If I can come in for a minute, I can explain. I just have a few questions about a parrot."

He shuffles, shifting weight from one foot to the other like he has to pee.

"Please," I add. "I only need a few minutes of your time."

The doc opens the door a snitch wider, and a ginormous tabby cat slinks past McMahan's moccasins to investigate me. I stoop to pet him. Based on the tabby's size, I figure it's definitely a him.

"Hello, there, you're a friendly kitty. What's your name?"

"Sam," the doc answers automatically.

Sam's purr could rival a V-8 engine.

"Is your parrot with you?" McMahan asks. "Is this an emergency?"

"No," I answer honestly. "I understand you're an expert in treating parrots, and I just have a few questions. I promise it will only take a few minutes."

I insinuate myself further inside the house by moving forward while I pet Sam. The doc takes a step back and doesn't try to stop my progress.

"Could we sit down?" I nod toward the living room, where a big-guy recliner is positioned in front of a large-screen TV. I was right. The voices are coming from the TV. The doc was watching a football game.

"Only for a minute." He ambles toward the TV. McMahan turns down the volume, but doesn't shut off the game. A sign he really believes he'll be rid of me in minutes. I sit on a couch cattycorner from his recliner. All the furniture is made for really big people. I sit forward on the cushion. The only position that allows my feet to touch the floor.

"Some friends and I were at Stillwater Cove this past Thursday," I begin. "We were part of a search party looking for an endangered Hyacinth Macaw parrot. Unfortunately, we found it. Dead."

I watch him closely as I speak. His breathing is audible. His meaty fingers curl around the arms of his recliner. It looks like he has the chair in a death grip.

"One of my friends took the parrot's body to the Feathered Friends Clinic. The vets there said someone gussied up the parrot after it died, trying to make it look more presentable before it was dumped for us to find. We know the parrot was smuggled into the country. Do you suppose the smugglers use the same hidden compartments for money laundering and transporting animals? Did the parrot spend too much time hidden away? Did it suffocate? Is that what killed it?"

The doc shakes his head, rapidly rotating it as far as his thick neck allows. "Why are you asking me about some dead parrot? How would I know what happened to it?"

"I heard you were one of the few Lowcountry vets who treats parrots. In fact, I heard treating exotic pets is your specialty."

"I don't know what you're talking about," he sputters. "Parrots aren't exotic pets."

"Do you know Archer Highsmith?"

"I don't believe so. No, that name doesn't sound familiar. I'd like you to leave now."

"Really, I'm puzzled. You don't know Archer Highsmith? He's the guy who signs your paychecks for treating the exotic pets that arrive every so often at Stillwater Cove."

The vet stands. His whole body is trembling. His complexion is splotchy with patches colored a deep red. I'm afraid he'll have a heart attack. Do I dare push him further?

"You need to leave," he growls.

"But I haven't even introduced myself. I'm Kylee Kane. I'll bet Archer has mentioned me. You've heard my name, right? Maybe in the context of breaking the necks of busybodies like Maury Campbell?"

McMahan's face now has a polka-dot quality. The red splotches appear even more startling now that his face's fleshy canvas is a ghostly white.

"Get out!" he shouts.

"Are you sure? I know you're not the one laundering money and smuggling endangered species into the country. That's Archer Highsmith. He's using you. He needs a veterinarian to treat animals, keep them healthy for illegal buyers. I bet if you told the authorities what you know, you'd get a sweetheart deal. You haven't really done anything wrong. Surely, caring for animals isn't a crime. In exchange for your testimony, I bet you'd go scot-free."

The doc rocks forward, and his chair propels him upright. He makes a beeline for me. His monster size makes his surprisingly fast approach look all the more threatening.

Time to go. I jump up, sling my purse over my shoulder.

Should I pull out my Glock?

No, not enough time. It would only frighten him more. People do foolish things when they're scared. The doc seems more frightened than angry.

I try to dodge past him, but his bulk makes it easy for him to block my feints.

"Hey, you want me to leave, I'm leaving. I just asked some questions. You didn't want to answer. Fine. Nothing to get excited about."

The doc's ham-sized fist encircles my right arm. It tightens like a blood pressure cuff that's gone berserk. God, I hope he's throwing me out of the house.

No such luck.

He drags me down a hall. I kick, and my shoe catches one of his tree-stump legs. He doesn't flinch. Doesn't even grunt in protest.

We're inside his home office. Computer, printer. A desk covered with papers and a black satchel. The doc pins me against the wall with his broad backside. My arms are free. I try to reach around him. Scratch at his eyes.

Crap. He's too wide. I can't reach any vulnerable areas.

"Come on," I cajole. "My fiancé knows I'm here. Let me leave. I'll go quietly. You can get back to your football game."

I can't see what he's doing. All I hear is his labored, staccato breathing. Or is it mine?

Can I get to my Glock? My over-the-shoulder purse hangs near my left hip. Can I suck in my stomach enough to wiggle my right hand between our bodies…open the bag…get the gun. I exhale. Here goes.

When he suddenly moves, and I'm no longer pinned, I'm out of air and unbalanced by his abrupt shift. I'm still wobbly when the doc pivots and slings one of his massive arms across my body. I'm imprisoned. I watch helplessly as his free hand brings a very large needle toward my arm.

"This will sting a little," he says.

Really, he's shooting some scary crap into me, and he's telling me it won't hurt? Much.

Chapter Fifty-Six

Archer

Saturday 6:30 p.m., December 21

I look down at Kylee laid out on the vet's living room couch, seemingly casket-ready. Her clothes are demurely arranged. Interlaced hands fold over her stomach. Of course, if she were in a casket, her wrists and ankles wouldn't be tightly taped. Perry didn't use duct tape. This stuff is blue and has a rough exterior texture. It's wider than duct tape, too. I assume Perry uses it to immobilize the limbs of animals after he's operated on them.

Kylee's death-bed appearance is also spoiled by her brown eyes. The eyes roam, and every so often, one of her fingers or a muscle in her jaw twitches.

"What did you give her?"

Perry is a blubbering mess. I'm sorely tempted to use Kylee's gun—in plain sight, since I dumped her purse—to kill Perry. Then I could torch the house. Let them go up in smoke together. The authorities would have fun sorting through the ashes to figure out what happened.

Perry stifles his sobs long enough to answer my question. "I dragged her to my office and opened the satchel I take on emergency calls. I keep vials of a sedative and muscle relaxer inside. I filled a syringe with double what I'd give a Great Dane and injected her. She's conscious, but I imagine her thinking is muddled. She can't grasp what's happening."

"How long will she be like this?"

Perry shrugs. "I'm not sure. I looked up what happens if a dose is accidentally given to a person. I gave her a big dose because she's bigger than a dog. Best guess is she'll start to come out of it in a couple hours, but she'll be real groggy and uncoordinated. Since I was unsure how long it would be before she could move, I used the tape to keep her still."

"Any idea how long this drug will stay in her bloodstream?"

I don't want her to die until the drug is undetectable. I wish Perry had forced opioids down her throat. It would be hard, but not impossible, to sell Kylee as an accidental overdose victim.

"I know what you're thinking," Perry stammers. "You're talking about killing her and want to know if an autopsy will find the sedative in her bloodstream. I told you I won't kill people.

"Can't you just keep her tied up and take her to Andros with you?" he pleads. "You could let her go there. She couldn't prove anything. You could claim she was a stow-away. You had no idea she was on your yacht."

I glare at Perry. "No. That won't work. You killed Kylee when you doped her up. All you had to do was kick her out of your house. I listened to the recording. The woman was fishing. She had no evidence, and you didn't confirm a thing.

"What did you think would happen after you drugged her? You'd just say, 'Sorry, my bad, I didn't mean to temporarily turn you into a vegetable, the needle just slipped. Of course, we have to kill her."

Perry sobs and drops into his recliner.

"Do something useful," I order, "look up the drug you gave her and find out if it's part of an ordinary autopsy tox screen."

I dismiss Perry, and study the contents of Kylee's purse, spread out on a nearby coffee table. There's a wallet, a cell phone, a digital recorder, her Glock, and keys to her car and her boat.

I pick up Kylee's cell phone. It's off. She must not have wanted phone calls to interrupt her badgering of stupid Perry. I wonder if the phone's password protected? My guess is no. She'd want to be able to open the phone quickly. A thumbprint? Facial recognition?

I start the phone and press one of Kylee's thumbs to the screen. Nope. I aim the phone at her face. Bingo. It unlocks. Glad Perry didn't tape her mouth shut. That would have played havoc with the phone's facial recognition.

I look at incoming text messages. None recent.

I hear Perry's labored breathing and look up. "It's not part of an ordinary tox screen," he says. "It wouldn't be ordered unless there was a reason to suspect it."

"Good," I say and turn back to Kylee's phone. Time to check her voicemails. There are three. I play the first.

"Hi, Kylee. It's Beth Reiner. Just wanted to let you know I emailed you and attached that detective's report on Babsie. Let me know you got it. I'm eager to hear how it compares with your backgrounder on that Queensbury woman. I'm certain their shared Saskatchewan ID dodge is no coincidence."

Dammit. Looks like Lisa will soon be outed as Babsie's sister. That will bring her usefulness as a Stillwater Cove director to an end. Mick had the goods on Lisa before he arranged for Quentin and I to become Stillwater Cove owners. Lisa and Babsie were grifters. Both thought their latest marriages would deliver pots of gold. They didn't account for smart stepkids.

I move ahead. "Got your voicemail," the woman begins. I recognize Alysha's sexy voice. "I agree. Maury's talk with that banker gives more credence to Archer Highsmith's possible involvement in money laundering. I'll talk to the powers that be. It may not be enough to get my superiors to search Archer's yacht when it leaves port. Will keep you posted."

Dammit to hell.

The risk of a Coast Guard search may not be imminent, but it has notched up.

Thanks, Kylee. Should have killed you sooner. What kind of misery will the last voicemail bring?

"Hello, Ms. Kane," a deep male voice says, "this is Wally from Wally's Marine Repair. That electrical panel is good to go. Shouldn't have any worries about the bilge pump either."

CHAPTER FIFTY-SIX

Thank God. A message with promise. It gives me an idea.

I'll need help. Quentin and Jack, time for you to earn your keep. I hope Quentin paid attention to those lessons I gave him when he bought his cabin cruiser. He'll need them.

And Perry. Maybe I should give him a sedative. Kylee needs to stay in the doc's care a bit longer.

"Why don't you turn on the TV, Perry? We're just going to sit back and relax."

Chapter Fifty-Seven

Archer

Saturday 8 p.m., December 21

I force Perry to give Kylee a second sedative dose. His hands shake as he injects the drug.

"I'm giving her half the previous dose. I'm afraid any more will kill her." He glares at me. "You don't want her dead yet, right?"

"No, I need her to stay alive," I say. "She needs to drown. Will this dose keep her docile for a few hours?"

"Yeah, docile or comatose."

What am I going to do with Perry? I can't trust him anymore.

Next month's problem.

I leave my car at Perry's and drive Kylee's Mustang to the Downtown Beaufort Marina. Jack is sending a couple men to the doc's house to retrieve my car.

I don't want Perry, that monster-sized helping of Jell-O, to drive my Vet. He'd wreck it en route to the Beaufort bridge. That is if Perry could actually squeeze behind the wheel—a big if.

I park as close as I can to the docks. Getting Kylee from the parking lot to her boat won't be easy. She can't walk. Even if she could, I wouldn't risk freeing her feet. One of Kylee's kicks left a mega bruise on Perry's calf. One of the many physical and mental horrors he whined about before falling completely to pieces. What an idiot.

I leave Kylee in the Mustang's trunk and walk to her sailboat. While she remains in la-la land, I did apply some of Perry's sticky surgical tape over her mouth. I don't want her screaming bloody murder if she comes around.

Putting Kylee in a fireman's carry for the trek to her boat isn't an option. I'd be huffing and puffing, and I doubt bystanders would buy that I'm helping an inebriated friend. Especially if her mouth, wrists, and feet are taped.

I'm hoping Kylee uses a wheeled cart to bring supplies onboard. If so, I can dump her inside and wheel her to the boat. No risk of a hernia or of looking like a kidnapper.

What luck. Her cart is in plain sight. No need to search. I check the boats in nearby slips to see if anyone's above deck or walking on a nearby pier. Thank heaven none of the marina occupants have strung Christmas lights on their boats. Transients aren't likely to cart seasonal crap on a holiday cruise.

The nearest boats are totally dark. No signs of life. I hope their owners are out for leisurely dinners and won't return until Kylee's stored below deck.

I heave Kylee into her container, which sort of looks like a laundry hamper. If she's attempting to struggle, her muscles aren't cooperating. What tiny movements I see look like uncoordinated twitches. Do her eyes seem a bit more focused? If her mental haze is lifting, she must be furious her brain no longer commands her body.

Though I doubt she can process anything I say, I bend down and whisper in Kylee's ear, "Whew, wish you'd decided to diet a bit for a wedding dress. You're not exactly a featherweight."

I am enjoying myself. This woman has caused me so much grief.

Once I dump Kylee below deck, I set about familiarizing myself with her Island Packet sailboat. I've sailed one before, but it's been years. While I have time, I need to figure out exactly how to disable the electrical panel and disconnect the bilge pump. I also need to switch off the River Rat's transponder.

I don't want surprises once we start on our evening cruise. No sails. This isn't the time. Besides, if Kylee were taking a short shake-down cruise to make sure all her boat repairs were good, she'd motor. There's virtually no wind, and it's hard to tack in the Beaufort River's narrower confines.

I check the time. Too early to leave. I want to rendezvous with Quentin and Jack at eleven. By then, most boats should be snug in their slips. Cold December nights this close to Christmas aren't very tempting for moonlight sails. Especially since there is no moon tonight.

What am I going to do for the next couple hours? I realize I'm hungry. The Chatty Cathy at the marina said Kylee brought groceries aboard the other day. Let's see what she's got in her cupboards and refrigerator. I step over Kylee on the cabin floor.

"Are you hungry? Guess not."

The cupboard is pretty bare, with the exception of a bag of Fritos and an unopened container of cheese dip. The refrigerator yields fresh fruit and a six-pack of Guinness beer. The freezer has three varieties of Lean Cuisine.

"A little schizophrenic in our diet, aren't we? I'm glad Lean Cuisine counters your Frito intake. Otherwise, I'd have more trouble carting you around."

I munch on Fritos and cheese dip while I nuke a Lean Cuisine and drink one of her dark beers. When the frozen dinner's ready, I pick up a paperback by Tami Hoag. A bookmark in the middle of the mystery tells me Kylee's only halfway through it. Too bad she'll never know who done it. I eat, read, and periodically check my watch.

Ten o'clock. Time to go topside. Almost no wind. Heavy cloud cover and a new moon make the Beaufort River look like ink. Ink that seems to absorb all the glitter of the Christmas lights strung on boats and private docks along the shore.

I untie the bumpers and slowly leave the slip. My running lights are on. Not about to get stopped for a stupid navigational violation.

Once I'm in the main channel, I call Quentin. "Are you ready?"

"Yeah, no problem. I brought Jack along like you said. GPS coordinates are programmed in. We'll be there ahead of you, waiting. You're in an Island Packet sailboat with River Rat painted on the stern, right?"

Quentin chuckles. "Little chance we'll get you mixed up with some other sailboat. Of course, I don't expect to see any boat traffic tonight."

"I'm counting on it," I reply. "Should be at our rendezvous in half an hour."

I hear no noise from below deck and take that as a good sign. Kylee's doped and tied up. She shouldn't give me any trouble. At least not until we untie her so she can go down with the ship. She is a U.S. Coast Guard Captain, after all. Isn't that what they're supposed to do?

The GPS location I gave Quentin is one I studiously avoid when piloting Wavedancer. Along this small section of Port Royal Sound, the water's too shallow for my yacht. But Quentin's and Kylee's boats can both maneuver in water as shallow as five feet.

I'll anchor Kylee's boat beside Quentin's while we take the last-minute steps to scuttle the River Rat. Quentin is towing one of the Wavedancer's lifeboats to our rendezvous. I need it for my final exit from the River Rat. Sorry, Kylee, there's no lifeboat for you.

Chapter Fifty-Eight

Kylee

Saturday 10:30 p.m., December 21

I'm conscious. Kinda. I couldn't make sense of anything for a long while. Unfortunately, that's no longer my problem. I realize I'm tied up on the floor in the River Rat's main cabin. And I know Archer Highsmith has commandeered my boat and plans to kill me.

But how?

He must want it to look like an accident—like Maury's death.

We're cruising along at a relatively slow speed. I feel zero turbulence. Must be little or no wind and no waves or chop. These conditions aren't exactly ripe to make my death look like a boating accident. I'm an experienced sailor. Without a gun pointed at my head, I'm unlikely to do something stupid enough to capsize the River Rat in calm water.

I concentrate very hard on my toes, then my feet. It's like that relaxation meditation people suggest to relax your body so you can fall asleep. Only I'm trying it in reverse to wake my body up.

Whoopee, I can nudge my ankles apart. A little. Whatever medical tape the vet used to tie me up is no match for duct tape. This stuff will stretch. That would be really good news if my muscles actually obeyed every command my brain sends them.

At least my ability to think has improved. I'm coming out of the fog. Just not as fast as I'd like.

The River Rat's motor stops, and there's a splash. An anchor tossed overboard? Men's voices, and this time, it definitely isn't from some TV.

Archer isn't alone. Footsteps. Three sets? I see a leg. Someone's climbing down into the cabin. It's Archer. Quentin is close on his heels. Oh, Lord, Jack, the security thug, is next. Never did learn his last name. Guess I never will.

The three men ring me and look down with sneers and leers.

Quentin chuckles. "You can't scuttle the boat and make it look like an accident if she's wrapped up in blue tape like a piñata."

"I can break her neck," Jack offers. "Be even easier than Maury's."

Archer shakes his head. "No, has to be a different cause of death. Too suspicious to have two broken necks."

"So, what's the plan?" Quentin asks.

"Kylee's going to drown," Archer replies. "Let's move her topside and toss her in the lifeboat so she's out of the way. We have some work to do before we can scuttle the sailboat. Later, we'll peel Perry's gaudy tape off Kylee and hold her head underwater till she's gone. Jack can have the honors if he wants."

Archer stares at me. I try to keep my face slack. Hope to appear somewhere between neutral and confused. Gee, Archer, I don't have the faintest idea what's in store.

"Don't worry, Kylee," Archer says. "Your last words will be to your fiancé. Of course, they can't sound as if you have any idea they are your last words."

Archer takes my phone out of his pocket. "You're sending Ted a final text to explain your tragic decision to take your sailboat out tonight. Don't suppose you can help me out here, Kylee? Do you use endearments? Sweetie? Honey? No, not your style."

Okay, asshole. It doesn't matter what you text.

Ted will know I didn't send it. I hate cell phones and texting. I only text if Ted's in a meeting and I need his immediate attention. Otherwise, I phone. If he doesn't answer, I leave a voicemail.

Archer frowns in concentration as he mentally composes a fake message.

He starts typing, then looks at the screen. "How does this sound, Kylee?" He looks down to read the text. "Taking short cruise to check electrical repair. Make sure River Rat shipshape. C U in AM."

It's okay for me to look confused. That matches Archer's expectations. But I truly am confused. Electrical repairs? The River Rat hasn't had any electrical repairs.

Slowly, the light dawns. Wally, my go-to electrician, must have texted or left me a voicemail to say he finished the electrical work. Only Wally didn't add that the work was on the Campbells' Soup Can, not my sailboat. Archer thinks an electrician just repaired the River Rat.

Crap. He must be planning to sabotage the panel and make it look like a botched job. A wire that's come loose? Wires crossed? Is he going to blow up the River Rat? If so, why drown me? Easier to leave me onboard, so the sailboat and I go out together with a bang.

"Why don't you just blow up the boat with Kylee inside?" Quentin asks.

Is he reading my mind?

"I'm no expert in blowing shit up," Archer replies. "We'd have to cut a fuel line and that might be easy to detect. Plus, I don't want to blow myself up by mistake. I have a better plan. We're going to run the River Rat aground in these shoals and tear a big hole in her hull. An electrical failure and bilge pump disconnect will help her sink. To help matters along, we'll tie a rope to the River Rat's mast and capsize her. The incoming tide will help."

"The sailboat will sink. No problem. When they find Kylee's body, they'll figure she was either swept overboard or tried to swim for it and didn't make it. Let's get Kylee out of the way. Jack, you get her feet. Quentin, take her arms. I did the heavy lifting getting her on the boat."

Quentin slips his hands under my armpits. I'm almost sitting for a second before Jack grabs my ankles. My body sways, butt bouncing against stairs now and again as they jostle me up top.

I'll have bruises, too. Like Maury.

I gasp when cold night air invades my lungs, goosebumps scurry up my arms. I'm wearing the same slacks and cardigan sweater I wore to the doc's. Not exactly the best choice for outdoor attire on a chilly December night.

I'll feel even colder when Jack plunges my face underwater.

But Archer doesn't know me. He doesn't understand how much I hate texting, and he certainly doesn't know I was too slow a swimmer to compete in high school. His ignorance gives me a slim chance.

Quentin and Jack unceremoniously dump me into a lifeboat tied next to the River Rat. It's one of those inflatable black jobs with wide round sides. Any thoughts of rolling out of the lifeboat and struggling out of the doc's medical tape vanish. I can't roll out. Probably a bad idea anyway. Wait for the chance.

I can't see the men anymore, but I pick up snatches of conversation.

"Kylee blabbed about money laundering...Coast Guard buddy." Archer's voice.

"Load cash tonight?" Quentin's voice.

"Not on Wavedancer." Archer.

"Your boat temporarily. Under tarps. Transfer offshore...any Wavedancer search...come up empty."

"Depart dawn?" Quentin.

"Close ... we can get." Archer.

Alysha must have called me back, left a voice message. She's taking my money-laundering suspicion more seriously. It's making Archer antsy. He isn't loading the cash on Wavedancer in case there's a Coast Guard search. He's stashing it on another boat temporarily—Quentin's cabin cruiser? They'll meet up offshore to transfer the money to Wavedancer. And they're hauling ass come dawn. Smart.

Crap. How can I stop them? Okay, my first goal—stay alive.

Chapter Fifty-Nine

Archer

Saturday 11 p.m., December 21

"Quentin, use your boat's fish-finder sonar to locate a big-honking submerged rock," I say. "Shouldn't be a problem in these shoals at low tide. Pick a rock that rises a couple feet above the River Rat's five-foot draft. Then, we'll do what we did with Maury's golf cart. I'll back the River Rat off, aim her, tie off the tiller to keep it on course, and goose the sailboat to full speed. That's when I jump off.

"And you'd better pick me up quickly," I add. "While the water's not freezing, my nuts won't know the difference. The fifty-five-degree water will feel like an ice bath."

"What happens after we run the sailboat aground?" Quentin asks. "Her mast will be sticking straight up, just waiting for some fisherman to spot it? And what about the tied-off tiller?"

"Once she's damaged, I'll climb back onboard and get rid of any signs it was rigged," I answer. "Then, we'll give the boat a little nudge to make her capsize. I'll tie a rope to her mast, and we'll use your boat to pull her over. I've already monkeyed with the electrical and the bilge pump. The hull will fill quickly with water. The tide is turning. As it starts rushing in, the River Rat will sink out of sight. At least until the next low tide."

"Wait, you've still got a rope tied to the boat's mast," Jack says. "Ain't that a big clue?"

"This is where you come in, Jack," I answer.

"Hey, I can't swim. Not about to slide around on some sinking boat."

"You didn't let me finish," I continue. "While I'm untying the mast, you cut all the tape off our out-of-luck captain. Hold her head underwater till she's gone, then row over in the lifeboat and pick me up. I'll be hanging on to the mast."

God, Almighty. A lot of things have to go just right. Damn Kylee for making us speed up our timetable to leave by dawn.

Chapter Sixty

Kylee

Saturday 11:30 p.m., December 21

I don't see the crash, but the sound sickens me. The rip in the River Rat's hull must be huge. I'm glad I can't see these monsters drag her down.

Anger and grief make my chest feel like it's in a vice. I love that boat.

Don't let them see tears on my cheeks. They'll know the drugs are losing their hold.

I fight back my angry tears. Archer thinks he can sell this as an accident. I can't see how. My Coast Guard buddies won't buy that I accidentally—and, certainly not purposely—ran the River Rat aground.

I know these waters. And Archer didn't pour liquor down my throat to try and up my blood alcohol. He must believe it'll be called an accident because no one can prove otherwise. It's night, no moon. Investigators could be encouraged to decide I had a lot on my mind, tragically got careless for a few moments.

The fake text to Ted tells a different story. Has he already alerted the Coast Guard? He'll know I didn't send that text. He'll know Wally did the electrical work on the Campbells' boat, not mine. Ted will shout to the heavens that I've been kidnapped.

No matter what Ted does, will people react quickly enough to prevent

Archer's escape? By dawn, he will be steaming full speed ahead toward Andros. If he's smart, and he is, Archer will arrange one more transfer of the cash before he approaches the Bahamas. Offload it to another carrier before the Coast Guard stationed on Andros can search his Wavedancer.

I try to listen. All I hear are grunts and splashes. I have no sense of how much time has elapsed. I wish I could maneuver to see my watch. It's waterproof and one of the few possessions Archer left me.

I have no idea what they're doing. But my dread builds. I imagine I'll be the center of attention soon.

Am I ready?

A boat motor roars. Another loud splash. Waves rock my lifeboat prison. The big waves gradually peter out, and quiet returns. The remaining ripples gently nudge the lifeboat. Their sounds almost soothing.

"Ready, slut?"

Jack. I recognize the thug's voice. Jack, as in Jack the Neckbreaker. Jack, who can't wait to hold my head underwater till I take my last breath.

I playact. I'm nothing more than a drugged ragdoll.

"I'm cutting these tapes off now," Jack says. "Don't try to get frisky. You ain't going anywhere. Hell, it doesn't look like you have enough spunk left to get frisky. That takes some of the fun out of it."

Jack pinches my forearm. Hard.

I clamp my teeth together, fight the scream that wants to escape. I have to act like I can't feel it, though it hurts like a sonofabitch.

Jack pulls out a pocket knife and slices through the tape, binding my ankles together. I don't try to move them apart. Next, he cuts the tape holding my wrists together. I don't move a muscle. Saving my strength, my concentration. I'll need every bit of it.

Take slow, calming breaths. No hyperventilating.

Jack's hands slide under my armpits, and he drags my head and torso up over the lifeboat's gunnels. I'm half in, half out.

Calm breaths. Deep, calm. I'm ready.

He puts a hand on the back of my head and shoves my face into the cold, salty water. I close my eyes. Salt stings my scraped chin. A self-inflicted injury acquired in my tussles with the doc.

I flail a little. Listless movements from unresponsive muscles. Jack expects it.

Okay, it's time. I go totally limp.

Jack doesn't let up his pressure on the back of my head.

I count silently. Calmly.

Pretend it's a Coast Guard rivalry.

Women are betting I can hold my breath longer than some two-hundred-pound male, who looks like Tarzan or maybe his ape.

Always had good lungs. Love the water and swimming, but I'm slow. If they'd had swim marathons, I could have competed. Not a swim-team event. So, I joined the Y's synchronized swim club. Performances demand underwater stamina, breath control.

One minute gone. Jack keeps pressing down. I stay limp, calm. I've made it more than three minutes. In slightly different circumstances.

Two minutes gone. Jack's pressure lessens. He wants to see if I raise up.

"She's dead," he yells. "Do I just dump her in the water?"

"Yeah," Archer replies. "Hurry up and row over here. Pick me up."

An oar splashes in the water. I wait for two more strokes. My lungs are burning. Have to chance a breath or risk fainting. I slowly turn my head, bring my mouth just above the water. Thank God, it's calm. I can't afford to suck in any water when I breathe. I might gag or cough. Normal reflexes. I breathe in the delicious cold air. Slow. I take another long, even breath.

My light-headedness eases.

The hard part is over. Except for playing dead. My arms float out from my sides. My butt and legs have begun to sink, dragged down by my shoes. But I've always been a good floater. A live floater.

Just a little longer.

The water feels like liquid ice. I wish I could say I've regained full strength. I'd be lying to myself. I simply can't risk swimming. No, I'll have to try for a free ride. I'll grab onto a strap on the side of the lifeboat and let them tow me back to Stillwater Cove.

They pulled a lifeboat all the way from Stillwater Cove. That means they're accustomed to feeling some drag. I pray they won't notice a little more.

Chapter Sixty-One

Archer

Sunday 12:15 a.m., December 22

Jack paddles the lifeboat close, then reaches down in the water to help pull me up and over the gunnels.

I'm pleased. Everything's going to plan. The River Rat is quickly sinking. The incoming tide will make the sound deeper soon. I untied the rope I'd wound around the mast to help capsize the sailboat.

Yes, it looks like an accident. Pilot error. And I see the pilot's body floating away. The tide will move her, too. It doesn't matter if she sinks or floats.

"Come on," I call out to Quentin. "Angle your boat closer so Jack and I can climb aboard."

His cabin cruiser closes the distance, then Q hauls in the tow rope hand-over-hand. Finally, the lifeboat gently bumps the side of Quentin's boat. I let Jack scramble out first. Then, I reach up and take Quentin's hand to climb onboard.

"Good job." I clap Quentin on the back. "Let's head to Stillwater Cove. We only have a few hours to get the money loaded on your boat. Earlier, I called the captain I keep on standby for the Wavedancer. He says she'll be ready to leave by five a.m."

I take a final look at the rapidly sinking sailboat. My three-way torture—a tear in her hull, electrical and bilge pump failures, and our sideways yank on her mast—was too much. I no longer see Kylee's body. She sunk even faster than her sailboat.

Quentin turns the cabin cruiser away from the shipwreck and toward our Stillwater inlet. I'm relieved. Except for Mick. My boss will be furious at losing his sizeable Stillwater Cove investment. He thought it could be a smuggling base for many more years. He won't lose his yacht, though. We'll figure out how to change her registration once we get to Andros. And he probably won't lose the houses Quentin and I lived in. They were leased from one of Mick's shell companies. Not assets the government can seize.

But he won't be able to recoup the money spent on the Stillwater security force.

Wonder what's going through Jack's head right now. He may be dim-witted but he must realize the curtain is coming down tonight on the Stillwater Cove operation. When the owners discover two of their directors—Quentin and me—have vanished, not to be heard from again, they'll probably hire a management company to clean up the mess.

Not quite sure if Lisa Queensbury can survive without arranging her own vanishing act. That depends on whether anyone picks up Kylee's investigation into the Hullis Island thefts and connects the thief, Babsie, to her sister, Lisa, the fence.

I chuckle. Maybe the new board will rehire Welch HOA Management. A small bone tossed to Ted for the loss of his fiancée and his firm's security consultant.

"Jack," I yell to make sure he hears me above the noise of the cabin cruiser's motor and the wind as we slice through the water. "I want you to know Mick will take care of you after Quentin and I leave this morning. Mick will find you another position in the organization."

"Yeah, okay," Jack responds. "Appreciate it."

"But I need you to do one last job for me," I add. "I want you to arrange another fatal departure. One that will leave Lowcountry animal lovers with one less veterinarian to care for their pets."

Chapter Sixty-Two

Kylee

Sunday 1 a.m., December 22

As the lifeboat begins paddling back to Quentin's cabin cruiser, I jack-knife into a dive. First job. Get rid of excess baggage, I toe off my loafers and struggle to peel off my trousers. The legs are plastered to my flesh. I finally succeed. My cardigan proves easy to discard.

I surface for much-needed air and to track the cabin cruiser. Quentin's hauling the lifeboat back to his boat, which is idling until everyone is onboard. I swim a few breaststrokes. Can't risk freestyle and splashing. No one's head turns in my direction.

Several more breaststrokes take me very close to the cabin cruiser. The tide is helping. It's going the same direction I want to go. Not fighting it. The longer it takes for Archer and Jack to get settled, the closer I can get to the lifeboat before they quit idling and take off.

Everyone's on board. Best guess: I'm ten feet from the back of the lifeboat. The cruiser will move before the tow rope jerks the lifeboat forward. The pitch of the cabin cruiser's motor rises. It's my make-or-break chance. I swim like I'm going for the gold. My muscles scream, my skin feels on fire reacting to the cold.

One more stroke. One more stroke. One more stroke.

My right hand grabs the lifeboat strap just as the tow rope jerks the boat forward. The rough strap saws into my hand, and my arm feels like it could be yanked right out of its socket. I have to get a second hand on the strap. I fight the force of the water, pushing my free hand away.

My left hand grasps the strap. Now, I'm holding on with two hands. But it's too early to sing hallelujahs. No way I can hang on for the entire trip. Water relentlessly rushes up, splashing between my face and the lifeboat. I swallow seawater and cough. There has to be another solution.

Can I jam an entire arm through the strap? Force it in from above? Then I won't have to hold on. My captive arm will paste me to the lifeboat, and it'll keep my head above water.

The strap is a rough plastic weave. It acts like a cheese grater on my skin as I force my left arm down. Shit.

I make it. Now, I just hope my arm won't be torn off, and I can wiggle it out when we near Stillwater Cove. When my would-be killers slow the boat, it'll be easier for them to spot me. I'll have to disappear.

My body insists the water's freezing; my mind knows better. At this time of year, the ocean water near shore only cools to fifty-five or sixty degrees. At these temperatures, I'd need to be in the water an hour or two before hypothermia would become a problem. At the cabin cruiser's speed, the entrance to Stillwater Inlet is maybe five minutes away.

Plastered against the lifeboat's gunnels, I'm hidden from sight. Plus, the men should be looking forward, not back. Once I feel the cabin cruiser slow, I'll drop off. Swim underwater until I'm a safe distance from the boat.

My position isn't exactly comfortable. The strap's abrading the skin on my upper arm and doing its darndest to cut off circulation. I shift my position slightly and waggle my fingers. I need to keep feeling in them for my upcoming swim.

Hang on. Hang on. Hang on.

Finally, the sound of the motor changes. Thank God, I can't wait to free my arm. The slowdown should make it easier to yank my arm free. I use my right hand to pull on the strap, opening up a small amount of space to extract my left arm.

Time to disappear in the inky water. I close my eyes, then dive. No point trying to see anything in the murky water. The salt would just burn my eyes. I think I've oriented myself in the right direction. Aggressive underwater breaststrokes pull me forward. My left arm tingles. Blood's returning. I come up for air.

What now? I'm freezing. A soaked bra and cotton briefs are my only clothes. I have no weapons. I'm now officially in Stillwater Cove, where armed thugs would love to take down any intruder. Even one in her underwear.

* * *

The Campbells' boat. Safety for a little while. I quietly breaststroke to the pier where the Soup Can has its slip. I put my palms on the dock and try to lever my body up. My arms shake. My muscles refuse. I can't lift my body more than a foot.

I want to cry. My legs are cramping. My taffy arms have been stretched to the breaking point. I bite my lip to keep from sobbing. I've come this far. And I just can't do it.

Quit sniveling, you wimp. There are towels and blankets six feet away. Are you just going to hang on the dock in freezing water and give up? You can do it. One more try.

I flop the top half of my body on the dock. My feet still dangle in the water. I wheeze like a beached whale. Will my tortured breathing carry across to the Wavedancer's pier? Will someone hear me? Damn, I can't stop.

Marshaling my last ounce of willpower, I fishtail my butt and legs onto the dock. Then I rest again. Maybe a minute later, I brace my arms on the dock and rise onto my knees. More minutes pass before I stagger to my feet. Luckily, the Soup Can hides me from the pier where Quentin's tying up his cruiser, and Archer and Jack are shouting orders at guards. The noise gives me cover.

I crawl onto the Soup Can deck and half climb, half fall down the stairs into the salon. No way I can turn on a light. The marina's scarce safety lights offer only faint glimmers through the Soup Can's portholes. Less helpful than a sputtering candle.

My hands grope at surfaces as I stumble toward the Campbells' master suite. Inside, I find the head and pat shelves until I find towels. I strip off my wet undies and rub every inch of my skin—even the scrapes—with a big beach towel. My rewards—warmth and tingles as circulation improves.

I stagger to the bed, wind the bedspread around me, and curl my body into a tight ball. A cocoon. I break down, sob, clench my fists. My tantrum ends with a tear-soaked face and nonstop hiccups.

I lay still. My mind blank. Then, finally, I tell myself to move.

Come on. Do something. The Soup Can has a radio. Should I call the Coast Guard?

No. The security guards monitor everything, including emergency radio traffic. Okay, no radio. No cell phone, either. Archer was quite joyful about dumping my phone in the ocean along with my purse and gun. Too bad the Campbells don't keep spare cell phones on their boat.

Maybe I'll think better if I'm not naked. While I was on the Soup Can the other day with Grant, I noticed Velma and Maury left some clothes in their master. Unfortunately, there's no way I can squeeze into any of Velma's clothes. Maury's too-big clothes will have to do.

I end my pity party and scoot off the bed. My hand brushes the nightstand, and something bulky falls to the floor. A flashlight? Yes, one was sitting there the other day. I scramble off the bed and drop to my knees, my arms sweeping the floor ahead of me. Might as well be blindfolded.

Eureka, I found it. I hope it has batteries. I aim the light down to keep it from reaching the portholes. Yes!

I cup my left hand around the flashlight to restrict its beam as I search the master's closet and drawers. To clothe my lower half, I choose a pair of Maury's boxers and black sweatpants with elastic cuffs and a drawstring waist. At least, they won't fall off.

Up top, I opt for three layers. Since Maury's underwear selection doesn't include bras, I pull on an undershirt, a fleece pajama top, and a large black sweatshirt. I cap it all off with Maury's multi-pocketed camouflage fishing vest.

Now I'm clothed. Still no plan. Anything to use as a weapon? I remember Maury's toolbox and picture a big, heavy wrench. The Campbell safety kit should have a flare gun.

I make judicious use of the flashlight to locate the toolbox and safety kit. I tuck the flare gun, two flares, and the big wrench in my fishing vest's pockets.

Did Ted open the fake text Archer sent? That turd Archer didn't send it until around midnight. Another clue I wasn't the sender. But, by midnight, Ted may have turned off his phone and gone to bed. No need to leave his cell on for emergencies. His company has an after-hours service. If there's a true emergency, it pages Ted. So, I can't count on the Coast Guard riding to the rescue anytime soon.

What do I know about Archer's and Quentin's plans, and is there any way to put a monkey wrench in them?

One, I know they have to move the cash from the maintenance barn to the marina.

Two, the cash will be loaded onto Quentin's smaller cabin cruiser rather than Wavedancer.

Three, Quentin will leave ahead of Archer, and they'll rendezvous at a pre-set GPS point offshore to transfer the cash to Wavedancer for the longer ocean voyage to the Bahamas.

I have no means of transportation so I can't get to the maintenance barn and try to sabotage the truck bringing the cash to the marina.

Once the truck arrives, the section of the marina where the transfer takes place will be crawling with security guards. It would be suicidal to expect I could get anywhere near the Wavedancer, Quentin's cruiser, or the cash without being caught. Even if I were willing to sacrifice myself, I couldn't do any real damage. Yeah, I could shoot the flares, but any fire I start would be quickly snuffed out by the gaggle of guards. In the movies, I could shoot a flare directly into the truck's gasoline tank and trigger a big explosion. This isn't the movies.

A gasoline tank. That's what I'm forgetting. Quentin said his cabin cruiser would practically be running on fumes by the time they returned to the marina. He'll have to gas up before he can sail away with whatever money-laundering treasure they've amassed.

That leaves two big questions. Will Quentin gas up while security guards are fetching the money from the maintenance barn? And will he be alone?

The gas pumps are on my side of the marina, one pier down from the Soup Can. If Quentin decides to gas up before the money's loaded, I may have the perfect monkey wrench.

I steal some rope from the Soup Can's deck and an empty gas can to compliment my weapons stash. Last chore? Untie the Soup Can and ready her for a fast getaway.

That saying "an eye for an eye" translates nicely into "a boat for a boat."

My borrowed clothes provide pretty good camouflage, but my curly, white hair is drying. Any light hitting it will turn me into an easy target.

Shit. I have to do it. Maury wasn't just working on his boat's electrical systems; he was greasing gears. And I know where he left the grease.

Yuck. I massage a generous glob of grease through my short hair. It's no longer fly-away. I must look like a fifties-era greaser minus the cool, black leather jacket.

Chapter Sixty-Three

Kylee

Sunday 2 a.m., December 22

I creep down the pier toward the marina gas pumps and crouch behind a pile of old canvas boat covers that maintenance hasn't hauled away. The discarded canvas doesn't totally hide me, but Quentin won't be expecting to see anyone. He has no reason to scout the area. Stillwater Cove security has the whole marina area locked down, and, well, I'm dead.

Looking across the marina basin to the Wavedancer and Quentin's boat, I see lots of activity. But it doesn't appear the money has arrived. No truck. Mostly, it looks like the Wavedancer is being readied for departure. Quentin and Jack are talking.

God, I hope whenever Quentin comes to gas up, he doesn't bring that little weasel. I can take one man down by surprise. Not two.

Okay. Quentin's getting back in his cruiser. He slowly backs out of his slip and turns his boat toward the gas pumps. Jack, the murdering rat, stays on the pier. He's talking with Archer now. Quentin is alone.

I have a death grip on Maury's big wrench. Too cold for my hands to sweat, but my heart's trip-hammering. Quentin's taller than me. I need to creep up while he's bending down to tie his cabin cruiser to the pier. He won't want his boat to float away while he's gassing her up.

Me either. I have other plans for her.

Quentin hops from his boat to the pier, holding the bow line he plans to loop around a cleat. I tip-toe forward, then leap. My wrench clubs the back of his head. An oomph sound escapes. He staggers, but doesn't go down. Heads are hard. The wrench didn't knock him out. I wallop him again, choosing a sweet spot between his skull and vertebrae. This time he's out, but still breathing. Not sure how I feel about that.

I grab the rope slipping through his fingers. Can't let his cabin cruiser float away. I pull the rope to bring the boat tight to the dock and tie off the bow line. Then I jump to the boat's deck to grab a stern line and secure it to a cleat. If anyone glances from across the way, the cabin cruiser needs to look exactly as it would if Quentin were filling her gas tanks.

I drag Quentin's body to my former hiding place behind the pile of torn canvas and retrieve the gas can and sturdy rope I left there. I start a pump to fill my gas can. Once it's filled, I'm ready. I climb aboard the cabin cruiser with my tools.

My first task is to figure out exactly where to point the helm so it'll smash headfirst into the rock and concrete jetty that helps protect Stillwater's harbor and keep its channel open. I also need to figure out her controls. Once the helm's position is set, I tie off the steering wheel. It should stay on course. No deviations.

I head to the cabin cruiser's open backend and pick up my gas can. I splash gasoline everywhere. I'm going to make dang sure this boat won't transport anything. Cash included.

But my plan will attract a lot of unwanted attention. As soon as I shoot the flare, I need to run like crazy for the Campbells' boat.

I start the engine. I'd love to crank her up to full speed for her encounter with the jetty, but that's not an option. If the boat took off at high speed, I'd have to leap in the water to escape. That wouldn't let me shoot the flare gun.

No, I have to settle for flames and the cabin cruiser's unpleasant but not catastrophic encounter with the jetty. She probably won't sink or explode, but she'll need extensive repairs to be seaworthy.

The motor's humming and the cabin cruiser's straining to move forward as I jump to the pier and untie the cleats. Then, she's off. Not fast, but steady. I aim the flare gun and shoot. Light streaks through the night as the flare arcs to its target. Whoosh. The gasoline catches. The fiery cabin cruiser lights up the marina as it travels toward its planned collision.

I'd love to watch, but need to run. I pound down the pier to the Soup Can, jump onboard, and start her up. Wally left the keys where I told him to when he finished installing the new electrical panel. I know she has a full tank of gas. The Soup Can's not a speedster, but I'm hoping she can get me out of this cove and beyond rifle range before anyone can follow.

Archer's yacht isn't a chase boat, and I've crippled Quentin's cabin cruiser. Do they have a backup? A lookout boat outside the harbor watching for the Coast Guard or other interference?

I hope not.

Chapter Sixty-Four

Archer

Sunday 3 a.m., December 22

What the hell is Quentin doing? His cabin cruiser is aimed straight at the jetty. My God, it's on fire! Is Quentin on it?

Before I can process what's happening, another boat leaves its slip and rockets toward the harbor entrance.

The Soup Can. The Campbells' boat. It has to be Kylee. How the hell did she survive? How could she be here?

I turn around. Jack's behind me.

"Heard from the gatehouse," he says. "Sheriff's deputies just came through with warrants to search the maintenance barn and any suspect vehicles or boats capable of hiding a kidnap victim."

I shake my head.

What now? Give up? Hope Mick will provide good defense attorneys?

Jack pulls out his gun. "Mick says he's sorry you screwed up. He can't risk you or Quentin trying to ease your pain by giving him up."

Jack laughs. "By the way, I'm not the dimwit. You are, for thinking Mick wouldn't have a watchdog to pull the plug and eliminate loose ends. "

"Wait…"

Chapter Sixty-Five

Kylee

Sunday 3 a.m., December 22

Men are yelling and shooting at the Soup Can. I ignore the marina's no-wake restrictions and gun the Campbell boat toward the harbor entrance. Go. Go. Go.

There's plenty of light courtesy of Quentin's flaming cabin cruiser beached on the jetty. Not the resounding crash I'd hoped for. No big explosion either. Guess the fire I set hasn't reached the cabin cruiser's gas tanks. A pity.

More shots. A couple hit. Fiberglass splinters. Please don't hit the gas tank. Another minute, and I'll be out of range.

I zoom through the harbor entrance. No pursuit boats. Where do I go now? Try to make Beaufort without Archer or Jack coming for me? Beach the Soup Can on an island and run to the nearest house for help?

I laugh. Are you stupid? Use the Soup Can's radio.

The bad guys already know where I am, guess I should let the good guys in on the secret. I make an emergency call to the Coast Guard and check behind me one more time.

Good, still no boats.

My radio call is answered. "Patching you through to Captain Reed. He's right on your doorstep."

"Captain Reed, this is Kylee Kane. I'm just outside the entrance to

Stillwater Cove's harbor. I'm in a thirty-five-foot boat with the name Soup Can painted on her stern."

Bright lights swarm over me like flies on a tasty carcass.

"We see you. Coming up fast on your port side."

A loud boom interrupts him. The sky turns yellow and orange as flames lick upwards.

"My, my. What have you been up to, Captain Kane?" Reed asks.

The Coast Guard cutter's air horn blasts. Once, twice. "Coming alongside to board."

In seconds, the cutter sidles up to the Soup Can, and I spot Alysha and my old friend Captain Harvey Reed on deck. The cutter secures the Soup Can, and two sailors come onboard.

"Glad you could make it," I yell.

I hurry through a quick synopsis. "You're just in time. They're smuggling millions of dollars."

Captain Reed orders the sailors who are now aboard the Soup Can to move her down Port Royal Sound, out of harm's way.

"Get your retired butt over here," he adds. "While you look like something no respectable cat would drag in, your brain appears to be functioning. You can pinpoint locations for our search and seizure operations.

"By the way, your fiancé has been raising holy hell. Ted called the young lady who runs the marina store. Rousted her out of bed to tell her you'd been kidnapped. She described a guy who looked like Archer, showing a keen interest in your boat. She saw him drive away in a red Corvette with a vanity plate 'AimHigh.' That prompted the Sheriff's Department to join in. Deputies are at the gates."

* * *

"This is the US Coast Guard," Captain Reed's voice booms over the cutter's loudspeaker. "Everyone stay where you are. Raise your hands. We need to see you have no weapons."

In the chaos, no one even tried to reach Quentin's cabin cruiser to put out the fire before it exploded. A large truck—the one carrying the cash?—sits alongside the pier with its back doors wide open.

About half of the security guards ignore the captain's orders and scurry toward their vehicles. Rats on a sinking ship. The hired captain of the Wavedancer and a few crew members stand on deck, hands waving above their heads. They'll plead ignorance. "We were hired to move the boat from point A to point B, never had a clue about any secret cargo."

I look for Archer. Where is he? Has Quentin come around?

With sirens blaring and lights flashing, three sheriff's vehicles race to block the exit of the fleeing guards.

The Coast Guard cutter's bright lights make the scene look like a play. This one will have a happy ending with the villains in handcuffs. I ask permission to get off the cutter.

"Just a few minutes more," Captain Reed says. "You don't look like one of them, but you don't look like law enforcement either. If there's any last-minute shooting, I don't want to be responsible for you getting air-conditioned by friendly fire."

The Coast Guard and sheriff's deputies work steadily to sort out the mess. All the security guards give up their weapons. That's when I spot a man, face down, not moving. He's dressed like Archer Highsmith. Is he trying to play dead?

I tell Captain Reed, and he agrees to accompany me off the cutter to ID the man. We walk toward him. It's Archer. He's been shot in the head. Definitely not playing dead.

Who killed him? There wasn't any gunplay after the Coast Guard arrived, and Archer wasn't the type to commit suicide. Besides, there's no gun near him.

"You should try to capture Quentin," I say. "He must know who's behind the money laundering, who's sending the cash to Stillwater Cove."

Reed gives permission for Alysha and two other armed Coasties to accompany me to the gas pumps where I clobbered Quentin.

There's no bullet hole in Quentin, but the angle of his head tells me his neck's been snapped. A trademark move of Jack's.

CHAPTER SIXTY-FIVE

"Sure you didn't do this?" Alysha asks.

"No, he was breathing the last time I saw him. The security chief, Jack, must have killed him. Broken necks are his trademark. Jack must be somewhere inside Stillwater. No boats left after I took the Soup Can out of here, and sheriff's deputies have the gates blocked.

Alysha radios Reed, and he relays the information to the sheriff's deputies.

"The deputies brought an ambulance along," Alysha says. "You will be examined. Don't bother trying to protest."

* * *

A medic takes my vital signs, probes my body. Asks me how many fingers he's holding up.

Then, he gives his verdict. "She's beat up. Some ugly skin abrasions and bruising, but she's not seriously injured."

"Good to hear," Alysha replies, then holds up a finger to signal silence as she listens to her radio. "Wait, there's news about that thug Jack."

Reed's voice booms. "The man you described as the Stillwater security chief is dead. He had an airboat hidden at the edge of the marsh. He apparently had a contingency plan to escape through the marsh if both the marina and land exits were closed. He came screaming out of the wetlands into Port Royal Sound, riding high on his airboat. He entered the sound right where Lieutenant Jackson had stashed the Soup Can for safekeeping.

"The idiot started shooting at the Soup Can," Reed continues. "He must have figured you were onboard, Kylee, and unarmed. I imagine he hoped to trade his airboat for the Campbells' cabin cruiser. He must have been surprised when the lieutenant returned fire. The surprise couldn't have lasted long. He was exposed, and Lieutenant Jackson's a good shot."

"I'm not sorry Jack's dead," I admit. "But I wonder if there's anyone left who can finger folks at the top of the food chain. The ones providing the millions for this smuggling operation."

"Not your worry," Alysha says. "I think you have company."

Ted scrambles out of a sheriff's vehicle and runs my way. I stumble toward him. My reserve of adrenalin is long gone, and my muscles can do little more than quiver. Ted crushes me in a bear hug.

"Kylee, my God, I was so scared. I knew you'd been kidnapped. I didn't know whether you were alive or dead."

"I'm alive," I whisper, "thanks to you for firing up the Coast Guard and the Sheriff's Department."

Ted won't let go of my arms, but he takes a step back to look me over. He laughs. "It appears nothing is broken, but I do hope that won't be your hairdo for the wedding."

I laugh, too. Then, I think of the River Rat, and tears flow once more.

"Oh, Ted, they scuttled the River Rat. I loved that boat. Everything I own went down with her. Oh, no. My wedding dress. It's gone, too."

The floodgates open. I can't quit crying. Ted holds me. "I'm taking you home."

Chapter Sixty-Six

Kylee

Sunday Noon, December 22

I wake in Ted's comfy king bed and try to blink away an entire attic's worth of cobwebs. My mind's hazy. Every inch of my body aches. That might include my eyelashes. Blinking isn't helping much. My eyelids act like sandpaper.

What time is it?

I raise my wrist. No watch. Ted must have taken it off when he put me to bed. I have no clear memories of anything that happened after we left Stillwater Cove.

I run a hand through my hair. Oh, yuck. Gross!

Grease slimes my fingers. That's it. I have to get up and shower, throw these sheets in the trash.

* * *

It's twelve-thirty when I go downstairs and find Ted pouring a mug of coffee for me.

I frown. "Aren't you supposed to be picking your father up at the airport about now?"

"Grant's doing the honors," he replies as he walks over, kisses my cheek, and hands me the coffee mug. "There are advantages to having a son who drives. We cancelled the Hullis Island brunch. We're doing dinner at the club instead."

"I'm glad I left some clothes here," I say. "I won't need to wear Maury's sweatpants and undershirt to dinner."

Ted laughs. "Yeah, not a good look for you."

"I was about to come upstairs and wake you," he adds. "We have a one-thirty date with the Beaufort County Sheriff and the DA. I think Captain Reed will be there, too. I promised you'd be right on time. Only way I could talk the powers that be into letting me bring you home last night. They're all quite eager to hear your story. For that matter, me, too. I won't yell at you, but I hope you realize going to that creepy vet's home alone was plain stupid. And you aren't stupid."

I inhale a big slug of coffee. "In hindsight, not one of my finer decisions."

Ted shakes his head. "Kylee, your determination is one of the reasons I love you. But, please, at least tell me when you're about to venture out on a limb. I could have gone with you. If you thought two people would have spooked the vet, I could have sat in the car while you questioned him. You're making me go prematurely gray."

I touch the hair at his temples. Mostly black. I can practically count the few gray threads. "Looks good on you, distinguished. Besides, you need a little gray, so my white hair doesn't make me look like your mother."

I drop my hand. "I'm really sorry, Ted. I know you must have been crazy with worry. It was stupid. And believe me, I paid for it."

He kisses my forehead. "Thank heavens you hate texting and that Grant kept me up later than usual last night. My stomach dropped when I opened the text. I was certain you hadn't sent it. I knew Wally worked on the Campbells' boat, not yours. Plus, Archer used the letters C and U as shorthand for words. You rave about texting shortcuts and how people will soon forget grammar, spelling, and how to read an actual book."

With two big gulps, I finish my coffee. "Let's go and get this over with. You know I can go alone if you want to be here when Grant and your dad return."

Ted's sideways look tells me what he thinks of that. "Take all the time you want telling your story. I'm in no rush."

Chapter Sixty-Seven

Kylee

Sunday 1:30 p.m., December 22

T he conference room is packed. Ted had warned me to expect Sheriff Eileen Baker, District Attorney Glen Jenkins, Captain Reed, and Olivia Tucker, the smart young attorney who now represents everyone in our family.

Ted asked Olivia to attend in case questioning might put me in legal or civil suit jeopardy. Perhaps for blowing up boats that don't belong to me or intentionally damaging the Stillwater jetty?

The room holds five more people I didn't expect—Hullis Island Chief O'Rourke, Beth Reiner, Lt. Alysha Carter, Deputy Josie Muschel, and a stenographer.

DA Jenkins opens the proceedings. "Ms. Kane, Beaufort County will be turning the money-laundering investigation over to the federal government. All the folks who had a role in recent events have already turned in reports and answered questions. Hearing your testimony today won't influence them. We're hoping you can provide some missing puzzle pieces. We need to understand who has been engaged in illegal activities in Beaufort County. If the federal government has no interest in them, we need to decide if we should try them locally."

The DA looks around the room. "Everyone clear on why we're here? I'll ask the questions, but, if any of you feel some point isn't covered or needs clarification, raise your hand. Okay, let's start."

As a first order of business, the DA asks me to explain why I went to Dr. Perry McMahan's home, and what happened there.

Olivia interrupts my account to interject, "For the record, Kylee, did Dr. McMahan let you into his house? You didn't force your way in, correct?"

"Correct," I say. "It would be hard for anyone to force themselves into the veterinarian's house. He was blocking the door, and he must outweigh me by two hundred pounds."

"Dr. McMahan, who is in custody, says you had a gun," the DA notes.

Oh, crap. Maybe I should worry. I'm glad Olivia is here.

"Yes, but I never took the gun out of my purse. I have a concealed carry permit."

The DA nods. "Okay, continue."

I take my account up to the point where Dr. McMahan pokes a needle in me, then skip ahead to when my brain starts semi-functioning again.

"That's when Archer told Dr. McMahan to give me another injection, and I was out of it until I woke on the floor of the River Rat," I add. "Archer was sitting in my galley crunching on my Fritos and drinking my beer.

"He spoke to me, kinda like he was talking to himself. Enjoying the fact that he could say anything he wanted, and there wasn't a damn thing I could do. He told me he was going to scuttle my sailboat and kill me."

Nobody interrupts the next several minutes of my testimony until I come to the part where I fool Jack by holding my breath longer than two minutes. "You can really do that?" the DA asks.

"Yes, started training—accidentally—in high school, when I joined a synchronized swim club that required a lot of underwater gymnastics. Now, synchronized swimming is an Olympic sport, though it's been renamed artistic swimming."

My solo narrative concludes with my radioing the Coast Guard. The DA then gives Captain Reed, Alysha, and Josie leave to share the law enforcement response. Captain Reed and Alysha describe finding Archer Highsmith's and Quentin Teacher's bodies.

Olivia raises her hand. "Kylee, you did say Quentin Teacher was still breathing when you left him and ran for the Campbells' boat, correct?"

"Yes, he was alive, just unconscious."

It takes a good hour for everyone with knowledge of what transpired in Stillwater Cove to speak. Captain Reed and Sheriff Barker confirm they seized fifty million dollars in shrink-wrapped currency, predominately hundred-dollar bills.

While I figure we're done, two people—Chief O'Rourke and Beth Reiner—have yet to speak. The DA turns to Beth. "Ms. Reiner, can you tell us why you're here?"

Beth clears her throat. "After Ms. Kane and I spoke, I asked her to email me descriptions of the jewelry stolen from Hullis Island residents over the past two years. At the time, I thought what the heck, maybe I'll catch my stepmother wearing one of the necklaces. Kylee told me there wasn't enough evidence for the authorities to get a warrant to search the house. Then, it dawned on me: my sister, Marianne, and I own the house, and Dad's trust gives us the right to enter the house whenever we wish."

Beth takes a deep breath. "I drove to Hullis Island and waited until Babsie drove off. She was dressed to the nines and wearing heels. I figured she wouldn't return soon. I used my key to go inside and do a casual walk-through. On top of a dresser, I saw a diamond ring that looked like a match to one that was stolen. The ring was in plain sight. I didn't touch it. I simply called Chief O'Rourke and asked him to meet me at the house. He bagged the ring as evidence."

The DA turns to O'Rourke. "And what did you do?"

"I called Sheriff Baker, and she got a search warrant. The house search netted another piece of stolen jewelry inside a jewelry box."

I interrupt. I can't help myself. "Why would Babsie keep any of the stolen jewelry? Wasn't she fencing them to supplement her income?"

The sheriff shrugs. "The woman liked jewelry. Maybe she planned to take the pieces to another city and have the stones reset."

"Am I missing something?" Ted asks. "How does this tie into the Stillwater smuggling operation?"

"We're getting to that," the DA says. "When Babsie was arrested, she used her phone call to ring her sister, Lisa Queensbury.

"Lisa already knew Archer, Quentin, and Jack were dead. She suspected she'd soon be arrested as Babsie's fence. So, she took preemptive action. Her attorney came to me, asking for a deal. Lisa claims Archer blackmailed her to remain a Stillwater director to keep owners from being concerned about a board totally composed of newcomers. The owners considered Lisa's rich husband a member of their club and figured Lisa would alert her hubby if there was reason for alarm.

"When Archer and Quentin talked about the big boss, they didn't worry about Lisa listening in," the DA adds. "Apparently, they thought of her like a piece of furniture. Their mistake. Lisa listened closely and took mental notes on whose cash they were laundering. Criminals underestimate women, too. Lisa can ID the top boss."

"Isn't she taking a huge risk?" I ask. "This crowd didn't hesitate to kill Maury, who only had vague suspicions."

The DA nods. "Believe me, Lisa knows the score. She admitted she's only taking the risk because she foresees a fatal 'accident' if she stays mum. No loose ends. Still, Lisa will only name names if she and Babsie skate. She's angling to get them into witness protection. Luckily, that's not my call. The feds will decide what comes next."

Wow. My head's spinning. I hope Lisa isn't blowing smoke. She's an inventive chameleon. Maybe she will get another new name. I wonder if she even remembers the name on her birth certificate.

Chapter Sixty-Eight

Kylee

Tuesday 3 p.m., December 24

Mom, Alysha, and Josie are fussing over me.

"Sure you don't want a little blush," Josie asks.

I shake my head. "No. If I'm going to be a blushing bride, it's because I'm blushing. I do appreciate the foundation you applied. While I never use it, covering the scrapes on my skin is a good plan. Lots less photo retouching for Mom on all the pictures she's instructed Frank to shoot."

"Ready to put on your dress?" Alysha asks.

"I guess."

A hint of sadness creeps in. I wish I could wear the dress Alysha and Josie found for me. But, like the River Rat, it's gone.

While the boutique had a duplicate—the one I didn't try on—it was in a smaller size. Had it been a larger size, I'd have hired a seamstress to do a rush job taking it in. Spilled milk.

Alysha and Josie went on an emergency shopping expedition. I wasn't invited. They told me it would go better if I wasn't along. Plus, I had plenty of other obligations. Like spending time with my soon-to-be father-in-law, having fun with family and friends at last night's rehearsal dinner, and catching up on sleep—at Mom and Frank's house. Mom was insistent I needed to rest so I'd look less like a zombie on my wedding day.

I tried on several dresses my friends brought on loan and finally picked a hunter-green number. Josie and Alysha also found a pair of low heels in my size. I'm grateful.

"Ready," I tell my friends. "Bring on the dress. Let's get this show on the road. I'm ready for my honeymoon."

Alysha and Josie carry in an unopened garment bag and set it on Mom and Frank's bed.

"We're not going to do everything for you," Josie says. "Get her unzipped and put it on."

I unzip the garment bag.

What? It's my bridal dress. The one I loved and lost.

Josie and Alysha laugh and clap. "It's your size. Put it on."

"How did you manage this?" I ask.

"We called the manufacturer. Got the owner and described how your heroics stopped a multi-million-dollar money-laundering operation but cost you a live-in sailboat and your wedding dress. She overnighted the dress. No charge. Plus, she sent along a suitcase full of clothes for your honeymoon."

I hug my friends. I can't believe it. Tears run down my cheeks.

"Oh, no, you don't," Mom says. "Stop the waterworks. I'm not walking a teary bride down the aisle."

* * *

Arms linked, Mom and I walk toward the chapel altar. I smile. A man I love with all my heart is waiting for me. No tears. I'm walking toward a future I totally embrace. I can't wait for it to start.

A Note from the Author

My love affair with the South Carolina Lowcountry made it a no-brainer to pick this location as my retired Coast Guard heroine's home. The dozen years we lived in the Lowcountry are chockful of fond memories. My biggest challenge has been inventing names for fictional HOAs, since most of my original ideas were already taken.

While I'm positive Beaufort County has no more homeowner association (HOA) feuds than other regions, the number and diversity of single-family home and condo communities make it perfect for this series. I also should note that Nick, my fictional deputy sheriff nemesis, is not meant to reflect on the competence of any law enforcement officer or the professionalism of the Beaufort County Sheriff's Office. However, if I let my fictional LEOs promptly solve local mysteries, my heroine would have nothing to do.

How do I feel about HOAs? Like all human collectives, their potential for good or harm depends on the ethics, personalities, and agendas of those in power. I admire the vast majority of individuals who volunteer for HOA boards and committees. I've met many wonderful people while serving as an HOA secretary, vice president, and president. Fortunately, for my series, I've also come across a few less than altruistic owners who are quite adept at generating the conflict every mystery novel needs.

If you enjoyed this book, PLEASE rate it and write a review on your favorite online bookseller website. Two sentences will do the trick, and it will mean the world to me.

Acknowledgements

Thanks to Mark Nowling for help with cell phone and video doorbell options, and to Stephen Schabel, VP, Director, The Center for Birds of Prey, The Avian Conservation Center, for background information. Any mistakes with technology or avian information are mine alone. I also owe a continuing debt of gratitude to Peter Kristian, General Manager, Hilton Head Plantation Property Owners Association, and Kevin McCracken, General Manager, Keowee Key Property Owners Association, for helping me understand homeowner association management challenges.

Jacquelyn Molnar won a reader contest to name the HOA featured in this novel, while Martha Steele, who won a drawing to name a character in my third HOA Mystery, gifted the option to her granddaughter, who now shares a name with a continuing character, Deputy Sheriff Josie Muschel. Reader Annie Potts deserves credit for Kylee's imaginary parrot's name.

As always, I'm indebted to fellow authors, friends and family, who read and critique my manuscripts. Their input and encouragement is invaluable. Hats off this time to Beta readers Howard Lewis, Donna Campbell, Cindy Sample, Gwen McPhail, Meredith Fuchs, and especially my husband, Tom Hooker.

My agent, Cindy Bullard, Birch Literary, along with Level Best Books, my publisher, and editor Shawn Simmons also deserve credit for seeing this book through to publication.

I can't say enough about subscribers to my Once-in-a-While newsletter. Visit my website: https://lindalovely.com and click on the *Contact Me* tab to join the fun, including book news, research finds, and fun reader contests.

About the Author

Beyond the Gates is Linda Lovely's twelfth mystery/suspense novel. Whether she's writing cozy mysteries, historical suspense or contemporary thrillers, her novels share one common element—smart, independent heroines. Humor and romance also sneak into every manuscript. Her work has been recognized as a finalist by such prestigious awards as RWA's Golden Heart for Romantic Suspense and Killer Nashville's Silver Falchion for Best Cozy Mystery.

Lovely is secretary of the six-state Southeast Regional Chapter of Mystery Writers of America. She also belongs to Sisters in Crime, the Authors Guild, and International Thriller Writers. She lives on a lake in Upstate South Carolina with her husband, and enjoys swimming, gardening, long walks, and, of course, reading.

AUTHOR WEBSITE:
  https://lindalovely.com

SOCIAL MEDIA HANDLES:
Facebook: https://www.facebook.com/LindaLovelyAuthor/
BookBub: https://www.bookbub.com/profile/linda-lovely
Amazon: https://amazon.com/author/lindalovely
Barnes & Noble: http://www.barnesandnoble.com/s/Linda+Lovely
Goodreads:
https://www.goodreads.com/author/show/4884053.Linda_Lovely
BlueSky: https://bsky.app/profile/authorlovely.bsky.social
Instagram: https://www.instagram.com/LindaLovely3

Also by Linda Lovely

HOA Mysteries:
>#1-*With Neighbors Like These*
>#2-*Neighbors To Die For*
>#3-*A Killer App*

Brie Hooker Mysteries:
>#1-*Bones to Pick*
>#2-*Picked Off*
>#3-*Bad Pick*

Historical Romantic Suspense:
>*Lies—Secrets Can Kill*

Smart Women, Dumb Luck Romantic Thrillers:
>#1-*Dead Line*
>#2-*Dead Hunt*

Marley Clark Mysteries:
>#1-*Dear Killer*
>#2-*No Wake Zone*